THE GRAND GAME
BOOK 7: ANCIENT DEBTS

THE GRAND GAME

BOOK 7: ANCIENT DEBTS

TOM ELLIOT

COPYRIGHT

THE GRAND GAME

Thrust once more into the heart of the Game, can Michael survive?

At long last, Michael emerges from isolation. The Kingdom has not changed much since his last venture, but he has. Will he be able to conceal the truth of what he has become? Will he be able to fulfill his many obligations? And most importantly, can he reconnect with his old allies?

Join Michael on his epic journey and find out!

PRAISE FOR THE GRAND GAME:

"Interesting portal litrpg. Well-paced and the start of a new series. Curious to see where it goes..." —**Tao Wong on goodreads.com.**

"... Great action, great storyline and I honestly binge read it, start to end..." —**Alex Kozlowski on goodreads.com.**

"Smart MC. Great Tension. Full of Action." —**CookieCrumble on RoyalRoad.com.**

"Everything I look for in a LitRPG." —**CosmereCradleChris on RoyalRoad.com.**

"Oh I liked this very much!" —**The Enlightened Beard on amazon.com.**

"One of the best in this category this year." —**kindle customer on amazon.com.**

AUTHOR'S NOTE

Dear Readers,

Thank you for reading the Grand Game. This is a self-published book. Even though care has been given to the review and editing of this novel, some mistakes may have slipped through. If you spot any grammatical errors or typos, please get in touch with me via email.

This book also contains game-like elements. They are generally unintrusive and integrated into the story, but beware, they exist. Otherwise, I hope you enjoy Michael's story.

Happy reading!
Tom (**TomLitRPG.com**)
Support me on PATREON

CONTENTS

MICHAEL'S EVOLUTION

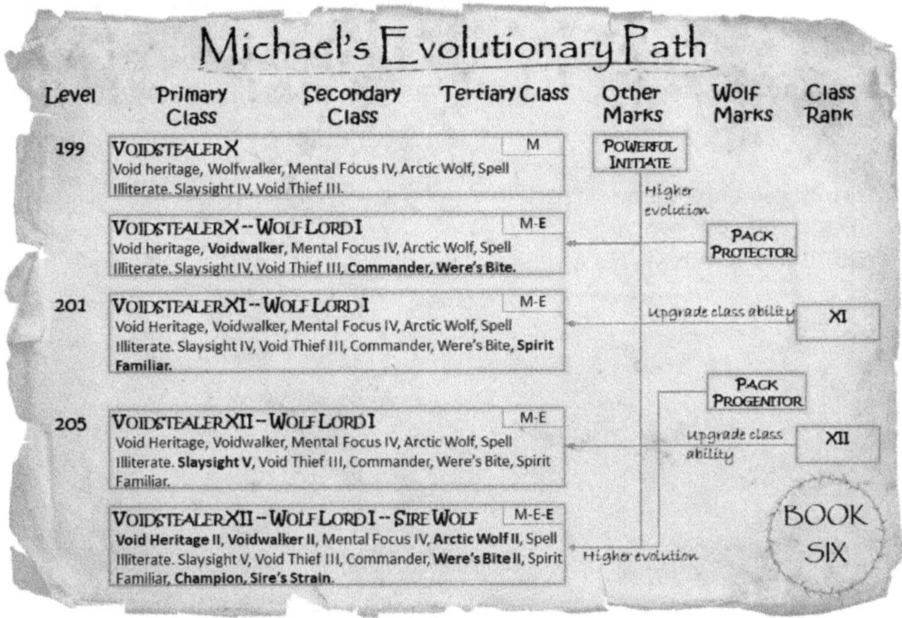

As always, Michael continues to grow during his adventures in the Forever Kingdom. The chart above only illustrates his latest achievements (as accomplished over the course of the last book). If you wish to view Michael's earlier evolutionary charts, please visit my site at the link below.

tomlitrpg.com/michael

THE SYSTEM OF THE GRAND GAME

The universe of the Grand Game continues to expand with every book in the series, and at this point, it no longer makes sense to include all the maps, charts, and diagrams in each new book.

If you wish to learn more about the world of the Forever Kingdom or understand the system of the Grand Game better, please visit my site at one of the links below.

tomlitrpg.com/game-lore
tomlitrpg.com/world-lore
tomlitrpg.com/glossary

MICHAEL AT THE END OF BOOK 6

Player Profile: Michael

Level: 211. Rank: 21. Species: Human. Lives Remaining: 4.
Ghost's Lives Remaining: 3.
True Marks: Powerful Initiate.
True Marks (hidden): Worthy Adversary, Wolf Protector, Wolf Progenitor.
False Marks (fabricated): Lesser Shadow, Lesser Light, Lesser Dark.
Followers: 2 / 200. Active Pacts: 0 / 20.

Faction Data: Forerunners

Office held: Faction Leader. Sectors claimed: 0 / 2.
Players pledged: Ceruvax.
Non-players pledged: Pack of the Reach (500), Bane Wolves warband (2,000).

Active Buffs

denotes boosts affected by items.
Damage reduction (reduces damage incurred only):
Life: 15%. Death: 25%. Air: 55%. Earth: 55%. Fire: 55%. Water: 55%.
Shadow: 35%. Light: 35%. Dark: 35%. Nether: 100%. Physical: 46%*.

Resistances (negates damage and/or rebuffs spell effects):
Life: 7.5%. Death: 12.5%. Air: 27.5%. Earth: 27.5%. Fire: 47.5%*. Water: 27.5%. Shadow: 17.5%. Light: 17.5%. Dark: 17.5%. Nether: 70%*. Physical: 0%.

Benefits derived from Items

Damage: +30% damage (ebonheart), +40% damage (faithful).
Abilities: perceive tier 6 spelled wards (sorcerer's coif), move soundlessly (wayfarer's boots), hands immune to hazardous substances (wayfarer's gloves), spellhold: empty (mage's surprise), psi-feed (psi bracelet).
Immunities: blindness, tier 2 entanglement (unbound ring), tier 2 mind spells (stillness ring).
Skills: +4 ranks stealth (ranger's armor).

Attributes

Available: 2 points.
Strength: 28 (20)*. Constitution: 32 (24)*. Dexterity: 108 (84)*. Perception: 94 (90)*. Mind: 135 (123)*. Magic: 66 (46)*. Faith: 0.

Classes

Available (Michael): 0 points.
Available (Ghost): 10 points.

Primary-Secondary-Tertiary tri-blend: voidstalker (fabricated). voidstealer XII (hidden).
Ascendant Class: wolf lord (rank I, hidden), sire wolf (rank I, hidden).
Familiar: stygian pyre wolf III (unique, hidden).

Traits

void heritage II (wolf, hidden): +4 Dexterity, +4 Strength, +8 Mind, +8 Perception, +12 Magic.
voidwalker II (wolf, hidden): improved senses in all conditions, nethersight, immunity to blindness.
arctic wolf II (wolf, hidden): +10 Constitution, +4 Mind, +6 Strength.
were's bite II (wolf, hidden): 0 to 30% chance of granting another player the were-trait.
sire's strain (wolf, hidden): boosts your other wolf traits by +1 tier.

anointed scion (bloodline, hidden): bound to House Wolf.
secret blood (bloodline, hidden): conceals the wolf blood of yourself, your followers, and your familiar.

beast tongue: can speak to beastkin.
Marked: can see spirit signatures.
inscrutable mind: +8 Mind.
mental focus IV: increases effectiveness of Mind skills by 40%.
budding explorer: all key points in newly discovered sectors logged.
spell illiterate: cannot cast mana-based spells.
potion resistance II: potency of potions reduced by 2 ranks.
spirit talker: can speak to spirits.
bold blood: +1 attribute per level.
higher evolution: can evolve Class beyond master ranked.
commander: can share bloodline traits or blood memories with your followers.
champion: increases the strength of blood memories.
spirit familiar: can bind a willing spirit as your familiar.
mage-host: +10 Mind, +10 Magic.

spirit familiar (Ghost): mirrors player attributes and level, and shares ability slots with them.
psionic being (Ghost): retains telepathic skills and abilities from her former incarnation as a dire wolf.
free spirit (Ghost): can roam an unlimited distance from her host, but only within the same sector.
born again II (Ghost): grants your familiar 2 additional lives, will resurrect in spirit vessel.

Skills

Available skill slots: 0.
light armor (current: 159. Constitution, basic).

dodging (current: 192. Dexterity, basic).
sneaking (current: 208. Dexterity, basic).
shortswords (current: 201. Dexterity, basic).
two weapon fighting (current: 173. Dexterity, advanced).
thieving (current: 141. Dexterity, basic).

chi (current: 179. Mind, advanced).
meditation (current: 211. Mind, basic).
telekinesis (current: 184. Mind, advanced).
telepathy (current: 214. Mind, advanced).

insight (current: 221. Perception, basic).
deception (current: 204. Perception, master).

channeling (current: 204. Magic, basic).
elemental absorption (current: 110. Magic, master).
null force (current: 77. Magic, master).
null life (current: 31. Magic, master).
null death (current: 51. Magic, master).
nether absorption (current: 200. Magic, master).

magma maw (Ghost) (current: 61. Magic, master).
stygian claws (Ghost) (current: 78. Strength, master).
ash armor (Ghost) (current: 65. Constitution, master).
telepathy (Ghost) (current: 77. Mind, advanced).

Abilities

<u>**Constitution ability slots used:**</u> **10 / 24.**
load controller (10 Constitution, expert, light armor).

<u>**Dexterity ability slots used:**</u> **56 / 84.**
crippling blow (Dexterity, basic, shortswords).
minor piercing strike (5 Dexterity, advanced, shortswords).
improved backstab (10 Dexterity, expert, sneaking).
improved trap disarm (5 Dexterity, advanced, thieving).
superior lockpicking (5 Dexterity, advanced, thieving).
superior set trap (10 Dexterity, expert, thieving).
whirlwind (5 Dexterity, advanced, two weapon fighting).
greater fade (15 Dexterity, master, sneaking).

<u>**Mind ability slots used:**</u> **71 / 123.**
superior mass charm (10 Mind, expert, telepathy).
stunning slap (Mind, basic, chi).
windborne (10 Mind, expert, telekinesis).
heightened reflexes (10 Mind, expert, chi).
twin astral blades (5 Mind, advanced, telepathy).
long shadow blink (10 Mind, expert, telekinesis).
quick mend (10 Mind, expert, chi).

fortified mind (10 Mind, expert, meditation).
astral bite (Ghost) (5 Mind, advanced, telepathy).

<u>**Perception ability slots used:**</u> **36 / 90.**
superior analyze (10 Perception, expert, insight).
improved trap detect (5 Perception, advanced, thieving).
conceal small weapon (Perception, basic, deception).
superior facial disguise (10 Perception, expert, deception).
superior ventro (5 Perception, advanced, deception).
lesser imitate (5 Perception, advanced, deception).

<u>**Other abilities:**</u>
adept slaysight (hidden) (Class, elite, telepathy): paralyze, shatter, sleep, terrify, blind.
superior void thief (hidden) (Class, expert, any void skill and telepathy): steal, siphon, negate.
manifest (Ghost) (Class, basic).
diresight (Ghost) (Class, advanced, telepathy).
direshield (Ghost) (Class, advanced, telepathy).

<u>**Known Key Points**</u>

Kingdom Sector 1 (Nexus) safe zone.
Kingdom Sector 12,560 (wolves' valley) nether portal and safe zone.
Kingdom Sector 18,240 nether portal 1 (guardian tower), and nether portal 2 (Draven's reach).

Dungeon Sector 101 (scorching dunes) exit portal and safe zone.
Dungeon Sectors 102, 103, and 104 (haunted catacombs) exit portals and safe zones.
Dungeon Sector 105, 106, 107, 108, and 109 (guardian tower) exit portals.
Dungeon Sector 14,913 (candidate's dungeon) exit portal and safe zone.
Dungeon Sector 73,102 (Draven's Reach) one-way entrance portal, safe zone, and exit portal.

<u>**Aetherstone Bracelet Stored Points**</u>

sector 24,401 safe zone.
sector 12,560 (wolves' valley) safe zone.
sector 18,240 nether portal 1 (guardian tower).

<u>**Equipped**</u>

<u>**Weapons**</u>
ebonheart (+30% damage).
faithful (+40% damage).

<u>**Armor & Clothes**</u>
sorcerer's coif (perceive tier 6 wards).
ranger's kit (+40% damage reduction, +4 ranks stealth).

bomber's belt (2 x acid bombs, 3 x smoke bombs, 2 x ice bombs, and 3 x fire bombs).
belt of the chameleon (5 x rank 4 nether protection crystals, 11 x rank 4 disease protection crystals, 9 scent concealment crystals, 5 x mental concealment crystals, 4 x rank 6 disease protection crystals, 2 x rank 5 poison protection crystals, 1 x rank 4 strength enhancement crystals, 0 x rank 4 dexterity enhancement crystals, and 2 x rank 4 magic enhancement crystals).
wayfarer's boots (legendary item, +8 Dexterity, move soundlessly).
wayfarer's gloves (legendary item, +8 Dexterity, hands immune to hazardous substances).
cloak of the Reach (legendary soulbound item, +10 Magic, +20% fire magic resistance, +20% nether magic resistance).

<u>**Rings & Accessories**</u>
goliath's ring (+8 Strength).
acrobat's ring (+8 Dexterity).
sharpshooter's band (+4 Perception).
hale stone (+8 Constitution).
savant's ring (+4 Mind).
troll's talisman bracelet (+6% damage reduction).
gift of the unbound ring (immunity to tier 1 and 2 entanglement spells).
band of stillness ring (immunity to tier 1 and 2 Mind spells).
aetherstone bracelet (3 / 5 stored locations, 2 stones charged).
simple potion bracelet (2 / 3 full heal potions).
mage's surprise (+10 Magic, spellhold: trigger-cast tier 5 spells).
psi bracelet (legendary item, +8 Mind, psi-feed).
veteran's trapper's wristband (0 / 200 trap-making crystals) (<u>triggers</u>: pressure plates, sound glasses, tripwires, motion pins, and remote control. <u>elements</u>: lightning, poison clouds, fire, spring-coiled daggers, bear-trap clamps, small explosives, blots of darkness, and ice. <u>guides</u>: reflect, split, and funnel.)

<u>**Other**</u>
backpack, large bag of holding (200 slots), **hunter's alchemy stone**.
pioneer's compass (soulbound, attuned to safe zone).

<u>**Ghost**</u>
shadow's friend (+4 ranks stealth).

<u>**Backpack Contents (Key Items)**</u>

<u>**Money**</u>: 23 golds, 5 silvers, and 3 coppers.
1 x coil of rope.
tavern bill of ownership.
Tartan token.
Vivane token.
Kesh Emporium access card.
cat claws.

spectacles of ward seeing (detect tier 4 wards).
BHG ID (junior member, 1 / 10 active jobs).
1 x rank 6 cure disease potions.
commune rod.
greater trap detect ability tome.
enchanted leather armor set (+20% damage reduction, -35% Dexterity and Magic).
2 x acid bombs, 7 x smoke bombs, 8 x ice bombs, and 4 x fire bombs.
2 x rank 4 cure poison.
mirror shield (reflect tier 4 spells).
phoenix's feather shaft (soulbound).
small bag of hiding (tier 6 concealment ward).
stygian shortsword, +3.
stygian shortsword.
netherstone.
a sealed missive (from Farren).
Blood Talisman.
small bag of hiding containing 100 x possessed finger bones.

Miscellaneous Loot

4 x legendary items.

Alchemy Stone Contents

(14 / 500 ingredients stored).
4 x orbs of petrification, 10 x Shadow ectoplasm.

Bank Contents

Money: 1,655 gold, 0 silvers, and 0 coppers.
2 x full healing potions.
2 x full mana potions.

Tavern Money: 9,850 gold, 0 silvers, and 0 coppers.

Open Tasks

Heist in the Dark (steal chalice from the Power, Paya).
A Perverted Trial (stop the Triumvirate abuse of the Combat Trial).
Brokering Peace (establish peace in sector 12,560 within 4 months).
Brotherhood Obligations (report to the brotherhood after 4 months).
Restore the Nexus Guardian (replace Kolath with Adriel).
Revive the Guardians (awaken Draven's brethren).
Locate the Lost Prime (find the hidden Prime).
Resurrecting Death (make Adriel a scion again).

If you wish to view Michael's earlier player profiles, please visit my site at the links below.

tomlitrpg.com/michael

Chapter 439: In the Kingdom Again

Transfer through portal commencing...
Leaving sector 73,102.

...

...

Passage completed!

You have entered sector 75,172 of the Forever Kingdom, an open sector forming part of the Forever Kingdom's Eastern Marches. This sector is under the control of the Devil Riders, whose claim is yet young.

The following restrictions apply to this region's safe zone: only Devil Rider faction members may teleport into and out of the safe zone, only Devil Riders may purchase new buildings in the safe zone, and only Devil Riders civilians may trade in the safe zone.

Incoming sector-wide announcement...
Fair warning to any members of the Silent Blades and Reaper Clan stupid enough to venture here: if you are found—and you will be—you will be hunted down and summarily executed.
Signed, The Devil Himself.

I stepped out from the portal, my stride firm and my body relaxed.

I had lost count of the number of ley lines I had traversed during my time in the Game, but the experience had stood me in good stead, and no longer did I find the transitions as jarring or disorienting.

Dropping into a crouch, I studied my surroundings. I was in a chamber of some kind. An empty, lightless room. Tattered banners decorated the walls, dirt collected in the corners, broken furniture littered the floor, and a thick layer of dust coated everything.

A chill wind wafted in through the rattling shutters—they'd been left unsecured and open—but no light. It was dark outside.

"Looks like Adriel called it correctly," I murmured. *"This place has been long abandoned."* The building housing the portal anyway, not necessarily the sector.

"Can I manifest then?" Ghost asked.

"Not yet," I replied. Creeping to the nearest window, I peered out and beheld a collection of dark buildings—as unlit and decrepit as my current environs.

Sitting back, I rubbed my chin thoughtfully. It seemed that not only had the portal tower been abandoned, but so too had the surrounding town. There was still one last check to perform, though.

Sending psi rippling outwards, I activated my mindsight.

Tendrils of my will flooded the space around me, forming a net of about four hundred yards in diameter. A net that none but the most adept of minds could evade.

Still, my mindsight failed to uncover anyone.

The town was as deserted as it appeared—which was exactly what Adriel had predicted. According to the lich, there had been nothing of import in the town, except for the exit portal itself.

In Adriel's day, it had been a thriving community, yet its economy had centered around the dungeon. But with Draven's Reach being closed for centuries, it was no wonder the town and surrounding region had been abandoned.

"You can come out now," I murmured to Ghost.

The pyre wolf did not need telling twice. Eagerly, she began manifesting, enfolding me in trails of black smoke. Leaving my familiar to her spell, I turned my attention to the sector welcome messages.

Most of the information in the Game alerts came as no surprise.

According to Adriel and Farren, Draven's Reach exited onto a collection of open sectors collectively referred to as the Eastern Marches. An open sector was one that bordered another, allowing anyone to pass freely between by simply walking across the boundaries.

Strangely enough, despite open sectors being the most common sector type in the Forever Kingdom, this was my first visit to one. The previous two Kingdom sectors I'd visited—well, three if you counted the nether-infested one—had all been closed sectors without any physical means of entering from without.

Still, it was not the fact that I was in an open sector that intrigued me. I'd know to expect it, after all. No, it was the rest of the information that I found fascinating—and troubling.

Devil Riders? Silent Blades? Reaper Clan?

The first was obviously a faction, and at a guess, so were the other two. Considering the sector-wide announcement—*and really, 'the Devil Himself?' Who styled themself such?*—the Riders appeared at odds with the Blades and Reapers. While I had no idea who the factions were, it was clear I'd entered a region in conflict.

Still, not my problem.

I didn't expect to remain in the Eastern Marches long. Crucially, there was no shield around the sector, nor was the controlling faction established enough to prevent anyone from teleporting into or out of the sector. And that meant there were no major impediments to me returning to the guardian tower and discovering how my stranded allies were faring.

Some careful prep work was called for, though.

Work I intended on starting as soon as Adriel and Nyra arrived. Dropping into a more comfortable position, I returned my attention to the exit portal.

Just under a minute had passed since I'd left the dungeon, which meant my companions would be emerging soon. There was no way for me to communicate with Adriel and Nyra on the other side, of course, but we'd decided beforehand that they would delay their own transitions by two minutes.

Ghost has taken the form of a level 211 stygian pyre wolf.

"*Ah,*" the pyre wolf breathed. "*I smell grass, trees, and earth.*"

I smiled. "*It feels good to be out of the dungeon, doesn't it?*"

"*It does.*" She wrinkled her nose. "*But the scents here are different from the valley.*"

"*Do you still remember your old den then?*"

Ghost tilted her head to the side. "*Only vaguely,*" she admitted. "*I recall the warmth of it and the embrace of the Pack. This place feels cold.*"

My smile faded. "*What about Draven's Reach? Did it feel... cold, too?*" One of my biggest fears was how the arctic and dire wolf packs would adjust to life in the dungeon. Would they hate it?

"*Of course.*" The pyre wolf flopped down beside me. "*But the Pack carries its own warmth. It'll do.*"

I nodded, hoping she was right.

✳   ✳   ✳

Almost exactly on the two-minute mark, the portal spun open, and Adriel marched out. A magic shield buzzed around the lich, and her hands brimmed with magic. Clearly, the former Death scion had come prepared for the worst.

Her gaze fell on me and Ghost, sitting at ease beneath the window. "It's safe?"

I nodded in confirmation.

Lowering her hands, Adriel let her spell fizzle out and stepped out of the way just as Nyra stumbled through.

Unlike my own transition and Adriel's, Nyra's was a mess. Her eyes white with fear, the hapless apprentice missed one step, caught herself, then stumbled again and collapsed into a heap on the floor.

My lips twitched, but somehow, I refrained from smiling.

Jerking back to her feet, Nyra spun in a circle, her dagger held in a white-knuckled grip.

"We're alone, Nyra," I said gently. "There is no one close by."

The young sniper whipped around, and spotting my relaxed posture, her own tension eased. "That was..." She licked her lips. "That was something."

"It was," I agreed. "But don't worry, they get easier. The first jump is always the worst."

Adriel snorted. "You should have prepared her better."

"I had a lot on my mind," I said defensively. Before she could respond, I turned back to Nyra and gestured at the naked blade in her hand. During her panicked entry, she had only just missed running it up against Adriel's shield. "You can put that away."

"Oh... right." Sheathing the blade, Nyra began dusting herself off. "Where are we?"

"Exactly where Adriel said we'd be—in the Eastern Marches."

Striding up to me, the lich peered out the window and into the lightless sky. "The town is abandoned?"

"It is."

Sitting down on the other side of Ghost, she inhaled deeply. "The air feels... different."

I smiled. "Ghost said almost the same thing."

Looking down at the pyre wolf, Adriel stroked her coat. "I never thought this day would come, you know. I expected to live out my life in Draven's Reach and, when the day came that I tired of existence, to pass away quietly. To be out..."

I nodded solemnly. "I know what you mean. I was only stuck in Draven's Reach for a few weeks, but even so, I feared Ghost and I would never escape. For you, stuck there for centuries"—I shuddered—"it must've felt like hell."

"Not hell," Adriel said softly. "It wasn't so bad as that. But limbo, certainly." Her eyes brightened. "That, though, is all in the past. I'm out again, and the future looks promising. Tell me, what have you learned about the sector? Is it unclaimed?"

I shook my head. "The owners are a faction named the Devil Riders," I replied as Nyra joined us. "But there is nothing stopping me from teleporting away."

Adriel's eyebrows rose. "There isn't? That must mean their claim is still new."

I nodded. Closing my eyes, I recited the Adjudicator's message verbatim to her.

"Hmm, that's interesting," the lich said. "I gather you haven't heard of the three factions before this?"

"I haven't," I confirmed.

"They must be fighting over the sector," Adriel mused. "It's the only explanation for the newness of the claim. However, why anyone would bother trying to hold this barren place is beyond me. Without Draven's Reach to bring in players, there is little of value in the region."

"A lot could have changed in a thousand years," I pointed out.

"Hmpf. Not that much," Adriel said scornfully. She narrowed her eyes. "Still, we'll have to be careful. There's no telling when the Riders' claim will mature."

"That bit has me worried, too," I admitted.

"You will have to move quickly, then," Adriel said. "Get the items you need, jump to the tundra, and then back here again before—"

"I'm sorry," Nyra blurted. "But what are you two talking about?"

I glanced at my apprentice sympathetically. Only a few days ago, everything Adriel and I spoke of would've been a mystery to me, too, but during the journey to the archlich's court, Adriel and Ceruvax had taken it upon themselves to cram as much Game lore into me as they could. The net result was that I understood the intricacies of sector ownership better than I ever had.

Yet I'd forgotten my apprentice lacked the same knowledge.

I glanced questioningly at Adriel, but she waved me on. "You do it." She smiled. "It'll be a good test of your knowledge on the subject."

Rolling my eyes, I turned back to Nyra. "You recall what I told you about factions and sectors?"

She nodded. "Only factions can claim sectors."

"Correct." Laying my hand on Ghost's head, I idly ran my fingers through her coat while I spoke. "But no claim occurs instantly. Ownership is always transferred gradually. And like with everything else when it comes to the Game, the stages of ownership are clearly defined."

"What are they?" Nyra asked.

I held up my right hand and ticked off points on my fingers. "New. Young. Mature. A new claim is anywhere between a day and a month. A young one ranges from a month to a year. And anytime a faction holds a sector for longer than that, the Adjudicator considers their ownership complete."

"Ah," Nyra breathed. "So, that's what the Adjudicator meant by 'young claim.' The Riders have owned this sector for less than a year."

I nodded. "The problem, though, is we don't know how much less."

The young woman frowned. "Why's that a problem?"

"Because the Game grants the owner progressively more control as their claim matures," I replied.

"After a year," Adriel said, finally interjecting, "a faction can stop anyone except its own members from teleporting into or out of a sector."

Nyra nodded sagely. "I understand now. So, we must leave quickly or risk being trapped here."

"Exactly," I said.

"So, when do we leave?" She looked around—searching for another portal, I thought. "And how do we do that?"

Adriel and I exchanged glances. "That's where it gets more... complicated," I said.

Nyra stared at me expectantly, waiting for me to go on.

I took a deep breath. "Neither you nor Adriel can accompany me to the guardian tower—at least, not right away."

"Why not?" the young woman demanded, her voice rising while the lich stayed silent. She knew all this already.

"Because Adriel is the only mage amongst us," I said quietly, "and she doesn't know the coordinates of the sector we need to get to. Therefore, she can't open a portal for the three of us."

"B-but... but what about that aetherstone bracelet you showed me," Nyra protested. "I thought it held the coordinates we needed."

Adriel sighed. "That's the thing, girl. I can't use it."

Nyra stared at her blankly.

Adriel's lips twisted. "Have you forgotten? I'm not a player. And that bracelet is a Game artifact."

I said nothing. Even as a non-player, Adriel could open portals to any sector she knew, but what she couldn't do was read the aether coordinates of a sector she hadn't visited from a Game item.

This was one of the big drawbacks to traveling with companions. They could not hop from sector to sector as easily as I could with the aetherstone bracelet. Ordinarily, this wouldn't be a problem, but without a mage who could use the bracelet...

"Oh," my apprentice said, shoulders sagging. "So, what then? Do we stay here?"

"You and Adriel do," I said. "But it will only be for a few days. Safyre should still be in the tundra. After I make contact with her, we'll come back to fetch you and Adriel." I glanced at the lich. "Unless you know another sector where you think it will be safer to wait?"

The lich hesitated, then shook her head. "My information is centuries out of date, and the places I know may be in a worse condition than this sector." She glanced around. "Better for us to wait in this remote corner of the world."

Nodding, I rose to my feet. "Then I guess I better head out."

Chapter 440: Venturing Out

I wasn't able to leave for the tundra immediately, of course.

First, there was the small matter of the other Game message patiently waiting for my attention. It had arrived as soon as I'd stepped through the portal, but caught up with scrutinizing the surroundings, I'd not attended to it.

I did so now.

Congratulations, Michael! You have completed Draven's Reach.

You have accomplished the feat: <u>Apprentice Dungeoneer</u>! Requirement: complete any 3 dungeons. You have been awarded an additional life! This life may be assigned to yourself or your familiar.

"Huh," I murmured, "curious."

"What's that?" Adriel asked.

"I just earned the apprentice dungeoneer feat," I said, scratching my chin thoughtfully.

Nyra frowned. "That's a good thing—isn't it?—but you don't sound all that pleased. Why's that? I thought all feats were a welcome bonus."

"They are," I agreed. "But it so happens, I've already earned the *master* dungeoneer feat." I'd gained it in Draven's Reach after slaying my first elite. "This feels like"—I shrugged—"a step backward."

Adriel laughed. "That's because you're doing things in the wrong order."

I smiled. "I suppose that's true." I doubted there were many players foolhardy enough to enter an elite dungeon as early as I had. Still, the additional life was welcome, and seeing as I already had four, I had no hesitation in bequeathing the new life to Ghost.

Your familiar has been awarded 1 additional life. Total lives remaining: 4.

The pyre wolf's ears flickered up as she felt the change. *"Thank you, Prime."*

I inclined my head. *"It's no more than you deserve."* I glanced at Adriel. There were four more matters for me to attend to before I could get going. "What about my blood awakening?" I asked, addressing the most pressing issue.

"Ideally, you should awaken your blood straight away," the lich said, "but given the circumstances, I'm not sure that is wise..." She pursed her lips in thought. "How much did the ritual combat awaken your blood?"

"Enough to gain three lesser blood memories." I paused. "Or one greater one."

The lich's eyes widened.

I grinned. "I would ask which you think I should acquire, but from your expression, I take it that awakening a greater blood memory is the way to go?"

Adriel nodded emphatically. "It is. You remember the spell Loskin used on you before you killed him?"

"The power word?"

"That's the one. All power words are greater blood memories, and if you ask me, each is worth more than any number of lesser ones." She paused. "And that's not counting how your champion Class would further empower it."

My eyes narrowed. "But would I even be able to use a power word? It's a spell, right? And if you recall, I'm—"

"Spell-illiterate," Adriel finished for me. "Trust me, I haven't forgotten that particularly nasty trait of yours. Blood spells—all blood memories, for that matter—are not true spells or abilities. None of them use mana, stamina, or psi. This is part of what makes them superior to Force abilities."

My brows drew down. "That's an interesting—"

Adriel waved her hand dismissively, cutting me off. "Sorry, I'm getting sidetracked. None of that's pertinent right now. We can discuss the relative merits of Force abilities and blood memories some other time. The important thing to note is that it's your blood that fuels your awakened memories, and in the case of a power word, it is your blood that will perform the casting. Even as spell illiterate as you are, you will be able to use it."

I nodded slowly. "Then, assuming I awaken a greater blood memory, how long will it take me to recover?"

"Three days," Adriel answered.

I winced. "That long?"

"Yes," she replied firmly. "And not a minute less. The process is strenuous."

I sighed. "I see. Then, I suppose you're right. I will have to leave awakening the blood memory for later." Withdrawing the Blood Talisman from my pack, I considered it for a moment.

To reach my allies in the guardian tower, I would have to first find a merchant. Unfortunately, I couldn't use the aetherstone bracelet to go *directly* to the tundra because the artifact could only be activated from inside a safe zone, and this sector's safe zone had already been locked down by the Devil Riders.

That left me with only two options.

The first being walking across the sector's boundary to an adjacent sector in the hopes of using *its* safe zone to teleport out. That, though, required the neighboring sector to be unowned—something Adriel and I considered unlikely since the Game messages had already made clear there were at least three rival factions present in the region.

The second option was more promising.

There was more than one way to travel between sectors, and if I found the right merchant, I could buy the items necessary to take me to the nether-infested sector. From there, it was only a short hop into the guardian tower.

Still, searching for a merchant meant wandering the sector and interacting with other players. This was not something I wanted to do with either Nyra or Adriel in tow. My apprentice was too low-leveled and lacked deception, while the lich's mere presence would set tongues wagging.

Then, too, there was the Blood Talisman to consider.

It, more than anything else I carried, was irreplaceable, and I was loath to travel with it on my person. "I'd better leave this with you, then," I said, holding out the Blood Talisman to Adriel.

"Bury it, rather," Nyra blurted before the lich could take it.

Raising one eyebrow, I looked at her questioningly.

"As long abandoned as these ruins appear, no one will come here in search of buried treasure," the young woman explained. She gestured to Adriel. "However, if someone, uh, uhm..." Her face flushing, she made stabbing motions with her hands.

"Kills me, you mean?" Adriel asked with a wry grin.

Nyra nodded mutely.

The lich laughed. "You're right. Players are more likely to rifle through my pockets than some dusty ruins." She smiled lazily. "But you're assuming they'd be able to slay me in the first place. Do you think I'm so easy to kill?"

Nyra's face grew more heated. "I didn't mean to suggest—"

"Relax, girl. I'm only teasing. Your suggestion makes sense. We should bury the blood talisman." Adriel withdrew her phylactery. "And this with it."

"Agreed," I said, glancing at Ghost.

Correctly interpreting my request, the pyre wolf rose smoothly to her feet and headed to the darkest corner of the room, where she proceeded to dig, her sharp stygian claws tearing through the rock underfoot.

"Bury this when she is done," I said, handing the talisman to Nyra. After a second's thought, I handed her the bag containing the possessed's bones as well. Just in case...

You have lost a Blood Talisman and a small bag of hiding containing 100 possessed finger bones.

My apprentice took the items, and I sat down cross-legged.

"What are you going to do in the meantime?" she asked curiously.

"The second thing I need to do before I can leave—save the portal's coordinates so I can return to it when I need to."

✳   ✳   ✳

As an added precaution, I removed all my stored coordinates from the aetherstone bracelet before saving the portal's. If I somehow lost the bracelet, I did not want anyone using it to visit the wolves' valley or worse yet, discovering the hidden nether-infested sector.

You have unetched the aether coordinates of sector 12,560's safe zone and sector 18,240's nether portal.

You have etched an aetherstone with the aether coordinates of Kingdom sector 75,172's nether portal.

Currently stored aether locations: 4. Charged and unetched gems: 1. Uncharged gems: 0.

Reconfiguring the bracelet did not take long; I'd already charged the gems with mana during my time in Draven's Reach. In fact, it took me longer to complete my third chore—weaving a disguise around myself.

You have cast facial disguise, assuming the visage of Jasiah, a level 152 human duelist. Duration: 3 hours.

Adriel's eyebrows rose in mock surprise. "What, no Taim? Have we seen the last of the intrepid explorer?"

I grinned. "I doubt it, but I don't want to use an alias recognizable to anyone from Draven's Reach. If any New Haveners somehow manage to exit the dungeon, they could inadvertently—or even deliberately—give me away."

The lich rolled her eyes. "Your paranoia knows no bounds, does it?"

I threw her an affronted look, but before I could defend myself, she went on, "So, who are you supposed to be this time?"

"Jasiah," I replied, "a rank fifteen duelist, and someone who should be low-leveled enough to go unremarked."

Such would only hold true as long as no one studied my spirit signatures, though. My facial disguise did nothing to conceal my Powerful Initiate Mark. Given that, all I could do was to *try* not to attract attention and hope no one looked at me too closely.

Even just thinking about the matter made me want to wince. My disguise was flimsy, I knew that. But it was the best I had, and under the circumstances, I had no choice but to make do.

The lich nodded. "Wise choice."

"Thank you," I muttered and glanced at the far corner of the room.

Ghost and Nyra were nearly done. Stamping on the ground, my apprentice was doing her best to hide the fact that the soil had been recently disturbed.

"Why did you bring your spirit vessel with you?" I asked Adriel suddenly. "Wouldn't it have been safer to leave it back in Draven's Reach?"

The lich shook her head. "My phylactery and I are bound by the same limitations as Ghost and her Cloak—both must be in the same sector at all times."

"I see," I said and glanced out the open door of the portal tower.

"You best get going," Adriel said, catching my look.

"You'll look after Nyra?" I prompted.

"Of course," the lich replied. "I'll make sure she doesn't get into any trouble." She pursed her lips. "And seeing as how we have some time on our hands, I'll further her education while we wait for your return."

I hid a smile. If I knew Adriel, that meant Nyra was in for a rough few days. *It'll do her good.* "You'll take her north then?"

"I will," the lich replied. "Three days ought to do it. If things are as I remember in the foothills, that should be ample time for some serious training."

According to Adriel, sector 75,172 was the northernmost of the sectors that made up the Eastern Marches, and in her day, the northern foothills had been sparsely populated by rock trolls. The creatures were solitary in nature and usually hard to find, but Adriel was certain she'd be able to locate a few.

"Be careful," I warned.

The lich smiled. "I've survived this long without you looking over my shoulder. What makes you think I can't manage a few more days on my own?"

Wisely, I refrained from further comment, and seeing that Nyra and Ghost were done, I waved the pair over. *Time to take care of the last chore.*

"Nyra, before I go, there is one last thing to attend to."

She looked at me expectantly.

"The Forerunners. I should add you to the faction before I leave. There wasn't time to attend to the matter in Draven's Reach, but I don't think we should delay further." I raised one eyebrow. "I assume you're willing to join up?"

"Of course," she said, clasping the arm I extended.

You have accepted Nyra, a player, into the Forerunners faction. Nyra is free to break her pledge of loyalty to the faction at any time and without consequences. As are you. However, until such time as the Forerunners disavow the sniper—or vice versa—she will be considered the faction's sworn woman, and her actions will reflect on it.

"All done," I said, releasing her hand. "Now, make sure to listen to Adriel. She'll see to your training."

Nyra nodded noncommittally, but I didn't fail to mark the rebellious cast of her gaze.

Sighing, I turned away. Adriel would straighten her out soon enough. "Let's go, Ghost," I said, heading for the door. "We have a merchant to find."

Chapter 441: The Eastern Marches

The Eastern Marches consisted of thirteen sectors. Sector 75,172 was the northernmost and, without a steady stream of players exiting Draven's Reach, was likely the most sparsely populated, too. This was largely why neither Adriel nor I had thought relocating to another sector a good idea.

In sector 75,172, the four of us would be easily missed. Elsewhere... perhaps not so much.

Still, there were ample signs that the sector had not always been the backend of nowhere. The road I followed south, while broken and cracked, had once been formed from good solid stone.

Large manor houses dotted both sides of the abandoned highway as well. Once, they must have been surrounded by their own sprawling, majestic estates. Now, only cobwebs, mice, and other vermin haunted their empty shells.

The countryside itself was flat and appealing. Except for the rolling hills to the north, the rest of the sector was arid grasslands, stretching away as far as the eye could see. According to Adriel, the upper ends of the Eastern Marches were largely infertile—which explained the lack of farms.

The southern regions—what Adriel had referred to as the lowlands— were a different story altogether. Fed by two major waterways and one massive lake, the lands to the south were rich, fertile, and densely populated—or had been in the lich's day.

The lowlands were also home to three of the Marches' four dungeons, and undoubtedly, this was another factor that contributed to the region's popularity. Certainly, it was in the lowlands that I had the best chances of finding the merchants I sought.

My first stop, though, would be the safe zone of sector 75,172.

Who knows, I thought wryly, *I might just get lucky and find what I need there.*

Ghost snorted. *"Lucky? You? Not likely, Prime."*

"I have been. A time or two, at least," I protested, then chuckled, conceding the point. *"But, I admit, my luck usually runs the other way."*

Still, if, by some happy coincidence, I did find the items I needed in the nearby safe zone, matters could turn out much simpler than I expected, and my companions and I could be gone from the region with none of the occupying factions any wiser.

Ghost paused in her step suddenly, drawing me out of my musings.

At first, I thought it was my words that had prompted her to stop, but then I saw her head swing to the left. Raising her snout, the pyre wolf sniffed delicately, tasting the scents on the wind.

"What is it?" I asked, sensing nothing myself.

For a drawn-out moment, Ghost stayed tense, not answering. Then, abruptly, she relaxed. *"Nothing. Just a hungry lion out hunting,"* she replied, resuming her stalk through the long grass. For reasons that escaped me, the pyre wolf preferred having the grasslands' sandy soil under her feet instead of the road's cold hard rock.

I nodded. *"Stay alert, anyway. We must be nearing the river by now."*

According to Adriel, the sector's safe zone was perched on the banks of the river. The safe zones of the other sectors in the Eastern Marches followed a similar pattern. It was one of the peculiarities of the region.

"I can smell it," Ghost said.

"What?" I asked, my brow furrowing.

"The river," she replied. *"And people."*

"Ah. Lead the way, then," I said, slipping in behind her.

✳   ✳   ✳

Less than ten minutes later, Ghost and I were crouched in the tall grass, studying the tiny village perched precariously on the raised bank of a mighty river. The settlement was a collection of about a dozen tiny hovels and looked far from prosperous.

There were no streets as such, just stretches of muddy ground separating the rickety structures. A handful of boats were drawn up along the water's edge, making clear it was the river that was the source of the residents' livelihood.

There could be no doubt the village was occupied either. The subdued candlelight peeking out of the hovels' shutters was evidence enough of that.

"How many minds do you make out?" I asked.

"Forty," Ghost replied.

That was the same count I'd arrived at. *"None of them are players, though."*

Ghost jerked her head towards the darkened building about a hundred yards farther north along the river. *"They must all be holed up in there."*

I nodded in agreement. The structure in question was a block-shaped building—four sheer sides of unrelieved stone holding up a uniformly flat roof—and was at least three stories high. No ornaments detracted from the building's lines either, and its starkness seemed a statement unto itself.

Here I am. Come at me if you dare.

The fort, which is what I marked it to be, sat directly atop the area where I expected to find the safe zone—on the western bank of the river as it turned southward. Unfortunately, I could tell nothing of its occupants.

The structure was shielded from my mindsight.

There were no external guards to offer any clues either. Not that it seemed that the fort needed any. All four of the fort's south-facing windows were barred by steel shutters, and they were so tightly sealed that no light seeped out. The single ground-level entrance was similarly guarded by a set of steel-studded doors.

Yet, it was not the physical defenses that concerned me so much as the magical ones. My sorcerer's coif revealed that all five of the fort's visible openings were covered by tightly knit tier four wards.

Whoever the fort's commander was, he clearly knew his business, and already, I could tell I would not be slipping in unnoticed.

"Can you see into the fort?" I asked Ghost.

She shook her head. *"I can't. The smells are confusing, too. There are people inside, that much I can tell. But there is also another stench. I'm not sure what it is, but it's both overpowering and... unpleasant."*

I sniffed at the air myself. I, too, had noticed the pungent odor on the wind, but I had put it down to the village. Fishing villages were notoriously foul-smelling, after all. I rubbed at my chin thoughtfully. Was the scent indicative of another player species, one neither Ghost nor I had run across yet?

It was certainly possible. But there were other possibilities, too.

Judging from its size, the fort was large enough to enclose the entirety of the safe zone—which, based on Adriel's information, I knew to be quite small—and a good portion of additional land besides. So, whatever was causing the smell wasn't necessarily in the safe zone... and that meant any number of creatures could be responsible for the scent.

I glanced at the pyre wolf. *"You're sure the stench is coming from the fort?"*

"Definitely."

"I see," I said. Sitting back on my heels, I considered my next step.

I had hoped to learn more about the so-called Devil Riders before venturing into the heart of their territory, but that didn't seem like it was going to happen—at least, not tonight.

I can always leave.

There were twelve other sectors in the region where I could get the items I needed, after all. My gaze drifted further right to study the river's opaque depths. The waterway itself was huge. Its far bank was at least two hundred yards away, and given the stillness of the water on top, I judged it deep enough to convey any number of river barges as it meandered lazily southward.

And south was where I would find the Marches' cities.

There was one significant problem trying to search them out, though.

My Power Mark.

Facial disguise—at its current tier—would conceal my identity, my level, and even my Class. But not my Marks. For that, I would need its tier five variant. Which was why I was leery of venturing into any city, much less one controlled by potentially hostile factions.

Until I upgraded facial disguise, I couldn't stop *any* passing player from seeing the mark Powerful Initiate had left on my spirit, and once that happened, word would spread.

Then, the region's Powers would begin hunting me.

I wanted to avoid all that if I could, but realistically, I knew the chances of doing so were slim. The next best thing would be to finish my business in the sector before the hunt began in earnest and leave the hunters ignorant of my true identity.

To do that, though, I needed to move fast: purchasing the items I required and vanishing before I could be detained or run to ground.

Doing that in the middle of a city would be hard.

Doing it in an isolated sector? Not so much.

This was why, despite the fort's daunting defenses, I was loath to move on to another sector.

So option two: *Stay and observe.*

I didn't know anything about the Devil Riders—or any of the other factions in the region for that matter. The wisest course, then, would be to lurk in the shadows and get a sense of how things stood before approaching anyone.

The only problem with this approach was that it wasted time—time I was not sure I had.

There was a third option, of course: sending Nyra into the lowlands to get what I needed. But this was an option I was reluctant to attempt, especially knowing how green my apprentice was.

I exhaled. Once again, it seemed there were no good options.

Ghost's ears pricked up at my sigh. *"Have you decided what to do?"*

I nodded heavily. *"I have. Tonight, we rest. Tomorrow, we begin surveilling the fort."*

The pyre wolf wrinkled her nose. *"For how long?"*

"For however long it takes to figure out what we'll be walking into."

The night passed without incident, and I awoke somewhat groggily with the dawn. Rolling upright, I glanced to my left and saw Ghost was also sitting up.

Something had disturbed us both.

"Aiyeeeeee!"

The pyre wolf's ears pricked at the distance shout. It was coming from the river. *"Trouble?"* I prompted.

"I don't know," Ghost admitted. Still on her belly, she inched closer to the water.

Edging forward myself, I parted the long grass and peered in the direction of the river.

There were five boats on the water, the same ones I'd spotted moored on the riverbank last night. I relaxed. *"It's only the villagers,"* I murmured. It seemed their day had already begun.

My gaze drifted north to the fort. Its doors and windows remained barred and locked. Clearly, those within were no early risers.

"I suppose we should get started," I said, stifling another yawn. Neither of us was likely to get more sleep now.

"What should I do?"

"Stay here and watch from the river's edge," I replied. The reeds alongside the river were dense and tall—which is why we'd chosen it for our overnight camp—and would better conceal the larger pyre wolf who lacked any stealth skills. *"I'll circle around and observe the fort from the other side."*

"Alright," Ghost replied, studying the surroundings doubtfully. *"And what will I be watching for?"*

"The villagers, the fort—anything out of the ordinary. I won't stray too far, so I'll be able to help if anything goes awry. And whatever you do, try not to get spotted."

"Yes, Prime."

✳   ✳   ✳

Four hours later, Ghost and I were thoroughly bored.

I was stretched out flat along the ground, and despite the morning sun beating down from high overhead, I was hidden from sight—not that there was anyone around to see me. Those inside the fort had not stirred yet, or if they had, they gave no outward sign of it.

"How much longer do we have to do this?" Ghost grumbled.

"For however long it's necessary," I replied wearily.

"But I'm hungry," the pyre wolf complained. *"And it's hot."*

It certainly was that.

One thing Adriel had not prepared me for was the intense heat. Perhaps she'd forgotten, or perhaps Draven Reach's cool temperate climes had spoiled me. Whatever the case, Ghost and I were already baking in the scorching heat. But there was no help for it. We would just have to bear through.

"*Can't we do something else, Prime?*" Ghost whined.

"*Like what?*" I asked, wiping away the drops of sweat rolling down my face.

"*Well, why don't you just go up to that building and knock?*"

"*I can't do that,*" I replied firmly.

"*Why not?*" she demanded querulously.

"*For one, we don't know how the Devil Riders will react. They're almost certainly not our enemies. Indeed, they probably have no clue who we are, but that doesn't mean they'll welcome us with open arms. In fact, given the tone of that sector-wide announcement, I'm inclined to believe they're the kind to attack first and ask questions later.*"

"*But what if you—*"

"*Then, there is my Power Mark,*" I continued, deliberately speaking over her. "*It alone will make them suspicious—perhaps even suspicious enough to call for help from whatever Powers rules their faction. And that, we want to avoid at all costs.*"

"*Oh, alright,*" Ghost said, deflating. But only a moment later, she spoke up again. "*But there must be something else we can do. Anything else. Please, Prime. Maybe, we could—*"

"*Well, you could always return to the Cloak,*" I snapped before I could bite back the words. The heat was making me irritable, too, it seemed.

Still, my retort silenced Ghost's protests as I knew it would. With a loud mental sigh—that she made sure I heard—the pyre wolf flopped back against the ground. Ignoring her antics, I kept my gaze pinned on the fort.

The northern face of the structure was a mirror of its southern one—four windows and one door, all locked and barred—and once more, I couldn't help but frown as I considered the fort.

Having walked the perimeter of the building twice this morning, I was sure the safe zone was housed inside the fort's depths. But while the fort was certainly large enough to house both the safe zone *and* the one thousand soldiers required to keep the Riders' claim valid, it had to be scorching inside. Were they not feeling the heat?

Metal screeched.

My focus sharpened. "*Ghost, you hear that?*"

"*I do, Prime,*" she replied, sitting up attentively. "*It sounds like a door opening.*"

"*I agree,*" I said, scanning first the door, then the four windows on my side of the fort. All five remained adamantly closed. "*Is it on your side?*"

"*No.*"

No?

Ghost's response left me momentarily stymied. The fort's east and west walls were blank slates, absent of any openings. I'd double-checked earlier to make certain of that. "*Are you sure about—*"

I broke off.

Something had appeared on the roof.

A large flying something.

A second, a third, and then a fourth followed in its wake. I groaned, finally realizing where the unseen opening was.

"There's a door on the roof," I told Ghost. Which perhaps explained its flatness.

"What are those things?" Ghost growled, ignoring my comment as her gaze fixed on the newly emerged creatures. *"They smell... disgusting."*

I wrinkled my own nose. I was closer than the pyre wolf to the fort—less than fifty yards away—and from this distance, the stench wafting off the creatures was more potent.

More joined the initial four until a full ten had assembled on the rooftop. From nose to tip, each creature was about the length of a horse. Their wingspans were thrice that, though.

In shape—if not in size—they resembled Gnat, but where Erebus' minion had been fleshless, these creatures were most assuredly not. Crimson leathery skin covered each giant bat. Their eyes shone a fierce red, and somehow, I got the impression that the heat bothered them not at all.

Reaching out with my will, I inspected the closest creature.

The target is Ectarr, a level 167 hellbat and demonic companion.

Hellbats are a rare subspecies with only one known spawning ground: the lava fields of Mount Torment. Unusually intelligent and more than a little magical in nature, they often bond for life with their chosen partner. They are not picky with who they pair with either and will often bond with the first individual—be it a bat or another creature—who impinges deeply on their consciousness.

Note: companions are alike yet different from familiars. Even more than familiars they are separate Game participants. They do not share their host's attributes, or their levels.

Companions do, however, partake from the same pool of lives and Class points as the player to which they are bound. Kill a player's companion, and he, too, will lose a life.

On the heels of the Adjudicator's response, ten bipedal shapes appeared on the roof, and I didn't need to analyze them to know what they were: players.

"Devil Riders and their rides," I muttered.

"Prime?"

"The hellbats are the players' pets," I explained. *"And if I had to guess, it's not just these ten that use them. The entire faction must."* I chewed on my lip. *"Which complicates things."*

"How so?"

"The river reeds are not going to hide you from those flying above," I replied, watching the Riders mount their hellbats. Where were they going? It didn't matter, though. The chance that the Devils would fly over the river and spot Ghost was too great. *"Time to unmanifest."*

"But—"

"No buts, Ghost," I said, cutting her off. *"They're about to launch. Do it now."*

"Yes, Prime," she replied meekly.

A moment later, I felt the pyre wolf's form begin to unravel, and I relaxed. Not only would the Devil Riders have been able to spot Ghost if they flew over her, but they could also hunt her down if they were so inclined. As fast as my familiar was, there was no way she was going to outrun an airborne pursuit.

Across the distance, I saw one of the players pause before jumping into his saddle. Backing away from his hellbat, he turned to face the river.

I tensed in sudden trepidation.

It was almost as if the Rider had sensed Ghost's casting, but he couldn't have...

Could he?

Ghost had not finished unmanifesting, and though I could not see her, I imagined she still was a nebulous—but very visible—cloud of darkness. A few more seconds and she would be safe. I only needed the player to do nothing for that long.

But I couldn't take the chance that he would cooperate.

Rising into a half-crouch, I drew psi and crept forward. There was only one surefire way to stop the Devil from interfering—presuming he could do so, of course, and I had no choice but to assume that—and it required me getting closer.

A wand dropped into the player's hand from wherever he'd kept it concealed in his sleeve.

It was all the confirmation I needed. The Devil was about to fling a casting at Ghost. I had to act. Whether or not I could've trusted the Riders enough to trade with them was all moot now. Releasing the weave I held ready, I dove into action.

The Devil's hand jerked up.

A fraction of a second later, I shadow blinked.

You have teleported 50 yards. You are hidden.

As I stepped out of the aether, I saw spelled energy gathering at the tip of the Devil's wand, threatening to burst out. Ebonheart was already in motion, though. It was a race to the finish.

But it was not a fair contest.

No spell was as fast as my black blade.

Almost too fast to see, ebonheart darted in and out, snuffing out the light in the Devil's eyes before any of his fellows could so much as register my presence.

You have killed Reinhart, a level 172 warlock, with a fatal blow.

His ties to life severed, the Devil slumped to the ground.

Around the corner of my eye, I saw a reddish shape blur forward. While the other Riders were still oblivious to the new danger in their midst, the dead warlock's demonic companion wasn't.

A hostile entity has detected you! You are no longer hidden.

Its eyes swimming with hatred, the hellbat lunged at me. I spun away, and its exposed throat sailed past. I made no move to stab at the creature, though. Instead, I drew more psi.

I'd eliminated the threat to Ghost, which was all that mattered, and now it was time to escape. Killing the hellbat would only hamper my efforts to do so. Backing away farther, I kept spinning psi.

"What—!"

"Who's that?"

"... did he come from?"

"Reinhart!"

The hellbat snapped at me again. Ducking low, I let its jaws close on empty air, still making no attempt to engage.

Rising back up, I found thirty-eight pairs of hostile eyes pinning me. They were in motion too, hellbats and players alike charging recklessly forward.

Unfortunately for them, I'd already bought myself all the time I needed. Releasing the psi in my mind, I let my will ripple outward and into their midst.

You have cast slaysight.

Sadly, given the mass of enemies converging on me, I had no time to finetune the casting, and so I released my spell without any specific targets in mind.

Acting indiscriminately, the slaysight spell invaded the weakest of the hostile minds around me, locking their limbs in place.

You have paralyzed 9 of 10 targets for 60 seconds.
Ghost has unmanifested.

Chaos ensued. The unfrozen players and hellbats, ignorant of their fellows' bespelled state, crashed headlong into their suddenly motionless bodies.

Not bothering to observe further, I spun around and headed for the roof's closest edge, drawing psi as I went. More cries and shouts rose behind me.

Ignoring them, I leaped off the building.

CHAPTER 443: WOLF ON THE RUN

I didn't fall to my death, of course. Midway to the ground, my spell finished, and I released it without ado.

You have cast windborne.

Borne upon a cushion of air, I landed softly, but I wasted no time in setting off, dashing farther north. I didn't look back. I didn't need to. My mindsight had already told me everything I needed to know: three pairs of closely entwined mindglows were in pursuit.

A trio of hellbats and their riders.

The doors to the fort were creeping open, too, and I knew it would not be long before I had more than the three airborne Devils to worry about. Drawing psi and stamina, I began casting my buffs.

"*Prime, what's happening?*" Ghost asked from the Cloak.

"*We're fleeing,*" I said tightly.

You have cast heightened reflexes.

"*I can see that, but why? I thought—*"

"*One of the Devils sensed your spell—my fault that. I should have figured out that they might do so. Anyway, I had to kill him.*"

"*Oh.*"

You have trigger-cast quick mend.

Before the pyre wolf could comment further, a fireball sailed across the sky, lobbed down by one of my hunters. Sidestepping left, I dodged it easily, but I was not at all reassured. I could no more outrun pursuit than Ghost could, and once more Riders took up the chase, the hail of incoming missiles would increase tenfold.

It was time to hide.

You have cast fade, blurring your form and making you 50% harder to see for 2 minutes.

The moment the buff was in place, I threw myself flat. The surrounding grass was only knee-high, but even that much would suffice to hide me. Wriggling like a worm, I burrowed deeper into the grass.

Six hostile entities have failed to detect you! You are hidden.

I exhaled softly. *Better.*

So far, my escape plan was going off without a hitch. But I knew I couldn't afford to stay still. Snaking through the grass as unobtrusively as I could, I kept moving.

A moment later, the earth shook as three enormous shapes hit the ground in a trio of thuds—the Riders landing. They'd touched down at the spot they'd last seen me which, thanks to my slow crawl, was already a half-dozen yards distant. They wouldn't find me in a hurry.

"Where is he?" a Devil demanded.

"Hiding," a second replied. "But he's close. Axyl can smell him."

Smell me? I didn't like the sound of that. Axyl had to be one of the hellbats, I realized.

Damnit. I should have used a scent concealment crystal before going in. It was too late for recriminations, though. For now, I had to concentrate on widening the gap between me and my hunters. Then, and only then, could I see to masking my scent trail.

"Karri?" the second Devil prompted.

"Working on it, Cor," the third Rider—Karri presumably—replied. "We'll have him soon."

Uh-oh. That didn't bode anything good either.

Worse yet, I could hear Karri chanting furiously under her breath. She was obviously casting, but what? *A revealing spell—or something worse?*

Damn and damn.

"Should I manifest, Prime?"

"No," I replied firmly. I still hoped to escape my hunters without revealing Ghost's existence or too many of my own abilities, for that matter. But I also realized that if I was going to have any hope of evading pursuit, I would have to take care of the three players and their companions—and fast. Already, I could sense more mindglows appearing on the roof.

Nothing for it then, I thought and drew psi.

It would've been perfect if I could simply sleep the trio and their pets, but my paralyze debuff was still active, and unfortunately, I couldn't have multiple slaysight effects active simultaneously.

Which left only mass charm and my blades.

Deciding I didn't want to show all my cards to the Devils just yet—the way things were going I would likely clash with them again—I rose into a crouch and shadow blinked.

You have teleported into Karrisen's shadow. You are hidden.

I emerged from the aether atop the Rider's hellbat. The creature stiffened, feeling the additional weight immediately. My target, though, remained oblivious.

Wrenching back her head with my left hand, I plunged ebonheart through the side of her throat just as the hellbat chirped in alarm.

You have killed Karrisen, a level 170 witch, with a fatal blow.
Five hostile entities have detected you! You are no longer hidden.

The black blade slipped into my mark without resistance. The witch had not seen to her defenses before setting out after me—a mistake that had cost her a life.

"He's here!" the first Rider exclaimed.

"I can see that, you fool!" Cor replied. "Get him!"

Tugging on the reins he held, Cor yanked his hellbat around while his fellow—more wisely—ordered his mount aloft. The dead Devil's demonic companion, meanwhile, reared up on her legs, flinging me off.

Tucking in my limbs, I controlled my precipitous flight and rolled back to my feet as I hit the ground, only to find myself facing Cor charging me down with a drawn shortbow pointed unerringly at my heart.

The rider released.

I dodged.

This time, not even my speed was enough to spare me entirely, and the shaft lodged deep in my right shoulder.

Corrigan has critically injured you!
You have failed a physical resistance check! Your right arm has been crippled. Your health is at 60%.

Agony rippled across my shoulder as the arrowhead tore through muscle and sinew to scrape against bone. The next instant, my right arm went limp, causing my fingers to open and ebonheart to fall free.

I ignored both my incapacitated arm and the dropped blade. Cor was still rushing headlong at me, a triumphant grin on his face. Karrisen's mount was only a step behind, while the other Devil was still winging aloft.

No doubt, he was building height to crash down on me in a calamitous dive. But for now, he was no threat. Gritting my teeth, I unsheathed faithful with my left hand. Then I waited.

A frown flickered across Cor's face as he realized I was not going to drop down and die. Yanking back on his hellbat's reins, he nocked another arrow.

He'd left it too late, though.

His mount was not going to stop in time.

You have cast piercing strike, doubling the damage dealt on the next attack.

Sidestepping to the right, I slashed outward with faithful as the hellbat rushed past. The startled archer raised his bow to fend off the blow, but the wooden implement was no match for bright steel—nor for the fury of my blow.

The bow snapped.

Leather armor tore.

And a second later, Cor's head flew free.

You have killed Corrigan, a level 174 parthian archer, with a fatal blow.

A furious red shape crowded my vision. Knowing what it was, I tucked my head into my chest and braced myself as best I could.

Magx, a level 160 hellbat, has hit you. Your health is at 50%.
You have been knocked down. You are <u>dazed</u> (reaction time slowed). Duration: 3 seconds.

I flew backward. Even having expected the blow—and accepting it as the price for killing Cor—it hurt. But despite the pain, I managed to keep faithful clenched in a white-knuckled grip.

Magx was not done with me, though.

Rushing onto my downed form, the hellbat trampled me with its taloned feet while simultaneously slashing at me with its clawed hands.

Magx has attacked you. Your health is at 47%.
Magx has attacked you. Your health is at 44%.
...

"Prime, let me manifest!" Ghost cried.

"No," I growled. Making no attempt to shield myself from the furious assault from above, I drew psi. The spell formed more slowly than was its wont, courtesy of my dazed state.

In the meantime, more blows rained down, but the pain barely impinged on my awareness. I'd grown used to psicasting under even the most difficult of circumstances.

The last spell weave snapped into place, and I blinked out.

You have teleported onto Axl.

I emerged atop Cor's hellbat, still flat on my back. The creature stiffened beneath me. Ignoring it for the time being, I righted myself. Twisting my body around, I scissored my legs to grip the creature's sides and heaved my torso erect.

Axl's head whipped around to nip at me, but I was ready for it. Smashing the pommel of faithful against the hellbat's snout, I caused it to flinch. And before the creature could recover, I buried the gleaming blade hilt-deep into its muscular neck.

You have critically injured Axl. Your target is bleeding.

It was not a fatal blow, far from it, but I was sure I'd struck a major artery. Wrenching faithful free, I rolled off the unwilling mount and left it to bleed out on its own.

I hit the ground hard, and the arrowhead, still lodged in my shoulder, was driven deeper still.

Your health is at 34%.

Biting back a yelp of pain, I rolled onto my back and craned my neck up, taking stock of the battlefield. Axl was stumbling around on my left, mewling in pain and no threat. High above, the last Rider had begun his dive, while up ahead, the other hellbat, Magx, was charging me down.

I squeezed my eyes shut. The battle was far from decided, and everything could still go pear-shaped. Inhaling deeply, I took a moment to consider my next move.

Flee, hide, or attack?

But it was a false choice really. I couldn't flee as I was. And with the blood pouring out of my shoulder, even a half-blind man would be able to track me. *Attack it is.*

My eyes snapping open, I drew psi.

Magx drew closer. I waited.

The hellbat ran over me again, stomping first onto my legs, then my torso, before coming to a stop with its feet splayed on either side of my head. I winced at each impact but, concentrating on my casting, didn't otherwise react.

This time, though, the creature didn't bother to pummel me with its hands and feet. Instead, it opened its mouth wide and lowered its head.

Perhaps it was a bid to keep me in place and prevent me from fleeing like I had before. I didn't care. The move was an unlooked-for opportunity, and altering my plans on the fly, I readied faithful.

The hellbat's head drew closer.

Still, I waited, not moving until the creature's red eyes were within inches of my own.

Now.

In one smooth move, I thrust my left hand upward, driving the sharpened tip of faithful straight into the surprised creature's mouth and out through the back of its skull.

You have killed Magx with a fatal blow.

The hellbat collapsed, blood pouring out of its mouth and all over me. Trying not to gag, I dragged myself out from under the corpse and searched the skies.

The last Devil had pulled out from his dive and was circling high above. He seemed more circumspect than his dead companions, and if I had to guess, I'd say he was trying to figure out if I was dead or still a threat.

It was the time for my last gambit.

Releasing the casting I held ready, I swamped the Rider's mind with my will.

You have charmed Amatein, a level 166 lancer.

The spell executed flawlessly, and I wasted no time in relaying my instructions to my new minion. *"Jump,"* I ordered the Rider as I staggered upright again.

Obedient to my will, the lancer freed his feet from his stirrups and threw himself into open air.

You have taken hostile action against your minion!
Control of target lost.

Abruptly coming to his senses, Amatein screamed as he tumbled in freefall. Whipping around, the hellbat dove after the falling player. But it was too late to save the Rider.

His death was already a foregone conclusion.

Wrenching the arrow from my shoulder, I drew more psi. It was time to heal up, recover my weapons, and quit the area.

Chapter 444: Snaring Foxes

Amantein has died.
You and Ghost have reached level 212!
Your sneaking has reached rank 21 and your chi rank 18.
You are hidden.

A few seconds later, ebonheart was back in my sheath, and I was crawling away from the bloodied battleground. The two remaining hellbats evinced no interest in me. One hung around its dead companion, whining mournfully, while the other had collapsed on its side, gasping its last breaths.

I, myself, was far from hale and had more than a few ministrations to perform. First, though, I had to make sure I couldn't be easily found again. Tugging free an enchantment crystal from my belt, I crushed it in the palm of my hand.

You have activated a single-use enchantment, completely masking your scent for the next 4 hours.

There. Now, they won't be able to sniff me out. Glancing over my shoulder, I examined the bloody trail I was leaving in my wake. *Time to take care of that,* I thought and released the spell I'd been preparing during my retreat.

You have restored yourself with quick mend. Your health is at 54%. Your right arm is still crippled.

I also had another instance of the spell ready — the trigger-cast version — and without hesitation, I activated it as well.

You have restored yourself with quick mend. Your health is at 74%. You are no longer crippled.

"Ah," I exclaimed, exhaling in relief as the hole in my shoulder closed. I was still covered in an assortment of cuts and bruises, but none of my injuries were life-threatening or serious enough to hamper me.

Beginning another casting, I finally looked up and took the time to study the new cloud of Riders gathering above the fort. The air was thick with them, making it difficult to separate individual mindglows or even shapes.

"How many do you make out?" I murmured.

"Three hundred," Ghost replied confidently.

I grunted. If I went by the minimum numbers required to secure a safe zone, that had to be nearly a third of the fort's full strength. Whoever was in charge was not mucking about. Instead of sending his Riders piecemeal after me, he was gathering them into an unassailable force.

One that even a Power would have trouble facing.

I sighed. It could only mean one thing. One of the players on the roof had seen my spirit signature and had read my Power Mark. It was the only explanation for why anyone would send so many players after what was only a lone intruder.

You have restored yourself with quick mend. Your health is at 94%.

"You think they're all for us?" Ghost asked.
I nodded. *"I'd bet on it."*
"What do we do?"
"The only thing we can—hide."
There would be no outrunning the gathering force, and even hiding would prove problematic. It could be done, though—with some careful preparations.

Glancing down, I studied my footprints. They were barely perceptible, but any able scout would still spot them. And while I had no way of concealing my tracks, I *did* have a means of leaving none.

Opening my mindsight, I scanned the surroundings. Despite the recent battle, not all the local wildlife had fled, and there were more than a few targets to pick from. Selecting one, I shadow blinked.

You have teleported into the shadow of a level 12 prairie fox. You are hidden.

"Boo," I whispered, causing the fox to yelp and bolt.
Ignoring the fleeing animal, I studied the surrounding terrain. I was in a natural fold in the land. The shallow dip was not large enough to conceal me on its own, but that was what my stealth was for. If I remained still and unmoving, even a master scout would have trouble sensing anything amiss.

It'll do, I thought, deciding against performing further hops across the landscape.

My chosen spot was close to the battlefield—only forty yards away—but that was not necessarily a bad thing. The Riders would expect me to have fled farther afield than that, and I doubted they would search the nearby surroundings as thoroughly as they should.

Or so I hoped, anyway.

I glanced in the direction of the fort again. The Devils were still gathering, their numbers growing by the minute. *How many are going to be enough?* I wondered.

I sighed. It didn't matter, though. For now, staying put was the best recourse. *And who knows, I might learn something.*

Lowering my head, I saw to the rest of my preparations.

✳   ✳   ✳

Axl has died.
You have restored yourself with quick mend. Your health is at 100%.

In the end, the Devil Riders did not set out until their total force numbered six hundred—three hundred players and the same number of hellbats. Not all headed after me, though. A full half—one hundred and fifty players and their mounts—peeled off south, heading for the river.

Frowning, I watched them go. Why had the Devil commander sent so many in that direction? Was it to find whatever the warlock Reinhart had sniffed out earlier?

Possibly.

I bit my lip, but I wasn't convinced the other Devils could know what had caught the warlock's attention. I'd killed him too quickly for that.

Refocusing on the small army heading my way, I watched them fly closer. Reaching the site of the battlefield, the three hundred did not land as I expected. Instead, they remained airborne, circling the area.

Multiple hostile entities have failed to detect you! You are hidden.

Craning my neck up, I studied the players. The Devils were grouped together in ordered wings of ten hellbats. Flying in formation, they cut huge circles in the air, and despite the distance separating us, I could see many faces were turned downward, inspecting the terrain.

Abruptly, a wing veered away, heading north. Another followed, choosing a different heading. Then, more wings followed, each covering a different direction until only a single group remained.

The command group? I wondered.

Reaching out with my will, I analyzed the players left behind.

The target is Titus, a level 195 human heavy lancer.
The target is Asha, a level 191 human heavy lancer.
The target is Canara, a level 191 elven ranger.

...

...

The target is Leafbright, a level 206 elven blight druid.
The target is Zultan, a level 203 orcish hellbringer.
The target is Malikor, a level 258 human paladin.

I whistled soundlessly. The lowest-leveled player in the group was rank nineteen. Additionally, they were accompanied by no less than *three* elites.

Definitely the command group.

What's more, each of the ten players bore a telltale Mark.

...bears a Mark of Mammon.

"Mammon," I whispered. It was not a Power whose name I recognized.

"Who's that?" Ghost asked.

"A Power in the Devil Riders' faction, perhaps even its ruler." I pursed my lips. *"All the players in the wing are pledged to him."*

"Is that bad?"

"Hmm. Possibly. The Mark means all ten are either followers or Sworn. As followers, they will be stronger than most other players of the same level, but other than that, they'll be no different and not of any great concern. It's the Sworn we have to worry about."

I fixed my gaze on the group's probable leader—Malikor. The paladin was covered from head to toe in lacquered red armor. For a human, he was truly huge—seven feet tall, at a guess—and his mount was equally large. The elite had a massive broadsword sheathed at his hip, a round shield across his back, and a pair of throwing axes stashed in his saddle.

"You see him?" I asked Ghost.

"The giant human in red armor?"

"That's the one. He, at least, is almost certainly a Sworn. Or worse yet, an envoy. Killing him will alert Mammon immediately."

"So, what do we do?"

"For now, only watch, wait, and hide. There is no upside to tangling with a force that powerful. And they look as if they're about to land." Falling silent, I observed the graceful descent of the hellbats while I renewed my buffs.

You have cast heightened reflexes, load controller, fade, and trigger-cast quick mend.

The ten creatures touched down in a close-knit group around the bodies of their dead fellows. Dismounting immediately, six of the group—lancers and warlocks mostly—peeled off to form a defensive cordon while the three elites and the ranger stayed in the center of the formation.

"Zultan, Leafbright, talk to me," Malikor growled. Despite his clipped tone, the paladin's words still carried to me forty yards away.

"We've only just landed," the elf replied reproachfully, her voice soft and warm as a summer's breeze. "Give us a minute."

"Work faster then!" the paladin snapped.

Not bothering to reply, the two spellcasters began chanting. Seeing that none of the enemy group were attempting to search the vicinity, I judged the risk of a few slow, controlled movements to be minimal. Reaching out with my right hand, I brushed aside a few errant stalks of grass to better view the Devils.

Lost in the midst of their spells, the two spellcasters had closed their eyes. Malikor himself stood unmoving next to them, arms folded and his visor still down.

The ranger, meanwhile, was moving quiet-footed from corpse to corpse, inspecting the wounds and the footprints I'd left behind. In the background, Amantein's mount—the sole survivor of the skirmish—kept up its mournful pining, but none of the Devils paid it any heed.

Wrapping my left hand around the hilt of faithful, I refocused on the two elite spellcasters. For now, they were the biggest threat. Tense with anticipation, I waited for the pair to complete their spells.

This was the moment of truth. Either I was discovered and forced to flee again or my defenses would stand up to scrutiny of their magic.

Zultan has cast burning gaze.

On the heels of the Game's message, the orc's eyes flared an ugly red. I wasn't sure what his spell had done, but it was a safe bet that the hellbringer had somehow enhanced his sight.

Staying where he was, Zultan pivoted around in a slow circle, and as his eyes passed over me, another Game alert dropped in my mind.

You have passed a mental resistance check!
A hostile entity has failed to detect you. You remain hidden.

I loosened my grip on faithful. *So far so good.*

The orc turned to Malikor. "The area's clear. As far as I can tell, anyway. But like I've told you before, revealing spells are not my forte. If you want to be certain, bring in the scouts."

The paladin grunted, but with his visor down, I couldn't read his expression nor gauge if the response was one of agreement. Saying nothing, he turned to the druid whose chanting was winding down.

Leafbright has cast nature unchained.

Her spell finished, the blight druid stretched out her arms. In response, the grass beyond the Rider cordon rose.

No, not rose, *grew.*

Even from as far away as I was, I could see each stalk thicken and lengthen until it resembled not grass but sticks of wiry bamboo. Leafbright was not done yet, though. Raising her arms skyward, she caused the circle of unnatural vegetation to grow larger, expanding first ten yards beyond the Devils, then twenty, thirty, and forty.

"What's going on, Prime?" Ghost asked.

I was just as puzzled. *"I'm not sure,"* I replied, watching the encroaching vegetation.

"Should we flee?"

"Not yet," I replied, not moving even as the magical forest of bamboo eclipsed me. Despite their supernatural origins, nothing about the overgrown stalks screamed of danger, and for now, I was content to wait and see what happened next.

The spell expanded, causing the grass beyond me to grow as well. How far the casting extended, I couldn't tell. The bespelled grass, pin-straight and at least eight feet tall, obscured everything from view.

At a yelp from the right, my eyes darted sideways.

A prairie fox has died.

I was sure the prairie fox's death was no accident. Somehow, Leafbright's spell was responsible.

The bamboo around me shivered, and my gaze jerked back to them. The stalks were no longer standing erect. Curling in on themselves, their upper ends were looping over until their tips pointed downward.

My eyes narrowed. Was this the true purpose of the druid's spell? To weaponize the vegetation? Staring at the sharpened ends of what suddenly looked like over a dozen deadly blades pointed my way, I readied myself to dodge.

But contrary to my expectations, the bamboo stalks did not stab down.

Instead, they began to exude a fine mist of glowing pollen.

My alarm grew. Whatever was in the pollen, I knew I didn't want it to touch me. I still refused to move, though. My void armor was sure to protect me, and I thought it better to trust in my defenses than to act precipitously.

A pollen seed floated lower. Avidly, I watched as it touched naked skin.

You have failed a magical resistance check!

A blight pollen has devoured 0.009% of your health (life magic damage reduced by 15% due to void armor).

A carnivorous bamboo stalk has leeched a fraction of your life force.

The pollen vanished, taking with it an infinitesimal portion of my health, and, if the Game message was to be believed, transferring the same quantity to the bamboo stalk which had birthed it.

Bloody hell, I thought, eyeing the millions of other spores following in the wake of the first.

The damn plants want to eat me.

The plants could not eat me, of course.

Not unless they had more to work with than devouring pollen. Lowering my head, I turned my face away from the sea of descending seeds and waited for my void armor to do its work.

You have sustained life damage.
You have sustained life damage.
...
...
Void armor charge remaining: 95%.

It didn't seem to matter where the pollen settled. Indirect contact, whether through my armor or cloak, was sufficient for the damnable things to suck away my life.

Void armor charge remaining: 90%.

I tensed at each contact, but there was hardly any pain, only a tiny pinprick hardly worthy of notice. But truly, the pollen was terrifying—or would have been, if not for my void armor. The tiny monstrosities were everywhere, leaving nowhere within the bamboo forest safe. Once Leafbright's spell ran aground, every living creature inside would be dead.

Except me.

Void armor charge remaining: 70%.
Void thief triggered!
You have acquired the channeled spell, <u>nature unchained (stolen)</u>, from Leafbright and will retain memory of it for the next 12 hours.
Nature unchained (stolen) is a tier 5 spell that causes all vegetation within 100 yards of the caster to awaken and turn carnivorous. The awakened vegetation will grow to gigantic proportions and release a swarm of symbiotic pollen seeds that will devour any nearby living creatures, further enlarging the host plant. The vegetation will remain awake for as long as the caster channels the spell.

Void siphon and negate activated!
A blight pollen has failed to harm you. You are immune to this spell.

I would have laughed if I didn't think the Devil Riders would hear. Not only had I survived, I'd gained a powerful spell, too. Now, all I had to do was wait for the casting to end.

Might as well put the time to use.

Closing my eyes, I considered my new attributes. I'd gained two from the last encounter and had carried over two more from Draven's Reach. I didn't have to deliberate too long about how to invest them either.

Your Dexterity has increased to rank 88. Other modifiers: +24 from items.

With not much else to do, I turned my attention back to the command group. The bamboo stalks still obscured my line of sight. My mindsight, though, was unimpaired. However, to my surprise, none of the Riders nor their hellbats' mindglows were visible anymore.

Hmm. I turned my gaze skyward, but just as I suspected, it was empty. Whatever else the Devils were, they were noisy—well, except for the ranger; she looked capable enough—and I doubted they'd managed to sneak away.

Which could only mean they had shielded their minds.

I bit my lip. *That'll complicate things if it comes to a fight.* I shook my head. It would do more than that, especially with three elites on their side. Battling the command group was out of the question—for now, at least.

Closing my eyes, I set about channeling mana. I would only remain immune to the druid's spell for as long as my void armor remained active, after all.

✳ ✳ ✳

Your null life has reached rank 4.
The spell, nature unchained, has dissipated.

Leafbright kept her spell going for a full five minutes—far longer than I could have managed. Eventually, though, the bamboo shrunk back to ordinary stalks of grass, returning the command group to my line of sight.

"Is it done?" Malikor demanded.

Leafbright nodded. "Nothing is out there, nothing living anyway," she said, her melodious tone at odds with the destruction she'd just wreaked. "The area has been scoured."

Nodding sharply, the paladin removed his helmet, revealing a bearded face, square jaw, blond hair, and cold blue eyes. "Good. Now, can someone tell me what the hell happened here?"

Malikor had thrown the question to the group at large, but it was the ranger to whom he looked.

The elven woman rose to her feet. "One man did all this," she said, gesturing to the corpses.

"I know that," Malikor replied impatiently. "How?"

"With his blades," Canara replied succinctly.

The paladin stared at her. "That's all you got for me? Our interloper killed everyone with his swords, and then he got away scot-free?"

"But he didn't get away scot-free," the ranger corrected mildly. "Our foe was injured. Badly, too, I'd say."

The orc, Zultan, snorted. "That can't be right. The intruder bore a Power Mark. What challenge could three riders and their companions pose for him?" He spat contemptuously. "Nothing, that's what. Corrigan was an idiot to chase after the Power on his own like that."

Leafbright threw him a reproachful look. "The lieutenant didn't know what the intruder was. The three left before Aguir could report what he saw."

Zultan grunted. "It was still reckless. The fool is an officer. He is paid to think for himself."

Canara shrugged. "Be all that as it may," she said, gesturing to a blood-spattered spot. "Cor's people fared better against the intruder than they had any right to expect. This here is the Power's blood."

Leaning over, Malikor studied the grass. "You're sure?"

The elf looked at him in affront. "Of course, I am."

The blond-haired man's eyes narrowed thoughtfully. "That's… interesting."

"Why?" Zultan demanded.

Ignoring the question, the paladin glanced at the druid, who had moved on to inspect the skirmish's sole survivor—Amantein's mount.

"What does Ormeen have to say?" Malikor asked.

Leafbright had placed her hands on either side of the hellbat's head. Without looking up from the distraught creature, she shook her head. "I can't get much from him. His thoughts are too scattered. And you know, Ormeen, he was never the brightest to begin with."

"But you must have got something," the paladin pressed.

"A smattering of images," the druid admitted. "They're disjointed, but from what I can tell, Ormeen thinks Amatein fell."

Zultan barked a laugh. "Fell! That's ridiculous."

Canara gestured to the mangled and nearly unrecognizable corpse beside the hellbat. "Amatein *did* hit the ground hard."

"Hard enough for the impact to have killed him?" Zultan asked.

"Harder," the ranger replied.

Malikor sighed. "So, what are we saying? Our mysterious interloper somehow jumped onto the roof of the fort, assassinated Reinhart—and why him?—froze nine others, fled, killed five more, then disappeared? None of that makes any sense to me. Does it to anyone else?"

"Maybe," Canara said, frowning.

The paladin whirled to face her. "Explain."

"You've got the sequence wrong," the ranger replied. "I don't think our 'guest' was trying to enter the fort when he was interrupted by Reinhart's patrol. I think he was *leaving*. Reinhart probably sensed him, which is why he was killed." She shrugged. "Corrigan and the others must've gotten in the way, too, somehow."

The other three stared at her. "You think he was *in* the fort?"

"He must've been. Why else would he have been on the roof?" Canara countered.

Leafbright bit her lip. "To get into the fort, the interloper would've had to bypass our wards and avoid detection, making him a highly skilled thief."

"And we know who has plenty of those," Zultan said with a scowl. "The damned Blades."

"Is that what you think he was?" Malikor asked. "A Blade?"

The ranger nodded. "I do." Walking to another seemingly nondescript spot, she gestured the others over. "See this?"

"See what?" Zultan grumbled.

"The blood," Carna clarified.

"We see it," Malikor confirmed. He looked up at the ranger. "Is there supposed to be something significant about it?"

The elf rolled her eyes. "Yes. It just ends. One moment our interloper was leaking blood, the next his trail goes cold." She stomped on the ground with her booted heel. "This here is where he didn't want to be tracked further."

Comprehension dawned in Malikor's eyes. "Then, he is good enough to defeat even your skills," he murmured.

"He is," Canara admitted.

"Further evidence that he is a bloody sneak!" Zultan exclaimed.

The ranger nodded solemnly. "I think we got lucky detecting him. If not for Reinhart's patrol, he would have gotten away cleanly. As it is, I suspect he's already crossed the river and back in Blade territory."

"But what did he want in the fort?" Zultan asked, his face wrinkled in confusion. "It's little more than an outpost. Little of value is stored within."

Malikor's eyes narrowed. "That's the question, isn't it?"

"Perhaps he was hunting," Canara suggested.

"Hunting what?" Malikor asked.

"You, of course," the ranger replied. "Have you forgotten? You are Mammon's envoy. *You* are the most valuable thing in the fort. If our mystery guest killed you, the Blades would have a much easier time reclaiming the sector." She gestured to the other two elites. "Then there is Leaf and Zul. As Sworn, they, too, were also likely also marked for elimination."

"So, why didn't he?" Leafbright asked. "Eliminate us, I mean?"

Canara sighed. "I don't know. Perhaps, the wards on your chambers defeated him, or perhaps, he got unlucky."

"So, not a thief, then. An assassin," Malikor muttered. "Not your typical Blade."

"Could he be a new recruit?" Leafbright wondered.

"He must be," the paladin agreed. "Such a high-level assassin would not escape the notice of Mammon's spies for long. They would've got word to us before this."

"Which brings us to another important point," Leafbright interjected. "What do we tell Mammon?"

All eyes turned to the paladin—the envoy, rather.

"Nothing yet," Malikor said after a moment of prolonged silence.

"Nothing?" Zultan asked, stomping closer to the paladin. "We're his Sworn. It's our responsibility to inform our lord about the rogue Power running around in his territory. He'll surely want to know!"

"We tell Mammon nothing," the paladin reiterated firmly. "Not until we've confirmed Aguir's report." He stared hard at the orc, who backed away hastily.

Leafbright's eyebrows rose. "Not that I disagree with your stance, Mal... but do you think Aguir was mistaken?"

"That or he was deceived," Malikor replied. He gestured to the corpses. "Does this look like the work of a Power to any of you? How many Powers do you know who would need to flee from ten players? Ten! Or get injured while fighting six?"

No one had an answer for him.

"Still," Zultan finally volunteered, a trifle sullenly I thought, "forging a spirit signature is damn near impossible. There can't be many who can pretend to be a Power."

"It's possible, nonetheless," Malikor retorted.

"You believe he is a deception player then?" Leafbright asked.

The envoy nodded curtly. "I do." He met each of his subordinates' gazes in turn. "And until we hear differently, that's the official line. Our mystery guest was a player, a high-leveled one to be sure, but a player, nonetheless. I've no intention of going crying to our lord about a *potential* Power sighting. He would be most displeased if our report turned out to be false."

"If not to report to Mammon, what's our response?" Canara asked.

"We take every precaution conceivable," Malikor replied. "If this *was* the work of a Blade, it can only be a precursor to an attack."

"They would have to already be in position to launch their assault," Leafbright mused. "Even if the assassin succeeded, their window of opportunity would've only been sixteen hours—at best."

"Exactly," Malikor agreed. "Which is why I want our people out in force, patrolling the river. No Blade is to sneak by, clear?"

"Clear," the other three echoed.

"What percentage of our people do you want to deploy," Zultan asked, all business now.

The paladin rubbed his chin. "At least half. You will command the eastern river patrols and Leaf the western ones. I'll guard the fort. I meant what I said. We may not be able to stop the Blades from crossing, but we'll damn well know when they do."

CHAPTER 446: CIRCLING AROUND

The Devil command group did not linger long after that.

Mounting their hellbats, they flew swiftly back to the fort, no doubt to put their plans into effect.

Staying where I was, I ruminated over what I'd learned. The Riders' conversation had certainly been enlightening. I now knew for certain that all three elites were Sworn, and in addition, Malikor was an envoy.

More importantly, I'd learned that the neighboring sector to the south was under the control of a rival faction—the Silent Blades. And the good news was that Malikor didn't seem too keen to report the presence of a Power to his boss, Mammon.

That gives me time, I thought.

How to use it, though?

From the sounds of it, this sector had recently belonged to the Blades, which perhaps explained its 'young' designation. What's more, it appeared that the Riders feared the Blades would attempt to reclaim it.

That's my lever, I decided.

"We cross the river?" Ghost asked, following my thoughts.

"We do," I confirmed.

"You think those Blades will help us?" she asked doubtfully.

"Help may be stretching it," I allowed, *"but if we can convince them our interests are aligned, I don't see why not."* I paused. *"Besides, I don't think we have much choice but to seek them out. If we can't secure the Blades' aid, we'll have to venture into the lowland cities, and that I think will be even more risky."*

"But how will you hide your Power Mark from the Blades?"

I grimaced. *"I don't think I can."*

I sensed Ghost's uncertainty. *"But... won't that just draw the attention of their faction's Powers?"*

"Let's hope not," I replied grimly. *"Because then we'll have two factions on our heels, not one."*

✳ ✳ ✳

Cutting a wide arc around the fort, I made my way swiftly to the river. Soon, I expected Malikor's promised river patrols would set out, and I had to cross before that happened.

That was not to say the river was unguarded.

The other half of the Devil force I'd spied setting out earlier hadn't returned to the fort. Instead, they had settled alongside the river's northern shore in evenly spaced squads of ten.

Still, one hundred and fifty players and their hellbats were hardly enough to cover the entire length of the river, and there were gaps in their cordon—which was why I had to cross now, before the envoy reinforced their numbers.

Multiple hostile entities have failed to detect you! You are hidden.

Stretched out flat on my tummy, I inched through the grass. The nearest Rider squad was fifty yards to my left, and although I deemed the likelihood of being spotted to be slim, I wasn't about to take any chances. Continuing my ponderous crawl to the river—it was only ten yards away now—I listened with half an ear to the nearby players.

"... think the Blades will attack?"

"I doubt it, but what do we know? We're just grunts."

"Yeah, command really seem to have their panties in a bunch this time."

"Now, there's an image," the second chortled. "I wouldn't mind seeing some of them in their undies, let me tell you. Especially, that—"

"Eew, Meng, that's gross!" the first exclaimed.

"Admit it, Pel, you were thinking the same thing," Meng said smugly.

Before the other player could reply, a third intervened. "Get your mind out of the sewer, soldier!"

"Yes, sarge," Meng replied unrepentantly. "But you don't fool me. I caught you staring at Leafbright just the other day, too, and I swear, you were panting."

"Shut up, Meng!" the sergeant barked. "Or I'll break that damn ugly mug of—"

Multiple hostile entities have failed to detect you!

Shaking my head in amusement, I slipped unseen into the river.

The water was pleasantly cool, and if not for the surrounding danger, I would have reveled in its touch. Staying beneath the surface, I waded deeper.

Adriel had labeled the Marches' lake and twin rivers the region's lifeblood, and everything I saw only confirmed that view. The water teemed with life—which, I suppose, explained why the villagers didn't bother trying to farm the less hospitable land.

When I was a safe distance from the shore, I came up for air. A quick breath and a look to orient myself, then I ducked beneath the surface again.

Multiple hostile entities have failed to detect you!

I smiled. *So far so good.* Spreading my arms, I swam strongly toward the southern shore. Soon, I expected, I would be out of the Riders' reach. The Marches' waterways acted as more than a source of trade and food. They also served to divide its sectors.

Adriel had not been able to recall all the details of the region's geography, but she'd remembered enough to tell me that the rivers were invariably the most contested sector borders, and the Game alert that dropped into my mind midway through my swim only reinforced the truth of that.

You have entered sector 75,175 of the Kingdoms, an open sector forming part of the Forever Kingdom's Eastern Marches. This sector is under the control of the Silent Blades.

The following restrictions apply to this region: only Silent Blades faction members may teleport into and out of the sector, only Silent Blades

may own buildings in the safe zone, and only civilians with the necessary trade permits may access Nexus' banks and global auction.

"Well, well," I mused. The Adjudicator's message confirmed my suppositions. Sector 75,175 was a mature sector firmly under the control of the Riders' rivals—the Blades. The alert implied more than that, though.

Unlike the Riders, the Blades had not limited trading rights to their own people. It suggested a greater degree of openness on the part of the second faction, and dared I hope... a willingness to trust?

Maybe I won't even need to parley with the Blades, I thought as I came up for air again. *Maybe I'll find a neutral merchant to—*

You have passed a Perception check!
You have detected a hidden entity.
You have detected a hidden entity.
You have detected a hidden entity.

...

...

In an eyeblink, a plethora of Game messages swamped my mind, simultaneously demanding my attention. Snapping alert, I studied the far shoreline as the seemingly random collection of distant lines and curves resolved themselves into recognizable shapes.

Players.

Scores of them, hidden in the reeds. *Waiting for me,* I thought, dread curling in my stomach.

✳   ✳   ✳

A second flurry of Game messages followed hard on the heels of the first.

A hostile entity has failed to detect you!
A hostile entity has failed to detect you!
A hostile entity has failed to detect you!

...

...

Not a reception committee then, I thought, letting myself sink back to the river bottom. Those hidden in the reeds were *not* lying in wait for me. In fact, they seemed to have no idea I was even nearby.

Because while I had uncovered the stealthed players, they had not found me, in turn. None had so much as stirred since the first Game alert had dropped in my mind.

All this told me one thing: my sneaking outstripped the waiting players' Perception.

This was another bit of Game lore imparted to me by Ceruvax and Adriel. To receive an alert from the Adjudicator—even if it was only one concerning a failed Perception check—one had to *first* pass an unseen check. In the past, when I'd received 'failed' Game messages, it was only against foes whose stealth did not far exceed my own Perception.

The Game mechanic made sense, too. Sneaking would be of limited use if every time a player failed to uncover a hidden player he was alerted to that fact!

The two-check system—unseen and seen—did not only apply to Perception checks either. It applied equally to other aspects of the Game where being alerted to a failure could prove advantageous.

The question now, I thought, sitting on the riverbed thirty yards from the shore, *is what do I do about the waiting Blades?*

And I was all but certain those on the south shore were Blades. The Devils' conversation implied their foes were stealth-based players. Their chosen faction name did so, too.

Did I reveal myself?

Doing so would be a show of good faith. But I couldn't afford to assume the Blades would be friendly. If I revealed myself and they proved to be otherwise, the consequences could be disastrous.

Waiting is wiser, I decided, floating back up.

Most of the Blades were visible in my mindsight but not all. I noted those carefully. Breaking the surface gently, I drew in some air, then silently swam farther downstream, intent on circling around the waiting players.

While the water did a good job of concealing me, it also restricted my movements, and when I finally made contact with the Blades, I preferred to do so with solid ground underfoot.

You have detected a hidden entity.

...

...

As I swam, I took count. There were two hundred Blades hiding amongst the reeds. Each was covered in mud and grass and lay still and unmoving in their own bit of hollowed-out ground. Given the players' preparations, I could only conclude they'd been at their silent vigil since before dawn, and perhaps all night, too.

Was Malikor right? Were the Blades about to launch a counterattack against the Riders? Given the numbers the rival faction had deployed along the river, it certainly seemed a possibility.

Hmm. If an assault *was* imminent, the Blades would be on high alert and no doubt suspicious of any interlopers. I would have to be doubly careful in how I approached them. Reaching the end of the Blade line, I crawled back onto the shore.

Multiple hostile entities have failed to detect you!

The reeds made for excellent cover, not just for the Blades but for me, too, and I crept confidently through them and past the hidden players. I had no intention of disturbing them.

For one, it would be hard to have any meaningful discussion under the watchful gaze of the Riders on the opposite shore, and for another, if this many Blades were gathered here, I was sure they had to have a base nearby.

I only needed to find it.

* * *

Your insight has reached rank 23.

Before moving on, I made sure to analyze all two hundred Blades. Their levels were similar to the Riders with the lowest player being rank fifteen and the highest rank eighteen. But, surprisingly, there were no elites amongst them.

Uncovering the Blades' base was harder than I anticipated, though.

For one, there were no tracks to follow. Amazingly, none of the two hundred players had left a trail for me to follow. It seemed that amongst other things, the Blades were also expert woodsmen.

The terrain did not help as much as I hoped either. From a distance, the grasslands appeared uniformly flat—deceptively so—however, that was not truly the case, and there were more than enough folds in the land to hide even a sizable structure.

Around dusk, after hours of fruitless searching, I sagged to the ground, about ready to give up. I'd spent the better part of the day crisscrossing the lands south of the river yet had not stumbled across a single clue to point me to the Blades' base, nor had I run across anyone else to direct me—willingly or otherwise.

Perhaps I've assumed incorrectly. Perhaps there is no base to find.

"What's wrong, Prime?"

I sighed. *"This isn't going as well as I expected, Ghost. I can't find the Blades' hideout."*

"Maybe it's deeper in the sector?"

I grimaced. I'd limited my search to a five-mile radius around the stealthed players, reasoning that if their base was any farther, my chances of finding it were nil.

"If it is, I'm not going to find it," I muttered. *"This damn sector is just too damn big."*

"Maybe I can help?" the pyre wolf suggested hopefully.

It was on the tip of my tongue to refuse, but I stopped myself in time. Ghost's senses *were* more sensitive than mine. I glanced at the sky. It was darkening rapidly, too. And on the open plains at night, she'd be hard to spot. The risk would be minimal.

And truthfully, I wasn't making any progress on my own.

"Alright," I agreed. *"That sounds like a good idea. Let's give it an hour for night to fall."* Stretching out flat, I closed my eyes. *"Then, we'll search again."*

CHAPTER 447: STEPPING IN IT

Ghost has taken the form of a level 212 stygian pyre wolf.

Three hours later, I was wandering the plains again, with Ghost ranging ahead of me. We'd not discovered our target yet, but I was optimistic. My familiar had found a scent trail.

"It's gone again," the pyre wolf reported.

I paused. *"You're sure?"* I'd gotten no whiff myself of whatever Ghost tracked. Its traces were too faint for me to detect.

"Yes," she replied, sounding frustrated. Her shoulders sagged. *"It's disappeared."*

I pursed my lips. This was the fifth time the pyre wolf had lost the scent. At first, I'd thought she'd misstepped somehow, then that the player we tracked had masked their scent. Now, I wondered...

Narrowing my gaze, I scanned the terrain up ahead. The trio of hills and the deep dip resting at their feet were familiar. We'd visited the area multiple times already, having approached it from different directions, and it was here—always—that Ghost lost the scent.

"The area is shielded," I murmured, feeling a stir of excitement at the realization.

Ghost wrinkled her nose. *"What?"*

I glanced at her. *"There has to be a ward about this place,"* I replied. *"That's why you keep losing the trail when we get close."*

The pyre wolf's gaze sharpened. *"The Blades' base is here."*

I nodded. *"It must be."* Reaching up, I rubbed at the side of my head.

You have activated a sorcerer's coif.

I waited a heartbeat. Then another. But no glowing lines of magic appeared in my sight.

Frowning, I lowered my hand. *"That can't be right,"* I murmured. *"There are no wards."*

Looking just as puzzled, Ghost sat down. *"Maybe the spell is too powerful to detect?"* she suggested.

I shook my head. *"The ward would have to be tier seven for that."* I met her gaze. *"Too powerful for any player to set."* Could there be a Power nearby? I wondered.

I bit my lip. It was a possibility but not likely. If the Blades had a Power nearby, surely they would have launched their counteroffensive already? Or was there more going on here than I was aware of?

"What do we do now?" Ghost asked, echoing my own thoughts.

I sighed. Retreating would be the prudent choice. But that meant going back into the Riders' territory or heading into the lowlands—both of which were also fraught with risk.

"We keep searching," I pronounced. *"But carefully."*

An hour later, I was still in the area, moving about with the wary gait of someone who *knows* there is danger nearby but just can't seem to find it.

Crouched small, I crept forward a few careful steps. Fifty yards to my right, Ghost inched forward on her belly. We'd spread out for obvious reasons. If I ran into danger, I'd teleport to my familiar. If she did, she would unmanifest.

Staying motionless, I scanned the vicinity with every means available to me—sight, smell, sound, mindsight, and even trap detect—but nothing turned up anything amiss. No alerts dropped into my mind. No Game messages triggered.

And yet, the back of my head still itched.

"Again," I ordered, ignoring the telltale premonition of danger as I had for the last hour. Following my own command, I ranged forward once more.

I kept the trio of hills and the deep dip beneath them in my sights. We were yet to enter the area itself, but it had not escaped my notice that the dip was perfect for a hideout. It was large enough to conceal a sizable camp. *If there is a base,* I thought, advancing once more, *it will be there.*

Snick!

At the soft click beneath my booted heel, I froze. But it was too late. I'd already misstepped.

You have triggered a trap!

A split second later, I backflipped, attempting to throw myself out of harm's way.

It didn't work.

The ground shifted—not just in the immediate vicinity, but all around me, in a twenty-yard radius. Dirt shot upward. The grass churned. And from beneath, a checkered cloth bearing the dull sheen of metal emerged.

Not a cloth—a net. A steel net.

As if it had a life of its own, the net flung itself after me. I was quick, but it was faster, and while I was still midair, the thing wrapped around me like a second skin.

You have failed a physical resistance check!

A shackling net has enveloped you. You have been <u>snared</u>. Duration: infinite. The debuff will remain in effect as long as the net stays in place.

Oof! I hit the ground hard. With my hands and legs trapped immobile by the net, I was unable to break my fall.

"Prime?" Ghost called from afar, concern lacing her tone.

"I'm alright," I panted, even as the net wrapped tighter around my neck. The thing really did seem to be a living creature, and while it didn't appear to be trying to strangle me, it was doing its damnedest to stop me from moving.

But as frustrating as that was, the trap was purely physical in nature.

It did not inhibit my psi abilities. Gathering my will, I prepared to escape its clutches.

You have detected multiple hidden entities!

I paused in my psicasting. Sure, the latest Game message was further cause for alarm, but it was *also* an opportunity, and on impulse, I let the spell I was casting dissipate. Opening my eyes, I bent my head backward.

Ten shapes were creeping toward me.

Where they'd come from I couldn't tell, but it had to be from the hidden base I searched for. Even better, they didn't appear to be aware they were under observation. *"Don't move, Ghost,"* I murmured, not letting my eyes rest too long on any of the advancing players. *"We have company."*

"What are you waiting for then? Get out of that net!"

"No," I said, finally articulating the impulse that had led me to abort my escape. *"The ones approaching have to be the Blades we came here to find, and what better way to meet them as I am—seemingly defenseless?"* If nothing else, it would be a test of how far I could trust the faction.

"Are you certain?"

"Yes, and don't worry, if it comes to a fight, we can handle them." Reaching out with my will, I analyzed the three players at the forefront of the group.

The target is Deklan, a level 175 human rogue.
The target is Cine, a level 180 elven greenblade.
The target is Yara, a level 176 orcish knife hand.

I smiled to myself. The trio's levels were nothing unexpected, and increasing the violence of my struggles, I feigned ignorance as the group dispersed to surround me.

"You hear that?" Ghost asked abruptly.

Caught up in my pretense, I'd heard nothing. "No, what is it?"

"A grinding noise. It's coming from the hill."

A prickle of unease shot through me. *"I can't look right now. Tell me what's happening."*

"The hill, it's.... moving."

Moving?

"A part of the hill is moving," Ghost clarified before I could ask. *"It's a door, I think."*

A door in the hill?

I'd been wrong, I realized. The Blades' base was not in the dip but inside the hill. *Clever.*

A second later, the pyre wolf's emotions spiked with fear—not for herself, but for me. *"More players are emerging."*

"How many?" I asked, suppressing my own alarm.

"Hundreds," she replied.

I closed my eyes. Hundreds was a bit more than I bargained for.

"Flee, Prime," the pyre wolf urged worriedly.

"No," I said firmly. Ten. A hundred. It didn't matter. I needed information on the Blades, and given the circumstances, this was the best way to get it. *"Let's see how this plays out."*

✳   ✳   ✳

Cine is no longer hidden.

The shadows wrapped around the elven Blade fled, and he materialized in front of me. Keeping up my pretense, I froze in feigned shock.

Cine smirked. "Well, well. What do we have here?" he drawled as the other nine in the leading group unmasked themselves. There was no sign of the players Ghost had spotted emerging from the hill, and I assumed they were deliberately keeping themselves out of sight. The ten alone were sufficient to defeat me, though.

That is, if I really were Jasiah, a rank fifteen player.

You have passed a mental resistance check! An analyze attempt by a hostile entity has failed.

Cine has failed to pierce your disguise.

I almost smiled, as right on cue, the familiar tingle of a failed analyze attempt washed off me.

"Let me go!" I panted in what I hoped was a suitably panicked voice.

I didn't really expect my disguise to hold up indefinitely. Eventually, someone would think to check my spirit signature, but before that happened, I hoped to convince the Blades to hear me out.

The elf chuckled. "Oh, we won't be doing that."

"What do you think, Cine," Deklan mused, toying with a slim stiletto, "should we cut him first?"

"Definitely," Cine replied. Striding forward, he squatted before me. "Why did Malikor send you?" he asked, glaring at me in a manner I assumed he meant to be intimidating. Unfortunately for him, I'd stared down much bigger foes.

"He didn't," I whined, intensifying my futile struggles. "I'm not a Rider."

The elf snorted. "Sure, you're not. How did you find us?"

"I–I t-tracked... you," I said with wide, vacant eyes.

Deklan laughed. "Impossible. A rank fifteen chit like you couldn't track a Blade."

"I ev–v–vaded y–your people at t–the rrr...river," I stuttered.

Cine's eyes narrowed. "How do you know about the cordon? Does Malikor have spies in—"

"Back!" Yara barked suddenly.

The elf's eyebrows shot up as he glanced over his shoulder at the orc, but he didn't heed the command. "What's gotten into you, Yara? Don't tell me you're afraid of this Rider scum?"

"He bears a Power Mark, Cine," Yara growled. "Whoever that bastard is, he's no rank fifteen player!"

The elven Blade fell back, his mouth opening in shock.

"Impossible," Deklan snarled.

I sighed. The gig was up and sooner than I expected.

"I'd listen to the orc," I said smoothly as I abandoned my charade, "she's smarter than you two idiots."

The rogue's eyes narrowed as he noted my sudden change in demeanor, but he paid it no heed. "Shut your mouth! If you don't, I'll gut you like a pig," he said, brandishing his stiletto.

"Trying that would be a mistake," I replied mildly.

"Who said anything about trying," Deklan spat, taking a threatening step forward. "We've got you trussed up good."

I laughed. "You don't."

The rogue raised his blade, but before he could do anything foolish, Cine intervened. "Stop!"

Freezing in place, the rogue glared at the elf.

"Yar is right," Cine continued, unperturbed by Deklan's heated look, "the bastard is a Power."

"But—" the rogue began.

"Back off, Dek," Cine ordered, rising to his feet. "I won't ask again."

Grudgingly, the rogue stepped back, and Cine turned back to me, his expression grim. "Now, tell me who you are and what the devil you're playing at. Because, by Blythe, Power or not, I swear we'll cut you to pieces if you don't!"

Chapter 448: A Meeting of Blades

"Who's Blythe?" I asked lightly, ignoring Cine's glare.

For a drawn-out moment, no one answered. I couldn't tell if that was because my question had caught them off-guard or if they had been struck speechless by my audacity.

Yeah, right.

"Blythe is our lady and the leader of the Silent Blade faction," Yara replied finally.

I inclined my head in her direction, or tried to anyway, but the net still ensnaring me made that hard. "Thank you."

"Don't pretend you didn't know that already," Deklan growled.

"I'm not a Rider," I said, striving to keep my voice free of exasperation. I'm a stranger to the Marches. I landed here by... accident."

"More lies," Deklan scoffed.

"I'm not lying," I said evenly.

"But you don't deny you're a Power," Cine interjected abruptly.

I glanced at him. "I don't."

His eyes narrowed to slits. "So, why shouldn't I kill you?"

"Well, for one, you'd find that hard to do," I replied blandly. "And for another, I can help the Blades regain the sector the Riders stole from you."

Deklan snorted. "What, all trussed up like that, *you're* gonna help us?"

I shrugged. "Looks can be deceiving."

The rogue opened his mouth to retort, but before he could, Yara spoke up. "How?"

"How?" I echoed.

"How can you help us against the Riders?" she elaborated.

"Surely, I don't have to spell it out?" I asked. "I'm a Power. What more is there to tell?"

None of the Blades looked impressed by my response. Cine even went so far as to shake his head. "You may bear a Power Mark," the elf stated, "but that does not make you a Power. And no Power I've ever met would allow themselves to be captured the way you have. In fact, I'd hazard to guess that you're not even rank thirty yet."

I kept my face smooth, but internally, I winced. It seemed I'd erred in feigning helplessness. I opened my mouth, ready to change tack.

Before I did, Cine stepped back. "And whatever you are, you're still an intruder. There's only one way to deal with those." Raising his voice, the elf shouted, "Kill him!"

✳ ✳ ✳

Cine's order did not catch me entirely flatfooted.

Regardless of what the Blades thought, I was not easy prey. My buffs were cast, Ghost was primed and alert, and my escape spell was ready.

No sooner had the words left the elf's mouth, than I cast.

You have teleported into Ghost's shadow.

Stepping out of the aether, I dropped flat onto the ground and wrapped myself in shadow.

You are hidden.

Fifty yards away, I heard Deklan curse. "The bastard's gone!"
"I can see that!" Cine snapped. "Find him!"
"Cine, you fool, what did you do that for?" Yara rasped. "We could've—"
"Shut up!" the elf snarled. "Or are you forgetting who's in charge?"
The orc snorted. "You won't be for long, once Tyelin hears about this."
Even from across the distance, I saw Cine's face turn purple with rage. "Do as you're told, Yar, or it's you who will be facing his wrath."
Wordlessly, the orc spun around to face the other seven silently waiting players. "You heard the *commander*," she said, somehow managing to make the word sound like an insult, "spread out and find the intruder."
Turning away from the ten Blades, I scanned the surroundings beyond. Yet, I still failed to spot any of the players Ghost had seen leaving the hidden base earlier.
"Where are they?" I asked.
"The other Blades went to ground," Ghost reported, not needing to be told who I meant. *"But before they did, they dispersed."* She paused. *"I think we're surrounded."*
I nodded thoughtfully. The news was not unexpected. What was, though, was that the hidden Blades were not visible in my mindsight. It likely meant the cordon the players had formed around me was larger than four hundred yards in diameter.
"How many did you spot leaving the base?" I asked.
"I'm not sure," Ghost admitted. *"Sorry, Prime, I'm still not great with numbers. A hundred maybe? Or two?"*
"Hmm," I murmured. Against those numbers, it would be safer to flee than to fight. The question, though, was fleeing wise? I'd not drawn Blade blood—deliberately so.
After the mishap with the Riders, I'd gone out of my way not to do so, not wanting to anger a second faction. But, in hindsight, that might have been a mistake.
Cine spoke truly, I acknowledged.
No Power I'd ever met, not even Loken at his most affable, would tolerate the disrespect I had during my pretense, and I'd messed up in approaching the Blades from a position of weakness instead of strength.
It was too late to go back and rectify the situation, though.
Still, I was not about to let myself be hounded across this sector and however many others the Blades controlled. Attacking Cine's people might earn their enmity, but it was better than being run to ground like prey.
It was time for a show of strength.
That at least might make them wary of tangling with me further.
"Ghost, here's what we do."

                              ✳   ✳   ✳

A minute passed, and still, the Blades failed to find us.

Not that their search was a thorough one. Spreading out, they thrashed at the bushes with their weapons.

I could tell from the muttered comments of some, and the tentativeness of others, that at least half of Cine's people lacked night vision. But despite this, no one released a magelight—something I would've found suspicious if I didn't already know about the *other* Blades hidden nearby.

Whatever the case, given the haphazard manner of their search, Cine's people were not going to find me, and I suspected they didn't expect to, either.

The Blades were obviously trying to flush me out and into the waiting arms of their hidden comrades. It was a cunning ploy and might have worked too, if Ghost hadn't spotted the emergence of the rest of the Blades earlier.

I turned to my companion. *"Ready?"* I asked.

"Ready," she replied, her gaze fixed on the nearest of the searchers, a pair of human Blades twenty yards away.

"Go," I ordered softly.

With all the stealth of a natural-born predator, Ghost rose to her feet and slunk silently up on her targets. I stayed where I was watching.

Fifteen yards. Twelve. Ten. And still, the pair didn't notice the giant wolf creeping up on them from behind.

I snorted. *And these two fancy themselves rogues?*

But perhaps, I was being unfair. The darkness camouflaged Ghost nicely, and the duo lacked my own night vision.

Eight yards. Six. Four.

Now, I silently urged. Any closer, and even half-blind as they appeared, the pair were bound to notice the pyre wolf. But Ghost didn't need me to tell her what to do.

Right on cue, she pounced.

The pyre wolf's large frame arced through the air. Her massive paws made contact with her target's shoulders. A split second later, her jaws closed on the back of the player's neck, and he collapsed with nary a squeal.

The perfect takedown.

Ghost has killed Walsh with a fatal blow.

"Wha—?" Walsh's companion cried.

He didn't get much further. Spinning around, Ghost leapt off the corpse and directly at the second player, and he went down hard.

But not before shrieking loud enough to wake the dead.

Petre has been knocked down.
Ghost has activated astral bite.
Your familiar has critically injured her target.

Cine, Yara, Deklan, and the others were not slow to react. Weapons were drawn, and eight pairs of eyes jerked in the pyre wolf's direction.

**Multiple hostile entities have attempted to analyze your familiar.
Secret blood triggered!
Ghost's true Class has been concealed, and instead, she has been identified as an unknown stygian of level 212.**

I chuckled softly. Since gaining the sire wolf commander Class, I'd known my secret blood trait would hide Ghost's true nature, but what I hadn't known was how it would accomplish that.

Misidentifying the pyre wolf as a stygian, though...

... that was perfect.

"A stygian!" a Blade cried.

"Powers above!" Deklan swore. "Where did it come from?"

"It's the intruder's doing, you idiots!" Cine growled. "He's a summoner. Kill it!"

Ghost has killed Petre.

As one, the remaining eight players converged on Ghost, but she didn't stay to meet them. Sticking to the plan, she bolted back the way we'd come and toward the river.

"After it!" Cine howled.

"No, you fool!" I heard Yara mutter, but not so loud that any of the others picked up on it. "Don't you realize this is a ruse?" But despite her reservations, the orc followed after her companions. Wisely, though, she hung back.

Smiling, I waited until the players were out of earshot, then I began chanting. Until I completed my casting, my familiar was on her own. But I had faith in the pyre wolf. She would do her part, leading the Blades on a merry chase while I did mine—readying the stolen spell.

"*Good luck, Ghost,*" I murmured before turning my attention inward and doing my best to speed up my spellcasting.

✳   ✳   ✳

A little later, I stopped chanting and opened my eyes.

**Spellhold enchantment activated.
You have successfully stored the <u>nature unchained</u> spell in the ring, mage's surprise. This spell may now be trigger-cast when required.
Note: nature unchained is a channeled spell. After it is initially triggered, the casting will draw from your mana pool in order to remain active.**

The stolen spell was finally ready to be cast. It had taken over a minute to prepare, which time I'd only gained thanks to Ghost.

Next time, store the damn spell immediately, I chided myself. Turning my attention outward, I glanced in the direction of my familiar.

The pyre wolf was not only alive and well, but she was still leading the Blades astray. Even better, she'd drawn some of their hidden players out into the open.

By the looks of it, Ghost had managed to jump the unseen cordon and was now dashing across the grasslands with two dozen players in tow.

She had not escaped unscathed, though.

Even from this distance, I could spot the burn marks and scars riddling her torso. Reaching out with my will, I inspected the pyre wolf.

Ghost's health is at 50%.

Wincing at the damage she'd incurred, I rose into a half-crouch and loped silently across the plains in her direction.

With their attention fixed on the sprinting pyre wolf, none of the pursuing Blades noticed me. What the hidden watchers were doing, I couldn't say, nor did I care. After I reached Ghost and activated Leafbright's stolen spell, there would be time aplenty to deal with them.

"Ghost, head back my way."

Mutely, the pyre wolf arced around, a long line of players trailing behind her.

You have detected multiple hidden entities!
Multiple hostile entities have detected you! You are no longer hidden.

The concealed Blades spotted me at nearly the same time I did them. I had anticipated being uncovered though, knowing I was moving too fast for my stealth to hold under scrutiny.

And besides, I wanted to draw my foes out. The more of them that converged on me and Ghost the better.

"There he is!"

"Get him!"

From all around me, dozens of players emerged from the long grass. Not slowing down, I glanced over my shoulder. Ghost had been right. The Blades *had* formed a cordon around us. Taking a quick count, I estimated we were facing about eighty foes.

Not bad odds. Not bad at all, I thought. *We can—*

You have triggered a trap!

The instant the Game alert arrived, I threw myself forward into a somersault. The trap was not unexpected. In fact, what surprised me was that it had taken me this long to run into another one.

After the sorcerer's coif failure, I'd come to the conclusion that the Blades had forgone wards in favor of traps, camouflage, and cunning. In hindsight, I'd realized that for a faction of their supposed specialization, this was the ideal way to conceal their base.

The whole region was probably seeded with traps, which was why I'd ordered Ghost to head back the way we'd come and not toward the hill where I expected the concentration of traps to be greater.

Still, my attempt at evasion was not entirely successful.

You have dodged a bear clamp trap.
You have failed to dodge a fan of knives trap. 3 of 5 knives have struck you.

One after the other, the trio of steel blades thudded into my calf, causing pain to shoot up my leg. I grimaced. The triple strikes hurt but were far from life-threatening. Completing my maneuver, I hit the ground hard and slumped into the long grass.

And stayed down—deliberately.

"*Prime?*" Ghost cried in alarm.

"*I'm alright,*" I assured her. Gritting my teeth, I yanked out the knives. "*They're scratches, no more. But better our foes don't know that.*"

"*Ah,*" she exclaimed in relief. "*You want to lure them closer?*"

"*Yes,*" I replied, watching the rapidly approaching Blades through my mindsight.

Having seen my collapse, most of the players had abandoned even the appearance of caution and were racing headlong towards me. *Like hunting dogs catching sight of a wounded stag.* No doubt, they wanted to be in on the kill—and share in the experience gain.

I smiled. Little did they know what awaited them.

Ghost reached me well ahead of the pursuing Blades. Skidding to a halt beside me, she flopped down on her belly and let her tongue hang out, panting heavily.

"Now?" she asked.

"Not yet," I replied, watching the players through my mindsight. Nature unchained had a range of a hundred yards, and while most of the Blades were inside that distance, a few stragglers remained outside. Chief amongst them was the orc, Yara.

"How much longer?" Ghost growled, her gaze fixed on the closest Blade. A real sprinter, he'd opened the distance between himself and the rest of the pursuing pack. Foolishly so.

"Take him," I ordered, not answering her.

Ghost sprang. Belatedly realizing his danger, the sprinter skittered back. Too late.

The pyre' wolf's formidable form hit him hard, her stygian claws raking through frail armor, and her magma maw biting into soft flesh.

Your familiar has killed Uglas.

In less than a handful of seconds, the Blade was dead. His fate only seemed to spur his fellows on, though. Howling and shouting, they dashed closer. Most had bladed weapons in hand, a few crossbows, and fewer still carried slings and other short-ranged weapons. Only a handful bore wands or staffs.

Not many magic users, then. Good.

"Now?" Ghost growled, scrutinizing the racing players.

"Just a little—" I began.

Grayson has teleported 23 yards.
Starblaze has chain-jumped 30 yards.
Ghost has passed a mental resistance check! Ogando has failed to charm your familiar.

The air popped, and suddenly, out of nowhere, two Blades appeared on either side of Ghost. Near simultaneously, the Adjudicator reported the failed attempt on her mind.

I bit back a curse. *Psicasters.*

Whirling around, Ghost turned to face the Blade flanking her on the left. The player lunged. But the pyre wolf's snapping jaw was quicker, and before her foe could skewer her, she trapped his hand in an iron grip.

Magma jaws closed, crushing bone, mangling flesh, and charring skin.

Your familiar has crippled Grayson!

The player shrieked, loud enough to disguise the movements of his partner, who—cunningly—had waited to launch his own assault unseen.

Unseen by Ghost that is. I, on the other hand, was watching him keenly and was primed to react.

You have teleported into Starblaze's shadow.

Before the glittering tip of the player's stiletto could plunge into Ghost's rear, my own blade ripped through his throat.

You have killed Starblaze with a fatal blow!

At the same time, Ghost leaped forward, disemboweling the still-screaming Grayson.

Your familiar has killed Grayson.

Her mouth dripping blood and gore, Ghost turned to stare wordlessly at me. *"Yeah, now,"* I muttered in acknowledgment of her unspoken question and, reaching into the ring on my right hand, drew out the spell stored within.

Mage's surprise activated. Spellhold casting released.
You have trigger-cast nature unchained.

A wave rippled across the sea of grass. Centered on Ghost and me, it expanded rapidly, transforming the thin stalks of grass into wiry sticks of bamboo. Equally, I ignored the passing mindglows
Shouts of consternation and confusion rose from the Blades.
Ignoring them, I turned to Ghost. Just like there had been when Leafbright had cast nature unchained, there was a small patch of unaffected ground at the spell's epicenter. Within its confines, Ghost would be safe, as would any foe who managed to reach the spot.
"Stay here, and deal with any Blade who arrives," I ordered. Assuming the players were familiar with the spell—and I had every reason to presume they would be, it belonged to a bitter rival, after all—they would know where to head to find safety.
"Where are you going?" Ghost asked.
"To deal with those who flee the other way," I replied.
The pyre wolf bobbed her head. *"Be careful."*
"You, too," I called in farewell, and plunging into the enchanted vegetation, I began casting.

✳   ✳   ✳

You have fully restored yourself with quick mend.
A blight pollen has failed to harm you. You are immune to this spell.

I rushed through the bamboo forest, ignoring the glowing pollen falling all around me. I, of course, still retained my immunity to the nature unchained spell and had nothing to fear from it. Equally, I ignored the mindglows I sensed.
They would not survive long.

It was the Blades near the spell's outer rim that concerned me. If they were quick to react, they could flee the casting's confines before they became too debilitated. Then, too, there were those who had been outside the casting's area of effect when I'd released the spell.

Like Yara.

To drive my point home, I would have to kill them all fast, *before* they had a chance to recover.

Reaching the boundary of the enchanted forest, I slowed my steps. Twenty mindglows were gathered on the other side. It seemed like I was too late; the Blades were already regrouping. From the sounds of it, Cine and Delkan were not among their number. Worse luck, Yara appeared to be in charge.

I hefted my swords. Still, twenty players—non-elites, all—I could handle easily. I just had to take care of them before more gathered.

I checked my buffs. They were in place, and I was as ready as I could be. Still, I hesitated a moment to consider the psi skills I'd observed the Blades use earlier and what it boded for the upcoming fight.

I could expect the players to be resistant to my telepathy, I reasoned. What's more, they were likely experts with those blades they bore, and undoubtedly, they had a few tricks of their own up their sleeves.

I sighed. Perhaps, this battle would not be as easy as I assumed. Still, I had one advantage the Blades could not so easily counter. Darkness and my wolf senses. I would have to maximize their use.

But to begin with, something familiar.

Closing my eyes, I drew psi.

✳   ✳   ✳

You have cast slaysight.

Casting slaysight had two purposes. One, it would serve as a test of my foes' mental defenses, and two, even if the spell only partially succeeded, it would distract the Blades.

Gathering the psi I'd marshaled in my mind, I flung it into the middle of the twenty Blades. Then, edging up the forest's boundary, I peeked through the bamboo to observe the spell's effect.

The first thing I noticed was that there were thirty players, not twenty as my mindsight had reported. Ten Blades had shielded their consciousness. *Damn.*

That was not the only surprise in store for me either.

Your mental intrusion has been detected!

A second before my will could crash into my foes' minds, a stocky gnome cried out. "Ware everyone! A spell's incoming."

"Wha—?"

"The bastard is attacking our minds!"

Interesting, I mused as I waited to observe the spell's outcome. The gnomish Blade had sensed my casting *before* it hit. Still, that did not prevent slaysight from doing its work.

4 hostile entities have passed a mental resistance check!
3 targets are protected by psi shields and are immune to mental manipulation.
You have paralyzed 3 of 10 targets for 60 seconds.

"Deke, what's wrong? Your face..."
"He's been paralyzed!" the gnome replied curtly.
"Gajan, too!"
"Mase as well!"
"It's the intruder," Yara snapped. "Zheck, Tum, find him! The rest of you, retreat! He must be hiding in that damned forest."
I sighed, deflating slightly. Slaysight's performance left a lot to be desired. But to be honest, I'd been expecting something like this. *Let's see if charm does any better,* I thought, drawing more psi.

You have cast mass charm.

"He's casting again," the gnome warned.
"Casting what?" Yara demanded.
"A... charm spell, I think," he reported.
The orc cursed. "Damnit! Zeek, get a shield—"
But it was too late. The weaves of psi I'd sent forth had reached my chosen targets. Delving into their minds, it assaulted their defenses.

You have charmed 5 of 10 targets for 20 seconds.

My second psi spell performed better than the first, but that was only because I'd taken care to exclude the mind-shielded players from my targeting. Some of the Blades still managed to resist, though.
"The spell is finished!" the gnome cried.
"How many did he get?" Yara snapped.
"Five!"
"Five?" Yara asked incredulously. "By all that is holy, how did he—"
Not waiting to hear what else she had to say, I ordered my new minions into play. Simultaneously, I slipped quietly out of the bamboo forest. It was time to take a more direct hand in matters.

✳   ✳   ✳

22 hostile entities have failed to detect you! You are hidden.

I stalked unseen through the long grass.
Yara was still snapping orders while the rest of the Blades were backing away from the five players I'd bespelled. Disappointingly, my minions had not managed to kill any of their former comrades yet.

I didn't shadow blink, nor did I use windborne, but I suspected I would need both abilities soon enough, as an escape mechanism if nothing else. If I was being honest, I was a bit worried the gnome might sense my psicasting.

So, instead, I crept up on the three paralyzed Blades. Not trusting the bamboo forest and what it may hide, the rest of the group had backed away—leaving the trio unprotected—and I went unnoticed.

Reaching the first paralyzed victim, I unbent from my crouch and slit her throat.

You have killed Ester, a level 166 human with a fatal blow.

Then I did the same to the other two.

My eyes fixed on the rest of the Blades, I eased the last of the corpses quietly to the ground. Thanks to the darkness, my kills had gone unseen.

Nog-dog has cast mental freedom. You have lost control over 5 charmed entities.

My brows rose at the Game message. It was not entirely unexpected. And once again, it was the gnome—Nog-dog—who was responsible for fouling my plans. Still, I'd come off better from the exchange. The enemy had lost three of their number and didn't even seem to know it.

Time to rinse and repeat.

Drawing more psi, I cast again—once more making sure to only target the unshielded players.

You have cast slaysight.
You have paralyzed 5 of 10 targets for 60 seconds.
Your mental intrusion has been detected!

"Yar!" Nog-dog shrieked. "He's done it again!"

"Done what?" the orc growled.

"Cast paralysis!"

"Dammit, Zeek!" Yara spat. "I thought I told you to shield everyone?"

"I'm working on it," a human player retorted. "But the spell takes time, and I have to cast it one by—"

"No more excuses," Yara growled. She spun around to survey the darkness. "How did he do it, anyway?" she muttered.

"Do what?" a confused Nog-dog asked.

"Cast paralysis again. His first spell should still be—" The orc fell silent, her eyes narrowing as she noticed the missing trio. "He's killed them," she whispered.

"Killed who?" a perplexed Nog asked.

Ignoring him, Yara raised her voice. "On guard, people, the intruder is close. Lake, Stern, magelights! Thieves, lay down some traps, and everyone else, watch the damn perimeter!"

CHAPTER 450: MAKING A POINT

My lips quirked upward in amusement as I listened to Yara's frantic orders. They told me much about the Blades' capabilities and confirmed many of my own guesses as to their skills. They also made another thing clear: I was not going to finish off my foes as quickly as I wanted to.

And if I could not make an impression on the Blades by how quickly I killed them, that left the next best thing: making them think I toyed with them.

But I couldn't afford to suffer any serious injury in the process; that would defeat the entire point of the exercise. *Which means employing utmost care.*

Right, slow and sure it is. So, what's step one?

Checking up on Ghost.

Reaching out with my mindsight, I reached across the expanse of the bamboo forest to the pyre wolf. From the limited number of mindglows near her, I could tell she was only moderately engaged. *"How are you faring, Ghost?"*

"Urgh, these players are no challenge, Prime," she complained. *"It's like killing cubs!"*

I chuckled. *"That's because the forest has already taken its toll. I take it you don't need any help then?"*

Ghost snorted. *"Of course not. The players stopped coming through a while ago, and I'm almost done with the last two."* She paused. *"What about you?"*

"Things are a bit trickier out here," I admitted. *"I may need your help soon. How many have you killed so far?"*

"Fifteen," she reported proudly.

I nodded thoughtfully. Ghost's fifteen, plus the two that she still sparred with, and the three I'd killed made twenty. Closing my eyes, I called up the waiting Game messages.

Cine has died.
Moonhide has died.
Anvil has died.

...

...

Deklan has died.

Tallying up the death notifications, I realized fully half of the Blades had been killed by the bamboo forest. *Perfect*, I thought in satisfaction. It meant the twenty-six players under Yara's command were the only real threat remaining—my gaze drifted to the hills in the distance—assuming, of course, no more reinforcements emerged from the Blades' hidden base.

"I'm dropping the nature unchained spell," I warned Ghost. *"As soon as you can, circle around the players I'm watching and wait."*

"What will I be waiting for?"

"Any Blade who thinks to make a break for their base." I paused. "Or any reinforcements that the base may send."

"Got it."

Trusting Ghost to do her part, I turned back to Yara's group. They'd formed a tight-knit circle, with only Yara, Nog-dog, and a few others enclosed within. Magelights hung above the players, and though I could not see them, I was sure the ground was seeded with plenty of traps.

Surprisingly, the orc had chosen not to have her people retreat to their base. I shrugged. Yara's reasons didn't matter. Only the fact that I faced twenty-seven primed and ready players did.

Time for step two.

Closing my eyes, I drew psi.

✳   ✳   ✳

I could've tried using nature's unchained against the Blades again, of course. But I didn't. Mostly because the first iteration had drained the greater part of my mana, and even though I was committed to taking things slow, meditating would take entirely too long.

I was also loath to approach the players, too.

I was fairly certain that the Blades were better than me when it came to thieving. I'd failed to detect their earlier traps, and I was sure I would not be able to do so now either. I *could* blink in, bypassing whatever traps the Blades had laid along their perimeter, but that would leave me trapped in their midst.

No, thank you.

I had more than a few bombs left in my backpack, but would a Power stoop to using mere bombs? No, he or she wouldn't.

Which left the next best thing: my only ranged offensive ability, telepathy.

Unfortunately, the player Zeek had finally managed to shield the consciousness of all the surviving Blades, which limited my options to slaysight-shatter or... astral blade.

Shatter was less than ideal in these circumstances, especially with someone like Zeek around—*and who knew who else?*—to renew any broken mental defenses. And astral blades wouldn't work *either*, not if Zeek's mind shield spell functioned the same way mine did.

But did it?

Zeek was casting his spell over his allies, which was something I couldn't do with my own psi shield variant. *So, if it's not the same spell, perhaps it doesn't afford the Blades the same protection.*

I shrugged. There was only one way to find out.

Concealing my hands behind my back, I let a psi dagger manifest in each. It was impossible to mask the blades' luminous aura entirely, but once they flew free, it would not matter if the players spotted them.

"He's attacking again, Yar!" Nog-dog screamed right on cue.

Damn gnome, I grumbled. His warning, though, would make little difference. Flicking forward my arms, I let the daggers fly at my chosen target.

"What's that—"

The cry cut off, mangled into something unintelligible as my two ethereal blades struck the player, causing splotches of angry purple to spread across his face.

You have injured Tomlin, a level 153 human skull-cracker, inflicting psi damage. Nerves at the point of contact have been weakened. Inflict further psi damage to deaden them entirely.

I smiled in satisfaction. The astral blades had worked. Unlike my own mind shield, Zeek's did not protect its subjects from nerve damage.

"Where did that come from?" Yara demanded sharply.

Fingers pointed into the night, most at empty spots of nothing. A few, though, managed to correctly pick out the position I'd fired from. Of course, I was no longer there, having relocated the moment the astral blades had left my hand.

Multiple hostile entities have failed to detect you!

"I don't see anything," Yara rasped. "Zheck, what do you see?"

"Nothing," groused the troll so addressed.

My smile widening, I slipped further into the darkness. *Yes, this will work,* I thought.

It will work nicely, indeed.

✳   ✳   ✳

A wolf in the night, I stalked the Blades, firing slivers of purple death as I circled them. Yara's people did their best to find me, using magelights, revealing spells, and even sending players out in pairs to search the night.

But in this one instance, at least, the Blades were completely outclassed. Buffed by fade and hidden by the darkness, I was impossible to find.

And one by one, the Blades fell.

Tomlin has died.
Zheck has died.
Tum has died.
...

I sensed Yara's frustration, but she was helpless to stop the slow attrition of her people. Eventually, she did the only thing she could and ordered a hasty retreat to the Blades' base.

But as withdrawals went, it was messy. The group's cohesion crumbled, transforming the players from the fighting unit they'd been under Yara to panicked individuals fleeing for their lives.

And ripe prey for Ghost and me.

Nog-dog has died.
Haversk has died.
...

We picked off the Blades one by one, preventing any from reaching the safety of the trap field circling their base until, finally, only Yara remained.

"Stay back," I ordered Ghost as I approached the orc. Standing stiffly to attention, she stared unseeing into the night.

"What are you waiting for, you bastard?" Yara yelled into the darkness. "Go on, finish it. Butcher me like you did the rest!"

"Terming it that is hardly fair," I objected mildly, letting the shadows wreathing me dissipate.

You are no longer hidden.

Yara spun around to face me. I watched her curiously. The orc gripped the hilt of her sheathed blades tightly, but she refrained from drawing them.

I smiled. *Smart of her.* "If you recall, I did not pick this fight."

Yara spat to the side. "Cine was always an idiot. But that's no reason to kill all of us."

I shrugged. "A point had to be made."

She scowled. "And what point is that?"

"That I am what I claim," I replied, my voice turning frigid. "A *Power*." Tilting my head to the side, I studied her coldly. "Or do you still doubt?"

Yara's shoulders sagged. "I don't," she whispered.

"Good. Then, when you get back, let your superiors know if they wish to parley, they can find me along the western border of this sector. I meant what I said: I can help your faction reclaim sector 75,172 from the Riders—for a price."

"Get back..." Yara echoed. "You're letting me go?" she asked hopefully.

My lips curved upward. "In a manner of speaking, I am," I murmured as I drew psi.

You have teleported into Yara's shadow.
You have killed your target with a fatal blow.
You and Ghost have reached level 215!
Your telepathy has reached rank 22 and your chi rank 18.
Ghost's magma maw and ash armor have reached rank 7 and her stygian claws and telepathy rank 8.

CHAPTER 451: DEALING WITH THE FAMILIAR

No more Blades emerged from the hidden base in the hills.

Perhaps there were no more inside to do so, or perhaps those inside were unaware of the deaths of their fellows. I didn't know, but nor did I make the mistake of approaching the base again.

I had eight hours.

That was about how long it would take the Blades to resurrect and report what had happened, and I had a lot to do in that time. *"Let's go, Ghost,"* I said, plotting a course southwest.

The pyre wolf looked at me curiously. *"Where are we going?"* she asked, clearly realizing we were heading deeper into Blade territory and not back north to the Rider sector where Adriel and Nyra waited.

"To the river," I replied. From the mental map I had of the region, I knew the river flowed due south until it reached the lake at the heart of the Marches. If we kept heading south, we'd eventually hit the lake and cross into the lowlands, but I had no intention of going that far yet.

"You plan on doing as you told the orc?" Ghost asked, guessing my intentions.

"I do," I replied. *"We'll wait on the banks of the river for our visitors."* Assuming Yara's superiors took up my invite, of course. It was maybe optimistic to believe that they would, but I was still hesitant to head into the lowland cities.

"What if they prove hostile?"

I shrugged. *"Then it's only a short hop into the river. Once we're in the water, even if the Blades kill us, we should be able to die outside their zone of control. But let us hope it doesn't come to that."*

Bobbing her head in agreement, Ghost followed silently in my wake.

✳ ✳ ✳

It took us three hours to reach the river.

Drawing to a halt, I surveyed the dark expanse of water. Both it and the adjacent shores were empty. Ghost and I were likely the only ones around for miles.

It seemed we were far enough south to have passed beyond the reach of the Blade and Rider cordons facing off against each other across the river but not so far south that we'd reach the Marches' more populous regions yet. *Good.*

Standing on a slight rise, I studied the river. *"That's a good spot,"* I said, pointing out a dense clump of river reeds less than fifty yards away.

Ghost studied the waterlogged area dubiously. *"I really have to hide in there?"*

My lips twitched. *"I know it looks unappealing, and it's probably going to be uncomfortable, but me teleporting onto you is my best chance of escape if things go awry."*

The pyre wolf's shoulders sagged as she began heading down the hill. *"Very well, Prime."*

I called her back. *"You don't have to go just yet, Ghost,"* I said, sitting down cross-legged in the grass. *"We've ample time before our guests arrive, and in the meantime, we can see to your leveling."*

The pyre wolf's ears pricked up curiously. *"My leveling?"*

I nodded. *"Yes, I think it's past time we used some of those Class points of yours, don't you?"*

Ghost's mouth dropped open in a wolfish smile. *"I do,"* she said, flopping down beside me.

Grinning at her eagerness, I turned my focus inward and called up her Class upgrade interface.

Assessing familiar's suitability for a Class upgrade...
Class points available: 10.
Familiar's rank: 3.
Upgrade requirements met.
Your familiar may advance her Class to rank 4 at this time by improving an existing Class benefit or by selecting a new one. Do you wish to proceed?

Ghost had been in more than a few scrapes since becoming my familiar, and I had gained a fair sense of her capabilities and weaknesses. Honestly, I should have upgraded her abilities before this, but for one reason or the other, I'd not had the chance to do so.

Better late than never, I thought, willing my response to the Adjudicator.

Commencing Class upgrade...
3 new Class benefits are available, and 2 of 5 existing benefits are upgradeable.
New benefit: <u>maul</u>. This buff increases the damage Ghost does with her claws by a multiplier determined by her Strength for 5 minutes.
New benefit: <u>gnaw</u>. This buff increases the damage Ghost does with her maw by a multiplier determined by her Magic for 5 minutes.
New benefit: <u>death magic</u>. This skill grants Ghost access to death magic.
Existing benefits that may be upgraded: <u>manifest</u> and <u>born again II</u>.
Existing benefits not available for upgrade: <u>astral bite</u>, <u>diresight</u>, and <u>direshield</u>. These abilities require a telepathy skill of rank 10 to advance.
Choose Ghost's rank 4 Class benefit now.

"Ah," I murmured.

"What?" Ghost asked, looking at me expectantly.

I recited the Adjudicator's response to her, describing the options on offer. *"It's curious that manifest can be upgraded,"* I said. *"I wonder what doing so will do?"*

"Make me bigger?" Ghost suggested, her tail thumping excitedly at the notion.

I chuckled. *"That's possible,"* I allowed, *"And upgrading the ability is certainly something we should keep in mind, but what do you think of the other options?"*

Ghost scratched the back of her ear with a hindleg as she pondered the question. *"Maul and gnaw sound useful...."* she began, even while sounding distinctly unenthused by the prospect of both.

"But?" I prompted when she didn't go on.

"But I do enough damage with my claws and teeth as it is," she replied.

I nodded, unsurprised by her response. *"And how do you feel about death magic?"*

Her ears perked up. *"Now, that's more interesting!"*

I hid a smile. I was just as intrigued by the idea of Ghost possessing death magic as she was, but... *"Another skill, Ghost? You sure you want that?"*

She shrugged. *"Acquiring the skill should cost only one Class point."*

"That's true," I said, nodding thoughtfully. *"It's certainly one of the advantages of using your Class points on skills. Unlike abilities, they won't require ongoing investment."* I paused. *"But what about manifest?"*

"The chance to upgrade it will come again, won't it?" Ghost replied. When I nodded, she went on, *"Death magic might not reappear, though."*

"Also true," I conceded. *"Alright, you've convinced me. Death magic it is."* Closing my eyes, I willed my response to the Game.

Upgrade complete. Class points remaining: 9.
Ghost's Class has advanced to rank 4.
Ghost has gained the advanced skill: <u>death magic</u>.

After spending a not-insignificant period as a spirit creature, Ghost has a strong kinship with the afterlife. This has left her with an affinity for death and has allowed her to acquire the death magic skill. However, as a familiar, Ghost does not have access to its full school of spells. She may only cast touch-based death spells and those without any verbal or somatic components.

Note: your familiar may possess a maximum of 6 skills. Remaining skill slots available: 1 / 6.

"Well, that's frustrating," I murmured after relaying the Adjudicator's response to Ghost.

"But the skill is still good, isn't it?" she asked worriedly.

"Definitely," I assured her. *"Although its use is more limited than I anticipated."* I had envisioned the pyre wolf as one day being able to cast spells of the same magnitude and power as Adriel. Unfortunately, it looked like that would not be the case.

Shrugging off my disappointment, I turned back to Ghost. *"We still need to get you an ability to train the skill. Shall we go again?"*

Ghost nodded, and without further ado, I called up her Class upgrade interface once more.

After a moment, a new list of benefits appeared.

3 new Class benefits are available, and 2 of 5 existing benefits are upgradeable.

New benefit: <u>bruiser</u>. This trait makes Ghost stronger.

New benefit: <u>fire magic</u>. This skill grants Ghost access to fire magic.

New benefit: <u>gnaw</u>. This buff increases the damage Ghost does with her maw by a multiplier determined by her Magic for 5 minutes.

Existing benefits that may be upgraded: <u>manifest</u> and <u>born again II</u>.

Choose Ghost's rank 5 Class benefit now.

My lips turned down at the options on offer. *"Urgh, none of these look appealing."*

The pyre wolf bobbed her head in agreement. *"What do we do?"*

I rubbed my chin. Ghost didn't need fire magic—magma maw already gave her access to touch-based fire spells—gnaw was a repeat, and bruiser looked like a straight Strength boost. *"Time to see what improving manifest does, I guess."* I glanced at her. *"You happy with that?"*

"I am," she replied.

"We chose manifest," I murmured, directing the thought to the Adjudicator.

You have upgraded Ghost's manifest ability to <u>greater manifest</u>. The second tier of this ability allows your familiar to leave her spirit vessel and take physical form as a <u>greater stygian pyre wolf</u>.

When in greater stygian pyre wolf form, Ghost gains the trait: <u>pyreborn</u>. This form pushes the essence of the mature phoenix woven into your familiar's being to the fore, granting her +50% fire magic resistance, +50% damage with all fire-based attacks, and the special manifest variant: <u>explosive entry</u>. Explosive entry allows Ghost to emerge in the physical plane amidst a concussive blast 5 yards in diameter.

Greater manifest, additionally, increases the distance from her spirit vessel that your familiar may materialize to 10 yards. Note: there is no restriction on unmanifesting. Ghost may disassociate no matter how far she is from Cloak of the Reach.

Greater manifest consumes psi or mana and can be upgraded with Class points. Its activation time is average or instantaneous (if using explosive entry). This is a Class ability and does not occupy any attribute slots.

Upgrade complete. Class points remaining: 8.

Ghost's Class has advanced to rank 5.

Ghost's physical form has changed to that of a greater stygian pyre wolf.

I rocked back. "Well, well, now *that* is more like it."

This time I didn't need to tell Ghost what changes the Game had enacted. She'd sensed them for herself. *"I feel… different,"* she marveled, running her tongue along her magma-formed teeth.

They looked noticeably bigger… and sharper. Her coat, too, had changed, gaining a half-seen shimmer of red. *"You are,"* I confirmed, *"and deadlier, too. That Class point was certainly well spent."* I paused. *"Shall we upgrade manifest again?"*

Ghost's eyes twinkled. *"Yes, please."*

Closing my eyes, I called upon the Adjudicator again.

3 new Class benefits are available, and 1 of 5 existing benefits are upgradeable.

New benefit: <u>sneaking</u>. This skill grants Ghost access to stealth.

New benefit: <u>draining bite</u>. This ability lets Ghost leech a portion of her foes' life with each bite.

New benefit: <u>pinning paw</u>. This ability allows Ghost to knock down her foe in a single hit.

Existing benefits that may be upgraded: <u>born again II</u>.

Existing benefits not available for upgrade: <u>astral bite</u>, <u>diresight</u>, <u>direshield</u>, and <u>greater manifest</u>. Greater manifest requires a magma maw, stygian claws, and ash armor skill of rank 10 to advance.

Choose Ghost's rank 6 Class benefit now.

I exhaled noisily. "Well, so much for that idea," I muttered, then went on to describe the options on offer to Ghost. "*I'm afraid it's going to be a while before you can upgrade manifest again.*"

"*That's alright, Prime. Greater manifest is powerful enough on its own.*"

"*True,*" I agreed reluctantly. "*What do you think of the other choices?*"

"*Sneaking sounds—*" she began.

I shook my head, stopping her. "*I don't think choosing another skill is a good idea.*"

"*Why not?*" she asked, lowering her head in disappointment.

"*Well, for one, you have only one skill slot left, and two, while I admit sneaking is a great skill to have, you don't really need it. We've been managing well enough without it, and truly, any time we need to stay concealed, it's better if I do the sneaking and you stay unmanifested.*"

"*Oh. That makes sense I guess.*"

"*Besides which,*" I went on, "*draining bite is the ability you want. Unless I'm very much mistaken, the spell is from the school of death magic. Not only that, but it will also grant you a form of life leech.*" I met her gaze. "*It's the healing ability you've been missing.*"

Ghost didn't look fully convinced, but I could tell my words had piqued her interest. "*Alright, Prime, if you think it's the right choice...*"

"*I do,*" I said firmly.

"*Then, let's do it.*"

Saying nothing further, I relayed our wishes to the Adjudicator.

Ghost has gained the basic spell: <u>draining bite.</u>

This ability allows Ghost to leech 10% of the damage she inflicts from a single bite attack, restoring her own health in the process.

This spell has no verbal or somatic component. Its activation time is very fast. It consumes mana and can be upgraded. You and Ghost have 45 of 46 Magic ability slots remaining.

Upgrade complete. Class points remaining: 7.

Ghost's Class has advanced to rank 6.

I peered at the pyre wolf. "*What do you think?*"

Ghost's eyes were closed as she absorbed the new knowledge the Game had gifted her with. "*It was the right choice,*" she pronounced.

I nodded in satisfaction. "*I think so, too.*"

Ghost opened her eyes. *"We go again?"*

My eyes narrowed thoughtfully. The pyre wolf still had seven Class points remaining—a sum that seemed ample—but upgrading just *one* of Ghost's abilities from basic to elite would require four points all on its own. *"Better not,"* I decided. *"Let's see how your new abilities perform before deciding anything further."*

She rose to her feet. *"Then, I guess it's time for me to head into the reeds."*

I smiled at her obvious distaste at the notion. *"It is. Get what rest you can. It will be at least another five hours before our expected company arrives."*

"Will you rest, too?" the pyre wolf asked as she slipped down the slope.

"I will," I confirmed. *"As soon as I take care of my own leveling."*

You have successfully stored the <u>nature unchained</u> spell in the ring, mage's surprise.
Your Dexterity has increased to rank 94. Other modifiers: +24 from items.
You have slept for 4 hours.
You have cast facial disguise, assuming the visage of Jasiah.

Dawn crept over the plains with me sitting on the grassy knoll and Ghost dozing in the reeds. Nine hours had passed since I'd slain Cine and Yara's people, and I was on high alert. If the faction's representatives were going to appear, it would be soon.

The entire venture with the Blades was a risk, but I was reluctant to spend more time in the Marches than I had to. It was true, I knew nearly nothing of the faction, their goals, and the alliances. It was also true I could be courting disaster by remaining a stationary target for their Powers.

But I was gambling that the Blades' leaders would want to recover their lost sector more than they desired slaying an errant Power. Only time would tell if I'd chosen right, though.

My mindsight pinged.

My gaze shifted to the left. A mindglow had slipped across the boundary of my mental circle of awareness, approaching, funnily enough, from the south—the opposite direction from which I'd expected a visitor to appear. Was the sector's safe zone in that direction?

Probably.

Reaching out with my will, I inspected the unknown consciousness.

The target is Tyelin. He is a level 260 human artful burglar and bears a Mark of Blythe.

I stroked my chin thoughtfully. The player was still not visible, hidden by the intervening folds in the land, but the fact that he'd chosen to approach unaccompanied and openly boded well.

But he might not be as alone as he seems.

Who knew how many others were hiding nearby? And there was the Blade's level to consider, too. At his rank, Tyelin would be no push-over.

"*Heads up, Ghost,*" I murmured. "*We have company.*"

Through our familiar bond, I felt her snap alert. "*The player approaching from the south?*"

"*Yes,*" I replied. "*Do you sense any others?*"

A drawn-out pause followed. "*No.*"

I relaxed slightly, glad for the pyre wolf's confirmation of what my own senses were telling me. "*You know the plan,*" I said, rising to my feet. "*Let's stick to it.*"

"Good luck, Prime."

Folding my hands in front of me, I set myself to wait for the visitor.

✳ ✳ ✳

A few seconds later, a slim figure materialized on the plains.

Even across the hundred-and-fifty-odd yards separating us, I could tell his gaze was fixed on me. Tyelin made no move to conceal himself, yet he slipped so unobtrusively across the ground that the grass was barely disturbed.

The Blade's hands rested at his sides—in plain sight just like mine. He bore no obvious weapons either and was dressed plainly in a cotton shirt, dark gloves, and pants.

Unarmed and *unarmored*?

Was that a sign of arrogance or a gesture of friendship? *No way to tell.* Tyelin's stride was easy and relaxed, and even though it was obvious I watched him, he appeared unperturbed by my regard. I turned my attention to the visitor's face.

It was as... forgettable as the rest of him.

With dark hair, brown eyes, pale skin, and an easy smile on his lips, Tyelin was not someone anyone would give a second glance to. Yet, he was a rank twenty-six player and therefore could not be nearly as harmless as he appeared.

"He has no scent," Ghost said suddenly.

Before I could respond, Tyelin's face tightened fractionally—had he sensed Ghost's sending?—but his expression smoothened over so quickly, I couldn't be sure. Still to be safe, I ordered, *"No talking. There are listeners."*

The Blade came to a halt before me. "So, Yara spoke truly," he said conversationally. "You *truly* are a power. I had my doubts." Not waiting for a response, he went on. "Unless that is as much a lie as everything else about you?"

"A strong accusation," I replied mildly. "And certainly not the best way to begin an alliance."

Tyelin smiled. "You're assuming I'm here for that."

I shrugged. "Why else would you be here?"

"Curiosity perhaps?" he asked, drumming his fingers against the side of his face in pretended thought. "Or... maybe I'm simply here to kill you."

I snorted. "All by your lonesome? And before you suggest you're not, don't forget who you're talking to. I know for a fact that you are." The lie rolled smoothly off my tongue. Saying no more, I kept my face impassive as I watched closely for his reaction.

Tyelin laughed easily, showing no unease, confusion, or even any hint of hidden smugness. "You're right," he said ruefully. "Even if you are not what you pretend to be, I daresay, given how convincingly you've played at being a Power, you're no easy foe."

I matched his smile with one of my own. "You're right about the last bit, anyway."

"You took a chance slaughtering all Cine's people like that, though," Tyelin said, and even though the words were lightly spoken, I didn't fail to mark the hint of coldness in the Blade's tone. "What makes you believe we'd let you get away with it?"

Here it was, then. The masked threat. The outrage—feigned or otherwise—of the big bad faction at the lone player who'd dared kill their players. It was as predictable as it was tiring.

I folded my arms. "Nothing. I did what I had to, what *your* commander foolishly forced me to."

"So, you're blaming Cine?" Tyelin asked, the smile never leaving his face.

"I am," I said, not backing down.

The Blade's smile broadened. "Lucky for you then that Yara said much the same." He paused. "She was most upset, though, that you killed her. She believes that was uncalled for."

I grunted. "I was making a point." *And buying time.*

"A well-made one, too," Tyelin said judiciously. "You made a strong impression on Yara and the others. They're all convinced you are what you say."

I didn't miss the implications behind his phrasing. The other Blades might be convinced, but he wasn't.

Tyelin spread his arms. "Tell me one thing, though. I hate inconsistency. It smacks of laziness. What possessed you to choose the visage of a rank fifteen player?" He rolled his eyes. "Really, who is going to believe a player of that level capable of acquiring a Power Mark?"

Despite myself, I couldn't stop my expression from freezing.

I'd had no inkling that the Blade had analyzed me. That he had was obvious. Less obvious was how much he had seen. Had Tyelin pierced my deception? Had he seen beneath my false guise to my true identity?

The Blade chuckled. "Didn't think I could analyze you, did you, *Jasiah*?" he asked, driving the point home. He eyed me lazily. "Should I call you that? Or is there some other name you prefer?"

I smoothened my expression, hiding my unease. "Would you prefer to see my true face?" I asked with false sincerity—there was no way in hell I was going to reveal my actual appearance and name to this player.

But Tyelin evinced no interest in my suggestion. "Not necessary. You are a deception player, of course. And like with most of your kind, it is almost always impossible to tell if the face you're seeing is the *real* one." He paused. "And besides, I need not know who you truly are for us to come to terms."

I cocked my head to the side. "Then you *are* here to deal?"

"I am," he replied succinctly.

I waited for him to go on, but when he didn't, I narrowed my eyes. "You mind if I ask why? You clearly don't trust me—or my appearance."

"I don't," he replied bluntly. "But in my world, trust is scarce. I would even go so far as to say non-existent. Its lack, however, does not preclude business from being conducted."

"And what world is that?"

"The underworld, of course," he replied as if that much should've been obvious to me and perhaps it should have. *I will have to remember to ask Adriel about it.*

"In the underworld, one never knows with whom one is striking a deal," Tyelin continued, oblivious to my confusion. His eyes turned cold. "But believe me, we have ways of handling those who deal falsely."

"I'm sure you do," I said, ignoring the barely veiled threat in his words. "Let's get down to business, then."

"We'll get to that in a minute." He stared hard at me, seeming to will the truth from me. "First, I need to know: are you truly a Power?"

"Yes," I said and left it at that.

The Blade stared at me searchingly. Whatever he saw in my expression seemed to satisfy him because he did not question me again. "Then I have a proposition for you."

"Go on, I'm listening."

"Lady Blythe wants to meet you. I'll escort you to the sector's safe zone. There, my lady will lay out the terms of your agreement and what she requires of—"

"No," I interjected.

Tyelin raised an eyebrow. "No?"

"No, I will not accompany you to this sector's safe zone," I said icily. "Doing that will put me at your Power's mercy." Even more than I already was.

To his credit, the Blade did not attempt to dispute my statement. "Then we have nothing further to discuss," he said, turning around and walking away.

I let him go a few steps, then called out after his retreating figure. "I don't buy it, you know."

Pausing, Tyelin turned around. "What's that?"

"Your act," I said, gesturing at him. "You would have not come all this way if your Power didn't want something from me, *Envoy*." The last was a guess—an educated one—and, from the involuntary tic of Tyelin's cheek, a correct one.

"Who said anything about being an envoy?" he asked neutrally.

I smiled. "What, did you think you were the only one with analyze?"

Tyelin's face remained blank, but I could see my response had struck another nerve. Clearly, he'd no more felt my inspection than I had his.

"You're guessing," he stated flatly. "Based on my Mark."

"I'm not, *Tyelin*. Congratulations on your level by the way. Rank twenty-six is not something many achieve. It's a dead giveaway, though. At that rank, you're either a Sworn or an envoy, and given your cockiness"—I shrugged—"it's easy to deduce which."

After a palpable moment of silence, Tyelin laughed with what appeared genuine amusement. "I'm not the only arrogant one here," he said. "Your Mark... Powerful Initiate, do not think I do not know what it means, nor how most earn it. Assuming the Mark is not a forgery, your *true* rank is likely no greater than mine." He paused. "And perhaps even lower."

I shrugged, neither confirming nor denying his assertions. "I guess you'll have to remain wondering as to the truth," I replied blandly, and before he could respond, I added, "But enough of this posturing. Shall we get down to business?"

Marching back to me, the envoy sank down into the grass. "Let's."

"You told Yara that you can help us bring down the Riders," Tyelin said, beginning without preamble once I'd seated myself opposite him.

I inclined my head. "I did."

"Tell me how," he demanded bluntly.

"Malikor has deployed a significant portion of his forces outside the Riders' fort," I began. "I can tell you where and—"

The envoy slashed his hand downward. "We already know about that. It's not enough."

I started again. "In that case, I can assist your own forces when you begin your assault—"

"We don't need help with that either," he interjected.

My eyes narrowed. "Then what *do* you need? You clearly have something in mind already."

Tyelin sat back. "I do. How good is your deception? Is it good enough to hide your Power Mark?"

For a moment, I was thrown by the apparent randomness of the question. But it was not random, not really. Ever since he'd arrived, the envoy had been focused on my deception. Was whatever the Blades wanted related to the skill? *Possibly.*

"Well?" Tyelin asked, interrupting my musings.

I took another moment to ponder how truthfully to answer. "It isn't," I admitted finally, seeing no way to conceal the truth.

The envoy frowned. "That is a problem." Setting his hands on the ground, he pushed himself to his feet. "And it leaves us with nothing more to discuss."

I stared at Tyelin, shocked by the abrupt end of the conversation. This time, I didn't think it was a ploy.

"I leave you one final word of warning," the envoy continued. "Given the circumstances, Lady Blythe will forgive you for slaying her people, but she will not tolerate your presence in her territory further. You have one hour to—"

"Wait! Just tell me what you need done."

Tyelin shook his head. "I'm afraid I can't, not if you're incapable of doing what we need."

"Let me be the judge of what I can and can't do," I snapped.

"I can't," he retorted primly. "The risk of you revealing—"

"If you can get me to a merchant, I can do what you want," I said, to forestall his departure which I sensed was imminent.

Tyelin's eyes narrowed. "Do what? Hide your Power Mark?"

"Yes."

Tyelin stared at me piercingly, but I could see my response had confused him. A merchant was likely the easiest thing for most players to get hold of, and he had to be wondering why I needed one and how it would help me do what he needed.

"Explain," he said finally.

"I won't," I replied. As much as I might need the Blades' help, I would not trust them further than I had to. "But if you can provide me with access to a merchant," I went on, "I give you my word that no Rider—not even Malikor—will figure out my identity." It had to be for some ploy against the Riders that the Blades required a deception player. I had figured out that much.

For a long moment, Tyelin said nothing as he weighed up my words. "Your word," he mused as he sank back to the ground. "A trite notion, and one that's not worth much in the Game."

I opened my mouth in rebuttal, but he spoke over me. "But a Pact. That's a different story entirely. Are you willing to swear one?"

I threw him a wary glance, but inwardly, I was smiling. Tyelin had not refuted my suggestion, which meant he was considering it. And that alone made the entire conversation worthwhile. After all, it was solely for access to a merchant that I'd come to the sector.

If I play my cards right here, I thought, *I might get everything I need from the Blades and without them ever realizing it!*

"A Pact?" I asked doubtfully.

"Yes," the envoy replied, seemingly pleased with himself for coming up with the idea. "A Pact will serve two purposes. One, it will confirm that you are indeed a Power, and two, it will provide me with assurances that your words are more than empty air."

Lowering my head, I pretended to consider the notion before nodding decisively. "Alright, I'll do it."

The envoy beamed. "Excellent." He waved his hand. "Go on, whenever you're ready."

Gathering my thoughts, I formulated the necessary words.

You, in the persona of Jasiah, have proposed a Pact with Tyelin, pledging that the next statement you utter will contain no falsehoods.

Saying nothing, I glanced at the envoy.

His eyebrows rose. "A novel way of doing it," he murmured as the Adjudicator relayed my words to him, "but acceptable, nonetheless."

Tyelin has accepted your proposal, sealing the Pact between you and him.

I began without preamble, enunciating each worth carefully. "Let me visit a trustworthy merchant, one with access to the Nexus auction, and I will be able to conceal my Power Mark from ordinary players."

Your Pact is closed.

Tyelin chuckled. "A most carefully worded statement."

I held his gaze. "Does it satisfy you?"

"It does," he said, still smiling.

"Good." I leaned forward. "Now, tell me what it is you need me to do."

Tylene did not quibble further. "Blythe wants Malikor dead."

I evinced no surprise at the request. "Mammon's envoy's suspicions were true then," I murmured.

"What?" Tyelin asked with a frown.

"Oh nothing," I said, dismissing my own words. "Just something I overheard the Riders' leaders talking about. They already suspect you have a plan afoot to kill them."

The envoy pursed his lips. "How did you hear that?"

I shrugged. "I have my ways."

Tyelin's eyes narrowed in obvious unhappiness at my refusal to share. "Will you heed my lady's request then?" he asked, dropping the matter.

"I have a few questions that need answering first," I replied smoothly. Now that there appeared little danger of Blythe's envoy walking away from our negotiations, I saw no reason not to probe a bit further into how matters stood in the Marches.

"Go on," he replied, his tone clipped. "Ask."

"If you haven't guessed already, I'm new to the region. I know nothing about your faction, the Riders, the Reapers, nor the balance of power in the Marches. Enlighten me, please."

Curiosity crossed the envoy's face. "How did you enter the Marches knowing so little?"

I waved aside his question. "Perhaps, I'll tell you—someday. But for now, what can you tell me about the source of your disagreement with the Riders?"

Tyelin tapped his lips with his forefinger as if contemplating how forthcoming to be. Finally, he shrugged and said, "Not so long ago, there was peace in the Marches, with the Blades controlling half the territories, and the Riders the other half. Then the Reapers invaded. They hit us first, gaining control of nearly all our lowland sectors in one fell swoop."

His mouth twisted distastefully. "The Riders did not sit idly by, and instead of banding with us against the Reapers as we proposed, they used the opportunity to steal our territory, too." He laughed darkly. "A foolish move for which they paid dearly. While the Riders were distracted, the Reapers hit *them*. Now, the Reapers control nearly all of the lowlands, leaving the Riders and us to fight over scraps on the outer edges of the Marches."

"I see," I murmured. "And how many sectors do the Blades control now?"

This time, he took much longer to respond. "One."

My eyes widened. "This one?"

"Yes," he replied shortly.

I winced. *Then the Blades are desperate.* That was perhaps the only reason Blythe had sent her envoy to approach me in the first place.

Seeming to sense my thoughts, the envoy scowled. "Don't think we are weak. This sector has been in our control for centuries. Neither the Riders nor the Reapers will ever gain a foothold here!"

I studied him thoughtfully. "And how long was sector 75,172 under your control before the Riders stole it?"

Tyelin didn't answer.

Sighing, I changed the topic. "Why is it that you need *me* to kill Mammon's envoy? Yours is a faction that should be replete with assassins."

"We don't need you to assassinate Malikor."

I frowned. "But you said—"

"Blythe wants him dead, true—but we already have a plan for dealing with Mammon's envoy."

"I see. Then you *don't* need me?" I asked skeptically.

"We do," he contradicted.

Impatiently, I waited for him to go on.

"We need you to smuggle something into the fort."

My frown deepened. "Really? That's all you want? Granted, the stealth of some of your people is a bit lacking, but yours, for instance, should be up to the task."

Tyelin's lips thinned. "Stealth is *not* the issue. Getting into the fort is. The place is ringed by wards that make it impenetrable. There is no way to sneak in."

"I find that hard to believe," I scoffed. "The wards are only tier four."

"Those are only the outer wards. The inner ones are tier six."

My eyes narrowed. "Then you want me to walk in through the front door," I surmised. "Bluffing my way in."

Tyelin nodded. "Something like that. You will have to assume the guise of one of the Riders. Everyone else, even the prole servants, are searched at the entrance."

Which was why, I guessed, they hadn't been able to smuggle the stuff into the fort in the first place. Tyelin's plan had at least one glaring flaw, though. "Surely, the Riders have installed Watchers at the entrances?"

"They have," the envoy confirmed. "But the Riders know our capabilities—and lack thereof—as well as we do theirs. They *know* the few deception players we do have are of little threat, which has made them complacent. The Watcher at the main gate is only tier five. If your deception is high enough to hide your Power Mark, it will be sufficient to defeat the Watcher."

"I see," I murmured. "And what is it I am supposed to be smuggling?"

"Cynacilin. It's a deadly magical poison," Tyelin replied promptly. "Our man on the inside will see to its use."

I raised an eyebrow. "You have a spy in the fort?"

"His name is Jone, but he is only a prole," Tyelin admitted. "He is one of the village fisherfolk the Riders forced into servitude after they took over the fort. Your job—your *only* job—will be to get the cynacilin to him."

I stroked my chin. The plan sounded feasible at least. Presumably, once Jone poisoned Malikor—and who knew how many other Riders—the occupying force inside the fort would be left too weak to resist the Blade assault that would undoubtedly follow. It did sound unnecessarily convoluted, though.

"Why doesn't Blythe take a direct hand in matters?" I wondered aloud. "With her help, you should be able to overrun Malikor's people."

Tyelin snorted. "If Blythe enters the fray, so will Mammon. And right now, we don't want that."

Translation: the Blades were not strong enough to defeat the Riders in an open confrontation.

Bowing my head, I considered Tyelin's plan more deeply. It still had more than a few holes in it. Like, how would Jone get the word out when the deed was done? What if he failed? And how did the Blades plan on getting inside? I assumed they didn't intend a direct assault. That would be foolish.

Still, when you got right down to it, I didn't think any of my concerns mattered. As long as I got what I wanted, what difference did it make if the Blades' plan for overthrowing the Reapers succeeded or not?

"So, just to be clear," I said, "if I agree to this plan of yours, you will let me visit a merchant? A *trustworthy* one?"

Tyelin smiled. "I'll do you one better. I will bring the merchant to you. An under-dweller, no less."

Under-dweller. The envoy clearly expected me to recognize the word, and truly, it did spark a flicker of recognition, but I couldn't place the memory. *Where have I heard that term before?*

"Will that suffice?" Tyelin prompted when I didn't respond.

Forced with no choice but to admit my ignorance or accept, I chose the latter course. "It will."

"You will have to swear to a Pact first," the envoy added casually.

I looked at him questioningly.

"You will have to vow to complete the task agreed upon: getting the cynacilin to Jone."

"Hmm, we'll have to word the Pact a bit more carefully than that," I replied.

"Of course," the envoy said. He leaned forward, betraying some of his eagerness. "So, shall we seal the deal?"

"There is still the matter of my price," I said mildly.

Chapter 454: A Favor for a Favor

Tyelin's lips twitched. "Ah. Your price. I was wondering when we would get around to that." He paused. "One thousand gold."

I laughed. "One thousand gold? For delivering a sector? Don't be ridiculous."

"But you won't be delivering us the sector," Tyelin declared. "All you'll be doing is smuggling in a packet of cynacilin."

"Which by your own admission, none in your faction can do," I retorted. "Assuming your plan works, it's my actions that will bring about the downfall of the Riders in the sector."

"That's right, *my* plan," Tyelin pointed out. "You'll be no more than a cog in the grand scheme of things."

"A *vital* cog," I said, letting a hint of smugness creep into my tone.

"Not so vital as—" Tyelin began.

"I can always walk away," I interjected. "Believe me, if I see no profit in this, I will."

"You're bluffing," the envoy accused. "You wouldn't have approached us if you weren't desperate yourself. No one who has managed to earn a Powerful Initiate Mark would so carelessly reveal themselves otherwise."

Saying nothing, I held his gaze and let him measure my resolve. The astute envoy was right, of course. I *was* bluffing. There was no way I would reject his offer. Gaining access to the merchant was everything I needed, but Tyelin didn't need to know that.

Let's see what else I can squeeze out of him.

That 'yourself' had been a revealing slip and confirmed my suspicions that the Blades were as desperate, if not more so, than me.

In the face of my continued silence, Tyelin's mouth twisted sourly. "What do you want?" he rasped finally.

"A favor," I said simply.

He frowned. "What sort of favor?"

"An equivalent one at a date and time of my choosing."

"Equivalent to what?" he asked.

"Equivalent to the sector I'll be earning for you."

The envoy scowled. "You want us to *give* you a sector?"

"No, and in the Pact that we form we can stipulate I want no such thing. But the Blades *will* give me something of equal value to sector 75,172—when I ask for it."

"What if we can't provide what you demand?"

"Then I'll ask for something else, but I will let the Adjudicator be the judge of whether your refusal is an honest one."

Tyelin bit his lip. "This is more than I can agree to."

I smiled. "Consult Blythe if you wish, but know that the clock is ticking. I will not wait forever for your answer."

Looking unhappy, the envoy pulled back his left sleeve to reveal a slim gold bracelet. Clenching his right hand around the item, he closed his eyes.

A farspeaker bracelet, I thought. That must mean the Blade's Power was also in the sector.

For a moment, I wondered why Blythe herself had not come to this meeting, but only for a moment. The Blades faction leader had to be wary of entangling with an unknown Power, especially one that was a proven deceiver.

From her perspective, there was no indication that I was not merely pretending to be weak in a bid to lure her in. And given how precarious her faction's position appeared to be in the Marches, she'd be doubly cautious. *No,* I concluded, *Blythe won't risk facing me herself, not unless I force her to.*

Which was the last thing I wanted myself.

The envoy's eyes opened. "My lady has agreed to your terms."

My smile widened. "Excellent."

✳ ✳ ✳

You, in the persona of Jasiah, have sealed a Pact with envoy Tyelin, acting on behalf of the Power Blythe. In exchange for delivering a package of cynacilin powder to the non-player Jone, Blythe will grant you a single favor at a time and place of your choosing. The favor will be equivalent to the worth of sector 75,172 to the Blades at the time the favor is called in.

It took over an hour for Tyelin and me to iron out the wording of the Pact. The sticking point had been the phrases "to the Blades" and "at the time." I'd argued—convincingly, I thought—against them before eventually conceding with pretended unhappiness.

The envoy had insisted on the phrases as a safeguard in case the Blades lost sector 75,172 again or failed to reclaim it in the first place. In that event, the favor I demanded would be worthless.

Of course, Tyelin didn't know about Draven's Reach.

Assuming sector 75,172 stayed in the hands of the Blades and the dungeon's existence became common knowledge, then the favor's value would increase tenfold... And while I didn't intend on ever reopening Draven's Reach for use by any but my staunchest allies, it was nice to have... options.

Arguing over the phrasing served another purpose, too, for me at least. Acceding to Tyelin's wishes when it came to the favor allowed me to insist that nothing in the Pact's wording would force me to perform the task the Blades required.

I could back out at any time.

Conveniently, this meant I would gain access to the merchant with no strings attached—for Tyelin, this appeared a minor point and one he was willing to concede in exchange for overruling me on the matter of the favor. For me, it was everything.

At the end, when we were both satisfied, we shook hands. "When can I expect your merchant to arrive?" I asked.

"He is already on his way," Tyelin said with a chuckle.

"Perfect," I murmured.

The envoy rose to his feet, and I looked at him curiously. "Where are you going?"

"To make arrangements for your insertion," he replied. "We will have to abduct a Rider and make sure to kill his hellbat before we 'disappear' him. It requires a deft touch, and I will have to see to the preparations myself."

I frowned, not sure how far I trusted the envoy to handle such things.

Seeing my look, he added, "Don't worry. Nicola knows where to find you."

Tyelin had mistaken the reason for my concern, but I didn't pursue the matter. "Nicola is the merchant, I presume?"

He nodded.

"Then I guess I'll see you shortly. You know where to find me."

He smiled. "That I do."

I watched the envoy walk away, saying nothing until he disappeared entirely from my mindsight. *"What did you think of that?"*

"I don't trust him," Ghost pronounced.

"Why?" I asked, keen to hear her thoughts on the matter. There was something about Tyelin that also made me hesitant to trust him. Yet I couldn't pinpoint why that was the case.

"I'm not sure," she admitted.

I sighed. *"Me neither."*

"If this merchant of his even turns up, we should purchase the scrolls we need and flee," she said.

I had half a mind to do just that. Yet...

"Prime?" Ghost prompted when I did not reply.

"Yet," I said, finishing my thought, *"he has done nothing to give us cause to expect betrayal."* I sighed again. *"I will not be the first to break faith."*

A pause. *"Then you intend to go ahead with the deal?"*

"I must," I murmured. *"The envoy's plan is a decent one. And besides, I gave my word. While that might not mean much to Tyelin, it does to me."*

"And if he proves treacherous?"

"Then we are freed of any obligations," I replied. Folding my arms behind my head, I lay back in the grass and set myself to wait for the merchant. *"But let us hope it doesn't come to that."*

✳   ✳   ✳

The sun hung high in the sky by the time the merchant, Nicola, appeared. He arrived without fanfare and on a wagon pulled by a pair of draught horses. Rising to my feet, I studied the slowly approaching wagon and driver.

Nicola was a middle-aged human, stout, but not gone to fat. Scars riddled his bare arms, and a thick cudgel was belted at his side. *Hmm, not your average merchant, then,* I thought, studying the man's grizzled face. He had a scraggly beard—more white than black—and the weatherbeaten look of someone who spent entirely too much time outdoors.

The wagon he drove was just as interesting. Its sides were boarded up and its top covered. I'd not seen a vehicle like it in a long time, and it immediately put me in mind of Hamish. And that, in turn, ignited a dormant memory.

It was Hamish who'd borne the Mark of an Under-dweller, I finally recalled.

A false Mark obviously—given that Hamish had, in reality, been Loken in disguise the entire time—but the comparison was noteworthy, nonetheless. Loken did nothing without reason, and I was certain he had not randomly chosen Hamish's Marks.

So, who are the Under-dwellers that even Loken decided to impersonate one?

A Shadow sect? *No, too obvious.*

Perhaps they were of the Dark, which would explain why I was only running across them in Dark-dominated territories like the Marches and Erebus' dungeon.

But no, Hamish had been pretending to be a Shadow merchant. Whoever the under-dwellers were, they had to be as welcome amongst the Dark as they were by Shadow.

And what was the Mark of *an* Under-dweller really?

I knew already that Marks signified allegiance to a Power—new or ancient. But the phrasing of the Under-dweller Mark hinted at it being neither. If anything, it almost sounded like a place.

Stranger and stranger.

Let's see what analyze can tell me, I thought, reaching out with my will to inspect the approaching player.

The target is Nicola, a human traveling merchant. He is a player and bears a Mark of Lesser Dark and the Mark of an Under-dweller.

My lips turned down. *Well, that tells me nothing.*

The merchant, meanwhile, had drawn to a halt twenty yards away. I strode forward. *Let's see what he has to say.*

Perhaps it would prove more enlightening than my speculation.

"He's alone," Ghost said, confirming what I myself had sensed. Nodding minutely, I drew to a stop beside the visitor's wagon.

"Are you him?" Nicola growled.

"What?" I asked with a frown.

"Are you the one Tyelin sent me for?"

"Ah, yes, I am."

Swinging himself off his high seat, the merchant planted himself before me and held out his hand expectantly.

I glanced down at it. His palm was empty.

"Well?" he demanded. "What's the delay? Hand it over!"

I stared at him. "Hand what over?"

"Your chit, of course," Nicola said, gesturing impatiently. "Give it here."

"You must be confused," I began slowly. "I have no chit to—"

The merchant harrumphed. "Are you or are you not a denizen of the underworld?"

"Huh... umm..." My words trailed off as I realized I'd erred earlier by letting Tyelin believe I knew what the hell he was talking about when he mentioned the underworld.

Nicola's eyes narrowed to slits. "You're not, are you?"

I shrugged apologetically. "I'm not."

The merchant swore ferociously. He didn't appear to be in any danger of stopping either, seeming to find new and more elaborate phrases to spew out every time he threatened to run aground.

"I don't know what half those words mean," Ghost said in horrified awe. *"Did he really just call you a—"*

"Look," I began, interjecting myself into Nicola's monologue—both to distract him and the all-too-fascinated Ghost, "why don't you just tell me what the issue is?"

Breaking off abruptly, Nicola stared at me. "The issue," he said scathingly, "is that I only deal with the underworld's denizens. Tyelin *knows* that. Why, by damn, did he send me here?"

I shifted. "Err, that might have been my fault."

Nicola folded his arms across his chest. "Tyelin thinks you belong to the guild?"

So, the underworld was a guild. "I may have given him that impression, yes."

The merchant's expression did not change, but one corner of his mouth twitched. Was he suppressing a smile? I thought so.

"Well, best of luck, young man," he said, turning around. "Tell Tyelin that next time he should—"

Placing a hand on Nicola's arm, I stopped him from walking away. "Hold on. Surely, we can come to some sort of compromise?"

The big merchant glared down at my hand. "I don't compromise."

"What's the big deal anyway?" I asked, ignoring his pointed look. "I have bought from one of your kind before."

"You have?" he asked.

I nodded. "Yes, his name was Hamish from—"

"Hamish," he muttered, then shook his head. "Nope. Never heard of him." He waved his hand dismissively. "Mind you, it makes no difference. Unlike *some*, my clientele is exclusive."

"Hmm, sort of like Kesh," I muttered under my breath, not expecting him to hear.

But Nicola's hearing was sharper than I thought. "You've dealt with Kesh?" he asked, swinging back to face me.

"I have," I said. Then, sensing his keen interest, asked, "You've heard of her?"

He snorted. "Every merchant worth his salt has." Distrust flared in his eyes. "But anyone can claim to know Kesh. It doesn't prove anything."

"True," I agreed. Withdrawing my Emporium access card, I flashed it under his nose. "But this does."

Nicola stared at the card, then squinted at me as if truly seeing me for the first time. He still, however, bristled with suspicion. "If you have access to that worthy's stores, what do you need me for? Kesh can supply you with everything I can and at far less of a surcharge."

I winced at his mention of a surcharge. Somehow, I didn't think Nicola's prices were going to be easy to swallow. Still, it was not like I had much choice in the matter.

"I'm in a bit of a predicament," I said, answering him forthrightly. "Circumstances prevent me from visiting Nexus right now."

His look turned sly. "That on account of your Power Mark?"

I sighed. "You could say that." I studied Nicola speculatively. His demeanor had softened, and no longer did his refusal to deal appear so adamant. *There's an opening here. Time to push.*

"So, it seems we're at an impasse. You won't sell to me, and I don't have time to go looking for another merchant. Looks like we have no choice but to wait for the envoy's return. Perhaps, he can resolve matters between us."

Nicola grimaced. "What, you mean spend the rest of the day waiting for that smug bastard to reappear? No, thank you."

I shrugged. "Then what? At a guess, it took you half a day to get here and will take you just as long to get back to wherever you've come from. A whole day wasted, and what do you have to show for it? Nothing."

The merchant's lips twisted sourly, no doubt realizing what I was driving at, yet the next words out of his mouth were not the ones I expected. "You have the look of a rogue about you."

I blinked. "I do?"

"A scrawny runt like you, in leather armor, and with a shortsword strapped at your side, what else would ye be?" Before I could respond, he leaned forward intently. "Tell me straight. Are you?"

"I've stolen a thing or two," I admitted.

"Answer the damn question," Nicola demanded, looking unimpressed by my response. "Yes or No?"

"Yes," I said bitingly.

"Good enough." Flicking his thumb up, he tossed me a small object.

I caught it easily.

You have acquired an <u>apprentice rogue's underworld token</u>. This is a writ of authorization, marking you as a minor denizen of the underworld. This item cannot be stolen, traded, or lost, even upon death. Note: if your membership is revoked by the guild, this writ will be destroyed.

Opening my fist, I studied the small round object in my palm. It was the size and weight of a gold coin. The numeral "1" was stamped on one side, and on the other side was a closed-eye symbol.

"What's this?" I asked.

"You're one of us now," Nicola replied, confirming my suspicions. "Show that to any underworld merchant and they will deal with you."

"And what exactly does it mean to be a denizen of the underworld?" I asked.

Nicola sighed. "You really know nothing, don't you?"

I didn't dignify that with a response.

"It means you are a member—a provisional one, anyway—of the underworld," he explained. "Which itself is a vast network of burglars, pickpockets, bandits, robbers, and the like that stretches across the length and breadth of the Kingdom."

My lips thinned. "A guild of criminals," I summarized.

"Not quite," Nicola disagreed. "The underworld deals in theft, but we do *not* deal in death. There are plenty of other guilds and factions for that sort of thing."

A thieves guild, then, I thought.

"Still, as you can imagine," he continued, "our members are not openly welcomed in the Kingdom's towns and cities. We keep to the shadows and away from those who fancy themselves the law."

I scratched my chin thoughtfully. Despite my initial misgivings, being a member of such a guild was certainly advantageous. After all, by the new Powers' reckoning, I was undoubtedly considered an even worse sort of criminal.

"How do the under-dwellers fit in?" I asked.

Nicola grunted. "They don't. The under-dwellers are... call us a band of traveling merchants. We roam the Endless Dungeon peddling our wares and are rarely, if ever, seen above ground."

"Hmm... so you're both an under-dweller and an underworld denizen?"

"I am."

"But you say the two are unrelated?"

"They are," he replied smoothly, but his eyes didn't quite meet mine as he said it, leaving me to doubt the veracity of his words. This was not the time to pursue the matter, though. "What's so special about the under-dwellers then?" I asked instead. "Tyelin made a point of mentioning you were one."

Nicola barked a laugh. "He did, did he? Well, we are known for our honor. An under-dweller will sooner suffer final death than break his word."

"I see." I rubbed my chin. "But that doesn't explain your Mark."

"The Mark is not just a designation, it is also the name of our patron."

I blinked. "The under-dweller is a Power?" The Game message certainly hadn't made it sound like that.

"We've ventured far enough afield," Nicola declared, changing the topic abruptly. "Let's get back to the matter at hand." When I didn't immediately respond, he demanded, "Do you want to deal or not?"

"One more question..."

Nicola's brows drew down.

"It's the last I promise."

Scowling, he stayed silent, which I took as acquiescence. "What are the rules?" I asked.

He stared at me.

"For the thieves guild, I mean."

"You intend on becoming a full member?" he asked skeptically. He pointed to the token in my hand. "And not just use that to trade with me?"

I shrugged. "Why not? My talents might be more suited to such a guild than you realize."

He snorted but didn't gainsay me. "I cannot properly induct you into the underworld. For that, you will have to visit one of the den chiefs." He eyed me thoughtfully. "You're from Nexus, you say?"

"As much as I am from anywhere," I replied lightly.

"Then the next time you are there, visit the 'The Crooked Man' inn in the plague quarter. Ask for Dinara and show him the token. He'll know what to do."

The Adjudicator has allocated you a new task: <u>The Seedy Side of Life</u>! The merchant, Nicola, has accepted you as a minor denizen of the underworld. Fulfill the thieves guild's requirements to become a full member. Objective: Visit Den Chief Dinara and complete your induction.

I smiled as I dismissed the Game message. "Thank you," I murmured.
He grunted. "*Now*, are you ready to shop?"
I grinned. "I am."

✶　✶　✶

You have entered a tier 7 shielded chamber.

A minute later, we were both sitting inside Nicola's wagon. All manner of items were crammed on the shelves lining three of the four walls. Craning my head left and right, I studied the wooden, box-like interior. It appeared tiny, especially with the hulking figure of Nicola crammed opposite me. A small table stood between us, and we sat on stools so low our knees were tucked beneath our arms.

"What's the shield for?" I asked.

"Privacy," Nicola replied laconically. "When you deal with one of my kind, your confidentiality is assured. No player will be able to scry into this room."

I nodded appreciatively. "And which kind is that? Under-dweller or underworld merchant?" I asked with a smile.

"Under-dweller," he replied quellingly. "Now, before we begin, let's see your gold," Nicola said.

"I don't carry much on me," I admitted. "Most of my wealth is stored in a bank. If you show me your keystone, I can—"

I broke off. Nicola was shaking his head. "What's wrong?"

He sighed. "I should have realized this would be a problem. I don't carry a keystone. No underworld merchant does."

I grimaced. No keystone meant no access to the funds I had stored in the Albion Bank. "Why's that?" I rasped.

"There is no guarantee of anonymity in transactions involving them."

My brows rose, ire forgotten. Loken, I recalled, had used his keystone to track me, but I'd considered that situation unique, a result of the trickery he'd employed. "Are you saying," I said slowly, "bank transactions are monitored?"

"Not ordinarily," he said, reassuring me somewhat, "but for the right price, and in certain situations involving ill-gotten goods of high value, the banks have been known to... reveal compromising information to affected parties."

"I see," I murmured, not liking the implications. "So, what are the alternatives?"

"Cold, hard cash is always best," he replied promptly.

"And in the absence of that?"

"We can barter. Or you can open an account with the thieves guild." He held up a hand, forestalling my follow-up questions. "And before you ask, I cannot help you with that. Only a den chief can authorize such."

I pursed my lips. "Barter it is then." Reaching into my backpack, I pulled out the four legendary artifacts I'd purchased in New Haven and laid them on the table. I watched Nicola closely as I did.

He didn't give much away, but from the almost imperceptible widening of his eyes, I knew I had surprised him. "Nice," he pronounced after carefully inspecting each object for a full minute.

I chuckled. "They're a bit more than that."

"Maybe," he said, conceding nothing. "What do you want for them?"

"First, tell me what they're worth."

He scowled, not liking that. "Five thousand gold for each," he said after a pause.

"No way," I said, thinking of the twelve thousand in gold that I'd paid for the wayfarer's gloves, which according to Kesh, had been the cheapest item in the set. "Thirty thousand gold—each. A legendary artifact is worth at least that much."

Nicola snorted derisively. "Is that how much Kesh charged you for one? You overpaid. I'll give you forty thousand for the lot, and that's only on account of how generous I am."

I didn't believe him. Sweeping the items off the table, I began packing them away. "Very well, if you don't want them, I'll sell them elsewhere. I have other stuff to trade."

"Whoa there," he said, stopping me before I could stuff the items back into my backpack. "No need to be so hasty. Sixty thousand."

Cocking my head to the side, I considered his offer. It was an incredible amount of money, and more than I expected to get. But then again, I had no way of ascertaining the true value of the four legendary items myself.

Still, considering the cost of the items I wanted to purchase, it was not like I had much choice about selling the artifacts. "How do I know you won't just overcharge me for the items I buy in order to recoup your 'loss?'"

"I guess you'll just have to trust me," he said with an evil-looking grin.

"Not a chance," I retorted. "I know the true cost of the stuff I want." Which I did—mostly—having purchased similar items from Kesh before. "We will agree on your 'surcharge' first." I paused. "Ten percent for—"

Bending over, Nicola clutched his stomach. He was shaking so hard that at first, I thought he was dying.

Then I realized he was laughing.

"Not on your life," he wheezed when he finally looked up. "Fifty percent."

"Ridiculous," I scoffed. "Twenty," I countered.

He shook his head, his humor fading. "You've no comprehension of the cost of doing business in the shadows, my friend. Fifty percent, and not a penny less. I won't sell at a loss."

I scrutinized his face, trying to pick out truth from lies. "Very well, I'll agree to your fifty percent"—Nicola began to smile—"but I'll sell you only three of the legendary artifacts. The last, I'll exchange for another legendary item, one useful to me."

He frowned. "What if I don't have such an item or if the cost is greater?"

I shrugged. "Then we begin negotiations anew. Deal?"

He pondered my offer for a moment, then nodded decisively. "Deal."

No sooner had Nicola agreed than I pulled out a slip of paper from my pocket.

"What's that?" he asked, eyeing the parchment.

Smoothing open the paper, I laid it out on the table. "My shopping list."

Leaning forward, the merchant studied what I had written.

<u>Ability tomes</u>

load controller tier IV,
piercing strike tier III, IV, & V
backstab tier IV & V,
whirlwind tier III & IV,
trap disarm tier III,
lockpicking tier III,
mass charm tier IV & V,
windborne tier IV,
heightened reflexes tier IV,
analyze tier IV & V,
trap detect tier IV,
facial disguise tier IV & V,
ventro tier III & IV.

<u>Other</u>

12 x upgrade gems.
4 x greater portal scrolls.
10 x acid bombs, 10 x smoke bombs, 10 x ice bombs, and 10 x fire bombs.
200 trap-making crystals.
10 x full healing potions.

Nicola's eyebrows rose. "That's a sizable list." His eyes flicked up to study me. "Have you been stuck in a dungeon or something?" he asked, only half-jokingly.

My lips twitched. "Something like that. Can you get the gear I need?"

Not answering, Nicola closed his eyes.

I waited patiently, assuming he was searching the stores and auctions he had access to. My list had been carefully curated, of course.

I'd not included everything I wished, only those items that wouldn't raise too many eyebrows. The shopping list, for instance, made no mention of a fade ability tome. To advance the ability, I planned on using an upgrade gem—even though the cost of doing so was exorbitant. There was a price to secrecy, after all.

Sometimes a literal one.

Also buried in the list was the thing I desperately sought—a portal scroll. Amongst the other requirements I'd scribbled down, the portal scrolls would barely draw notice, yet they were vital to my plans.

I'd first run across portal scrolls during my time in the wolves' valley, and even though I'd not ended up using the one I'd acquired then, I knew the scrolls required nothing from the user but mana. This was important because my spell-illiterate trait would not allow me to weave any spell myself.

And while the mana cost of a greater portal scroll was astronomical—to the average fighter anyway—thanks to my own not-insignificant investment in Magic, I had enough mana to use one.

"I can get everything on your list," Nicola pronounced at last.

I leaned across the table. "And the price?"

He held up a hand. "I can get everything *except* for a full complement of the upgrade gems you've requested. I can only source ten gems right now. Even as expensive as they are, they are much in demand."

I waved aside the comment. "How much?" I asked again.

"Forty-seven thousand gold."

I sat back, a surprised expression on my face.

"You think it too much?" he asked, noticing my look.

I shook my head. "On the contrary, it's about what I estimated." And indeed it was. "I'm only surprised..."

He grinned. "That I deal fairly?"

I matched his grin. "Yeah, that."

He chuckled. "I may drive a hard bargain, but once the deal is struck, you can trust me to be scrupulous in meeting the terms."

"I see that now."

"That brings us to the matter of the legendary artifact."

I nodded. I'd been in two minds about how open to be when it came to my equipment requirements, but seeing that Nicola had not tried cheating me, I decided to trust him a bit further. "I'm looking for any wayfarer pieces you may have."

"I'm familiar with the wayfarer set," Nicola murmured. "I can get you the gloves"—his gaze flickered to my hands—"but I see you have them already. I assume you don't want duplicates?"

I shook my head. "I need only the pieces I'm missing," I confirmed.

"Ah. Then, in that case, I can't help you," he said regretfully. "Are there any other legendary artifacts you need?"

I hesitated, then coming to a decision, I set down the psi bracelet. "Yes, either of the pieces that match with this."

Nicola sucked in a breath as he caught sight of the artifact. "The Three-is-One. This, too, I've heard of. It's a unique set, something almost *unheard* of." He looked up at me, his eyes shining with awe. "Where did you get it? This piece has been missing for centuries."

"I can't say, of course."

He smiled. "Stole it, did you?" he murmured.

I didn't correct him. "So, can you source the other two pieces?"

He shook his head. "Regretfully, artifacts like this are almost never put up for sale." His eyes growing distant, he said nothing else.

"But?" I prompted, guessing from his look that there was more to the matter.

He refocused on me. "But," he allowed, "I know the whereabouts of both remaining pieces."

I stamped down my excitement. "Tell me," I whispered.

"It won't help you," he cautioned.

"Let me be the judge of that," I replied.

Nicola shrugged. "They are in the keeping of a Power named Mai."

I frowned. "Never heard of him."

"I'm not surprised. Mai is a recluse who rarely ventures out of his home sector," Nicola said. "He is a collector, too, and has been searching for the last piece for a long time. Over the years, Mai periodically reaches out to the underworld seeking information on the whereabouts of the last Three-is-One piece." He shrugged. "If you're looking to sell, he's the one to approach. And if you're not, you'd be wise to tell no one else about what you have. Mai does not take rejection lightly, if you take my meaning."

"Thank you," I said softly. "I do."

"That still leaves the matter of our deal." Nicola gestured to the four artifacts still on display. "Since I've failed to live up to my end of the bargain, you can take one back."

I eyed the items on the table doubtfully.

"There is an alternative," he offered.

I looked at him curiously. "Go on."

"You can take the remaining money—thirteen thousand gold." He smiled. "That much gold will be hard to carry on your person, but I could issue you with a promissory note to be reclaimed when you visit Den Chief Dinara."

"But that will entail a visit to Nexus," I said, stating the obvious.

He nodded. "Which you may not be able to do any time soon. The other possibility is that I offer you something else from my stores."

I bit my lip. Buying more gear was tempting. There was still much I needed and things that Ghost did, too. But I didn't know what awaited me in the guardian tower, the wolves' valley, or Nexus, and until I reconnected with my allies—or a bank—I would have no ready source of funds.

"I'll take the money," I said finally. "Twelve thousand in a promissory note, and one thousand in gold coins."

Nicola nodded. "I can do that."

"And one more thing," I said, struck by a passing thought.

He looked at me questioningly.

"What can you tell me about cynacilin?"

"Cynacilin," Nicola mused, rubbing his chin consideringly. "I gather this has something to do with the envoy?"

"Hmm," I replied noncommittally. "What makes you say that?"

He laughed. "You will not find cynacilin on the open market—or any market for that matter. The alchemical powder is extracted from a rare plant, one that few have access to. And it just so happens the Blades number amongst those who do."

My eyes narrowed thoughtfully. So, the Riders would know immediately who was responsible for the assassination. Not that I could see how that would make any difference. "What does it do?"

The merchant shrugged. "Cynacilin is most famous for being a poison for which there is no known cure—magical or otherwise. The victim's only chance is to resist the powder's effects. If he or she doesn't, death is inevitable."

"I see. What are the poison's limitations?"

"It's not easy to make or prepare. I'm told the process to produce it takes years. And it requires an expert touch to apply."

"An expert touch," I mused. "Could I use it?"

He snorted. "Not unless you're a trained poisoner."

Interesting, I thought. *This Jone who I'm meant to deliver the smuggled package to has to be more than a simple fisherman.* Tyelin had failed to mention that.

I inclined my head. "Thank you, Nicola. You've been quite helpful." I gestured to the table. "I'm ready to conclude our deal if you are."

He nodded. "I am. Let's do it."

✳   ✳   ✳

You have lost 4 x legendary items.

You have acquired an underworld promissory note for 12,000 gold.

You have acquired 1,000 gold coins.

You have acquired 21 ability tomes, 10 x upgrade gems, 40 bombs, 200 trap-making crystals, and 10 x full healing potions.

You have acquired 4 x greater portal scrolls.

Each of these scrolls allows a spellcaster to open a portal for a party of 4 to any known sector key point. This item requires a minimum Magic of 40 to use.

Nicola did not hang around once our transaction was concluded. After saying his farewells, the merchant turned his wagon around and disappeared over the horizon.

"*That went well,*" Ghost noted.

I nodded. "*It did.*" The under-dweller had been an interesting character, and in the end, he had proved more trustworthy than I had expected. *Tyelin chose well.*

Remembering the envoy, I searched the surroundings, but there was no sign of Tyelin yet. It was only late afternoon, though, and we'd agreed to enact his plan at night.

He'll be back after dark, I guess.

Shrugging, I sank down cross-legged in the grass. I had a few hours to wait, and I knew exactly how to spend the time. Pulling out the upgrade gems and the ability tomes I'd purchased, I lay them out before me.

For a moment, I just sat staring at the items. This point had been a long time in coming. It had been over a month since I'd last had access to a merchant, and in that time, my skills and player level had grown exponentially.

Not so my abilities. They had remained stagnant.

It was finally time to address that lack. But doing so would call for some difficult decisions, too. Cupping my chin in my hands, I pondered my choices.

Which abilities did I upgrade?

CHAPTER 457: WORKING WITHIN ONE'S LIMITS

I began with Constitution.

Since I had only a single Constitution ability and limited slots available, it was the easiest attribute to attend to. Picking up the tier four load controller ability tome, I began to read.

You have upgraded your load controller ability to <u>greater load controller</u>. This ability increases the encumbrance of any foe within 5 yards by 50% for 10 minutes. Its activation time is very slow. Note: load controller only affects hostiles who wear armor.

This is a master ability and requires 5 more ability slots than its expert variant. You have 9 of 24 Constitution ability slots remaining.

"That was simple," I murmured as the new knowledge filtered into my consciousness. Ideally, I would've liked to advance the ability even further, but unfortunately, my light armor skill hadn't reached rank twenty yet. Acquiring load controller's elite variant would have to wait.

On to the next: Dexterity.

Here the choices I faced were much tougher, and before I made them, I wanted to be certain I understood the impact. Calling up an extract of my profile, I reviewed the status of my Dexterity abilities.

<u>Dexterity abilities ready for upgrade (56 of 94 slots used)</u>
Master abilities: greater fade.
Expert abilities: backstab.
Advanced abilities: piercing strike, trap disarm, lockpicking, whirlwind.

I only had thirty-eight Dexterity ability slots available—far less than what I needed to upgrade all the abilities ready for advancement. *Let's begin with the most important, then.*

Picking up an attribute gem, I willed my intent to the Game.

Creating ability tome...

...

You have acquired a tier 5 fade ability tome.

The gem crumbled to dust, leaving a small leatherbound book in its place. Wasting no more time, I opened the book and absorbed its knowledge.

You have upgraded the fade ability to <u>vanish,</u> which grants you true invisibility for 5 minutes. While invisible, you cannot be spotted by sight alone, nor will any actions you take break the spell. Note: this does not prevent your foes from locating you by other means—magical or otherwise—or from dispelling the buff.

Vanish is an elite tier ability and requires 15 more ability slots than its master variant. You have 23 of 94 Dexterity ability slots remaining.

I exhaled softly, marveling at the new knowledge settling in my mind. True invisibility was finally mine to wield. What's more, I would be able to activate vanish for a full five minutes. That was longer than many of my fights lasted. I grinned.

Hand-to-hand combat is going to be much easier now.

Unfortunately, there was a downside, too. Acquiring the elite ability had consumed a sizable chunk of my available ability slots, and with only twenty-three remaining, I had two choices.

One, advance backstab—my next most valuable Dexterity ability—two tiers, making it an elite ability as well. Doing so would cost twenty ability slots.

Or two, raise all my direct combat abilities—backstab, piercing strike, and whirlwind—one tier each, leaving me with a surplus of eight Dexterity slots for use elsewhere.

The second approach was the more conservative one and left me more prepared for 'normal' combat, whereas the first maximized the burst damage I could do when stealthed.

Then, too, there were the obvious synergies between backstab and vanish. *The benefits of such are too great to ignore,* I decided.

My choice made, I opened the backstab ability tomes.

You have upgraded your backstab ability to <u>greater backstab</u>.
You have upgraded your backstab ability to <u>deadly backstab</u>.
Deadly backstab increases the damage you inflict to 5x more than normal. You have 3 of 94 Dexterity ability slots remaining.

I whistled softly. Five times more damage was an incredible multiplier and meant even shielded mages would fall quickly beneath my blades.

Happy with my choice, I stored the remaining Dexterity ability tomes in my backpack. I might not be able to use them immediately, but keeping them on my person meant I wouldn't be caught out again. I smiled wryly. After all, who knew when I'd find myself trapped again?

Right, that's Dexterity done, I thought, chuckling softly. Next on the list was Mind. Turning my focus inward, I pulled up the applicable status report.

<u>**Mind abilities ready for upgrade (71 of 123 slots used)**</u>
Expert abilities: mass charm, windborne, heightened reflexes, shadow blink, quick mend, fortified mind.
Advanced abilities: astral blades.

With Mind, I had even more slots to play with—fifty-two to be precise—but that didn't make the decisions I faced any easier. I used all my Mind abilities extensively in combat—with the possible exception of fortified mind. What's more, all seven abilities were upgradeable to tier four, and three could even reach elite rank.

I simply couldn't afford to improve all of them, though. I chewed on the inside of my lip, considering what approach to take.

I should advance all seven abilities to tier four, I decided eventually. Considering the relative ability slot cost of each tier, this was the most effective approach.

My course set, I picked up the first book—the tier four mass charm ability tome.

You have upgraded your charm ability to <u>mass puppet</u>.
The tier 4 variant of this spell temporarily overrides the consciousness of 20 targets, forcing them to serve you for 30 seconds. Unlike charmed entities who will only obey basic commands, puppeted foes will follow complex orders as well.
You have 47 of 123 Mind ability slots remaining.

"Nice," I murmured. Pulling open the next book, I read it, too.

You have upgraded your windborne ability to <u>improved windborne</u>. The tier 4 variant of this ability allows you to slide along a current of wind, in any direction, up to a maximum distance of 20 yards and at 3x your normal movement speed.
You have 42 of 123 Mind ability slots remaining.

I smiled. "Also good." Next was heightened reflexes.

You have upgraded your heightened reflexes ability to <u>enhanced reflexes</u>. The tier 4 variant of this ability increases your Dexterity by +16 ranks for 20 minutes.
You have 37 of 123 Mind ability slots remaining.

That took care of my 'ordinary' Mind abilities. There were still my scion ones to attend to. Improving them, however, required the use of the upgrade gems. First up was astral blade.

Ability gem activated.
Creating ability tome...
...
Tome creation halted.

There are 3 expert variants available for the astral blade ability.
Variant 1: <u>astral shurikens</u>. This variant replaces your astral daggers with twin psi shurikens. The shurikens can only be thrown and will bounce from target to target doing progressively less damage each time.
Variant 2: <u>astral sword</u>. This variant replaces your daggers with twin psi swords. The swords cannot be flung, but they persist for longer in your hands than the more ephemeral daggers.
Variant 3: <u>astral spear</u>. This variant replaces your daggers with a single psi spear. The spear deals significantly more damage than the smaller daggers and can be thrown or wielded in one hand.
Choose your tier 3 astral blade ability tome now.

"Damn," I whispered, rocking back and forth as I found myself face to face with yet another—and this time, wholly unexpected—choice. I'd run across variants before, of course, and the three on offer now were as intriguing as the previous ones I'd encountered.

Rubbing the side of my face, I considered the choice before me.

The three variants appeared to build on the tier two spell, improving and specializing it further. The shuriken variant focused on ranged area-of-effect damage, the swords on melee damage, and the spear offered the versatility of being able to perform both melee and ranged attacks.

Given that, the decision was an easy one.

I used my astral blade spell almost exclusively for performing ranged attacks. This being the case, it made sense to specialize it further in this regard.

Closing my eyes, I willed my choice to the Adjudicator.

You have acquired an astral shurikens ability tome.

You have upgraded your astral blade ability to <u>astral shurikens</u>. This tier 3 spell manifests two psi shurikens in your hands. Each shuriken will bounce a maximum of 3 times to a random hostile less than 5 yards away from the previous target. At each bounce, the damage inflicted is halved. Note: both your hands must be empty to use this spell.

You have 32 of 123 Mind ability slots remaining.

"Perfect!" I exclaimed.

"I want that spell, too," Ghost said, sounding only a little envious.

I grinned. *"I think your astral bite variant is locked into the melee path already. But don't worry,"* I consoled her, *"I'm sure it will be equally good when we upgrade it."*

"If *we* upgrade it," she corrected.

"True," I mumbled apologetically. *"Unfortunately, I think we're going to be chronically short of Mind slots."*

"That's alright, Prime," she replied, *"you'll make better use of them than I would."*

Thanking her for her graciousness, I turned my attention to my other scion abilities. They were now all at the expert tier. *Time to advance them to master.* One after the other, I activated four more upgrade gems.

This time, there were no further surprises.

You have upgraded your astral shurikens ability to <u>superior astral shurikens</u>. The fourth tier of this spell increases the maximum bounce of each shuriken to 5 and the bounce distance to 10 yards.

You have upgraded your shadow blink ability to <u>extreme shadow blink</u>. The fourth tier of this spell allows you to teleport to any living entity within 100 yards, taking your shadows with you.

You have upgraded your quick mend ability to <u>improved quick mend</u>. The fourth tier of this spell increases the restorative effects provided by a quick mend to 30%.

You have upgraded your fortified mind ability to <u>improved fortified mind.</u> The fourth tier of this spell increases the portion of your psi pool available for psi casting to 75% while the remaining 25% forms a barrier around your thoughts.

You have 12 of 123 Mind ability slots remaining.

Wincing, I rubbed at my temples. The knowledge of the new spells sat heavy in my mind, and I could feel a headache coming on. Shaking my head to clear it, I refocused on the task at hand.

All my Mind spells were finally at the master tier—except stunning slap which couldn't be upgraded—and I could finally turn my attention to the last set of abilities requiring advancement: the Perception ones. Calling up another extract of my profile, I reviewed their status.

<u>**Perception abilities ready for upgrade (36 of 90 slots used)**</u>
Expert abilities: analyze, facial disguise.
Advanced abilities: trap detect, ventro, imitate.
Basic abilities: conceal weapon.

When it came to Perception, at least, there were no difficult decisions. I'd already made up my mind that I would upgrade both analyze and facial disguise to tier five and leave the other abilities as they were for now.

Opening the requisite ability tomes, I began to read.

You have upgraded your analyze ability to <u>greater analyze.</u>

You have upgraded your analyze ability to <u>powerful analyze</u>, enabling you to inspect entities of rank 40 and below. The tier 5 analyze variant will identify a target's level, race, individual Classes, follower classification, and the current status of their health, energy pools, buffs, and debuffs.

Additionally, when it comes to other players, powerful analyze will function like a passive ability. As soon as another player enters your circle of awareness, you will gain access to their analyze data without any active intervention on your part.

You have upgraded your facial ability to <u>master facial disguise.</u>

You have upgraded your facial ability to <u>mimic.</u>

The tier 5 variant of this spell physically transforms your face during casting, making your disguise impenetrable to nearly all forms of detection. In addition, the spell's duration is increased to 10 hours, and all your analyze data and spirit signatures can be falsified. Note: however, the extent to which you can replace your spirit signatures is limited. You may not assume the guise of a non-player or that of a Power.

You have 14 of 90 Perception ability slots remaining.

I exhaled slowly. It was finally done. I'd gained the abilities I needed to convincingly disguise myself from other players—but not just them. I suspected some Powers would also have trouble seeing through my false visage.

That was not all, though.

I'd also acquired the abilities I needed to make myself a true elite. Now, I could face players like Leafbright, Malikor, and perhaps even Tyelin, with confidence.

I'm ready, I thought. *No matter what the next few hours bring, I'm ready.*

Chapter 458: A Spy's Worth

Before setting myself to wait for the envoy, I renewed my disguise.

You have cast mimic, transforming your visage into that of Jasiah, a level 152 human duelist and concealing your Powerful Initiate Mark. Duration: 10 hours.

As expected, the experience was wholly different this time. Instead of using mere light and illusion to disguise me like the facial disguise spell did, mimic physically changed my entire face.

My bones shifted. My nose broadened. My eyes widened. And my skin tone changed. And when all was said and done, I did not only look like Jasiah, I *was* him.

At least, my face was.

The rest of me remained unchanged. *A pity,* I thought. My disguise would have been more complete if mimic could transform my entire body like the imitate spell did. But imitate was too costly. Worse yet, only its tier six variant was capable of hiding my spirit signatures. And even now, my deception was not high enough for that.

Mimic will do well enough, in any case. After all, concealing my Power Mark was more important than the completeness of my physical disguise.

Twisting my neck from side to side, I rubbed my cheeks, feeling out my new face. "What do you think, Ghost? How do I look?"

"The same," she replied dryly.

I rolled my eyes. "I know *that*, but can you spot any difference between now and before?"

"No."

"Ah," I said, deflating. "I guess the spell is working then."

"Just in time, too," she observed. *"We have incoming."*

Snapping alert, I let my awareness expand outward and noticed what Ghost had. Eleven players were approaching from the south.

But remarkably, that was not all I sensed.

Almost as soon as I became aware of the players, their analyze data scrolled through my mind.

The target is Tyelin, a level 260 human artful burglar and envoy of Blythe. His health and energy pools are at 100%, and he bears a Mark of Supreme Dark and Blythe. Tyelin is currently suffering no ill effects and is buffed by...

The target is...

The target is...

"Ah," I exclaimed softly to myself. Not only did I know the players' names, but I knew their levels, Class, current status, and Power allegiance. Their primary faction, while not explicitly identified, was obvious, too. They were Blades.

"Trouble?" Ghost wondered.

"I don't think so," I replied. While the players with the envoy were mostly higher-leveled than other Blades I'd met, none were elites. If Tyelin had intended on ambushing me, he would have brought at least a few rank twenty players to support him. *"This must be part of the envoy's 'preparations.'"*

The party drew to a stop a respectful distance in front of me. "Tyelin," I greeted.

The envoy nodded in acknowledgment. "I see your dealings with Nicola were a success," he said, no doubt having already noticed that the Power Mark was gone from my spirit signature.

"I got what I needed," I agreed.

"Then you're ready to work?" he asked brightly.

"I am." Running my gaze over the other silently watching players, I nodded at Yara. She was the only one I'd met prior to this.

The orc scowled back.

Ignoring her reaction, I addressed Tyelin again, "Why the escort?"

"Raiding party—not escort," he corrected.

My gaze flickered over the Blades again, this time noting their dark clothing, loosened face masks, and blackened weapons. "We're going to ambush a Rider patrol," I surmised.

Tyelin grinned. "That's right, and in the confusion, we'll substitute you with one of the Riders."

I nodded. It was a simple, if elegant, ruse. "I should not be the sole survivor," I stated.

"You won't be," Tyelin assured me. "From the Riders' perspective, the raid will be a failure. At least half of them and their companions will survive. You will be one of the unlucky ones, forced to walk back to the fort on foot."

"Then what?" I asked.

Tyelin handed me a rolled parchment. "That is a map of the Rider base. The shortest route from the main gate to Jone is also marked. You will find him in the servant's quarters on the ground floor. He doesn't know you're coming, but the code phrase you need is in there as well."

Unrolling the parchment, I perused the map. It contained an impressively detailed layout of the first two floors of the fort. Every room—including the demarcated safe zone area—was clearly labeled and described, and like Tyelin had said, a series of meaningless words were scribbled along the bottom.

"How did you get this?" I asked curiously.

He laughed bitterly. "You forget. Sector 75,172 was once under our control. *We* built the fort."

I nodded in appreciation. The map's detail made sense now. There was one glaring omission, though. "What about the third floor?" There was one. I knew that from observing the fort from afar.

Tyelin grimaced. "The Riders butchered it. What was once an elegant span of rooms is now a *stable*."

"A stable—? Oh. You mean for the hellbats."

He nodded sourly.

Forgoing further comment, I stuffed the parchment in my pocket. "Thanks. This will help immensely."

"Make sure to memorize the map before we cross the river," he added.

"I'll do that." I paused. "How do we communicate once we're separated?"

Tyelin threw me a quizzical look. "We don't," he replied. "Once you're inside the fort, you're on your own."

I snorted. "That's foolish."

He stared at me.

"What if I can't find this Jone?" I asked. "What if he isn't where you say he is? What of the other hundred-odd things that could go wrong? In fact, I will be surprised if everything *does* go to plan." I shook my head. "We should be prepared for the eventuality that things won't go as we want." I had had more than enough plans go awry to know that contingencies were necessary, essential even.

The envoy frowned, looking a little taken aback. "You're right," he conceded finally. "An oversight on my part." Glancing at Yara, he waved her forward. "Give him a bracelet."

Wordlessly, the orc placed a thin slip of metal in my palm.

This is a farspeaker bracelet. This item is 1 of 15 in a matched set of devices and will allow you to communicate through the aether with the other bearers while you both occupy the same sector. It has no minimum requirements to use.

"Satisfied?" Tyelin asked—a little bitingly, I thought—while I equipped the bracelet.

"Very," I replied evenly.

"Good," the envoy pronounced. "Then let's move. We don't have much time if we want to get into position before the patrol reaches the ambush spot."

❋ ❋ ❋

Ghost has unmanifested.
You have entered sector 75,172.

The Blade squad moved well. With Tyelin leading the way, they waded into the river, fording it with ease and managing to stay in formation the entire way. I followed a few steps behind, a part of—yet apart from—the group, observing everything but not interfering. The first stage of the envoy's operation was clearly theirs to perform.

Ghost had unmanifested before we'd set off. None of the Blades knew she was more than an ordinary summons, and I wanted to make sure it stayed that way. In the event that Tyelin betrayed me, the pyre wolf would make for an unpleasant surprise.

It was not that I *expected* to be betrayed, but like I'd told the envoy, it would be foolish to believe everything would go as I hoped. I couldn't see why the Blades would double-cross me, though.

They had everything to gain if our venture succeeded and lots to lose if it didn't. But admittedly, I didn't know all the dynamics in the region, and perhaps Tyelin foresaw some hidden profit in duplicity. *Or perhaps, he sees a way to defeat both the Riders and me,* I mused.

The Pact the envoy and I had formed did not guarantee my safety, after all. And from the Blades' perspective, there was no downside to slaying me once they regained the sector.

If Tyelin is going to double-cross me, it will happen after Malikor is killed, I concluded.

"What will you do if he does?" Ghost asked, listening in on my thoughts.

I smiled grimly. *"Teach him the true cost of betrayal, I suppose."*

A Wolf did *not* let his enemies go unpunished.

✳ ✳ ✳

It was just after midnight when Tyelin called a halt. "We're here," he declared.

Glancing around, I studied the terrain but saw nothing that set this spot of grassland apart from any other that we'd crossed in the last few hours. We had been traveling steadily north along the river, though. So, perhaps we'd finally reached the region the Riders' patrols covered.

"Jasiah," Tyelin called, "get down and stay out of sight." He paused. "You can do that, can't you?"

Ignoring his condescending tone, I shrugged and did as he asked.

You have activated a single-use enchantment, completely masking your scent for the next 4 hours.

You are hidden. Twelve neutral entities have failed to detect you!

The moment I vanished, the raiding party spread out and, one by one, duplicated my feat until only Tyelin was left standing in plain sight. Their concealment was better than the other Blades I'd encountered, and even after straining my senses, I failed to pick them out.

An elite squad, I thought in grudging admiration.

Surveying the area, the envoy nodded satisfactorily before crouching down.

"What now?" I whispered.

"We wait," Tyelin replied. *"The Rider patrol is almost here."*

Uncertain how he could be so sure, I nevertheless held my counsel and settled down to observe the forthcoming ambush.

✳ ✳ ✳

Whatever the source of Tyelin's knowledge, events bore him out. Not even a minute later, a V-shaped formation appeared on the horizon. The Rider patrol. Distant tiny specks though they were, I could nevertheless tell they were winging south along the river and heading in our general direction.

But *only* in our general direction.

Judging from the enemy's flight path, it seemed certain they would not overfly us. *Bad planning or bad luck?* I wondered. Still, I said nothing, waiting to see what Tyelin would do.

Almost a full minute after I'd spotted the Riders, the envoy did so himself. *"Incoming,"* he cautioned, speaking through the farspeaker bracelet. Contrary to my expectations, though, he gave no orders for the ambush party to relocate.

Assuming the whispered caution was not for my benefit alone—the other Blades had to be equipped with communication devices, too—I waited for their reaction.

There was no audible or visible acknowledgment from the squad, but that did not mean they did not respond. Where before the players exuded only watchful intent, now the air was filled with a sudden keenness, a whiff of predatory intent that had my Wolf instincts prickling. The hunt was about to commence.

And by all signs, the hunters appeared confident their quarry was within reach.

Thoughtfully, I turned my gaze skyward, wondering how Tyelin intended to bring the Riders down. The patrol was flying too high and too fast to be targeted from the ground.

It turned out, though, that doing so was unnecessary.

Almost as soon as I completed the thought, the Rider patrol banked sharply, making straight for us. At first, I feared we'd been spotted, but no war cries cut the air, and the hellbats flew lazily, not hurriedly.

They're going to land, I realized. *And almost on top of us.*

My prediction proved correct, and a little later, the ten hellbats hit the ground with a resounding thud—the closest less than thirty yards away.

Multiple hostile entities have failed to detect you! You are hidden.

I rubbed my chin thoughtfully. Tyelin's chosen ambush spot was no accident, and it implied much about his knowledge of the enemy's movements. *How many spies does he have in the Rider fort, I wonder?*

"Make ready," Tyelin commanded—somewhat unnecessarily.

The Riders, meanwhile, were dismounting.

"Jove, Troy, you're on watch," the patrol leader, a player named Mack, ordered. "Elly, get the magelights up. The rest of you, see to the hellbats. We're running behind schedule, so we're gonna have to cut our break short. Ten minutes, then we're back in the air."

Nine groans greeted this pronouncement. But the Riders complained no further as they set about their assigned tasks. Little did they know how close danger lurked.

"Yara, take your squad and circle left," Tyelin ordered. *"Mong, you have the right."* He paused. *"Jasiah, you still with us?"*

Where else would I be? I wondered. "I am," I replied evenly enough.

"Pick one," the envoy instructed.

Knowing what he meant, I ran my gaze over the Riders again—as unnecessary as this was. Courtesy of my upgraded analyze, I already knew everything I needed to know about each player.

"*Troy,*" I replied. He was one of the patrol's two scouts. The human Rider wielded a shortbow, not a sword, but I didn't think an occasion would arise where my lack of skill with the weapon would trip me up. More importantly, Troy wore light armor, which meant that even while wearing his face, I would not be completely without protection.

"*Yara, Mong, you heard him,*" Tyelin said. "*See to it.*"

"*On it, boss,*" Mong replied.

Sitting back—figuratively and literally—I got ready to watch the Blades work.

CHAPTER 459: TROJAN HORSE

The ambush went off without a hitch. Well, from our perspective it did, but from the Riders' vantage point, it must have seemed poorly executed.

Yara and Mong began by killing the mage, Elly. Then, in what was either a planned maneuver or a very liberal interpretation of their orders—I couldn't tell which—the two sub-squads killed not just Troy's hellbat but all of them.

Not unexpectedly, the Riders' initial response left much to be desired. Still, Mack should have managed things better. After the slaughter of the hellbats, instead of having his people stand their ground and regroup, he ordered them to scatter.

Which played right into Tyelin's hands.

Easily picking out Troy from the fleeing Riders, the Blades stripped him of his gear and trussed him up. *"You have two minutes,"* the envoy rasped. He and I were alone with the scout while the other Blades kept watch on the surviving Riders.

"Make him talk," I replied tersely while I reclothed myself in Troy's gear. *"I need to hear him speak."*

My own equipment was already in my bag of holding. This included the Cloak of the Reach, which had the unfortunate consequence of putting me and Ghost out of contact. The pyre wolf could still manifest, though—something she had strict instructions *not* to do.

Not replying, the envoy prodded the scout with the sharp end of his dagger. "Do you know who I am?" he asked mockingly.

Looking mutinous, Troy stayed silent.

With no change in expression, Tyelin prodded him again, this time burying half the blade's length in the player's naked torso.

Troy shrieked. "I know who you are, you whoreson!" he snapped. "Blythe's little bi—"

He broke off as the envoy drove the dagger all the way in and twisted viciously. "Tsk, tsk, where are your manners?" Tyelin inquired mildly.

"Malikor will kill you for this!" Troy spat.

The envoy laughed. "He will have to catch me first," he retorted mockingly. *"You've heard enough?"* he asked in an aside.

"I have."

"Oh, he'll catch you, al—" the scout began, but before he could finish, Tyelin broke his neck with a sharp crack.

Troy has died.

You have equipped a scout's kit, a ranger's cloak, 4 trinkets, the shortbow, <u>deadeye</u>, and other miscellaneous gear, gaining +25% physical damage reduction and +6 ranks in sneaking.

Ignoring the corpse at my feet, I studied my new attire. There was nothing spectacular about Troy's gear, but it fit well and provided a modicum of physical protection.

"Do your face," Tyelin said, gesturing impatiently. "Don't forget, we're on the clock now."

Nodding agreeably—I had eight hours before Troy resurrected—I drew stamina and set about reconfiguring my facial features.

You have cast mimic, concealing your Powerful Initiate Mark and transforming your visage into that of Troy, a level 167 human scout. Duration: 10 hours.

Stepping back, the envoy stared me up and down. "Good, you look the part."

"And sound it, too," I replied laconically in Troy's voice.

"Impressive," Tyelin agreed.

Bending down, I dipped my hand in the blood pooling beneath the corpse and rubbed it over my armor.

Tyelin raised an eyebrow. "What's that for?"

"To disguise my scent," I replied. While Troy's hellbat was dead and it was unlikely that any of the other Riders' mounts would recognize the scout's smell, there was no reason to take chances. Besides, the blood would also give me an excuse to be muddled about the course of the battle—if such became necessary.

Inspired by that thought, I dipped my hand in the dead player's blood again and smeared the left side of my face—and bits of my hair too—to create the appearance of a recently received head wound. Then, closing my eyes, I tinkered with my analyze data.

You have activated mimic's secondary effects, altering your player data. Falsified debuff: <u>concussed</u> (mental acuity reduced by 30%).

The envoy's brows rose higher, but this time, he declined to comment. Instead, he stuck out his hand, revealing a small object. "Here, stow this safely."

You have acquired a packet of <u>unrefined cynacilin powder</u>. This is an unprepared dose of the poison. You lack the skill necessary to use this item.

I frowned as I digested the Adjudicator's words. "Unprepared? Why is that?"

"Unfortunately, as powerful a poison as cynacilin is, it's not without drawbacks," Tyelin explained. "The poison has a short lifetime and will lose potency ten minutes after it is activated. But don't worry, Jone will know what to do."

"I see," I said noncommittally.

"Now, if that is all," the envoy said cheerfully, "we best get this show moving."

"Agreed," I replied, turning away. There was no point questioning Tyelin further. I suspected any answers I managed to extract from him would be far from satisfying. *Time to finish this and move on.*

"Good luck," Tyelin called from behind as I walked away.

Not bothering to reply, I kept walking.

✳ ✳ ✳

The Blades made sure to clean the scene before leaving. Primarily, this consisted of removing Troy's corpse. Still, I didn't hang around.

Feigning panic, I stumbled 'blindly' through the grasslands. In truth, though, I had my mindsight trained on the still-fleeing Mack and, with every passing minute, drew closer to him.

Around me, I sensed some of the other survivors. Knowing it would be easier to remain anonymous in a larger group, I thrashed loudly, attracting their attention. And so, when I did finally catch up with the patrol's erstwhile leader, it was with a party of four other Riders in tow.

"Mack, stop!" shouted Helen, one of the Riders accompanying me.

"Finally," I muttered under my breath. The patrol's leader had been glaringly visible for the last minute yet still had gone unnoticed by the others.

"Lieutenant," another Rider—Timmons—called. "Wait!"

This time, Mack responded. His eyes round with fear, he glanced over his shoulder. Seeing five familiar faces seemed to calm him, but he didn't slow down.

"The Blades are gone," Helen shouted, noticing what I had.

The lieutenant ground to a halt.

About bloody time.

Panting heavily, my party drew to a ragged stop before Mack. "You're sure?" he asked anxiously.

"Yeah," replied Gregor, the third Rider with me.

"Looks like they were just after the hellbats," Eric added.

"Seems that way," Helen agreed.

Mack scanned the five tired faces arrayed before him before his gaze eventually settled on me. "What's wrong with Troy?" he asked, at last appearing to regain control of himself.

"Head wound, I think," Timmons answered.

"He hasn't spoken much since we ran across him," Gregor added.

Mack frowned, but before he could inquire further as to my state, Eric interjected, "What do we do now, Mack?"

"We head back to the fort, of course," Helen said, answering in the lieutenant's stead.

"What about the others?" Timmons asked.

"What about them?" Gregor shot back. "They're either dead or heading north themselves."

"And our hellbats?" Eric protested. "Do we just leave their bodies lying there?"

"We do," the lieutenant said, finally taking charge. "We head north as fast as we can. Command needs to be informed."

No one protested, and in fact, most appeared relieved by the order. Swiveling about, and with a suddenly more confident pep to his stride, the lieutenant marched north. The rest of us fell in step behind him.

"We're on our way," I reported to Tyelin.

"Excellent," came the instantaneous response. *"Any complications?"*

"None."

"Good. Keep me informed."

"I'll do that," I replied, staggering after the others.

✳   ✳   ✳

It was a few hours' walk to the Rider fort, but even before the first hour was up, we were intercepted.

"Look!" Helen shouted, pointing skyward. "A patrol!"

"Not an ordinary one either," Mack muttered. "There's thirty hellbats in that formation."

He was right, I saw.

"Perhaps Command got wind of what happened?" Eric suggested.

"How?" Timmons demanded.

No one had an answer for him, but I thought perhaps I did. *"This your doing?"* I asked Tyelin across the farspeaker link. I didn't bother describing what I meant either. I was fairly sure the Blade squad was still shadowing us.

"Maybe," he replied, making no effort to disguise the smugness in his tone.

I held back a sigh. The envoy's latest addition to the plan was unnecessary, but there was nothing for it now but to see how events played out.

The thirty hellbats landed hard. "Lieutenant," the captain in charge ordered brusquely, "get your people mounted."

"Dyl, the Blades have crossed the river," Mack began. "We were—"

"Save your report for later," Captain Dyl ground out harshly. "Command wants to see you. Now."

"But—"

"Stow it, Lieutenant!" Dyl snapped, his eyes cold and unrelenting. "I gave you an order. Now, do as you're told and get your people mounted. We'll ride double until we reach the fort."

Shoulders sagging, Mack waved us toward the six waiting hellbats and their riders.

"This part of your plan, too?" I asked Tyelin bitingly. I couldn't see how it could be, though. The envoy had only given me a map of the fort's first two floors, and the hellbats, I knew, landed on the roof above the *third* floor.

"Err..." was the envoy's not-very-eloquent response.

Cursing silently to myself, I mounted the waiting hellbat and wrapped my arms around the Rider sitting in front, wondering all the while just how the hell I was going to improvise my way out of this latest wrinkle.

Chapter 460: Something Untoward

Traveling by air, we reached the fort considerably quicker than either I or Tyelin originally anticipated, and I couldn't help but wonder what this meant for the envoy's schemes. If he was planning on launching an assault soon—which I suspected to be the case—then the Blade forces had to be badly out of position.

Tyelin must be scrambling to recover right now, I thought, unaccountably cheered by the thought.

It made no difference to my own mission, though.

My only objective was finding Jone, earning my Pact-guaranteed favor from Blythe, and leaving before the Blades could double-cross me. All of which I could still do—provided nothing further untoward happened.

As we neared the fort, Captain Dyl's oversized patrol veered toward the roof and, just as I suspected, landed on it. "Dismount," he ordered, the moment we touched down. "Lieutenant Hog," he called to the Devil Rider officer waiting to greet us, "see that these six are taken directly to Command. Malikor wants a word with them."

The lieutenant snapped off a salute. "I'll escort them there myself, sir!"

Groaning internally, I slid off the hellbat. Contrary to my hopes, things looked like they were going from bad to worse.

"This way," Hog called, making for the large doors inset in the middle of the roof. With no other choice, I fell in line with the others and followed after the Rider lieutenant. For now, I had to stay in character, but once inside the fort, I would have to find a way to 'get lost.' No matter my confidence in my guise, I did not want to risk coming face to face with the Rider envoy.

Beyond the door was a short ramp that descended onto a wide, well-lit passage. Three narrow bands of metal stood a short distance beyond the ramp. Four feet apart from each other, they framed the corridor.

Those must be the Watchers.

Reaching the first Watcher, Hog stepped through without pause. Mack followed, then the others. Finally, it was my turn. I dragged my heels, intent on analyzing the Watchers before I passed through. The lieutenant, however, noticed me slowing down.

Whirling about, he pinned me with an unhappy glare. "Stop dawdling!" he snapped. "Didn't you hear the captain? The envoy is waiting. Hurry up, damn you!"

Not wanting to attract further attention, I ducked my head and stepped forward. The others had passed through the Watchers without incident. I expected no less.

Watchers activated. Scans commencing...

...

...

You have passed a mental resistance check.

You have passed a mental resistance check.

You have failed a mental resistance check.

Scans completed. The subject is wrapped in a tier 5 mimic spell and bears a Power Mark. Warning! Warning! Level 7 threat detected!

Uh-oh.

My eyes wide with horror, I stumbled out of the last Watcher. This time, left reeling by my abrupt unmasking, my clumsy footing was no act.

I curbed my rising dread. *All is not lost*, I thought desperately. *They don't know my name, not yet. No matter the cost, I have to—*

"Blade!" Hog yelled, the accusation ringing sharply down the corridor.

"Blade—?" a confused Timmons asked. "Where?"

"Him?" Eric asked, glancing in the direction of Hog's damning finger. "B-but... that's Troy!"

Mimic was still in place, which was the reason for their confusion. The spell served little purpose now, though. I had been uncovered. *Time to go.* Ignoring the six Riders, I spun around.

Only to be greeted by the sight of the wide double doors leading to the roof slamming close.

Defensive wards triggered! Activating fort defenses...

Doors sealed. Alarm sounded. Tracker locked onto target.

Aether portals opened. Summoning commencing.

Hellfire dome raised. Duration: 4 hours.

Psi-dampening field activated. Duration: 1 hour.

Communications locked down. Duration: 1 hour.

You are <u>hell-tracked</u> (revealing your location to all nearby Devil Riders). Duration: 1 hour.

Well. This certainly counts as something untoward.

Not only was I shut in the fort with who-knew-how-many Riders, but my mindsight had been snuffed out, and I'd been completely cut off from my psi. Worse yet, for the next hour—assuming I survived that long—the enemy would know my every move.

There was no two ways about it. The mission was over.

"Get him!" Hog ordered.

Reminded by the lieutenant's cry of the most immediate danger facing me, I spun back around. Luckily, it was only the six Devil Riders I had to contend with—for now.

Timmons, Gregor, and Eric were charging straight at me, while Hog, Mack, and Helen—archers all—were drawing back. Fortunately, or unfortunately, there were no spellcasters among the group.

I was undaunted, though.

Even hampered as I was, taking down the six should not unduly strain me. Sidestepping to the left to place the broad-shouldered Gregor between me and the archers, I drew stamina.

You have cast vanish. You are <u>invisible</u>. Duration: 5 minutes.

Gregor skidded to a halt. "Where'd he go?"

"He's still there, right in front of you!" Mack shouted.

"Query the tracker, you fool!" Hog added for good measure.

"And get out of the damn way," Helen snapped. "You're blocking my shot!"

Ignoring the Riders' comments, I stayed focused on Timmons and Eric. Both were still advancing, although they'd slowed their approach drastically. Unfortunately, I couldn't afford a slow, careful fight. More foes were bound to appear sooner or later.

I have to end this quickly.

Dashing forward, I held out my right hand. It was empty—I hadn't had time yet to retrieve the gear I'd stored in my bag of holding. Still, there was one item that I could always summon to hand.

You have recalled the sword, <u>faithful blade</u>.

Armed, I closed the remaining distance to Eric.

He *knew* I was there, but he couldn't see me or my blade. His face scrunched up in worry, the Rider raised his javelin defensively.

It did him no good.

Circling around the slower-moving player, I thrust faithful through his leather-armored back.

You have backstabbed your target for 5x more damage!
You have killed Eric with a fatal blow.
Five hostile entities have failed to detect you! You are hidden.

As Eric fell, Timmons swiped at me from the left, but I was beyond the reach of his searching broadsword and barely needed to dodge the blow. At the same time, two of the three archers fired.

Gregor, though, was still in the way.

You have evaded 3 hostile attacks.

"Ow!" Gregor cried. "You hit me!"

"Then stay out of my line of fire, you dumb ox!" Hog retorted.

I advanced on Timmons. He was better armored than Eric, but that meant little. Lunging blindly at me, the fighter swept his blade from left to right in a blow that would've cleaved me in two had it connected.

But it didn't.

Ducking beneath the glittering length of steel, I came up inside the fighter's guard and, once more, rammed faithful forward.

You have cast piercing strike.
You have backstabbed your target for 10x more damage!

Sharpened sword tip met thick armored steel plate—
—and plowed straight through.

Even heavily armored fighters were no match for my blades anymore.

You have killed Eric with a fatal blow.

An arrow whistled past. Throwing myself forward into a tumble, I bowled over Gregor who'd resumed his charge. With an outraged cry, the Rider fell on his face. Ignoring him, I kept rolling, building up momentum.

Another projectile hissed through the air, but it had been aimed too high and sailed harmlessly overhead.

"Shoot him!" Mack yelled. "He is coming this way!"

"I've tried!" Helen screamed. "That arrow passed right through his location."

"Aim higher," Hog ordered. "Or lower."

But it was too late. I'd already closed the gap to the archers. Rising smoothly, I empowered my limbs with whirlwind and got to work.

Lunging forward, I punctured Mack's gut.

Wrenching the blade out, I pivoted on my back heel and decapitated Helen.

Spinning to a stop in front of Hog, I rammed faithful through his heart.

Like marionettes with their strings cut, the three collapsed. I turned around. Only one Rider remained standing. Gregor. But the fight had seeped out of him already. His eyes wide and unseeing, the Rider turned and fled. Grimly, I chased after.

There could be no survivors.

✳   ✳   ✳

You have killed Gregor.

It did not take me long to run down the fighter. He'd fled in the wrong direction, after all. Hacking him down from behind, I wrenched out my bloodied blade and studied the still-sealed doors.

They didn't look like they would be opening any time soon.

Not bothering to inspect the doors further, I moved on to option two: using a portal scroll to escape. Reaching into my pack, I retrieved one but, for a drawn-out second, just stared at it.

The thing had cost a fortune, and given the wards and shields the Riders had activated around the fort, I was uncertain it would even work. But I had to try. And it was for emergencies like this that I had bought extra scrolls.

Here goes. Cracking open the seal binding the scroll, I drew on my magic. Yet even before I could begin feeding mana into the item, a Game message dropped into my mind.

Warning: the wards around this area prevent any unauthorized portals from being opened. You have failed to create a portal.

Item consumed. You have lost a greater portal scroll.

My lips thinned unhappily, but I couldn't claim to be surprised by the Game's response. I'd half expected it. Still, the scroll's failure left me in a quandary. My mindsight was also dead, which meant I wouldn't be shadow blinking out either. That left me with only one option.

Fleeing deeper into the fort.

I sighed. Doing that while hell-tracked would make surviving difficult... if not impossible. I had to try, though.

And the tracker spell was not infallible.

That much had become clear during the fight. While the Riders had known where I was, the tracking spell was not so precise as to betray my every movement. My ducks and rolls had fooled them.

I can use that.

Shouts and cries from farther down the passage drew my attention. I didn't have much time until the next group of Riders arrived. Still, there were a few preparations I could make.

Reaching into my bag of holding, I withdrew my cloak and ebonheart. Putting on the rest of my gear would have to wait until later.

You have equipped the <u>Cloak of the Reach</u> and <u>ebonheart</u>.

"Ghost, I need you," I said, the moment I was dressed. Thankfully, the defensive spells the fort had activated did not in any way impinge on my spirit bond with my familiar. I could still talk to her.

"What's wrong?" the pyre wolf asked, sensing the urgency in my voice.

"We're trapped in the fort," I said, not elaborating. Further explanations could wait.

"Did the Blades betray you?" she asked.

"I'm not sure," I admitted. It was a good question, though.

At least one of the Watchers on the roof doors had not been a tier five detection device as Tyelin had claimed. But had the envoy known that? After all, I'd not entered the fort through the main entrance like we'd planned.

Still, I could see no reason why the roof doors would be better protected than the main entrance. If anything, the converse should be true.

"It is something I mean to ask Tyelin when we next speak," I added. And there would be a next time, I vowed grimly.

"What do you need me to do?" Ghost asked, letting the matter drop.

I glanced down the corridor. Eight Riders—five mages and three fighters—had just appeared in sight. My vanish was still active, and they couldn't see me yet, but they knew I waited ahead and approached cautiously.

What they didn't know was that I wasn't the only threat they had to contend with.

The eight Riders advanced down the corridor in a tight-knit group, with the mages' shields touching and the fighters standing shoulder to shoulder. It was a good strategy against an invisible foe but was exactly the wrong approach to use with Ghost.

Ghost has cast explosive manifest. She has 90% mana remaining.

The pyre wolf emerged in a blaze of glory.
Where before she had always coalesced gradually out of streaming trails of shadow, this time her manifestation was sudden, quick, and as deadly as a raging bonfire.
And like a bonfire, she was clothed in flames aplenty.
Billowing clouds of flame mushroomed out from beneath her, enveloping everything within a five-yard radius.

Ghost has taken the form of a level 215 stygian pyre wolf.
3 of 8 hostile entities have been critically injured.
5 hostile entities have blocked your familiar's attack.

The three fighters shrieked as their skin charred, and their armor blackened. The mages flung up their hands, instinctively protecting their eyes even as their shields blocked the incoming fire damage.
Ghost herself was not unaffected.
The flames snapped at her as eagerly as they did at the Riders, but courtesy of her new pyreborn trait, her fire magic resistance was even higher than mine, and she weathered the firestorm mostly untouched.

Ghost has passed a magical resistance check!
Ghost has passed a magical resistance check!
...

The pyre wolf's explosive arrival was the opening salvo only, and no sooner had Ghost appeared than she was leaping onto the closest player.

Ghost has activated draining bite.
Ghost has killed Amagog, a level 170 player.

I did not stand idly by either.
Sprinting forward, I joined in the melee. A few of the Riders noticed, but they were in too much of a disarray to react effectively. Leaving the fighters to Ghost, I threw myself at the spellcasters.

You have cast whirlwind and piercing strike.
You have backstabbed your target for 10x more damage!
Sarocyx's shield has been destroyed!
You have killed Sarocyx, a level 164 player, with a fatal blow!

Killing the mages was almost laughably easy. Shattering their shields with ebonheart, I stole their lives with a follow-up strike from faithful.

Two hits. That was all it took to snuff out each Rider mage.

Easy.

Ghost fared no differently. After snapping the neck of the first fighter, she leaped onto the second, ripped out his throat, and then tore into the third.

You and Ghost have reached level 216!
Your sneaking has reached rank 22 and your chi rank 18.
Ghost's death magic has increased to level 6.

Ten seconds later, the battle was over, and just like that, eight Riders were dead. But there was still an entire fort of them to deal with.

"Let's go," I said. Sheathing my blades, I turned about and ran down the corridor.

"Where to?" Ghost asked, bounding after me.

"Don't know," I muttered. *"But I know we can't stay here."*

You are hell-tracked. Remaining duration: 59 minutes.

It did not take me long to figure out that our best chance of survival was to keep moving. If we stopped, the Riders would overrun us with sheer numbers.

Still, staying ahead of the pursuit was not going to be easy. The Riders had our location, and they knew the fort better than I did. But I still had a few tricks up my sleeves. Step one, though, was getting out of the entrance corridor.

The passage was a death trap.

It had been purposely designed that way, I suspected. The corridor had no exits on either its left or right walls. Still, the large barn-like doors from which the eight Riders had emerged were within sight, and I didn't stop my flat-out run until I crossed over the doorway's threshold.

Skidding to stop, I studied my surroundings. I was in a cavernous hall. There were three other exits, one set in the middle of each remaining wall. Bales of hay and water troughs lined the hall itself, and in the corners were what looked like bits of rancid meat.

"Eww, there's that reek again," Ghost whined.

I nodded absently. *This is a feeding chamber,* I realized. The hall was presently empty, but from beyond the door directly opposite me—an ordinary-sized one—I could hear the hue and cry of gathering players.

There were noises coming from the left and right entrances, too. Animal noises. *That's where the hellbats are stabled.* I glanced up. Only twelve feet separated the floor and ceiling, which meant... *the hellbats will be at a disadvantage in their pens.*

I hesitated, deliberating over my next course of action. My first instinct was to descend to the lower floors. Thanks to Tyelin's map, I had a good idea of their layout, and that would make staying one step ahead of the Riders easier. This floor was an enigma.

But.

The lower levels would be swarming with players. Smart, dangerous players who could track me. On this floor, there were only hellbats—for now anyway—and I already knew they lacked Ghost's intelligence. They would have a much harder time dealing with me.

Going into the stables might not buy me much time—the Riders would rally fast—but even a few minutes could make all the difference. And once the Riders' hell-tracked spell lapsed, the game would change completely.

Then the hunted would become the hunter.

Decided, I cut right across the halls, heading for the south stable wing.

✳   ✳   ✳

You are hell-tracked. Remaining duration: 58 minutes.

The hellbat stables were filthy and stank even worse than the feeding chamber.

Heaps of rubble—from the broken-down walls and destroyed furnishings—littered the aisles running between the hellbat pens.

The pens themselves—such as they were—were little more than wire mesh fences anchored by thick metal stakes driven deep into the floor. They were laid out in checkerboard fashion and covered the entire expanse of space before me, which judging from what I had seen of the fort from outside, had to be the entire southern half of the building.

The pens were full, too, each holding a single hellbat that barely had space to move. Why the creatures had to be confined in such a manner I had no idea, but confined they were.

And that afforded me an opportunity.

"Scout the room," I ordered Ghost, changing my plans on the fly as I drew to a halt just inside the entrance.

"Yes, Prime," she replied as she slipped down the stable's central aisle. Unlike me, Ghost was not invisible, and her passage sparked a furor of angry hisses and calls.

"Anything, in particular, I should be looking for?" she asked, ignoring the outcry from the trapped hellbats.

"Exits and players," I replied before turning my focus inward and investing my newly earned attribute points.

Your Dexterity has increased to rank 96. You have 5 Dexterity ability slots remaining.

I smiled. I'd gained enough ability slots to advance another of my Dexterity abilities, but doing so would have to wait. For now, I had something else in mind. Running my fingers along the blue rune on my wristband, I activated its enchantment.

You have removed 16 trap-making crystals from your trapper's wristband. Remaining trap-making crystals: 184 of 200.

Working swiftly, I embedded four crystals in the doorframe itself, two on either side.

You have concealed 4 <u>reflect</u> guides.

I peeked out the door, checking how much time I had. The feeding chamber was still empty, the massing players having not yet arrived. I suspected they were delaying their entry while they expanded the size of their force.

I smiled grimly. *The more the merrier.*

Retreating ten feet from the door, I drew up alongside one of the metal posts on the left side of the aisle. The nearby hellbats spat angrily at me from inside their pens, but I ignored them as I inserted three trap crystals into the post at waist height.

You have concealed a <u>reflect</u> guide.
You have concealed a <u>motion cone</u> trigger.
You have concealed a <u>lightning</u> element.

Crouching down, I placed myself at eye level with the embedded crystals and measured the angle to the right side of the door. Once the trap activated, the released lightning bolt would bounce back and forth between the reflection guides I'd placed, crisscrossing the aisle and wreaking havoc on the incoming players.

That was the idea, anyway.

Looks good, I thought, completing the final spell-linkage between the four crystals.

You have connected 2 reflect guides and 1 lightning element to a motion cone. A tier 3 trap has been successfully configured!

Perfect. Skipping across to the opposite side of the aisle, I set another almost identical trap. Only this time, I used a reflection guide on the left side of the door as its endpoint.

A tier 3 trap has been successfully configured!

Retreating to the next metal post, I set another two traps, making sure that their motion cones overlapped with the first two.

2 tier 3 traps have been successfully configured!

Sitting back, I took a moment to consider my handiwork. Each of the reflection guides I'd set on the door had been configured as an endpoint of a different trap. Assuming everything went as planned, the traps would activate near-simultaneously and unleash four lightning bolts that would turn the aisle into a killing field.

That should thin the Riders' numbers.

Withdrawing farther into the stable, I ran my thumb along my wristband again. The quad-lightning trap was to be my opening gambit only. I intended to place more traps—simpler ones—to slow down my pursuers further.

You have removed 2 trap-making crystals from your trapper's wristband.

The trap crystals fell into my waiting hands, and I set them on the floor.

"Prime, I've found something," Ghost called abruptly.

In the act of configuring the new trap, I paused. *"What?"*

"People," she replied and, before I could grow alarmed, added, *"I don't think they're players."*

I frowned. *"Why not?"*

"They're carrying no weapons and wearing no armor." A pause. *"They're barefoot, too."*

Servants, I thought. *"Where are they?"*

"Hiding in the rearmost pen."

"Alright, what about exits? Did you find any?"

"There are no other doors beside the one we entered through," Ghost answered, dashing my hopes.

"Damn," I muttered.

"But there is a hole."

"A hole?" I asked, perplexed. Why would there be a hole on the third floor of the fort? *"Where does it go?"*

"I don't know," Ghost replied, *"but it's in the same pen as the servants."*

"I see. Well, keep an eye on both for now. I'll be there soon." Returning my attention to the crystals, I quickly completed their spell-linkage.

You have connected a poison cloud element to a pressure plate. A tier 3 trap has been successfully configured!

The voices coming from beyond the doorway grew louder. Cocking my head to the side, I listened intently. The Riders had entered the feeding chamber. They would be here soon.

But I still had time to place a few more traps. Retreating down the aisle, I set my next trap.

You are hell-tracked. Remaining duration: 56 minutes.

Ghost has unmanifested.

6 tier 3 traps have been successfully configured! Remaining trap-making crystals: 170 of 200.

You have recast vanish.

You have cast load controller, gaining a 10-minute encumbrance aura that slows any armor-wearing foe within 5 yards by 50%.

You have upgraded your whirlwind ability to <u>improved whirlwind</u>. The tier 3 variant of this ability increases the speed boost provided by this buff to 2.5x more than normal. You have 0 of 96 Dexterity ability slots remaining.

I was ready and waiting in the middle of the stable by the time the first Rider poked her head into the room. Unfortunately, the players' precipitous arrival meant I had to forgo checking on Ghost's discoveries. I would do so later—assuming there was a later.

For now, my focus remained fixed on the Riders. Sadly, with my mindsight blocked, I could tell little about the players gathered outside the door beyond the fact that there were a *lot* of them. So, I did the next best thing: I listened intently.

"What do you see?" an unseen Rider whispered hoarsely.

"I see nothing," the player peering into the room—a scout named Maeve—replied, sounding peeved by the question.

"Why not?" another demanded. "The intruder is in there."

"I know *that*—" Maeve retorted.

Definitely peeved, I thought.

"—but I don't see him." Maeve swept her gaze across the room. "He must be hiding," she muttered.

"It's a Blade then," the first Rider pronounced.

"A Blade Power?" another scoffed. "There's only one Blade Power, and somehow, I doubt that Blythe has come all this way *alone* and unaccompanied."

"Then who do you—"

"Enough, you two," a third replied firmly. "It's the same intruder who killed Corrigan's squad. Has to be. Maeve, what about the hellbats?"

The scout shrugged. "They're in their pens and unharmed."

"What do they have to say?"

"The hellbats?" Maeve rolled her eyes. "Shing's thoughts are... annoyed. She's angry at being awoken early and is demanding food."

Shing was almost certainly Maeve's hellbat companion.

"I'm not interested in how hungry she is," the authoritative voice snapped irritably. "What does she have to say about the intruder?"

"C'mon, Titus," Maeve replied. "You know what the hellbats are like. Shing is aware he is around but has nothing more to add."

"But what do the others—" Titus began.

Maeve cut him off. "No idea. I'm no Leafbright. I can't tell what the other companions are thinking."

"Where are the Sworn anyway?" another Rider muttered. "They should be doing this. Not us."

"They're out on patrol, you idiot," someone else informed him caustically. "Or did you forget again?"

"Then Malikor should be the one leading us," the whiner went on, unrepentant. "How does he expect us to take down a Power on our own?"

"Malikor is busy reporting to Mammon," Titus interjected before anyone else could answer. "Do you want to be the one to interrupt that conversation?"

The whiner didn't answer.

Titus snorted. "I thought not." He raised his voice slightly, no doubt to address the group at large. "Right, we have our quarry trapped, so we'll do this slowly. Here's what I want..."

I stopped listening. The whispered conversation had revealed more than a few interesting tidbits—not the least being that their Power, Mammon, was at this very minute being informed of events—but the time had come for me to intervene.

Titus seemed intent on advancing cautiously into the room, and while only a few minutes ago such time-wasting would've pleased me, now I preferred they rush blindly into my traps.

Rising to my feet, I leaped over the adjacent fence and into an occupied pen. The hellbat hissed warningly. Undaunted, I advanced on the creature.

Let's see how quick they move once their companions begin dying.

✳   ✳   ✳

You have killed Tsang, a level 163 hellbat.

The hellbat shrieked loudly as it died, drawing the attention of the Rider scout. "Titus!" she screamed.

Still issuing orders, the Rider commander broke off midstream. "What?"

"He's killed a hellbat!"

"Whose?" he demanded.

"Does it matter?" Maeve snapped back.

Smiling grimly, I hopped into the next pen. Forced to keep its wings furled—or else risk damaging them against the fence—the occupant slowly tottered around to face me.

I waited until the hellbat completed its maneuver. Predictably, it lunged at me when it did. Sidestepping the snapping teeth, I buried both my blades in the creature's neck.

You have backstabbed your target for 5x more damage!
You have backstabbed your target for 5x more damage!
You have killed Nyx, a level 166 hellbat.

"Another one," Maeve squeaked. "He's got another one!"

"We should get in there," an anonymous Rider yelled. "Now!"

"No," Titus said firmly. "We're not ready yet."

Climbing onto the fence again, I flung myself into the next pen—

—and landed squarely on a hellbat's back.

Barely pausing for breath, I stabbed downward. Once. Twice. Thrice.

You have killed Inori, a level 173 hellbat.

"Nooo!" a Rider shrieked. "He's got my companion."

"Damnit, Titus, we have to move!" another player added.

"Don't forget what we face!" the Rider commander growled. "That is a Power in there. We have to do this carefully. Now, wait for your goddamn orders!"

"Stuff your orders," someone else shouted. "I'm not letting Lux get killed because of you!"

The Riders' burgeoning rebellion was music to my ears. Spurred on, I leaped at the next hellbat. Then the next. And the next.

You have killed Agulaz.
You have killed Neech-ta.
You have killed...

...

The rapid-fire deaths of the hellbats was too much for even Titus to stomach, and en-masse, the players charged into the stables.

✳ ✳ ✳

You have recast vanish.
You are hell-tracked. Remaining duration: 50 minutes.

My biggest concern in the upcoming fight was healing.

Without access to my psi, I didn't have any way to restore my lost health—except for the new potions I'd bought, and they were only a measure of last resort. So, this time, as much as I disliked the notion, it would be Ghost—not I—who would be in the thick of things.

"You ready?" I asked over our mental bond.

"I am," the pyre wolf replied promptly.

Sitting atop the fence of a slain hellbat, I scrutinized the incoming horde of players, noting levels and Class as their analyze data scrolled through my mind. Nearly a hundred Riders were already in the room, and yet more kept coming.

Damn, there's a lot of them.

But for now, the Riders' numbers meant little.

They were bunched up nicely and running straight down the central aisle. The mages had their shields up, and their warriors had cast their buffs, but no one was paying much attention to the immediate surroundings.

It made for an almost perfect ambush.

A hostile entity has triggered a trap!

A hostile entity has triggered a trap!
A hostile entity has triggered a trap!
A hostile entity has triggered a trap!

The lightning traps activated near simultaneously, and quicker than thought, four lethal bolts zigzagged across the aisle. Game messages cascaded across my sight as Rider after Rider was stunned, damaged, or both.

And that was only on the bolts' first iteration.

Bouncing off the reflection guides, the forked tongues of lightning returned to the head of the Rider column to inflict more damage. Then, they crisscrossed the aisle again.

And again.

And again…

Not all the Riders were stunned or damaged, of course. Many of the mages made it out of the kill zone before their shields collapsed. Then there were those who were fortunate enough to be at the back of the Rider mob or outside the stable when the trap was sprung. And finally, there was the lifespan of the reflection guides themselves to consider.

They only lasted five seconds.

But during those five seconds, the lightning traps wreaked destruction on a scale I'd rarely managed before.

63 hostile entities have died.

"Wow," Ghost remarked, observing the death and destruction through my eyes. *"Did you expect that, Prime?"*

I shook my head, just flabbergasted by the success of my ploy.

"Time for me to enter the fray?" the pyre wolf prompted when I said nothing else.

I hesitated, then shook my head again. The thirty-odd Rider survivors inside the stable were still reeling in shock, and as yet, I didn't know how many waited outside the door. *"We're going to do this differently than we planned,"* I murmured.

I wound back my arms. Traps were not the only tricks I had up my sleeves, and there were other ways I could inflict damage from afar. Flinging my arms forward, I threw the objects I'd primed.

You have ignited an acid bomb, creating an acid spill.
You have ignited a fire bomb, creating a small flame.
An acid spill has been set alight, releasing toxic fumes!

Fresh bedlam ensued as a thick plume of noxious green and yellow enveloped the Rider-occupied aisle.

Players shrieked, coughed, and cried as their eyes burned and their skins melted. Around me, the hellbats echoed their companions' tortured screams. Wisely, the players who had yet to enter the stables backed away from the door.

I was far from done, though.

My face hard, I didn't let up on my deadly assault. Extravagantly spending my supply of the deadly alchemical mixes, I lobbed them one after the other into the Riders' midst.

Until, finally, all the remaining Riders in the room were dead.

You have ignited 10 acid bombs and 10 firebombs!
31 hostile entities have died.

I was still not done.

Running lightly along the top of a fence, I cut a wide arc around the treacherous cloud occupying the main aisle as I made my way to the entrance. My original intent had been purely to buy time.

To seed doubt in the Riders' minds. To force them to delay and regroup.

But the overwhelming success of my ambush had afforded me a unique opportunity, and I was not about to let it go begging. Now, I saw a means of enacting my original plan, only on a larger scale.

If I eradicated Titus' group entirely, I doubted even the Rider envoy would be in a rush to pursue me.

Much would depend on Ghost, though.

✳ ✳ ✳

<u>You are hell-tracked.</u> **Remaining duration: 49 minutes.**

I slipped outside the stable's main doors to find the remaining Riders backing away. They had been aware of my approach, of course.

Multiple hostile entities have failed to detect you! You are hidden.

I swept my gaze from left to right, taking a swift count of their number. *Fifty.* The Riders lacked cohesion, though—Titus had died in the lightning trap—and they were more a mob than an organized force.

"*We can take them,*" Ghost pronounced.

Still studying our foes, I didn't respond. Despite the Riders' numbers, the fight seemed to have gone out of them, and while more than a few pointed weapons my way, the hands that held them wavered.

"*Should I attack?*" Ghost probed.

My gaze flickered to the open door on the right—the one leading to the floor below. Crucially, it was empty. No reinforcements were incoming—yet.

Seeing no reason to hold back, I dashed forward, rapidly closing the distance between me and the Riders. "*Go,*" I ordered.

The response was instantaneous.

Ghost has cast explosive manifest. She has 80% mana remaining.

Tongues of fire accompanied the pyre wolf's entrance in the 'real'. She'd chosen her emergence point well, too. Appearing amongst the farthest group of players, Ghost set to her task with a vengeance.

Cries of consternation rang across the feeding chamber as players began to die, and some of the Riders spun around to face the new threat at their rear.

Perfect, I thought. Ghost had split the enemy's attention nicely, and just at the right time, too.

Choosing a target at random, I leaped the final few yards to him. Half-turned away, the Rider was in no position to fend me off as I landed atop him and bore him to the ground. Battering aside his frantic hands, I rammed ebonheart into his chest.

You have backstabbed your target for 5x more damage!
You have killed Osmil.

Rolling off the corpse, I regained my feet. A spear swept in from the right. Fending off the weapon with ebonheart, I counterattacked with faithful.

You have critically injured Buldhar.

Not bothering to finish off my foe, I threw myself forward and beneath the next attack: a sparkling ray of frost aimed in my general direction.

It struck the spearman instead.

Buldhar has died.

Rising swiftly, I spun around to face my next set of foes—three axemen closing in fast from the right flank.

3 hostiles have failed a physical resistance check!
Yaczar, Meng, and Regil are <u>encumbered</u> (movement speed reduced by 25%).

I almost grinned as between one step and the next, the three Riders hit the edge of my encumbrance aura and slowed. Already, my upgraded abilities were showing their worth. Using the extra time afforded me, I drew on my stamina and empowered my limbs.

You have cast whirlwind and piercing strike.

Then I laid into the trio.

Ducking under a whistling axe, I buried ebonheart in the torso of Yaczar. Still, crouched, I pivoted around and cut out the legs from beneath Meng.

Regil chopped down. Rolling out of the way, I came up behind him, and before the axeman could react, I yanked back his head and cut his throat.

But despite my quick work, the skirmish had left me exposed, and the charge from a nearby orc caught me blindsided.

You have failed a physical resistance check!
Usark has <u>stunned</u> you for 3 seconds.

The air whooshed out of me as I hit the ground hard. *Damn.*

"Got you!" the orc chuckled, drawing closer. Flat on my back and helpless to move, I watched as he raised his hammer in preparation to smash down.

A dark shape, blurring through the air, struck him from the right.

Ghost has knocked down Usark.

Out of the corner of my eye, I saw Ghost dig into the Rider with tooth and claw. There was nothing I could do to assist her, though. I couldn't even turn my neck to the side to properly watch their tussle.

Then another dark shape blurred through the air.

There was nothing friendly about this one, though.

A slime tentacle has hit you!
You have failed a magical resistance check!
You have been <u>befouled</u> (speed reduced by 10% and life drained by 1% per second).

Snaking around my throat, the coils of oily darkness constricted.

A nightmare tentacle has drained 0.65% of your health (Force damage reduced by 35% due to void armor).

Involuntarily, I bucked. My back arched, and my mouth yawned, trying to release a scream that Usark's stun wouldn't let me.

There was worse to come, however.

A slime tentacle has hit you!
A slime tentacle has hit you!
A slime tentacle has hit you!

The three follow-up tentacles hit me in rapid-fire fashion, wrapping about my arms and torso. Then, they, too, began sucking away my life.

Even though I was still invisible, they seemed to have had no trouble anchoring themselves on me. *Hells! How am I going to—*

You are no longer stunned.

I moved immediately. Rolling to the left, I got my legs under me.

4 slime tentacles have drained 2.6% of your health (1.4% damage reduced).

Staying bent double—with the vague idea I'd be able to avoid being struck by further tendrils that way—I staggered forward. Or tried to. Hitting a hard surface—a fighter's armored breast, I realized, belatedly—I was violently flung backward.

"Bastard! We got you now!"

"I can see him!"

"Quick, kill him before gets away!"

Jerking my head upward, I looked around. I was surrounded, the Riders having used my momentary incapacitation to form a tight-knit circle around me. Worse yet, I'd been revealed. Or rather, the four tentacles sucking away at my life were giving away my position.

Beyond the circle, I spotted Ghost. She was frantically trying to break through with no thought for her own safety and was sustaining huge swathes of damage as a result. *"Unmanifest!"* I ordered her.

"But—"

"Now!"

She didn't respond, but I felt her spirit begin to unravel. I exhaled in relief. *"Good. When you're back in the Cloak, I want you to—"*

A fireball roared through the air.

My movements hampered by the tentacles, I barely stumbled out of the way.

You have evaded a fireball.
4 slime tentacles have drained 1.95% of your health (1.05% damage reduced, 1% resisted).

"Hey! Watch it, that hit my shield!"

"You said kill him! How am I supposed to do that if I don't—"

"No projectiles," someone else interjected firmly. "Melee weapons only. Fighters, get in there and finish him!"

4 slime tentacles have drained 1.3% of your health (0.7% damage reduced, 2% resisted).

Ten fighters—about a third of the remaining Riders—stepped into the open space around me. Watching them warily, I backed away from the closest. With my arms, neck, and torso bound, I was in no position to engage in swordplay yet. I would be, though.

Soon.

4 slime tentacles have drained 2.6% of your health.
Ghost has unmanifested.

"You see that? The stygian is gone! Where'd it go?"

"Who cares? It was a summon. The spell must have lapsed."

"I don't know... It didn't look like one—"

"Forget the damn stygian!"

4 slime tentacles have drained 1.95% of your health. (1.05% damage reduced, 1% resisted).

"Shouldn't we hit him with more disables?" someone else asked. "You know, just in case?"

"Good idea. Emery, Gale, target him with your—"

"*I'm back,*" Ghost reported breathlessly—and somewhat unnecessarily. "*What next?*"

"*On my word, I want you to manifest again,*" I replied. Taking my gaze off the approaching fighters for a split second, I focused on a group of spellcasters on my right flank. Emery and Gale were amongst their number. "*You see those mages?*"

"*Yes.*"

"*They're your targets. Kill them as quickly as you can.*"

"*What about you?*"

"*I'll be fine. Void thief is about to trigger.*" And no sooner did I voice the words, than the expectant Game messages flashed for attention.

Void armor charge remaining: 70%. Health remaining: 60%.
Void thief triggered!
You have acquired the channeled spell slime tentacles (stolen) **and will retain memory of it for the next 12 hours.**

Slime tentacles (stolen) is a tier 4 spell that grants the caster control of 4 Dark tentacle constructs. Once released, the tentacles will latch onto any hostile lifeforms in the vicinity, restricting their movements and injecting the victims with a foul darkness that both slows and kills. The tentacles will remain active for as long as the caster channels the spell.

My sigh of relief was more palpable this time.

Despite the efforts of my void armor, the tentacles had inflicted major damage. It could have been worse had I not resisted some of the spell's effects. Tier four or not, the tentacles were a lethal Dark magic construct.

But not to me. Not any longer.

Void siphon and negate activated!
4 slime tentacles have failed to harm you. You are immune to their effects.

A split second later, the coils of inky darkness loosened and fell lifelessly to the floor.

The advancing Riders paused.

"What happened?" a perplexed fighter asked. "Did you stop channeling the spell, Dona?"

"I didn't," an equally confused Dona replied. "He negated it somehow."

"But that means—" the fighter began.

His words cut off as I plunged ebonheart through his throat. *"Now, Ghost,"* I ordered.

Ghost has cast explosive manifest. She has 60% mana remaining.

Flames, accompanied by screams of agony, erupted behind me. Ignoring them, I waded into battle. Ghost and I had the upper hand again.

And this time, I didn't intend on losing it.

* * *

You are hell-tracked. Remaining duration: 43 minutes.

You and Ghost have reached level 220!

For achieving rank 22, you have been awarded 1 additional attribute point and 1 Class point.

Your light armor has reached rank 16, your thieving rank 15, and your null force rank 8.

Ghost's death magic has reached rank 2 and her ash armor rank 8.

A few minutes later, the battle was over.

I'd taken a few more hits during its course, reducing my overall health to just a fraction below fifty percent, but that mattered less than the fact that Ghost and I had triumphed.

The one hundred and fifty Riders that had formed part of Titus' group had been wiped out.

And just as importantly, Ghost and I had gained four levels. That equated to nine attribute points—and one Class point. All of which I intended to put to good use before the next encounter.

We might just survive this yet.

Cleaning my blades, I renewed my buffs. *"Ghost, check out the east entrance."* That was the one going down to the second floor. *"Don't show yourself,"* I warned. *"Get close to the door and tell me what you can hear and smell."*

I would've preferred to scout out the entrance myself, but hell-tracked would reveal my movements, and I didn't want to unwittingly force the Riders into another attack—not yet. Then, too, thanks to her draining bite, Ghost was in better shape than I was and therefore less at risk.

Cutting a circuitous path around the room, the pyre wolf slunk along the feeding chamber's right wall. Coming up to the doorway, she slowed further, dropping onto her belly as she inched forward.

"I hear four voices," she reported a foot from the door. *"They're coming from below."*

Four. Good. Four were no threat. *"How far away are they?"*

"*Not close,*" Ghost replied. "*It sounds as if they're at the bottom of a stairwell.*"

"*What are they saying?*"

Ghost listened intently for a moment. "*They're debating whether to come up and investigate or report to Malikor.*" She paused, cocking her head to the side. "*They seem uncertain about what happened to their fellows, but the silence worries them.*"

I grinned. Even better. "*Are they alone?*"

The pyre wolf wrinkled her nose. "*I can pick out eight... no, ten scents.*"

A full squad then. Titus' rearguard or sentries set to guard the second floor? I wondered.

"*They've decided.*"

I tensed. "*Go on.*"

"*They're sealing the doors at the bottom of the stairs. They're going to report to Malikor.*"

Chuckling softly, I sheathed my blades. My gambit had succeeded, and I'd bought some valuable time. But I didn't kid myself. The Riders *would* return, and when they did, it would be with a force many times larger than the previous one.

I would have to be ready.

"*Let's retreat to the stables,*" I told Ghost when she rejoined me.

The pyre wolf's bloody snout turned in my direction. "*What about the bodies?*" She nudged an armored corpse. "*Don't you want to search them?*"

I did, dearly, but I didn't think we had the time to spare. "*First, we regroup, and if the next force of Riders still hasn't found us by then, then we loot the corpses.*"

Shrugging, the pyre wolf followed on my heels as I led the way back into the south stable wing.

✴   ✴   ✴

The first thing I did on entering the stable was to re-equip all my remaining gear. Then, while Ghost kept watch, I saw to my player progression.

Your Dexterity has increased to rank 105. Other modifiers: +24 from items.

You have upgraded your whirlwind ability to <u>superior whirlwind</u>. The tier 4 variant of this ability increases the speed boost provided by the buff to 3x more than normal. You have 4 of 105 Dexterity ability slots remaining.

Opening my eyes, I rocked back on my heels and took a moment to savor the new knowledge filling my mind. Despite the recent success of my traps, the ability I'd chosen to advance was whirlwind, not set trap.

Mostly, this was because a tier four set trap ability would be of little help in my current situation—I was only carrying tier three traps. Upgrading the thieving ability would have to wait.

My most immediate needs taken care of, I glanced down and took stock of myself.

Your health is at 49%.

My throat, arms, and torso felt as if they'd been rubbed raw everywhere the tentacles had latched onto them, but importantly, nothing was broken. *I can still fight,* I thought stubbornly, and as much as I desired to sip a health potion, I resisted the idea.

"Any sign of movement?" I asked Ghost.

"None," she replied from where she sat crouched near the stable entrance.

Pursing my lips, I considered my next move. Ghost's earlier discoveries bore investigating, my Class point needed spending, and there were still the players' bodies to loot. However, I wasn't sure how much time I had. It would not take long for the sentries to report back to the envoy or for him to realize Titus' group was dead.

What Malikor would do then was debatable, but I figured the stable was the best place to weather the storm of his fury. As both elite and Sworn, I expected the envoy to have a devastating array of spells at his fingertips, but I was betting the penned hellbats around me would temper his response. He would not risk too much collateral damage to the Riders' companions—or so I hoped anyway.

Still, if I was going to survive the envoy's wrath—even the watered-down version—I would need every tool at my disposal. *"I'll be a while longer,"* I informed Ghost. *"I'm going to spend my Class point."*

Turning my focus inward, I called up the class upgrade interface.

You may advance your Class to rank 13 by improving an existing Class benefit or by selecting a new one. Do you wish to proceed?

I signaled my intent to do so, and more Game text filled my mind. This time around, though, I saw no reason to deliberate over the options.

While there were some interesting new benefits on offer, there was only one sure choice: upgrading void thief. Selecting it for advancement, I waited patiently.

Commencing Class upgrade...

...

Upgrade complete. Class points remaining: 0.

Congratulations, Michael, your voidstealer Class has advanced to rank 13!

You have upgraded your void thief ability to <u>greater void thief</u>. The fourth tier of this ability makes it easier for you to filch knowledge from your foes by reducing the damage that your void armor needs to sustain to trigger a theft from 30% to 20%.

The range of hostile spells that can be stolen has also expanded to include non-sustained area-of-effect spells. Additionally, the memory capacity of your void armor has improved, allowing you to remember your stolen knowledge for 16 hours instead of 12.

Greater void thief also provides you with a fourth method, called <u>redirect</u>, of disrupting your foes' attacks. Your mana's understanding of a stolen spell is such that, within 10 seconds of being hit, you can redirect the spell at a target of your choice.

Note: like its lower-tier counterparts, redirect is a passive ability and is dependent on a successful void theft to function.

"Ah," I exhaled softly. In some respects, redirect did what the mage's surprise ring did, except in a much shorter timeframe. It was a spell effect designed for immediate re-use.

Now, instead of simply negating incoming damage from stolen spells, void thief allowed me to bend them to my use, all without wasting any of my own mana—or time—forming the necessary spell weaves.

Definitely a worthwhile upgrade, I thought in satisfaction.

My player progression done, I refocused on my surroundings, but everything was still quiet both in the stables and outside. *Good, that means I can complete my other chores.* Spinning on my heel, I made my way to the back of the stables.

It was time to check on the servants Ghost had found.

The servants were gone.

But there was no doubt they'd recently been in the pen. Their scents still lingered in the air for one. For another, boxes filled half the small space, testament to the fact it had never housed a hellbat.

The servants, I suspected, had been using the pen as a storeroom. *So, how did they leave?* I wondered.

My gaze fell to the dark hole backed up almost against the wall. A rope disappeared down its depths, answering the mystery. Stepping forward, I crouched down for closer inspection.

The hole was square-shaped and barely large enough to squeeze a medium-sized human through. Its edges were smooth, and from the dust marks on the floor, I guessed that it was ordinarily hidden by the piles of nearby boxes. Frowning, I peered into the cavity's black depths.

The darkness was no obstacle to my sight, and right away, I made out the layer of bricks lining all four sides of the hole.

Not a hole then. A shaft.

Given how deep the shaft stretched, I estimated it went all the way to the ground floor. I rubbed my chin thoughtfully. Whatever the shaft's original purpose, it was no recent construction, and it had to have been built before the Riders took control of the fort. Struck by sudden inspiration, I lifted my head upward.

The patch of ceiling directly atop the shaft's location was lighter colored than the surrounding brickwork. *It's a chimney shaft,* I deduced. One that originally reached all the way to the fort's roof but that had been deliberately removed and concealed at some point in the past.

"Ghost," I called, "*About those servants... how many were there?*"

A pause. "*Two. Sorry, I didn't think to mention that before. Does it make any difference?*"

My frown deepened. "*I'm not sure, but I'm wondering if those servants really were servants.*"

"*What else could they be?*" the pyre wolf asked.

"Spies," I murmured. "*Tyelin's spies.*"

I pulled out the envoy's map. By my reckoning, the shaft was situated along the fort's south wall. According to the map, the spot directly below me on the first floor was occupied by the fort's kitchens.

The chimney wasn't shown on the floorplans, though.

Admittedly, that didn't mean much. If it had been part of the Blade's plan to betray me all along, there was no way he was going to tell me about his spies' secret network in the fort.

Of course, the shaft's absence from the map could *also* mean Tyelin didn't know about the shaft, but I highly doubted that. Still, at this point, whether he did was irrelevant. The more pertinent question was whether the Riders knew.

My gut was telling me they didn't.

And that allowed for some interesting possibilities.

I could use the shaft to escape whatever force Malikor sent to attack me next. Doing so would let me easily slip the Riders' noose and buy more precious time.

However, it would also reveal the Blades' hidden network, not that I cared much about keeping the Blades' secrets at this point, but a secret shaft that no one knew I knew about? That could come in handy in the future. Sadly, though, I could see no way to conceal my use of the shaft while I was hell-tracked. Still, I could not ignore it.

I rose to my feet, my decision made. I would use the shaft, but only after being forced to retreat. Until then, I'd remain in the south stables, letting the Riders believe they had me cornered.

✳ ✳ ✳

I didn't stay in the shaft-pen, but before leaving it, I made sure to slide some boxes over the hole. If nothing else, the sound of the heavy objects being moved would alert me if anyone tried using the shaft.

"Still no movement," Ghost reported as I exited the pen.

Frowning, I checked the status of my debuffs.

You are hell-tracked. Remaining duration: 37 minutes.
You are psi-dampened. Remaining duration: 37 minutes.

More than five minutes had passed since Ghost and I had left the feeding chamber. It was ample time for the sentries to have made their report, yet still, no response from Malikor was forthcoming.

What's keeping him? I wondered.

I had no idea, but I had no intention of hanging around doing nothing while I waited. Striding down the stable's central aisle, I rejoined Ghost by the barn doors.

The poison clouds from my bombs had long since dissipated, exposing the hundred-odd bodies lying atop one another near the entrance. Crouching down, I studied the corpses. Even in death the Riders' expressions, contorted limbs, and positioning betrayed their surprise and the suddenness of their demise.

"You're going to loot them?" Ghost asked.

I considered the question carefully for a moment, then reluctantly shook my head. Laid out as they were, the dead Riders made for an impressive statement—one beyond my own ability to replicate, and one that would perhaps instill fear in the hearts of those who came next.

Looting the corpses would only lessen that impact. Straightening, I drew my swords. Besides which, they had given me an idea.

"Prime?" Ghost prompted, her head swinging around at the sight of my drawn blades.

Not answering, I turned a slow circle, listening intently.

The hellbats were still hissing and shrieking their outrage. At a guess, there were nearly five hundred of the creatures in the chamber. But there was also the north stable wing to consider. Assuming it housed an equal number of hellbats, that meant... the Rider occupation force was at least two thousand strong.

A not-so-small army, I mused. One I was *not* going to defeat all by my lonesome.

Still, I could have a good go at it.

"I think it's time to expand our statement, Ghost," I mused.

You have recast vanish.

The pyre wolf's ears pricked up in confusion.

"The statement we began when we killed Titus' people," I explained as I renewed my invisibility.

"What statement is that?" she asked, no more enlightened.

I headed toward the closest pen. *"Woe to those who hunt us."* Leaping over the fence, I advanced on its occupant. *"Only death follows in our wake."* Drawing back my blades, I struck.

You have killed Xyactil, a level 149 hellbat, with a fatal blow!

I had no intention of slaying all the hellbats, of course. They would not serve as an effective deterrent in that case, but half of them?

Half of them, I had no compunction about killing. *"Take the pens on the right,"* I told Ghost. *"I got those on the left."*

✳   ✳   ✳

You are hell-tracked. Remaining duration: 27 minutes.

You and Ghost have reached level 221! Ghost's death magic has reached rank 3.

Your Dexterity has increased to rank 107.

Ten minutes later, Ghost and I were drenched in blood.

We had executed close to one hundred and fifty hellbats, all helplessly trapped in their pens and easily slain. It was grim work and earned us another level.

I, of course, worried that their companions' deaths would spur the Riders into attacking early, but I didn't let that stop me. Either Malikor sent an ill-prepared force to attack me or he waited and sent an overwhelming one. There were advantages to be had with both approaches.

But, admittedly, as the clock ticked down and no Rider force turned up, my concern grew.

The hellbats' companions had to be aware of their deaths. No doubt, it angered them. No doubt, it made them chaff at the bit. No doubt, it made them want to set aside their plans and charge up to the third floor.

But they didn't.

So, either the hellbats meant far less to Malikor than I'd believed or... Malikor was not in charge anymore.

Mammon was.

I knew my incursion had been reported to the Riders' Power, but would he see fit to handle the matter himself? Would he have dropped everything and teleported to this sector? Could he?

I didn't know, but I had to be prepared for the possibility. *If Mammon comes, I'll have to—*

"You hear that, Prime?"

At Ghost's question, my head whipped in the direction of the stable's main entrance. But the faint sound—the screech of wood on rock—was not coming from the barn doors.

It was coming from the shaft-pen.

Someone was moving the boxes I'd placed over the hole. Cursing silently and fearing the worst, I withdrew my blades from the hellbat corpse at my feet.

"Ghost, go to the feeding chamber and keep watch on the stairs," I ordered. *"Let me know the instant you hear the doors from below opening. This may be the Riders attempting a two-pronged attack."*

"What are you going to do?" she asked as she raced out of the room.

"Kill Malikor's hellbat," I replied grimly. I'd located the creature minutes ago but had held off slaying it, not wanting to overly anger the envoy. Now, though, there was no reason to hold back.

Hopping over the fence, I raced down the main aisle even while I listened with half an ear to the noises emanating from the rear of the stables.

Those in the shaft were moving carefully, trying to remove the blockage I'd placed over the hole as soundlessly as possible. It would take them a few more seconds yet.

Dashing into another pen, I struck at its occupant. The envoy's companion was both larger and stronger than the other hellbats, but that made little difference.

In its pen, it was as helpless as the rest.

You have backstabbed your target for 5x more damage!
You have backstabbed your target for 5x more damage!
You have backstabbed your target for 5x more damage!
You have killed Nyctaeus, a level 223 hellbat.

You and Ghost have reached level 222!
Your two weapon fight has reached rank 18.

Not pausing, I withdrew and sheathed my blades in one fluid motion. Then, I ducked out of the pen and back into the aisle.

"Did you hear that?" a voice whispered almost too soft for even me to hear.

"No," a second hissed back. "What was it?"

"A... hellbat, I think," the first said. "Sounded like it was dying." A pause. "Do you think *he* is still alive?"

"Can't be," the second refuted at last. "Jone and Cail said the Riders had him cornered. He must be dead by now."

My ears pricked. *Jone?* The same Jone I was supposed to deliver Tyelin's poison to? *Has to be.*

Dropping into a crouch, I padded in the direction of the shaft-pen. Whoever the two up ahead were, I was certain they were no Riders.

"Jone and Cail could be wrong," the first went on.

"Yeah, you think so?" the second scoffed. "They've never been before."

"They were wrong about the hole," the first pointed out. "The boxes were not supposed to be there."

The second chewed over that for a bit. "True."

Another drawn-out moment of silence followed, then I spotted two worried faces rise above the shaft-pen's fence.

The target is Tulvin, a level 180 half-orc seeker and...
The target is Hycrail, a level 175 human infiltrator and...

Blades. The pair were Blades. But that didn't necessarily make them friendly. Nothing in the overheard conversation implied one way or another whether Tyelin had betrayed me, but the two had clearly been talking about me. And they had known the Riders had attacked me.

And had done nothing to assist.

At best, that makes them neutral. At worst, enemies. Freezing in place, I waited while the pair scanned the room.

Two hostile entities have failed to detect you!

"I don't see anything," Hycrail reported.

"Me neither," Tulvin confirmed.

Hycrail rubbed his eyes irritably. "Damn dampening field," he whined. "Without my psi, it's like I am half-blind or something."

Tulvin nodded. "I know the feeling."

"Why did we have to move early again?"

Tulvin grunted. "Stop asking stupid questions. You know why."

Sighing, the human scanned the room a second time. "It's clear—as far as I can tell in this state, anyway." He paused. "We signal the others?"

Tulvin pursed his lips. "We have to," he pronounced. "The plan has gone to shit as it is. Time to get it back on track."

"Agreed," Hycrail said, and a second later, both vanished from sight— presumably to summon the 'others.'

I rocked back on my heels the moment they were gone, more perturbed than intrigued by the overheard conversation. *Blades in the fort.* That was the last thing I expected.

How had they gotten in anyway? With the Riders' defenses raised, no one should have been able to get in *or* out. Yet the Blades had managed it. Unless...

...they were here all along.

It certainly seemed the more likely possibility, especially if there were only a handful of Blades involved. But just how many 'others' were there? And more importantly, what did the Blades' presence mean for me?

"Prime," Ghost called.

"It's a false alarm," I replied absently. *"We're not being ambushed. The ones coming up the shaft are Blades, not Riders."* I sighed. *"Although what that portends, I'm not sure."*

Ghost did not respond immediately. *"Then those coming up the stairwell are Blades, too?"*

I blinked. *"The stairs? Which stairs?"* I asked, although I already knew.

"The doors on the second floor are opening," Ghost replied, confirming my suspicions. *"And there are scores of players waiting beyond."*

Riders and Blades. One group was coming through the shaft, the other up the stairs.

And Ghost and I were caught between.

I dared not trust the Blades, and the Riders could follow my every move. *"What's the plan?"* Ghost asked, echoing my own thoughts.

I hesitated a moment longer, then said, *"Unmanifest."*

"You sure?" she asked, her mindvoice thick with surprise.

"Yes," I said more decisively.

"But I thought the plan was to—"

"The plan has to change," I interjected. The shaft was compromised, unfortunately. With an unknowable number of Blades hiding somewhere beyond, I couldn't simply use it to escape the Riders.

But that was not to say I couldn't use the shaft, at all.

A more... creative solution was called for than the one I'd originally planned. *"For now,"* I told Ghost as her spirit began to unravel, *"we simply watch and wait."*

✳ ✳ ✳

Ghost has unmanifested.
You are hell-tracked. Remaining duration: 25 minutes.
You have recast vanish.

It didn't take long for things on the third floor to get busy.

First came the Blades, black-clad figures swarming out of the shaft by the dozens. Then, my sharp ears picked up on the tramp of hundreds of feet marching in lockstep. The Riders.

Sitting in a pen occupied by only a dead hellbat, I went still and tense. I was not sure what surprised me the most. The fact that the Riders' approach was as measured as it was or the Blades' numbers.

No way, that many of them have been hiding in the fort all along, I thought. Peering through the openings in the fence, I began counting but had to give up at two hundred.

The Blades did not stand conveniently still. Moving quickly, they spread themselves about the stable until I lost track of most of them. And still more kept emerging from the shaft.

A hostile entity has failed to detect you.

Swiveling my head upward, I studied the player who had perched herself on the top of the pen. The Blades, unlike the Riders, were not privy to my location. And from the earlier overheard conversation, it was clear that they, too, suffered from the effects of the psi-dampening field.

"This hellbat is dead," the Blade—a woman named Chia—hissed.

"A lot of them are," someone out of my line of sight called softly.

As yet, it appeared the Blades had not heard what I had—the slow tread of armored men and women making their way up their stairwell. What would they do when they finally recognized the threat? I wondered.

"Wow," Chia exclaimed as she scanned the main aisle. "That Power really did a number on the Riders. Look at all those corpses!"

"He didn't go down easily, that's for sure," a second Blade said, whistling in soft appreciation.

"How did he do it?" a third player asked.

"Traps," Chia pronounced decisively. "I've spotted at least three that are still active."

"Stupid dumb Riders," a Blade chuckled.

"Serves them right," someone else muttered darkly.

"Cut that chatter!" another Blade ordered. "Focus on your tasks. Once we get started, the Riders are sure to interrupt. Chia, find another pen. The rest of you, get into position, and mind the damn traps!"

My eyes narrowed as I recognized the Blade leader's voice. Yara. Like Tyelin and me, she had been part of the raiding party, and I could say with almost certainty, she'd *not* been in the fort when its defenses went up.

The conclusion was inescapable. The Blades had a way in—and out.

More worrying, though, was that if Yara was here, then so was the rest of the raiding party. *Tyelin is in the fort.* He had to be. By and large, most of the Blade players did not concern me. Blythe's envoy, on the other hand, would not be as easy to deal with.

And I was becoming increasingly convinced that I would have to deal with him. The Blades' presence here, the obviously planned manner of their maneuvers, and their secret means of entering the fort, all betokened one thing: I'd been betrayed.

It was obvious now that Tyelin had not needed me to deliver his poison. He could have done so himself—easily.

So, for what reason had the envoy sent me?

"*The wards,*" I murmured in belated realization. "*Tyelin needed me to trip the wards.*"

"*I don't understand,*" Ghost complained. "*Couldn't the Blades have done that themselves?*"

"*They could've,*" I agreed. "*But that would have spoiled their attack.*"

The more I thought about it, the more sense it made. The wards made a surprise assault... problematic. Not only would it have alerted the Riders, but many of the Blades depended on psi as much as I did. In fact, the psi-dampening field had probably been designed to combat the Blades, not me.

Then, too, if I had entered via the ground floor entrance as Tyelin had originally intended, it would have drawn the Riders' focus there, leaving the blades free to slaughter the hellbats on the third floor, which I was sure now was Yara's intent.

I was a mere distraction. A feint.

I swallowed angrily. I had been so caught up by the notion of the cynacilin poison, I'd not realized it. In fact, it would not surprise me if the entire story with Jone was utter fabrication. Tyelin had used it to distract me as much as he was using *me* to distract the Riders.

But not everything is going Tyelin's way, I thought, recalling Hycrail's previous words. The Blades had been forced to move 'early.' My entry through the fort's roof had thrown the Blades' carefully laid plans into disarray.

My face hardened. And I had every intention of spoiling them further.

"Yar!" a Blade hissed from the direction of the barn doors.

Unbending, I peeked over the top of the pen.

The Blade in question—a thief named Smythe—was signaling frantically to Tyelin's lieutenant.

"What?" Yara hissed back.

"Riders are coming!"

Swiveling about, the orcish woman broke off from the orders she was issuing to give Smythe her full attention. "Already?"

The thief nodded vigorously. "They're assembling near the stairwell."

"How many?" Yara demanded.

"Can't say," Smythe rasped. "A hundred? Two hundred? More are still spilling out of the entrance, and by the look of it, they know we're here. The mages' shields are up, and the warriors are practically glowing with all the buffs they've activated."

A variety of emotions—consternation, surprise, fear—flickered across Yara's face, but they didn't stop her from acting. "Begin!" she ordered.

"But we're not ready yet!" someone else protested.

"It doesn't matter," Yara ground out harshly. "We're out of time. Those of you still out of position, gather at the stable doors. We'll hold the Riders there!"

No one else argued, and almost as one, those Blades perched on the fences dropped down into their assigned pens while those still in the aisle hurried toward the main doors.

I shook my head grimly. Yara's orders were a death sentence. The Blades could not go toe to toe with the Riders and expect to survive. And from the look on the orc's face as she planted herself at the barn doors, she knew it, too.

"Which side do we join?" Ghost asked.

It was a good question and one which I was not ready to answer. While the Blades might be unaware of my presence in their midst, the Riders were most assuredly not and would not let me stay out of the fray. I would have to act.

But how?

Turning my head from left to right, I scanned the room. All about me, the hellbats were dying—a fact not lost on the Riders assembling in the room beyond. Spurred into action, they surged towards the stable, setting the floor trembling with the fury of their charge.

I didn't have much time. I had to act.

But did I help the Blades who had betrayed me or the Riders who could track me? My gaze fell on the shaft at the rear. Or did I flee?

"Prime?" the pyre wolf interrupted. *"What are we doing?"*

Rising all the way, I jumped lithely onto a fence post.

Multiple hostile entities have failed to detect you! You are hidden.

"As always, Ghost, we're on our own side," I said.

I tasted her eagerness at my pronouncement. *"We kill everyone then?"*

My lips twitched upward. *"That will not be possible this time, I'm afraid,"* I replied as I scanned the adjacent pens. Finding what I was looking for, I hurried over.

✳   ✳   ✳

The pen was occupied—not just by a hellbat but also by a Blade who was hacking away furiously at the creature. Remaining crouched in my chosen corner, I waited patiently for the player to finish.

It took longer than it should have, but finally, the hellbat gasped its last breath, and I rose to my feet. "Took you long enough," I whispered.

The Blade whipped around, his eyes wide and startled, but before he could release the warning bubbling in his throat, I slid ebonheart up and into his torso.

You have killed Mazeen with a fatal blow.

You have cast mimic, transforming your visage into that of Mazeen, a level 170 human scoundrel and concealing your Powerful Initiate Mark. Duration: 10 hours.

Easing the corpse to the ground, I quickly stripped it of the loose-fitting black outer garments that all the Blades had draped over their armor. Removing the Cloak of the Reach, I redressed just as fast, then shoved Mazeen's body under the wings of the dead hellbat.

The corpse wouldn't stay unfound, but it should go undiscovered long enough for the Blades to remain ignorant about what I'd done.

"Is this really necessary?" Ghost asked while I still held her cloak in my hands.

"Unfortunately, I don't see another way," I replied as I rolled up the Cloak. *"But don't worry, I'll let you out soon."*

Sighing heavily, Ghost didn't respond.

Taking her silence as agreement—if reluctantly given—I packed away the precious spirit vessel into my bag of holding. Exiting the pen, my gaze naturally locked on the barn doors.

Just as I'd expected, the Blade force gathered there was in tatters. Yara was already dead as were half of the players who had accompanied her. And at the forefront of the Riders cleaving through the Blades' ranks was a familiar figure in red.

Malikor.

Mammon's envoy was as heavily armored as the first time I'd seen him. Now, though, he also had his defenses up. Enveloped in a red dome and wielding a broadsword that glowed just as crimson, the paladin struck down another Blade. Wrenching free his sword, the envoy raised his head and stared directly at me.

Or rather, the spot I occupied.

Despite my new guise, I'd chosen to keep vanish active. Ignoring the nearby Blades surrounding him, the envoy leveled his sword in my direction. "You are a dead man!" he roared.

"Hells," someone to my right moaned. "It's Malikor."

"The Devil himself," someone else muttered.

Wrenching my gaze away from the envoy, I turned about to take in the room. Most of the Blades were done with their grim work, yet none of them seemed in any hurry to aid those being slaughtered at the entrance.

"We can't stand against them," another Blade said, echoing my own thoughts on the matter.

"Where's Yara?"

"Dead."

"Damn. So, what do we do?"

"Flee," I shouted, grasping the opportunity to shepherd them toward the right choice.

"Who said that?" a Blade demanded.

"Does it matter?" another interjected. "He's right! I'm going, too."

"No, wait you—"

"Zul ain't wrong, Dox. Let's get out of here."

Slowly, then in ever-increasing numbers, the Blades raced toward the shaft at the rear of the stable. Heaving a deep breath, I dropped my invisibility and turned back to the envoy.

Malikor was still glaring at me. Only now, he was muttering under his breath, too.

Bowing mockingly in the envoy's direction, I spun around and joined the Blades in their flight.

CHAPTER 466: THE DUES OF THE FECKLESS

You are hell-tracked. Remaining duration: 20 minutes.
Your deception has reached rank 21.

The Riders knew I was fleeing, of course. Indeed, they would be able to track the exact route I used. I didn't let it bother me, though. The Blades were guarding my rear, albeit unknowingly.

Shimmying down the rope after a player who didn't give me so much as a backward glance, I entered the shaft.

It was not what I expected.

Coarse gray bricks lined the sides the first three-quarters of the way down. The last quarter? Chiseled rock. The bottom of the shaft was *beneath* the fort.

That's how they did it, I realized as I dropped down onto solid ground again. The Blades had tunneled into the fort from below. Thoughtfully, I scraped at the floor with my boot. Paved brickwork lay beneath what seemed a decade's worth of accumulated dirt and grime. *Interesting. This is no recent construction. That must mean—*

"Psst! Mazeen, quit dawdling," a voice from above hissed. "You're leaving us hanging up here."

Waving apologetically at the Blades still stuck on the rope, I moved clear of the landing area and studied the room I found myself in. It was cramped and windowless and had only one other exit.

I pursed my lips. I was beneath the fort, that much was obvious. Yet I was still *in* the fort—as evinced by the psi-dampening field that remained active about me.

So, what does this make this place? Some sort of basement level? I wondered. *Has to be.*

The Blade behind me brushed past. Muttering under his breath about dawdling fools, he hurried through the exit. Unsurprisingly, all the other players had headed that way, too. Shrugging fatalistically, I followed on their heels.

✳   ✳   ✳

A narrow passage waited beyond. There was no lighting of any sort, and though that bothered me little, I could tell from the bitten-off curses of those in the fore and the rear that not everyone was managing as well as I was.

The corridor worked its way from east to west—following the fort's south wall—but it was not very long before it spilled out into a large chamber brightly lit by magelights.

Again, there was only one exit.

This time, though, the succeeding passage headed due north, into the fort proper, and in the *opposite* direction of where I wanted to go. Slowing my steps, I watched the Blade I'd been following disappear into the corridor beyond, then turned my attention to the room's other occupants.

That was the other thing different about this chamber. It wasn't empty.

Standing with their backs braced against the opposite wall, and with bared weapons in hand, were ten Blades—some of whom I recognized.

Multiple hostile entities have failed to pierce your disguise.

The leader of the player squad glared at me. "What are you waiting for, Maz?" Cine demanded. "You know your orders. Go see Tyelin!"

There was no trace of suspicion in Cine's expression nor any spark of recognition in his eyes. The elf had no idea who I was. Nodding placidly, I headed towards the room's northern exit.

Cine had clearly been reborn since our clash two days ago, yet I found it interesting to find him here, standing guard on what, to all intents, was an empty room.

Tyelin has demoted him then, I thought, concealing a smile. My gaze flickered to Deklan, the human rogue beside Cine. *And his cronies, too. Serves them—*

You have passed a Perception check.
You have pierced a veil of concealment. An illusion has been lifted. You have found a hidden trapdoor!

Midway into the room, my steps faltered. Caught by surprise by the Game message, I couldn't stop my gaze from jerking sideways to the newly revealed trapdoor.

Cine noticed.

"No, you don't," the elven greenblade growled. "No one leaves, not until we've done what we've set out to do."

"Ye, and don't think about making a dash for it," Deklan scoffed in the sneering manner I remembered so well. "The envoy's traps will chew you up and spit you out without breaking a sweat."

Tearing my gaze away from the trapdoor, I nodded submissively and continued on on my original trajectory. Yet even as I did so, my mind was awhirl with thoughts of the trapdoor. It had been cunningly concealed in the far south corner of the room, and I knew beyond a shadow of doubt that it marked the way out.

A backdoor. *That's how the Blades got in.*

And that's how I get out.

In my mind, I tried picturing the location of the trapdoor, the fort, and the river. They all fit neatly together.

The Blades had built a secret tunnel, I decided. And not just any tunnel, but one that delved beneath the river, connecting this sector and the adjacent one. *Sneaky,* I thought in admiration.

Yet, the tunnel's construction had to have been a massive undertaking. It would've taken years to finish, which meant the Blades had likely built it when they controlled both sectors—an exhibition of both cunning and forethought.

The Blades had both in spades. *No wonder they've survived so long.*

Unfortunately, that same cunning and forethought was also turned against me. With the exit so close at hand, I was tempted to fight my way to the trapdoor. But Deklan's words stopped me.

The Blades had trapped the exit.

Just like they had their camp near the river. I hadn't found *those* traps, and I doubted I was going to spot these either, especially since it seemed that Tyelin himself had set them.

So, as much as it irked me, I did as I was told and entered the north corridor.

✳   ✳   ✳

Fortunately—or unfortunately—I didn't get far.

I'd barely ventured a dozen steps into the north corridor when I caught sight of a crowd of Blades coming the other way.

"Back!" someone shouted. "Everyone back!"

The one doing the shouting, a player named Auris, was at the forefront of the advancing Blades. Standing shoulder to shoulder, they filled the corridor to the brim and were descending on me like a horde of angry black insects. Left with no other choice, I and the other Blades fleeing the stables, retreated into the trapdoor-room.

"What are you fools doing back here?" Cine roared. "I thought I told you to—"

"Shut up Cine," Auris snapped as she entered the room at the head of her own force of players.

"Auris!" the elf exclaimed. "You shouldn't be here. Your orders were to—"

"Orders change," another interjected, separating himself from the column of newly arrived Blades.

I stiffened, recognizing the speaker's voice almost at the same time as the Game fed me his analyze data. It was Tyelin. Blythe's envoy had finally arrived to take charge of matters.

Discreetly, I shrank farther back into the ranks of Blades around me. If anyone was going to be able to pierce my guise, it would be Tyelin.

"That is something I thought you would have learned by now, Cine," the envoy went on.

The greenblade shifted unhappily. "But you told me to follow your instructions to the letter. You said if I deviated even a—"

Tyelin didn't let him finish. "Tell me, Cine, did you bother to question any of Yara's people who passed by this room?"

His face devolving into confusion, the elf opened his mouth to reply.

The envoy sighed. "Don't tell me," he said, holding up a hand. "I already know. You didn't." Striding up to Cine, Tyelin stared him down. "But if you did, you'd *know* they're fleeing a counter-ambush. You'd *know* Yara is dead.

You'd *know* there are scores of Riders on their heels. You'd *know* that Malikor himself is in the stables!"

"M-Mammon's envoy," Cine stuttered. "He's here?"

Ignoring the question, Tyelin placed his face mere inches from the elf's. "That being the case, don't you think it would've been wise to halt Yara's people's flight and gather them together to guard the shaft?"

"Uhm—"

"Shouldn't you have at least ordered your own squad into the shaft-room to protect our rear?" Tyelin went on remorselessly.

"Err..."

Stepping back, Tyelin folded his arms across his chest. "Go," he commanded, his voice dangerously soft. "Take your people, and go secure the shaft."

Cine blanched. "But what about Malikor? My squad can't stand against Mammon's envoy. Shouldn't you—"

"Don't be a fool!" Tyelin hissed. "Malikor can't use the shaft. Or," he added sarcastically, "do you think Mammon's brave paladin is going to take off his armor and try to squeeze his big frame through that little hole?"

Cine licked his lips. "Well, when you put it like that, I guess not."

"Then go," Tyelin repeated. "None of the Riders have entered the shaft yet for fear of being ambushed, but if you keep dithering, you're going to find them waiting for you."

Cine's eyes darted to the other Blades in the room. "Shouldn't I take some reinforcements with—"

"SHUT UP AND GO!" Tyelin yelled, his temper finally snapping.

Saying no more, Cine beat a hasty retreat with Deklan and the others hard on his heels.

The envoy watched their departure for only a moment before spinning around to survey the packed room. "Haiken, come here."

The Blade hurried up to the envoy.

Placing his hand on the player, Tyelin drew him close. Unobtrusively, I inched forward, straining my ears to listen.

"Follow Cine. Take five squads and keep an eye on him and his men," the envoy ordered in a low voice. "You are not to enter the shaft-room yourself, nor are you to engage with the Riders." He threw the player a stern look. "Got it?"

"Got it," Haiken confirmed.

"Good," Tyelin continued. "Now, when Cine's squad falls"—his voice turned grim—"and make no mistake, they will fall, activate the shaft traps. Then retreat up the corridor, activating the traps placed there as you go."

I stifled a groan. Just how many damnable traps had the Blades set? Escaping was looking more problematic by the second.

"It will be as you say, Envoy," Haiken said.

"Good man," Tyelin said, clapping him on the back. "Now, go."

After Haiken hurried off, Tyelin called to Auris, "Secure the room."

"Yessir," she replied as she began ushering players into place.

"And when you're done with that, bring me the reports from the survivors. Before we move, I want to know exactly what disaster befell Yara."

CHAPTER 467: THE TENETS OF WOLF

You are hell-tracked. Remaining duration: 14 minutes.

Auris assigned the rest of the survivors of Yara's band and me to guard the west door. I fell into position willingly enough. Right now, I was exactly where I needed to be—in a room filled with scores of Blades and Tyelin, no less.

Nor was the envoy the only elite amongst the Blades. There were three others: Auris, Haiken, and a player named Lune. When Malikor and his Riders arrived—and I had no doubt they would—they would have no easy task getting to me.

"Anyone have anything else to add?" Auris yelled, addressing my group at large.

The Blade elite had been making her way down the ranks of the survivors, questioning Yara's officers about events in the south stable wing. I'd eavesdropped on their reports but heard nothing that would give me away.

"No, Boss!" I said, shouting back my response in time with the others.

Nodding peremptorily, and no doubt feeling the press of time, Auris hurried over to Tyelin to deliver her findings. While she was about it, I spotted another Blade slip in through the north entrance.

The target is Bern, a level 201 gnomish hunter and...

Another elite.
Frowning, I watched the gnome make his way over to the envoy. There were nearly six hundred Blades in the chamber already. How many others did Tyelin have spread out about the fort?

"More bad news, do you think, Maz?" the Blade on my right asked as he leaned over conspiratorially. He, too, was watching the envoy and the two elites.

I shrugged, not daring to speak.

"Not interested, huh? But you will be, I promise. If Mong suffered the same losses we did, then the battle is lost already."

Mong? I thought, my eyes narrowing. But despite my curiosity, I said nothing.

Disgruntled by my continued silence, the talkative Blade turned away in the hopes of striking up a conversation with his other neighbor.

More than happy to be ignored, I focused my attention on Tyelin, listening intently.

"... Attacked *after* you say?" the envoy was asking. "Are you sure about that?

"I am," Bern responded. "Malikor's people only entered the north stable after Mong's people started killing the hellbats."

Tyelin's brows crinkled. "Yet they hit Yara before she began. Why is that?"

"Perhaps it was because of the Power," Auris ventured. "The survivors did say nearly half the hellbats in the south stable wing were dead before they even got there."

"Hmm." Tyelin rubbed his chin. "And why would Titus have allowed so many companions to be slain?"

Neither Auris nor Bern had an answer for him this time.

"The only explanation," the envoy went on, "is that Malikor's dog had no say in the matter. Titus failed. He didn't kill our decoy. The bastard is still alive."

So, I was a decoy, was I?

Even though I had already guessed as much, the outrage I felt at Tyelin's words was no less. They were the final confirmation I needed too. My assumptions were valid. Tyelin *had* betrayed me—not perhaps by the letter of the Pact we'd sworn, but he'd played me false.

Still, now was not the time to indulge my emotions. Burying my anger, I returned my attention to the trio.

"But didn't the spies see him die?" Bern protested.

"They did not," Tyelin corrected. "They saw him unmasked and about to be hit by a concerted attack from over a hundred Riders and *assumed* he would die. Erroneously, it turns out."

Auris blinked. "So, where is he?"

Tyelin turned slowly about to study the room-at-large. "My guess would be... here."

* * *

I didn't react despite feeling the sudden urge to bolt.

Trusting in my disguise, I kept my face impassive as the envoy's eyes passed over me. Just one amongst many, that was all I was. There was no need to panic. None at all.

You have passed a mental resistance check!
Tyelin has failed to pierce your disguise.

There you go, I thought, not giving way to the heartfelt sigh that threatened to escape. *That wasn't so bad.*

"He's here, Ty?" Auris asked in a furious whisper, her hand dropping to the weapon by her side. "Are you sure?"

The envoy nodded. "I am."

"But he is hell-tracked!" Bern squeaked. "He'll lead Malikor straight to us!"

Tyelin shrugged. "Given the situation, that's not a bad thing. We've prepared the ground already. And besides, there is little we can do to rectify the situation now."

In the face of the envoy's calm, the tension eased from the other two. Not entirely, though.

"Shouldn't we place them under guard at least?" Auris asked, squinting suspiciously at the survivors of Yara's band.

"We don't have the people to spare for that," Tyelin replied. "And I don't think it's necessary either."

"Whyever not?" Auris demanded.

"I've taken the Power's measure," Tyelin said easily. "He struck me as a pragmatist. He'll know as well as I do that *we* are his best chance of surviving." Raising his head, he added, "You hear that, Jasiah? If you don't move against me, I'll leave you be. You've already done all I need of you."

I was unmoved by Tyelin's words. *Ha!* I thought, in the privacy of my mind. *I'm afraid matters will not so easily be squared between us as that, Envoy.*

"He can hear us?" Bern asked aghast.

Ignoring the strange looks the Blades not privy to the conversation were giving him, Tyelin scanned the room nonchalantly again. "I suspect so."

Bern did not look best pleased by the envoy's answer, but Auris had more important things on her mind. "Then the plan has changed?" she asked, lowering her voice even further. Despite this, her words still carried to me.

"It has," Tyelin confirmed. "Pull everyone in. Mong's people included, as well as those set to watch the summons on the ground floor. We'll make our stand here."

"What about the psi-dampening field?" a worried Auris asked.

"What about it?" Tyelin retorted. "There's only ten minutes remaining on the spell, and no matter how furiously Malikor's mages work, they will not be able to renew it for another few hours yet."

"Ten minutes is a long time," Auris cautioned. "Malikor alone can do a lot of damage in that time."

"Which is why we have the traps," Tyelin replied primly. "They'll force the Riders to slow their approach. They should not reach us before the field dissipates."

"But what if they don't slow down?" Auris countered.

The envoy grinned evilly. "Then their losses will be horrible. Truly horrible."

✳ ✳ ✳

It was an anxious next few minutes, not just for the waiting Blades but for me, too.

Refusing to trust Tyelin's glib words, I dared not lower my guard. No matter what he'd said, I was certain Blythe's envoy would strike at me the moment I was located.

As the clock ticked down on the psi-dampening spell, the tension in the room ratcheted up. At the eight-minute mark, more Blades rushed into the room. Mong's band. Watching intently, I took careful count while Auris redeployed them.

Eight hundred was the final tally—five of whom were elites.

Quite the invasion force.

But were the Blades' numbers sufficient to defeat the Riders?

I wasn't sure. Even discounting the hellbats, the fort was home to at least two thousand Riders. Crucially, though, Malikor had sent half his people to patrol the river, including his own elites—Leafbright and Zultan.

Factoring in the players I'd already killed, that put the Blades force at parity with the Riders. But the overall count of players mattered less than the number of elites did. With Leafbright and Zultan absent, how many did Malikor have supporting him?

Probably not enough. Whatever else Tyelin was, he was not foolish. He would not have come unprepared.

Chewing on this, I studied the chamber anew—the envoy's chosen battleground. Even with the addition of Mong's people, there was plenty of space. The middle of the room was occupied by Tyelin, his commanders, and a reserve force of four hundred.

The north door was guarded by Mong's band of three hundred and the east entrance by the remnants of Yara's band. The hidden trapdoor in the southwest corner of the room was unguarded—deliberately so.

There were no furnishings as such. Other than the dusty boxes stacked against the walls and the magelights clinging to the ceiling, the chamber was empty. *It's probably a storeroom,* I thought. *If an unused one.*

Given the room's layout, I didn't see myself escaping until the Riders arrived or the psi-dampening field dissipated. Which meant I had another decision to make. The same one, in fact, that I had avoided in the stables— choosing a side.

Did I help the Blades?

Aid the Riders?

Or stay out of it?

This time, though, the stakes were higher. It was not just control of the fort that would be decided in the upcoming battle but ownership of the sector itself.

Claiming the sector for myself was an impossibility. I had not the numbers for it. And, undoubtedly, it would serve my interest if the Blades won. Then the sector would revert in age, leaving me with greater freedom to come and go as I pleased from the region.

But the Blades had betrayed me. And I balked at the thought of seeing them rewarded for their treachery. Nor could I deny that the idea of helping Malikor and seeing Tyelin defeated had a certain appeal to it. Now that I had the portal scrolls, I didn't need the Blades, so why not see them punished?

The final option was to simply leave, letting matters between the Blades and Riders take their course without any interference on my part. It was by far the safest choice, too.

Biting the inside of my cheek, I pondered my options, and as I did, a surprising Game message unfurled in my mind.

The Adjudicator has allocated you a new task: <u>The Tenets of Wolf</u>! The Blades have betrayed you. Falling prey to Envoy Tyelin's machinations, you've been manipulated into doing the Power Blythe's bidding. But Wolf is no one's plaything. Nor does Wolf tolerate betrayers. Wolf does not betray weakness in the face of others or let any slight go unanswered. Pride demands vengeance.

That, though, was the old way, and Wolf is no more.

You, young scion, are the future. The time has come for you to determine what sort of Power you will be. Will you cleave to strength? Will you take a more pragmatic approach? Or will you forgive and forget?

It is in your hands to determine what path your House Wolf shall follow. There is no wrong way, but there are consequences with every choice, and your actions today will determine the tenets of the reborn House.

Objective: Respond to the Blades' treachery. Note: this is a time-limited task that will auto-complete in 1 hour.

Huh, I thought. *Curious.*

I rubbed my chin as I considered the Game message. In many ways, it gave me carte blanche. By my reckoning, I could do anything—including nothing—and I would still complete the task. In that sense, the Adjudicator's task seemed almost frivolous.

Yet, it was not.

In the past, my bloodline Mark had only strengthened when I'd adhered to the ways of Wolf. And while my Mark had never weakened, I'd know it would if I failed to respect the tenets of Wolf.

Now, the Adjudicator was giving me the responsibility for determining the way. *I* was being given the power to decide what type of Wolf scions would ascend in the future. It was a heavy burden but not one I would shrink from.

Still, the Game message did nothing to alter my course.

I had not ventured as far down Wolf's path as I had by forcing my actions in a direction foreign to me. No, I'd always acted true to myself.

And I would keep doing so.

I knew what I had to do, if not precisely how to go about it.

Step one, though, was simple enough: wait for the Riders' assault.

* * *

You are hell-tracked. Remaining duration: 5 minutes.
You are psi-dampened. Remaining duration: 5 minutes.

A collective sigh passed through the room as the five-minute mark came and went, and still, the Riders did not show.

Speculation had been rife during the agonizing wait about when Malikor's people would arrive, *if* they would arrive, and how they would choose to make their entrance. But now with less than five minutes on the clock, surely it was too late for the Riders to attack?

Most of the Blades seemed to think so.

The window of opportunity to take advantage of the psi-dampening field had passed, and weapons were lowered, jokes were traded, and cramped joints were stretched.

Of course, that was the moment Malikor decided to strike.

A resounding boom rocked the storeroom. It had come from the direction of the shaft. A second explosion sounded. This time, from somewhere beyond the north exit.

"They're coming!" Bern proclaimed unnecessarily.

"I need more than that!" Tyelin snapped. "Get me their numbers and disposition."

Swallowing unhappily, Bern hurried into the north corridor.

The shaft corridor flashed white. Once. Twice. Thrice. *Those are lightning traps activating,* I thought.

Hard on the heels of the Blades' defenses triggering, Haiken and his men rushed into the cavernous storeroom. "Cine's dead," he gasped. "And the bottom of the shaft's been captured."

"How many Riders did the traps get?" Tyelin demanded.

"None," Haiken replied grimly.

The envoy's face went blank. "None?" he repeated.

"Malikor has sent in the demons," Haiken explained. "They're leading the way."

My eyes narrowed. *Demons? What demons?*

"The summons," Tyelin whispered so softly I doubted anyone else heard him. "Of course. That explains the delay. Malikor has redeployed the creatures."

I frowned. This was the second time I'd heard Tyelin speak of the mysterious 'summons,' but there was also a third occasion when I'd heard mention of them—after I'd triggered the fort defenses.

'Aether portals' had opened then. And now... there were demons running about the fort. The two had to be related. But why did Tyelin seem afraid of the summons?

Animation returned to the envoy's face. "How far behind are the creatures?"

"Less than a minute," Haiken replied.

Tyelin's gaze flickered over the survivors of Yara's band. "Time to redeem yourselves," he told the group at large. "Hold the summons at the door. At any and all costs." He paused, his face uncharacteristically grave. "If we die here, while the sector is still under the Rider control, I don't need to tell you what will happen next." The envoy's gaze turned harsh. "We'll be slaughtered. Again and again. Over and over. Until final death. Don't let the summons in and that won't happen. But fail... fail, and none of us will live to regret it."

The players about me shifted, muttered, or swallowed nervously, but no one voiced any dissent.

The envoy spun away, seeming to dismiss us to our fate as he turned his attention to the north exit.

"You heard the boss!" Haiken yelled. "Let's keep the bastards out!"

Spines stiffened and weapons were clenched as the players spun around to face the door. My own gaze grew thoughtful. Tyelin's little speech had worked, but I wondered how much of it was true. The envoy did not strike me as someone who would put his own life in the hands of others, much less a bunch of players who had already failed him.

"It's a demon!"

At the cry from behind, I glanced over my shoulder to see Bern dash back into the room.

"Malikor is using—" he began.

"We know," Tyelin interrupted. "Now, get in line." Raising his voice, he shouted, "Four minutes, people! That's how long we have to hold them at bay! Then, I promise you, the tide will turn!"

✳　✳　✳

Objectively, four minutes was not a long time, but given the fear permeating the room, I got the distinct impression it was not going to feel that way soon.

Swinging about to face the shaft-corridor, I saw to my own preparations which, truthfully, did not amount to much. I was not about to use load controller—it might tip off the surrounding Blades as to my true identity—nor could I use enhanced reflexes or quick mend yet. So, sadly, all I did was draw faithful and prepare the single spell in my arsenal—slime tentacles.

My talkative neighbor—Emery—glanced at the blade in my hand. "Nice sword."

"Looted it off a Rider," I replied casually, no longer caring if my voice gave me away. Soon, it wouldn't matter.

Emery, though, didn't seem to notice anything amiss. "Let's hope *we* aren't the ones being looted soon," he grumbled.

Before I got a chance to reply, I spied movement in the corridor and got my first glimpse of one of the feared demons.

My initial impression was that of red. My second, too. A red so shockingly bright and uniform that it took me a moment to see past the color to the shape of the creature it hid.

The demon was humanoid, and if not for the luminous scarlet sheen of his nearly naked torso, I would have labeled him a minotaur. But he *was* red, from the tip of his gleaming tusks to his hooved feet.

What is it with the Riders and the color red, I wondered sourly. Around me, none of the Blades had reacted yet. But they did a moment later, when gale-force winds, appearing from nowhere, howled through the corridor.

"Another trap's been tripped!" someone shouted.

"That's Reg's ice storm!"

"Do you see it?"

"I don't— Wait! I do..." Momentary silence. "By god, it's Mammon. The Power himself has come!"

"Don't be a fool!" Haiken snapped, interjecting himself into the conversation before the speculation could get out of hand. "You fools know Blythe is keeping him away. Mammon won't come. That's just one of his alter egos.

Alter egos? My eyes narrowed, wondering what he meant by that.

"There's another!"

"And two more!"

I stared into the snowstorm that gripped the far end of the shaft-corridor. Ice and sleet were falling sideways, whipping relentlessly at the minotaur-like shapes caught in the storm's midst.

The demons were undaunted, though, and leaning forward, they stomped resolutely onward. My analyze did not trigger either, which meant that whatever the 'alter egos' were, they were not players. Forced to consciously reach out with my will, I inspected the foremost figure.

The target is Bulezu, a level 265 lesser demonic aspect of the Power Mammon. His health is at 90%, and he is currently suffering under the <u>chilled</u> debuff.

Aspects are spell constructs. Living facsimiles of a powerful entity, they can either faithfully replicate the entirety of a host or one particular aspect of them. The creatures must be summoned from the aether through pre-existing links with their host. This often requires extensive preparations and a fixed magical focus. For this reason, aspects are often employed defensively. Ascendant governors, in particular, favor their use and often summon aspects of themselves to enhance their sectors' defenses.

Depending on the strength of the summoning spell used to call an aspect into being, they can range from unthinking creatures to fully sentient individuals who can think and act independently.

So that's what Haiken meant by alter ego, I thought, frowning worriedly. Needing to understand the full magnitude of the threat, I reached out with my will and analyzed the trailing two figures.

The target is Benzein, a level 250 lesser demonic aspect of the Power Mammon. He is severely injured.

The target is Bulalayo, a level 254 lesser demonic aspect of the Power Mammon. He is barely injured.

"Damn," I muttered. "How many of these things did Malikor summon?"

"Six," Emery said, throwing me a sharp look. "Don't tell me you slept through the entire briefing?"

Six, I mused, not bothering to reply.

Three to clear this corridor, and another three to hit the north one? I wondered. But a moment later, that hope was dashed as two more figures appeared at the far edge of the snowstorm.

The target is Baseera, a level 263 lesser demonic aspect of the Power Mammon. She is near death.

The target is Bimal, a level 251 lesser demonic aspect of the Power Mammon. She is barely injured.

A shout erupted from the north door. "There's the demon!"

"It's alone!"

"Thank Blythe!"

"Silence," Bern snapped. "Remember your orders. First squad advance through..."

I stopped listening, my attention recaptured by the approaching aspects. The snowstorm had dissipated, and the momentum of all five demons— including the injured ones—had increased. We didn't have much time before they hit us.

"Five," Emery groused. "Why do we get to face five and they only one?"

I said nothing, but I knew why. Malikor had not forgotten me. At a guess, he'd sent the majority of the demons through the shaft-corridor because of my hell-tracked presence near the east door.

My gaze flickered to Tyelin. The envoy stood well clear of the shaft-corridor and was making no effort to reinforce us either. He'd suspected something like this would happen, I realized. Not that it would be demons obviously but that Malikor would focus his attack on me. *He's sacrificing Yara's people just like he had Cine's.*

"Bastard," I muttered.

"Hey, there's no call for that—" Emery began.

"Not you," I said. "Tyelin. The bastard is going to let us die alone. He is buying time."

Emery shrugged, surprising me. "I figured as much. But Ty's a sharp one. We may die, but we'll be back," he said confidently. "The envoy will see us through. He always does."

I'd no response to that and turned back to the advancing aspects. Thirty yards was all that separated us now.

A heartbeat later, there was an audible click. The leading demon—Bulezu—had stepped on another trap. Blue flames surged down the corridor in both directions, temporarily blinding me. Shielding my eyes and fearing the worst, I stepped back, but the inferno did not cross the threshold of the door we guarded. Stopping just short, they receded from whence they came.

"Haiken's work!" Emery shouted above the cheers of the surrounding blades. "He always times things perfectly."

Benzein has died.
Baseera has died.

"And look at that," Emery chortled, "he's got two!"

I nodded slowly as my sight returned. Haiken's trap had cleared out the two most badly injured aspects, but that still left three more for us to deal with.

Turning my gaze inward, I queried the status of my debuffs.

You are hell-tracked. Remaining duration: 140 seconds.
You are psi-dampened. Remaining duration: 140 seconds.

Not long now, I thought. Two more minutes and a bit, and I would be clear of the Riders' tracking and regain access to my psi.

But until then, I had to stay alive.

Chapter 469: Battling with One's Demons

Much to my surprise, the moment the blue flames vanished, the survivors of Yara's group charged into the shaft corridor—some of them, anyway.

I did not join in.

No matter what Tyelin had said about the danger of letting the aspects into the storeroom, there was no way I was going to try battling the three demons in the tight confines of the corridor, especially not with dozens of other players hampering my attacks.

Glancing left and right, I realized I wasn't the only one who thought entering the corridor was a bad idea. A third of the Blades assigned to the east door remained behind, including Haiken and his squads.

Huh, at least not everyone has bought into Tyelin's nonsense.

Facing forward again, I watched Emery and the others rush the demons. The sixty-odd Blades slammed into the three aspects like a tide crashing against a cliff—and broke apart just as easily.

Swinging their arms like battering rams, the red trio swept aside the Blades, hurling them into the adjoining walls with abandon. Bones were snapped, skulls were crushed, and limbs were torn off.

I winced even as I rued the players' foolishness.

Their charge had only bought a few seconds but had cost two-thirds of our defenders. "Yikes," I heard someone mutter, "that was stupid."

I couldn't have agreed more.

Trampling over the dead and dying, the demons resumed their advance. Many of the Blades glanced at Haiken for guidance, but he stayed tight-lipped, his eyes fixed on the aspects.

More stupidity.

"Back, everyone," I growled. "We need space to fight."

Haiken's gaze darted to me. I was openly disobeying Tyelin's orders—*and* encouraging the others to do so as well—but surprisingly, he did not rebuke me.

"He's right," the elite said, nodding jerkily. "Form a half-circle around the door. We'll let them in but keep them contained at the entrance." Snapping off further orders, he began chivvying the Blades into place.

About bloody time, I thought, turning back to the aspects. The trio was fast approaching, their faces devoid of expression and their arms held at the ready. Studying the creatures, I considered my own role in the forthcoming battle.

The demons had utilized no magic so far, but that didn't mean they had none. And their hammer-like fists were dangerous enough all on their own. A single strike had been enough to maim or kill. How would the players accompanying me fare against them? Well enough to stop the creatures?

I didn't think so.

A little help is warranted then.

Backstepping in time with the other Blades, I tapped into the pool of magic at my core and released the spell weaves held ready there.

You have cast slime tentacles.

Four lengths of wriggling black darkness materialized in the east doorway just as the aspects stepped through.

A slime tentacle has hit Bulezu!
A slime tentacle has hit Bulezu!
A slime tentacle has hit Bulalayo!
A slime tentacle has hit Bimal!

Darting through the air, the coil of oily darkness snaked around their chosen victims, the first two wrapping around Bulezu's arms, the third around Bulalyo's throat, and the last around Bimal's left ankle.

Unfortunately, the demons proved more resilient than I hoped.

2 of 3 targets have passed a magical resistance check!

Goddamn, I cursed as the tentacles around Bulalayo and Bimal unfastened and fell lifelessly to the ground. Still, I couldn't be too unhappy. I'd managed to slow one of the red trio. That had to be good enough.

Bulezu has been <u>befouled</u> (speed reduced by 20% and life drained by 2% per second).

"Good job to whoever did that!" Haiken yelled as Bulezu fell out of step with his fellows. "Everyone, focus on the other two." Not waiting to see if the Blades under his command heeded the order, the elite dashed forward.

Bimal's arm flashed down. Bulalayo's hands reached out.

Both missed.

Moving so fast that even to my eyes he was a blur, Haiken ducked beneath both attacks to strike at Bimal from behind with his needle-like blades.

The elite's daggers failed to penetrate.

"Feh!" Haiken spat. "They're resistant to physical damage!"

Watching intently, I sensed the Blades at my side who were about to step forward hesitate. I didn't blame them; Haiken's report would've given me pause, too.

The demons, meanwhile, had halted their advance to focus on their attacker. Bulezu, still plagued by the tentacles, drew back his arms while Bimal and Bulalayo spun around to face him.

Haiken was undaunted, though.

Ignoring the aspects' own maneuvering, he kept striking at Bimal. But the fury of his assault made no difference, and not a single blow penetrated.

Then it was the demons' turn.

Three sets of iron fists rushed at Haiken.

The elite, though, was not as oblivious as he appeared. A split second before the trio made contact, Haiken multiplied. Where before there had been one Haiken, now there were nine.

But that didn't stop the demons' attacks from landing.

In the twinkling of an eye, one of the Haikens—the original—disappeared in a spray of blood and guts. "Damn," I murmured, shielding my face with a gloved hand as gore rained down on me and those nearby. Why had the elite been so foolish as not to dodge? When I lowered my arm though, the sight that greeted me wasn't what I expected.

The other eight Haikens were still fighting.

My eyes widened in amazement. The Haiken who had 'died' was no illusion. The spots of red on my cheek was testament to that. *An interesting spell that.*

"What are you fools waiting for," the surviving Haikens snarled in unison. "Attack! If enough of us strike at them, one of us is bound to get through!"

The players around me surged forward. Not me, though. Haiken's demonstration, as impressive as it was, made one thing clear: blades alone were not the answer. My gaze darted to the trailing demon.

Bulezu is <u>befouled</u>. Remaining health: 76%.

Magic, on the other hand, seemed to work well enough. Unfortunately, I had no further spells to utilize. That left me with only three options.

Stay disengaged while I waited out my debuffs.

Swap out faithful for my stygian swords and enter the fray.

Or lastly, add Ghost to the mix.

I refused to expose my familiar, though. Despite her innate stygian nature, Ghost was susceptible to physical attacks. Mammon's demonic aspects would hammer her as easily as they did the Blades. And there was no telling what the players themselves would do if she suddenly appeared in their midst.

That leaves options one and two.

I didn't want to engage the aspects myself, though. It would only attract more unwanted attention. Deliberating further, I glanced over my shoulder and took stock of the situation at the north entrance.

Unsurprisingly, matters were altogether different there. The three elites—Auris, Bern, and Lune—were arrayed around the demon and keeping it pinned in the doorway. What's more, Bern and Lune—spellblades of one sort or the other—were using swords charged with ice while Auris wielded twin stygian daggers. All three were dealing damage.

The north demon would fall soon, I realized.

I turned back to the east doorway, where despite Haiken's best efforts, neither Bimal nor Bulalayo looked any closer to falling. Sighing, I sheathed faithful and withdrew my stygian swords from my bag of holding.

You have equipped a +3 stygian shortsword and a basic stygian shortsword. Your attacks will now deal necrotic damage.

My reluctance notwithstanding, I had to take the fight to the aspects. If I didn't, the demons would tear the Blade force at the east entrance into shreds. And while their fate did not unduly concern me, there were the Riders to consider. Malikor and his people could not be far behind.

Let's do this properly then.

Not caring who was watching—my disguise would be compromised soon enough—I activated my buffs.

You have cast load controller, gaining a 10-minute encumbrance aura that slows any armor-wearing foe within 5 yards by 50%.

Then I joined the fray.

*   *   *

I had deliberately not cast vanish.

In the close-quarters fighting around the east doorway, the ability would only increase the likelihood of me suffering an accidental strike from an 'ally.'

Besides, the less the Blades knew about my abilities the better. "Make way!" I shouted. "I can hurt them!"

The players in front of me glanced back and, seeing the naked stygian swords in my hands, hastily parted. I waded through, peripherally aware that somewhere to my left the surviving Haikens still danced about Bimal, while on the right, the tentacle-wrapped Bulezu flailed ineffectively at the nearby Blades.

Bulalayo, meanwhile, had spotted my approach and was swinging around to face me. Setting aside thoughts of the other aspects, I focused on the foe before me.

Up close, the demon loomed monstrously large. Nearly twice my height, the creature was forced to hunch his shoulders lest his horns scrape against the ceiling overhead. *Fighting like that will restrict his movements,* I surmised.

There was no time for further analysis, though.

Bulalayo had closed the distance and was already on the offensive. Activating my final buff, I rushed to meet him.

You have cast whirlwind, increasing your attack speed by 3x more for 3 seconds.

An arm speared forward. Sidestepping, I ducked out of the way.

A fist raced down. Twisting my torso, I evaded the blow.

A hoofed foot whirled around. Jumping, I leaped over the attack.

You have evaded 3 of 3 hostile attacks.

The demon's opening salvo had been blisteringly fast, leaving no room for thought nor time to counter. But Bulalayo had erred with his last maneuver, and for a single split second, his large frame was precariously balanced on one leg.

It was my moment to strike.

Darting forward, I drove the sword in my left hand through the demon's exposed flank. Facing the wrong direction, the aspect was helpless to counter, and toughened hide notwithstanding, my stygian blade penetrated all the way.

You have critically injured your target!

Throwing back his head, Bulalayo roared in anger as his stomach was ripped open. My lips curled up in satisfaction, but I didn't follow up with a second attack, even though the urge to do so was almost irresistible.

Given the demon's demonstrable speed and aggression, I suspected his response to my success would be nothing short of cataclysmic. Retracting my blade, I stepped back.

A precaution, I had cause to be thankful for only a moment later.

Seemingly more outraged than hurt, Bulalayo resumed his offensive, attacking with both fist and feet. Throwing blow after blow with abandon, he stepped up the tempo of his attacks.

Matching him for speed, I ducked, dived, and weaved.

You have evaded a bludgeoning fist.
You have evaded a stunning kick.
You have evaded a twin strike.

But despite the demon's disregard, the gaping wound in his side was no minor injury, and little by little, it tore further.

Bulalayo is now <u>bleeding</u>. Ongoing damage sustained. His health is at 80% and dropping.

Even in the midst of my foe's furious onslaught, my smile widened. There was no need for me to strike at the demon again—the wound in his gut would kill him soon enough. Only one thing was required of me from this point on.

Not getting hit.

As hard as Bulalayo was striking, even a glancing blow could prove fatal. Narrowing my focus, I let my awareness of the surroundings shrink to the demon's four limbs. For the next few seconds, nothing else mattered.

Nothing except for the motion of those four lethal appendages.

You have evaded an attack.
You have evaded an attack.

...

...

Sway. Dip. Retreat. Advance. Moving in sync with my foe, I mirrored his movements, avoiding each and every blow he threw at me.

All while he inched closer to death.

Bulalayo's health is at 73% and dropping.
Bulalayo's health is at 61% and dropping.

...

...

Despite my almost feverish focus though, I couldn't but help catch snippets of conversation from the surrounding Blades.

"... That Mazeen?"

"... Can't be..."

"Wow... he's fast."

"No way..."

"... see that?"

"How... doing that?"

"... must be... Power..."

My disguise had just become redundant, but I didn't let that fact trouble me. Bulalayo was weakening fast, and Bulezu also hovered near death. Only the fate of the last aspect—Bimal—was uncertain.

The elites can take care of her, I decided, executing a perfect backflip as Bulalayo's hands came crashing down on the spot I'd just occupied.

You have evaded hammer's fall.

Poised on the balls of my feet, I waited for the next attack, but somewhat to my surprise, none came. Going the way of his hands, Bulalayo's face slammed into the ground.

He's done for, I realized as the rest of the demon's body followed suit.

You have killed Bulalayo.

Chapter 470: Rue the Day

You and Ghost have reached level 223!
Your insight has reached rank 24, your dodging rank 20, and deception rank 22.
You are hell-tracked. Remaining duration: 30 seconds.
You are psi-dampened. Remaining duration: 30 seconds.

Ignoring the Game messages scrolling through my mind, I turned away from the downed aspect. On my right, a much-weakened Bulezu was being held down by a trio of Blades, while on my left, Auris had joined Haiken.

Only half of the east force's commander's copies still remained, but, on their own, the four Haikens more than sufficed to keep the demon occupied while Auris dealt damage to the creature.

The other Blades had backed away, leaving the aspects to the elites and me—and me to them, I supposed. Some of the players whispered fearfully and others muttered angrily, but the lesser Blades did not concern me.

The envoy did.

Feeling his eyes upon me, I glanced over my shoulder. Standing over the corpse of the fourth aspect, Tyelin was staring at me, his eyes narrowed to slits. I tensed, ready to ward off an assault, but the envoy made no attempt to attack, and I got the impression he'd been watching me for some time.

"RRR....EEEAA....DDY!"

At the distant shout carrying from beyond the north entrance, Tyelin's head whipped around to study the open doorway. My own gaze flew in that direction, too.

"WEAPONS! BUFFS! ADVANCE!"

It was the Riders. Malikor had finally come. And from the resounding thuds—the sound of marching feet—echoing above the shouted commands, I'd judged he'd brought every surviving Devil in the fort with him.

Tyelin must have thought so, too, because his face grew grave, but only for a split second. The next instant, the envoy's face smoothened into an expressionless mask.

My own brows drew down. *Tyelin is concerned but not scared.*

The envoy's ploy with the traps had failed, but then, so too, in a sense, had Malikor's with the demons. Neither traps nor demons had managed to inflict any meaningful damage on the opposing faction's forces.

Tyelin must believe the odds still favor the Blades. But only barely. Else, he'd be more confident. The envoy's gaze flickered back to me. "Truce?" he mouthed over the distance separating us.

I stared back at him, not at all surprised by the offer. Circumstances had changed for Tyelin, and right now, he needed me more than he needed another adversary—which I surmised was why the Blades had not attacked me.

But do I need the Blades?

For a heartbeat longer I held the envoy's gaze even as the Riders marched closer. Did Tyelin spy the calculation in my gaze?

Maybe. *Probably.* He was no fool.

The envoy's offer appeared genuine enough, but then so too had his prior overtures. And I was not in a forgiving mood.

"No," I called back and promptly faded into the shadows.

Multiple hostile entities have failed to detect you! You are hidden.

❋   ❋   ❋

Bimal has died.

The first thing I did was to cast vanish. The second thing was retreating to the southeast corner of the room. There, safely tucked away from prying eyes, I re-equipped the Cloak of the Reach.

"*Wow,*" Ghost remarked once communication was restored between us. "*What is that?*"

She meant Bulezu. The pyre wolf had spotted him the moment she could look through my eyes again. And truly, the red minotaur was hard to miss.

"*One of Mammon's demonic aspects,*" I explained absently, my own gaze fixed on Tyelin.

The envoy's eyes had tightened fractionally at my terse response before he'd turned away to spew out a slew of orders. Tyelin obviously had more important things to worry about than me lurking in the shadows.

And for now, I, too, was content to let him be.

"*How many demons did you kill?*" Ghost asked. "*I bet it was all of them!*"

I smiled. "*You'd lose that bet. I slew only the one. Two, if you count Bulezu, I suppose,*" I replied. While the tentacle-wrapped aspect was still alive, he would go the way of the others soon enough. "*But forget the demons. We've other things to concern ourselves with.*" Stowing away my stygian blades, I re-equipped ebonheart and faithful. "*The Riders are about to make an appearance.*"

The pyre wolf's interest sharpened. "*Through the north entrance?*" she guessed.

"*Yes.*"

I felt Ghost's attention turn to the Blades and more specifically the distance I'd placed between me and them. "*You've decided not to ally with Blythe's people?*"

I shrugged. "*They've left me little choice in the matter. As much as I may wish otherwise, the Blades can't be trusted. From here on out, we treat everyone in the room as hostile.*"

"*Got it. Kill everyone.*"

I chuckled. "*Not quite. The Blades may be untrustworthy, but they are still useful.*"

"*You have a plan then,*" she said.

"*I do. Here's what we'll do...*"

✳   ✳   ✳

I didn't get to relay the entirety of my plan to Ghost. In fact, I'd barely begun explaining when the Game message I'd been waiting for for what seemed like an eternity finally arrived.

You are no longer hell-tracked or psi-dampened.

A sigh crossed the chamber, echoing my own feelings on the matter. "At last," I murmured in time with the seven hundred-odd Blades in the storeroom, many of whom were voicing similar sentiments. They were no longer psi-dampened.

And nor was I.

"We'll have to finish this later, Ghost," I said. *"My psi is back."*

She said nothing, understanding immediately.

Without further ado, I drew on my will and took care of my most immediate need—healing the damage I'd sustained from the slime tentacles.

You have restored yourself with quick mend. Your health is at 79%.

Around me, I sensed many Blades busy with their own psicastings, buffing themselves or preparing attack spells.

"Kill the lights."

My brows rose in surprise as Tyelin's command hissed from the nearly-forgotten bracelet on my left arm. I was still connected to the envoy's farspeaker network.

Of course, I mused in belated realization. The spell preventing communications had been on the same timer as the psi-dampening field, and it, too, had just fallen away.

"Activate your night vision, people," Auris ordered aloud. She and Haiken had rejoined Tyelin and Lune at the north entrance. "Geck, douse the magelights."

Does Tyelin remember that I still have this? I wondered. Listening with half an ear to the ongoing conversation, I kept psi casting.

"Bern, how much time do we have?" the envoy asked.

Bern had left the room. I'd known that the instant my mindsight had been restored. I knew, too, that the elite rogue was currently about a hundred yards north of my own position. *He's in the corridor,* I guessed.

"Two minutes," Bern replied. *"Maybe more. They're marching slowly. Malikor doesn't appear to be in a hurry."*

The estimate made sense because none of the Riders were within range of my mindsight yet.

"Two minutes to contact, everyone," Auris repeated aloud, which I took to mean not all the Blades were fortunate enough to have their own farspeaker bracelets.

"The fool probably thinks he has us cornered," Lune said, peering out the doorway.

"He'll have placed a blocking force at the top of the shaft, too," Haiken said, not disagreeing.

Bern chortled. *"Little does he know how we got in."*

"We're not retreating," Tyelin rasped, his voice cutting across the chatter. *"And, Bern, watch what you say. Don't forget our visitor."*

You have fully restored yourself with quick mend.

"Sorry, boss," the rogue said contritely. *"Won't happen again."*

"See that it doesn't," the envoy said sharply. A pause. *"Jasiah, you're there?"*

Huh, so he didn't forget.

"Jasiah?"

For a moment, I contemplated not responding, but there was more to be gained by talking to the envoy than there was in remaining silent and hoping the Blades would let something slip.

"I am," I said slowly, even as I kept casting.

"Why did you refuse my offer?" Tyelin asked without preamble.

"Because you can't be trusted," I replied evenly.

"You're still angry about earlier?" the envoy asked, affecting surprise. *"This time will be different. This time, it's in my best interest to keep you alive and hurting the Riders for as long as possible."*

I snorted, not bothering to reply.

You have cast enhanced reflexes, increasing your Dexterity by +16 ranks for 20 minutes.

"What can I do to make you believe me?" he persisted.

"You can start by telling the truth," I retorted bitingly. *"Why did you send me here?"*

"I needed someone to trigger the fort's defenses," Tyelin replied so promptly I knew he'd been expecting the question. *"Someone who Malikor would not immediately associate with us, and someone who could keep the Riders distracted long enough for us to kill their hellbats."* Across the room, I saw him shrug. *"You fit the bill perfectly."*

"That couldn't be all of it, surely," I objected. *"When we first met, you put great stock in whether I was a Power or not. Why?"*

"Blythe needed me to verify your Mark," Tyelin replied. *"Forcing you to demonstrate you truly were a Power through a Pact was the easiest way to do that."*

I frowned, not at all pleased by how cleverly I'd been manipulated. *"And where is your Lady now?"* I asked.

"Making sure Mammon doesn't interfere with what goes on here. Believe me, that is for the best."

Best for whom? I wondered. I didn't pursue the matter further, though, and returned to the original topic of conversation. *"Things didn't quite end up the way you planned, though, did they?"*

"No, they didn't," Tyelin admitted. *"You were supposed to enter the fort through the ground floor. If you had, you would've faced the brunt of the Riders' defenses, including the summons, and no doubt you would have died in the process—neatly taking care of the problem of you."* He shrugged again, almost apologetically this time. *"You were too much of a wildcard to let live."*

I let his statement pass uncontested. *"And all that nonsense about the cynacilin?"* I asked casually. *"Was any of it real? Does Jone even exist?"* I already knew he did, of course, but confirming Jone's existence wasn't the purpose of the question.

Observing how Tyelin chose to respond was.

"Of course, he does," the envoy replied, sounding almost offended at the implication that he didn't.

You have trigger-cast quick mend.

"Really?" I asked skeptically.

"Really," he replied. *"The Pact demanded it. As for the rest... well, most of it was true."*

You have cast fortified mind.

"I knew it," I began. *"You're a—"*

"Ty," Bern interrupted. *"Sorry to intrude, but it's time to wind this up. The Riders are closing in on my position. Malikor has his mages upfront casting detection spells as well. I'm going to have to retreat."*

The rogue was not lying. A thick mass of mindglows had entered my mindsight only seconds ago and, as inexorable as a tide, were sweeping closer.

"Final chance, Jasiah," Tyelin pronounced. *"Are you with us or not?"*

"Not," I replied bluntly, rebuffing him for a second time.

"But I'm not against you," I allowed a moment later to soften the blow. *"I will not kill any of your people until you're done reclaiming the sector."*

Tyelin sighed. *"Good enough, I suppose."* Then, turning his back on me—literally and figuratively—he ushered his commanders closer. "Places, everyone. Time to make the Riders rue the day they stole this sector from us."

CHAPTER 471: DEADLY PROVOCATION

Bulezu has died.
You and Ghost have reached level 224!

I did not let the minute we had remaining pass idly by. First, I invested my new attribute points.

Your Dexterity has increased to rank 113. Other modifiers: +24 from items.

Then, I retrieved two of the ability tomes from my collection and began to read.

You have upgraded your trap detect ability to <u>superior trap detect</u>.
You have upgraded your trap detect ability to <u>greater trap detect</u>. Greater trap detect reveals and identifies all traps of tier 4 and below. Additionally, it increases your chances of spotting higher-tiered traps. You have 4 of 90 Perception ability slots remaining.

Closing my eyes for a moment, I savored the new knowledge. In hindsight, I realized I should've advanced my trap detection ability earlier, but I had precious few Perception slots, and I'd the vague notion of using them for ventro instead.

In my defense, I had *not* expected to encounter as many Blades in the fort as I had, nor to find them as entrenched as they were. But given my present circumstances, I knew I no longer had a choice.

Trap detect demanded upgrading.

And now it's time to find out just how well the thieves have fortified their chosen battleground. Activating my new ability, I surveyed the room anew.

Energy rushed into my eyes, sharpening my gaze, and from the edges of my vision, glowing dust particles swirled into being. After a second, they coalesced around multiple spots in the room.

You have spotted a trap! This is a dormant tier 4 stunning trap formed of 5 trap elements: 3 x lightning enchantments, 1 x pressure plate trigger, and 1 x remote key.
You have spotted a trap!
You have spotted a trap!
…
…

The storeroom was littered with traps, but surprisingly, they were not clustered around the entrances as I half-expected. Instead, they were liberally spread about the chamber. This was not the most curious aspect, though.

The Game had described all the traps as 'dormant.' What the Adjudicator meant by this was not hard to divine: the traps hadn't been enabled yet.

It explained why I myself had not triggered the things when I'd first crossed the room. More intriguing still was the mention of a 'remote key.' It was not a trap component I was familiar with.

The key must be how the Blades are keeping their traps inactive.

Why they had to do so was self-evident, but as interesting as I found the traps on the storeroom floor, they were not my main focus of concern. The ones set around the hidden trapdoor were. Craning my neck left, I studied the southwest corner of the chamber.

But, sadly, my upgraded ability was of no help. Even with it, I failed to spot anything amiss. To all intents and purposes, the hidden trapdoor was not trapped.

I knew that could not be the case, though.

Tyelin would not have left the Blades' escape route unprotected. I sighed. That meant the traps the envoy had set around the Blades' secret tunnel were beyond my ability to perceive.

They're probably tier five, I thought morosely. *Or even six.* Using the tunnel was still not an option.

It's a good thing you have a plan then, isn't it?

✳   ✳   ✳

The next few seconds passed with me watching the north entrance as avidly as the rest of the Blades. The heavy tread of the Riders' steel-clad boots was unmissable. They would enter the storeroom any moment now.

But only from the north.

I glanced at the east doorway again to be sure, but the corridor beyond was silent. It seemed Malikor had not deigned to use the shaft after all, and instead of attacking from two directions, he had chosen to concentrate his forces. That simplified things and gave me a viable escape route if such became necessary.

A heartbeat passed.

Then another.

Crouched and shrouded in darkness, I waited. So, too, did the Blades.

The rogues had scattered while I'd been about my preparations, spreading themselves around the storeroom, some hiding so well, I lost track of their locations. Their tactics reminded me once again that Tyelin was no fool.

Blythe's envoy knew better than to try and face the Riders head-on. Bunched together in the doorway, his people stood little chance against the heavily armored Riders. But cloaked in darkness and aided by their traps? Dispersed, and forcing the Riders to do so likewise? Well, then, the odds would tilt in the other direction.

A red-garbed figure appeared in the doorway.

A second followed, a third, then two more. The Devils had arrived.

"*Now,*" Tyelin hissed.

In response, a dozen objects were lobbed across the darkened room. *Bombs*, I realized watching the small stone-like projectiles arc towards the doorway.

They failed to have the desired impact, though.

A yard from the Riders, the bombs struck an invisible barrier and exploded prematurely.

12 bombs have ignited!
The targets' shields have blocked the attacks.

"Again," Tyelin ordered.

Another volley of bombs were launched, but they were no more effective the second time around than the first.

"Sergeant!" a voice barked from beyond the five motionless figures in the doorway. "Do you have the enemy in your sights?"

"No, sir! They're hiding."

Drawn-out silence.

My lips twitched upward in a smile. I got the sense that the Blades' tactics had confounded Captain Hesh—the one doing the shouting. Would he advance, retreat, or wait for further instructions?

Malikor had not appeared in my mindsight—his mind was shielded most likely—and I could only guess as to his position in the snaking Rider column in the corridor beyond, but I had no doubt he was somewhere close.

The silence drew out longer.

"Launch again," Tyelin commanded.

I rubbed my chin consideringly. Either Tyelin was trying to bait the Riders into entering the storeroom or hoping to destroy the shields of the five and do some real damage. My guess was that it was the former.

The third round of bombs were launched. Then a fourth. A fifth. A sixth.

A shield wavered. Another dimmed.

"Vanguard advance!" Hesh yelled, finally giving way to the Blades' provocation.

In response, the players under his command swarmed in. But the captain really should have given more thought to his order.

Some squads took Hesh literally and marched straight down the storeroom. Others interpreted his words as a command to secure the room and broke off to the left and right. Whatever the case, the Rider column lost coherence the moment they crossed the doorway.

Which was just what Tyelin wanted.

"Activate your traps," the envoy ordered. *"And strike at will."*

Change in state of spotted traps detected...
Auris has activated 20 tier 4 traps. Haiken has activated 35 tier 4 traps. Bern has activated 60 tier 4 traps.

A trap has been triggered!
Warux, a level 166 heavy lancer, is <u>stunned</u> (duration: 5 seconds).
A trap has been triggered!
A trap has been triggered!
...

Between one breath and the next, the room devolved into chaos as dozens of traps came alive and individual Blades sprang their ambushes. Not moving from my spot in the southeast corner of the room, I watched it all play out.

Malikor had not entered the room yet. Nor had Tyelin re-emerged from hiding, and until the two envoys showed themselves and the battle began in earnest, I had nothing to do but wait.

✳   ✳   ✳

It did not take Malikor long to appear.

All about the storeroom the Riders' vanguard was being slaughtered, some one hundred players, each ruthlessly cut down after being isolated and separated from their fellows.

It is what forced Mammon's envoy's hand, I suspected, and instead of entering in a more measured fashion, Malikor and the main body of Riders stormed the chamber in a rush.

As the sea of red flooded the room, Tyelin's voice rang out, "Phase two—begin!"

Immediately, the Blades retreated into the shadows. Most did, anyway. Some, too close to a Rider or caught out by a detection spell, were not fortunate enough to escape and were quickly slain.

Malikor himself ignored the chaos. Striding fearlessly to the center of the room, he swiveled his head from left to right. "Tyelin, you worm! Where are you?"

But despite his earlier shouted order, Tyelin's stealth was too good, and even I couldn't pinpoint his location. Realizing his foe was not about to show himself on his say-so, Malikor glanced over his shoulder and yelled, "Clear the traps. And get some damn magelights up!"

The mages behind him were already chanting, some invoking light, others casting revealing spells. Having little fear of either, I watched on, curious to see how Tyelin responded.

By my reckoning, there were already eight hundred Riders in the storeroom, with more pouring in every second. Their numbers were not unending, though. In my mindsight, I spied the tail-end of the column waiting to enter. At a guess, there were about a thousand Riders in total.

One thousand against seven hundred. Not great odds.

"*Now, Auris,*" Tyelin whispered just as a string of tiny lights floated up to the ceiling.

The response was immediate.

Auris has cast <u>winnowing scythes</u> of spell penetration.

From where the Blade elite sat concealed near the north entrance—*her* stealth was not as good as Tyelin's—a dozen enormous projectiles took flight. Each was as large as me and formed from two scythes joined together. Rotating about their center, the blades hummed ominously.

The twin-scythes arced upward across the chamber, and at first, I thought they'd been aimed at the magelights, but only a second later, Auris' projectiles began to sail down, heading straight for Malikor's honor guard.

Xul, a level 179 hellknight, has been decapitated!

The foremost scythe sawed through the armored player, first slipping through his spelled shield as if it wasn't there, then cutting through steel and bone without pause.

The rest of the honor guard reacted quicksilver fast, throwing themselves sideways or raising their weapons up high in a bid to dodge or deflect the trailing missiles.

To no avail. The scythes were not to be denied.

Amalu, a level 185 paladin, has been decapitated!
Zantis, a level 185 battlemage, has been decapitated!

Each projectile had been individually aimed, I realized. Twelve scythes. Twelve targets. *Not just a shield-penetrating spell then but a seeking one, too.*

Harvin has died.
Bast has died.
Fumansin has died.

None of the scythes had been aimed at Malikor, I noted. Most likely that was because the Sworn's defenses were beyond Auris' ability to penetrate. And in the end, it took the envoy himself to end the attack.

Malikor has cast <u>hellwinds of disruption</u>.

A fetid gust of air, reeking of sulfur and heat, surged out of the envoy's upturned palm. Hitting the projectiles dead-on, the conical-shaped storm shredded them into tiny scraps of metal.

6 winnowing scythes have been destroyed.

Despite the premature end of the assault, I judged Auris' spell a success. She'd killed half of Malikor's personal guards, all with a single spell.
And Blythe's elites were far from done.
"Your turn, Lune," Tyelin whispered.

Lune has cast <u>pulse of disruption</u>.

A wavefront of magical energy rippled out from the second Blade elite. It spread fast and far, encompassing not just the storeroom but the corridor beyond. And whenever it encountered a hostile, they were stripped of their magics.
I was not spared either.

Lune is attempting to dispel you!
Your spells, load controller, quick mend, and enhanced reflexes have been <u>disrupted</u> (dispelled and blocked from re-casting for 10 seconds).
Fortified mind has resisted disruption (this ability cannot be dispelled).

Mimic and vanish have resisted disruption (pulse of disruption only affects spells of tier 4 and below).

Between one instant and the next, the Riders' magelights were quenched, their weapons dulled—stripped of any enhancing magics—and most importantly, their casters' spell shields vanished.

"That's a neat trick," Ghost remarked.

I nodded in fascinated agreement. Lune had changed the complexion of the forthcoming battle entirely. Not only had the storeroom been plunged into darkness again but the enemy had been shorn of their protections and left largely defenseless.

And still, Blythe's elites were not done.

"Haiken, Bern, go."

Bern has trigger-cast <u>trap reconstitution</u>, restoring the enchantment crystals of all spent traps in the vicinity.

Warning: a tier 4 trap has been reactivated!

Warning: a tier 4 trap has been reactivated!

...

My eyes widened in amazement as glowing specks of red coalesced in the room again, marking the reappearance of dozens of traps. That was not all, though. Almost unnoticed, multiple Haikens appeared in a ring around Malikor.

Haiken has cast <u>nine lives</u>.

A moment later, the dagger-wielding elite was joined by *three* Tyelins, and I realized the envoy had cast a spell of his own this time, too. Although, admittedly, it was a bit underwhelming in comparison to his subordinates' castings.

Those have to be copies, I thought, studying the three identical Tyelins. *They can't be anything else given how—*

Tyelin has cast <u>phantom forces</u>, spawning two duplicate images of every ally in a 100-yard radius.

In an eyeblink, the three Tyelins became nine, and the nine Haikens became twenty-seven, while all around me, the other Blades similarly triplicated.

"Wow!" Ghost exclaimed in awe.

I nodded slowly, unable to articulate my own thoughts any better.

Wow, indeed.

Malikor and his Riders had not stood idly by while the enemy ran amok with their spells, of course.

But the castings of lower-ranked Riders were less... effective than those of the Blade elites. And unfortunately for the Riders, they had only one elite in their own ranks—Malikor himself.

Mammon's Sworn did his best to restore the balance, but he fell far short.

Malikor has cast demonic fury, doubling the damage dealt by all allies in a 150-yard radius.

Malikor has cast chained-to-combat, revealing all hostiles in a 100-yard radius and preventing them from retreating or hiding.

Admittedly, I felt a moment of trepidation as the paladin's spell washed over me, but my void armor was equal to the task of repelling it.

You have passed a magical resistance check!
Malikor has failed to <u>reveal</u> you!
Malikor has failed to afflict you with the debuff <u>no-retreat</u>.

The Blades themselves were not as fortunate, and nearly all seven hundred of them—and their accompanying images—were revealed. This did not daunt Tyelin and the others, though. The odds were firmly in their favor now, after all.

"Attack!" Auris yelled.

"Kill them all!" Bern shrieked.

The rooms devolved into chaos as the Blades and Riders threw themselves against each other.

"Time for me to go?" Ghost asked.

"Almost," I replied, unable to tear my gaze away from Haiken and Tyelin.

The pair and their images had engaged Malikor. Tyelin was even faster than Haiken, and although the envoy had been stripped of his stealth, his eight copies made it almost impossible for the paladin to strike the *real* Tyelin.

Malikor fought alone—his remaining guard already having been cut down by Haiken and Tyelin—but despite this, he was doing surprisingly well. Trusting his armor to turn away the Blades' attacks—which it mostly did—he fought offensively.

There was no blocking the paladin's massive broadsword either. Each time a Haiken or Tyelin failed to dodge, they were brutally chopped down. But it was anyone's guess as to who was actually winning.

Turning away, I studied the room at large. The rest of the Blades were faring much better. Dozens of Riders were down already, and those that remained all looked hard-pressed.

The Blades have this, I surmised. It was a view that was only further reinforced when a Game alert unfurled in my mind.

Control of sector 75,172 is being contested!

The current owner's defensive strength around the safe zone has dropped to below 1,000, leaving it vulnerable to takeover by a rival faction. The Devil Riders have 1 hour to reinforce the safe zone's defenses, failing which the sector will revert to unclaimed.

To claim sector 75,172 on behalf of the Forerunners, fortify the safe zone with 1,000 or more of your faction's soldiers. Note: your occupying force must remain in place for a minimum of 1 day before ownership can transfer to you.

A smile slipped onto my face. The Adjudicator's message was... illuminating, and I didn't fail to register its implications.

One hour from now, nothing would stop me from using my aetherstone bracelet—assuming, of course, the Blades' fortune didn't change, and they maintained control of the battle.

Theoretically, I could also force the sector to *stay* unclaimed.

However, doing so would require me to kill a large swathe of both Blades and Riders. And even if I managed that, eight hours from now most would only be reborn once more, requiring me to repeat the difficult feat again.

And again. And again. Theoretically possible, but practically... not so much.

Then, too, there was the matter of my new task, the tenets of Wolf. I'd already resolved how to go about it. Tyelin's betrayal would not go unpunished.

But my response would be measured.

And killing every Blade in the room was hardly that. It would only earn me Blythe's enmity—and another enemy I didn't need.

But if I let the Power claim the sector while *still* punishing her subjects... that was a justifiable compromise, and I could only hope Blythe saw it that way, too.

Yes, I thought. *This sector is best left to the Blades.*

Closing down the Game message, I began sliding along the wall at my back. *"Alright, Ghost. Let's get you on your way."*

✳   ✳   ✳

It took me almost a minute to work my way around the room to the north entrance. I managed the task successfully, though, and none of the players locked in combat noticed my invisible presence.

Peering through the doorway, I confirmed what my mindsight was telling me. The corridor was empty.

"It's clear," I informed Ghost. *"Go."*

Ghost has taken the form of a level 224 stygian pyre wolf.

The pyre wolf wasted no time in manifesting. Emerging unseen from coils of darkness, she bolted up the empty corridor and into the fort above.

"Be careful," I couldn't help calling after her.

"Always, Prime," she replied in an amused tone before disappearing from sight.

Alone once more, I spun about to face the room.

Aided by Bern's traps and Lune's dispelling spell, the Blades had slain fully a third of the Riders in the opening seconds of the battle. But since then, the tide of slaughter had waned, and the survivors had rallied.

Somewhat, anyway.

The Riders had restored their defenses and recast their buffs and were no longer easy targets. But their morale remained shattered, and while most still fought on, they did so in a lackluster fashion.

Malikor himself remained the only true obstacle to a Blade victory.

Propped up by his rage, the Sworn fought on with a viciousness that was unrelenting, and despite everything Tyelin and Haiken were throwing at him, he appeared in no danger of falling soon.

Yet he would fall. That much was inevitable.

Especially once Auris, Lune, and Bern joined in. The trio were presently stalking the chamber, aiding the other Blades with their kills, but soon, I expected they would turn their attention to Malikor.

For a moment, I was tempted to take a hand in the fight myself, but I held myself in check. The time to strike would come soon enough. For now, I had to remain a spectator.

Crouching down small, I renewed my buffs and kept silent watch on the battle while I waited on Ghost's return.

You have cast enhanced reflexes, load controller, vanish, and trigger-cast quick mend.

✳   ✳   ✳

"We have a problem."

For a split second, I nearly responded before realizing that the mindvoice disturbing my vigil was not Ghost's. It was a voice I didn't recognize, and it was coming from the farspeaker bracelet on my left wrist.

Frowning, I scanned the storeroom, trying to identify the speaker. *Who is—*

"Tell me," Tyelin ordered tersely, even as he ducked and weaved around Malikor.

"The patrols are on the way back."

Patrols?

"Which ones?" the envoy demanded.

"There's no way to tell, but at a guess, I'd say all of them," the unknown player responded grimly. *"Malikor must've issued the recall order the moment the communication lockdown was lifted."*

They were discussing the river patrols, I realized. The unknown speaker was a scout, one Tyelin apparently had the foresight to post outside the fort.

"Damnit," Tyelin cursed. *"How long do we have?"*

"Fifteen minutes before the squads I'm watching land," the scout replied solemnly. *"As for the rest, who knows?"*

"Auris, you heard that?" Tyelin asked.

"I did."

"We can't afford to drag this out any longer. I've deactivated the traps in the secret tunnel. Open the trapdoor."

A pause. *"You're sure?"*

"Yes, it's time to commit the reserves," Tyelin replied curtly. *"We have to finish this now. Bern, Lune, to me, quick as you can. We must kill Malikor before the patrols arrive,"* he finished grimly.

Tyelin was right, of course. The Blades *had* to kill Malikor—and fast.

Given everything I'd overheard and seen of the Riders, I was fairly certain they had more than one thousand players out on patrol—and the same number of hellbats, too. Then, there was Zultan and Leafbright to consider as well.

Once the Riders' elites returned, the Blades would definitely lose any advantage they'd managed to retain thus far. Tyelin's only hope for securing a victory was to kill Malikor and as many other Riders as he could before the incoming players reinforced them.

But what were the 'reserves' he'd spoken of? And how would they factor into the equation?

"Alright, boss. I'm on it," Auris said, darting across the room in the direction of the trapdoor while Lune and Bern cut straight for the center of the room and the epic fight raging there. *"I'll have it open in a—"*

An explosion rocked the room.

Auris has died.

My head whipped around to the right, my gaze not going to the messy remains of the former Blade elite but to the shimmering curtain of white that had appeared not far off from her.

A portal had been opened.

And standing before it was Zultan.

The first Rider elite had arrived.

✻　✻　✻

In hindsight, I realized it was glaringly obvious that the Rider elites would teleport in. Of course, the pair would come by the fastest means possible once Malikor contacted them. And not just them, every Rider patrol with a mage capable of opening a portal would do likewise.

And indeed, all around the storeroom, more portals were opening.

That I had not predicted such, was perhaps excusable. It was not *my* battleplan controlling things, after all. But why had Tyelin not foreseen this? Why had he not guarded against this eventuality?

I had half a mind to ask him, but before I could do, his voice hissed through the farspeaker bracelet again. *"Hells, Lune, why is your disruption field not up?"* the envoy growled.

"You said to join you—" the elite began.

"Hells," Tyelin swore, cutting him off. *"Just get it up. And quick!"*

"Working on it," the spellblade bit back.

More Riders stepped out of Zultan's portal, an entire squad's worth and their hellbats. They did not immediately move to attack, though. Instead, spreading out, they formed a defensive cordon around the Rider elite—who was chanting furiously.

That can't bode anything good.

Drumming my fingers along the hilt of my sheathed blades, I wondered if I should intervene, but before I could decide how to act, another familiar voice tore my attention away.

On the other side of the room, standing in front of yet another open portal, was Leafbright. And she, too, was chanting.

Both Rider elites had joined the battle.

Yikes.

"Lune!" Tyelin rasped, sounding half-strangled with frustration.

"Almost there," the elite replied. *"Another five seconds and I'll be—"*

Lune has imploded.

I lowered my head into my hands. The battle had turned in the Riders' favor—decisively, I thought.

And from the stunned quality of the silence emanating from the farspeaker link, I suspected the surviving Blade commanders thought so, too.

✳ ✳ ✳

"I've found Jone."

Given the unnerving happenings of the last few seconds, it took a moment for the sense of Ghost's words to penetrate.

"You have?" I asked, straightening. *"Where is he?"*

"On the ground floor," she replied. *"In what looks to be the fort's kitchens."*

The kitchens, I mused, locating it on the mental map I had of the fort. *That's not too far.*

"Do you want me to stay and keep an eye on him?" Ghost prompted, no doubt sensing some of the chaos in the storeroom through our familiar bond. *"Or should I return to you?*

I inhaled deeply, considering and discarding a variety of options.

"Return here," I said finally. *"We have work to do."*

Chapter 473: Negotiating Under Duress

As Ghost raced back to rejoin me, I surveyed the room.

That the battle had turned was obvious. Now, it was the Riders who fought with renewed vigor and the Blades who were disheartened. It was not the ordinary players who concerned me, though. Focusing on Zultan and Leafbright, I considered the pair.

The two Rider elites were still chanting. Besides Malikor and Tyelin themselves, they were undoubtedly the biggest threats in the room. If I was going to join the battle, it was them I had to target.

But which one to tackle first? I wondered.

Drawing psi, I began a casting while I pondered the question—only to be interrupted midway through again.

"Jasiah?"

It was Tyelin reaching out to me through the farspeaker bracelet. *"Yes?"* I murmured, not stopping my spellcasting.

"Are you still in the room?"

"I am," I replied. *"What do you want?"*

A pause. *"Help."*

I didn't reply immediately, surprised by the bluntness of his response. But I couldn't forget that the envoy was a consummate liar, nearly as practiced at obfuscating the truth as... well, me.

Looking across the room, I saw that he and Haiken had not broken off from their fight with Malikor. How wise that was, I wasn't sure, but between them, the pair had the big paladin locked down, stopping him from interfering in the wider battle.

"Please," the envoy coughed, almost seeming to choke on the word.

Admittedly, I derived a certain amount of pleasure at witnessing the envoy humbled so, but there was no faking the raw desperation in his tone, and my good humor faded quickly.

I had resolved to intervene in the battle, but my plans for how I went about that were still in flux. That the Riders had to be stopped from restoring their defensive strength above the minimum threshold of one thousand was obvious, but beyond that? I still wasn't sure what I would do.

And here was Tyelin asking—no, *begging*—for help.

Hmm. The Blades' straits must really be dire this time around. Deciding to maintain my silence, I weighed up the battle.

Could I sway the outcome?

I thought so. The Blades still had a numerical superiority when it came to elites—if a slim one. Bern was still alive. Having ducked back into the shadows, he was stealthily making his way toward Malikor. Adding myself to the equation—especially if I managed to neutralize one of the Rider elites quickly—would give the Blades a definite edge, no matter how many more enemy players spilled through the portals.

"If you don't aid us," the envoy added, seemingly too anxious to wait for my response, *"the sector will remain in the Riders' hands, and I know you don't want that."*

The envoy's voice, coming uninterrupted over the communication link as it did, gave me a second's pause. Wasn't Tyelin embroiled in a deadly fight?

Frowning, I let my gaze drift back to the skirmish in the center of the storeroom, but all five remaining Tyelins were still dancing about Malikor. Watching him, you'd never say he was fighting distracted, with only one-half of his focus on the actual fight. It was an impressive feat and made me doubly wary of trying to cross blades with Tyelin.

"My help will come at a cost," I warned.

"Name your price," Tyelin said, not quibbling, *"and I assure you my Lady will meet it."*

"Before we get to the matter of price, tell me about these reserves you mentioned."

This time the envoy was not as prompt in his response. Yet, he did not refuse to answer. *"There is a force of contract mercenaries waiting on the other side of the trapdoor."*

My eyes narrowed. *Mercenaries. "How many?"*

"One thousand under the command of a Blade named Banyen."

Ah. So that's how Tyelin intended to hold the fort after he captured it. *"I see. Is this Banyen on the farspeaker link?"*

"No. And before you ask: no, I don't believe the mercenaries are enough to turn the tide. If I thought so, I would open the trapdoor myself."

I opened my mouth to respond, then noticed Zultan had stopped chanting. Falling silent, I waited.

A second later, one of the Tyelins exploded.

I turned the orcish hellbringer's way. There was little doubt in my mind now that it was Zultan who had killed Lune and Auris. Whatever spell he'd used, it inflicted incredible burst damage—and I dared not let myself or Ghost fall prey to it.

Drawing my blades from their sheaths, I crept towards the orc. I didn't act yet, though. There was still the matter of my 'negotiations' with the Blade envoy. It was time to conclude.

"Alright, understood," I said to Tyelin. *"As to my price: two hundred thousand gold."* It was a ridiculous sum certainly, and I'd named it chiefly because nothing else had come to mind in the moment, and I knew I didn't have time to ponder the question further.

"Done," Tyelin replied promptly.

I winced. *Guess I should have asked for more. "You'll swear a Pact to—"*

"Of course! We can modify our existing Pact to—"

"No," I refused sharply. *"Let's not complicate matters further. We'll form a new Pact."*

Another reluctant pause. *"If you insist."*

"I do." Reaching out to the Adjudicator, I formulated the necessary words.

You, in the persona of Jasiah, have proposed a Pact with Blythe, pledging to help her Blades kill Malikor, Zultan, and Leafbright. In exchange, Blythe

will pay you the sum of 200,000 gold in the form of an underworld promissory note, which will be handed over to you within 24 hours.

"That's poorly worded," Tyelin protested. *"At the very least the Pact should require you to actually kill those three. Also, there should be a —"*

"There's no time to debate the matter," I declared. *"Accept the Pact as is or not. But if you don't, I walk away."*

Silence.

The Pact I'd proposed was unfair, I knew that. But I didn't care. Tyelin either trusted me to do as I said or he didn't. And if he didn't, I *really* would walk away.

More precious seconds passed as the envoy deliberated.

Then the ground shook.

Drawing up short, I ran my gaze over the room again. Cracks were spreading across the roof, floor, and walls. Someone had set a spell in motion. Tracing the spidery lines back to their source, I discovered a slim elf at the epicenter—Leafbright.

Urgh, what now? I wondered.

Leafbright has cast verdant growth.

Thick, fleshy vines burst through the largest of the room's new fractures and wormed their way in. Spreading rapidly, they covered all four walls, roof, and floor in a matter of seconds.

Glancing down warily, I studied the dense layer of vegetation underfoot. The new growth appeared harmless enough, but I suspected that was only because it was a precursor to something else—a second spell.

One I knew all too well.

I'd stolen it from the blight druid previously, after all.

"You better hurry making up your mind," I murmured resuming my advance on Zultan, *"because if Leafbright's next spell is what I think it is, you and the rest of your people don't have long to live."*

"Nature unchained," Bern whispered, also listening in.

My brows rose. *"So, you know it."*

"We do," Tyelin said tightly. *"Can you stop her?"*

"In a manner of speaking," I replied smoothly.

A pregnant pause. *"Cine reported you using the exact same spell on his command before,"* Tyelin said. *"I didn't believe him. But he wasn't lying, was he?"*

"He wasn't," I said, with a shrug. The truth would become apparent to the envoy soon enough anyway.

"What are you?" Tyelin whispered.

"Is this really what you want to be discussing now?" I asked in exasperation. *"Give me your answer."*

Tyelin didn't respond verbally, but he didn't have to. The Game message that dropped into my mind was answer enough.

On behalf of the Power Blythe, Tyelin has accepted your proposal, sealing the Pact between her and the Power known only as Jasiah.

"Excellent." My eyes flickered back to Leafbright. As expected, the elven druid was whispering furiously to herself again. I knew exactly how long she needed to finish her casting, which didn't leave us much time.

"Have your people withdraw to the north and east doorways," I ordered Tyelin as I drew stamina. *"They're to hold there and prevent any Riders from escaping."*

"You're going to cast nature unchained before Leafbright does?" Tyelin guessed, not asking me just how I was going to achieve such.

"Yes," I replied tersely, impatient to act now that my path was set.

"But that will kill us, too," Bern protested. *"Malikor's spell has us chained here. We can't retreat. Tyelin tell him!"*

"I suspect Jasiah has already worked out as much for himself," Tyelin said quietly. *"He plans on killing all of us."*

"I have, and I do, but not on purpose," I confirmed and released the spell I'd woven.

You have cast mimic, transforming your visage into that of Jasiah. Duration: 10 hours.

Since the Adjudicator had already dubbed me 'the Power Jasiah', I decided it best to keep up the façade.

"Why, you little—" Bern began.

"Look," I said, explaining as rapidly as I could, *"Leafbright's spell is an unlooked-for opportunity—and the surest path to victory. Even if every single Blade in this room perishes, which I doubt will be the case, you will still have the mercenaries waiting beyond the trapdoor. The sector will be yours."*

"What about our gear?" Tyelin asked softly.

"I get to take my pick. Call it the second half of my price." I paused, then added, *"But I promise to limit myself to only one item from every dead Blade."*

I was being magnanimous, I knew, but I didn't think my generosity was entirely unwarranted. The Blades would be doing their fair share to help, after all, and a little goodwill would not go amiss.

"And the Riders?" Bern demanded.

"Their gear I claim entirely," I replied firmly. *"Spoils of war and all that."*

Much to my surprise, Tyelin didn't argue. *"Go on. Do it,"* he said with a sigh.

Delaying no further, I did just that.

Mage's surprise activated. Spellhold casting released.
You have trigger-cast nature unchained.

I was watching Leafbright's face as I released the casting, and so, I didn't fail to observe her reaction.

An entire host of emotions ran riot across the elf's face. First, confusion. Then, shock. And finally, fear. Stunned into inaction, she watched helplessly as the surrounding vegetation came alive, but not under her direction.

The vines grew.

Wriggling free of their fellows, individual stalks pushed farther into the chamber, transforming the rugs of green covering the walls, roof, and floor into a deadly pincushion that extended not just upward, but downward, and even sideways.

A resounding cheer rose in the air.

It was the Riders—celebrating.

Most of them, it seemed, had not caught onto the fact that it was an enemy and not Leafbright who was transforming the already thick strands of vines into juggernauts of destruction. Some, though, were watching their Game alerts more closely.

"JASIAH?" Malikor bellowed, his voice echoing loudly across the chamber. "WHO IN DAMNATION IS JASIAH?"

"The rogue Power, the one who..." Leafbright whispered.

I didn't manage to catch the rest of what she said, but I'd heard enough to know she'd stopped chanting. Satisfied that the blight druid had been neutralized—somewhat, anyway—I resumed my advance on Zultan.

The vines shivered.

I smiled but didn't bother to look, knowing already what it portended: the pollen seeds were being released. And this time, there was no safe area. I'd not designated one. The only escape from the pollen's deadly touch was through the room's exits.

It occurred to me to wonder then how Leafbright had intended to use nature unchained. The spell did not distinguish between friend and foe, and if the druid had released it in the manner I had, just as many Riders would've died.

Maybe she planned on designating a safe spot around Malikor, one large enough to fit all the Riders. I shrugged aside the question. It didn't matter now. The spell was out of Leafbright's reach.

"Move, people," Tyelin shouted, his voice smaller and shriller than the paladin's but carrying across the chamber just the same. "Take your positions! Guard the doors."

All around the storeroom, the Blades disengaged with satisfying promptness and, like a gathering swarm of insects, raced for the exits.

"Stop them!" a Rider captain shouted.

But most of the Riders failed to heed his call. Instead of responding, they stared in bewildered fascination at the glowing mist of pollen whose not-so-tender mercies they were being subjected to—for the first time ever, perhaps.

Ignoring both sets of combatants, I fixed my gaze on Zultan. Although he looked as perplexed as Leafbright, he'd not stopped chanting. I would have to deal with him quickly.

"Ghost, you're following all this?" I asked as I completed my final preparations.

"I am."

"Good, then unmanifest. When the time's right, you can re-materialize in the room."

While both Ghost and I would feel the effects of nature unchained, I had my void defenses to protect me. The pyre wolf's draining bite would help her offset some of the damage from the spell, but her death magic skill was still new and couldn't be depended on entirely.

"On it, Prime," she replied.

Another Tyelin exploded, and again, it was Zultan's doing. Smirking in satisfaction, the orc began spellcasting anew.

My lips thinned unhappily. I couldn't delay further. Leaving Ghost to her task, I released the casting I held ready.

You have cast mass puppet.

Expanding outwards, strands of my will reached into the minds of Zultan's guard. Six of them lacked any mental defenses or mage shields, leaving them vulnerable to manipulation. Their mounts were similarly exposed as well.

Like a few of the other patrols, the orc's squad had brought along their companions. The creatures would be constrained within the limited space on offer in the storeroom, more so now after the vines' recent growth. But that concerned me little. I didn't need the hellbats to move far.

You have charmed 12 of 12 targets for 30 seconds.

All twelve of my designated targets fell victim to my spell. Better yet, my control over my minions was more nuanced than it had ever been before. Though my will overrode their own just as firmly, they retained enough of their minds to interpret complex commands.

"Attack," I ordered. *"Take down Zultan first and fight as a group."*

A pollen seed touched me.

A blight pollen has devoured 0.008% of your health (life magic damage reduced by 20% due to void armor).

A carnivorous vine has leeched a fraction of your life force.

Ignoring the damage, I watched my new minions. The bespelled hellbats had clamped their jaws around the closest of their surprised fellows. Disappointingly, puppetting the creatures seemed to have made no difference.

The players, on the other hand, were acting just as I hoped.

The bewitched fighters had formed a defensive line. Retreating behind it, the three archers fired shaft after shaft at their former squad leader—and from nearly point-blank range, too.

Not unexpectedly, their attacks did not get through the elite's shield. Still, the magic bubble encasing him dimmed noticeably.

Which, in turn, forced a response from Zultan.

"Fools!" the orc spat, breaking off from his spellcasting to berate the bespelled Riders. "How weak-willed are you idiots to fall prey to the Blades' trickery?"

"I don't think this is the Blades' doing," a mage objected, backing away from a tussling hellbat duo. "This spell is stronger than I've witnessed any of them cast." He licked his lips. "It must be that Power, the one who tripped—"

"The rogue Power?" Zultan scoffed. "*That* one has long since fled."

"But—"

The orc cut him off again. "If a Power was here, don't you think he would have taken a hand in the battle before this? No, this is the Blades' work. Nothing more."

Unlike the rest of the squad, Zultan appeared completely at ease, unaffected by both the turmoil in his own guard and the happenings in the wider battle.

Another salvo of arrows thudded in the elite's shield, causing it to dim further.

Zultan's eyes narrowed. "Can you wrench back control, Arie?"

"I've tried," the mage so addressed replied. "But the spellcaster's grip is too firm. I can't—"

"So be it," the orc said. Lowering his staff, he pointed it at the fighters. Spelled energy gathered at the end.

The fighters responded immediately, charging forward.

My brows rose in surprise, impressed by their initiative, even if it availed them little.

The first fighter staggered and fell, his legs burned out from under him by the flames fanning out from Zultan's staff. The other two managed to evade the attack, but the rest of the squad were pitching in too now. My minions would not survive long.

Still, they had done better than I'd expected, and the moment had come to launch my own assault.

Drawing psi, I launched myself forward.

You have cast windborne.
Ghost has unmanifested.

✳ ✳ ✳

You have cast whirlwind and piercing strike.

Invisible and borne up by a ramp of air, I closed the distance between me and my target at an astonishing rate. Despite this, I was ready when I reached my target and struck without pause.

First with ebonheart—

You have backstabbed your target for 10x more damage!

Your target's spell has blocked your attack.

—then with faithful.

You have backstabbed your target for 5x more damage!
Your target's spell has blocked your attack.

Then, I did it, again and again.
And again.
Each of my attacks was three times faster than usual, flawlessly executed, and courtesy of the windslide bearing me round and round, launched from a different direction. What's more, I remained hidden the entire time.

Multiple hostile entities have failed to detect you!
Multiple hostile entities have failed to detect you!
...

It took Zultan an entire second to realize he was under attack. Another to turn in my direction. Then yet another to realize the foe battering at his shield was invisible.
By then, his defenses were already in tatters.
Somersaulting off the windslide, I launched my final attack from above.

You have backstabbed your target for 5x more damage!
You have backstabbed your target for 5x more damage!
Your target's shield has been destroyed!

I landed lightly on my feet in front of the shocked orc. His eyes were wide with fear, and even though I was close enough to reach out and touch his nose, he still failed to spot me.
"What— Who...?"
Not troubling to respond, I buried ebonheart deep in his chest.

You have killed Zultan with a fatal blow.

You and Ghost have reached level 225!
You have slain a Sworn servant of Mammon!
You have passed a mental resistance check! Multiple hostile entities have failed to pierce your disguise.
Congratulations, Michael! You have successfully avoided Mammon's attention despite killing one of his Sworn servants.

Blood bubbled out of the orc's throat as he fell lifelessly to the floor. It was an ignominious end for the powerful caster, but I had little further time to spare him. Withdrawing my blade, I spun away and took stock of the battle.
The skirmish between my minions and the rest of the squad had not abated, but they, too, were of little consequence now, and I cast my gaze farther afield.
The greater part of the Blade and Rider forces were congregated around the north and east exits—the Riders trying to get out, and the Blades holding them at bay. I nodded approvingly. The Blades were performing the task I'd set them admirably.

"Good job with Zultan," Tyelin congratulated.

I glanced at the center of the room. Tyelin, Haiken, and Bern were still battling Malikor. The two Blade elites were not faring so well, though. None of Haiken's copies remained, and Bern was swaying listlessly. The pollen had claimed a heavy toll from both, I realized.

Malikor, though, was unaffected. None of the seeds seemed able to penetrate the heat haze surrounding the paladin. Each was burned away to nothing before it could land on his armored form.

As for Tyelin...

My eyes narrowed. He'd lost his copies, too, but the seeds were passing *through* the envoy as if he wasn't there.

Some sort of phasing ability? I wondered.

"Deal with Leafbright next," he added when I didn't respond to his initial remark.

My gaze flickered to the opposite side of the room. Leafbright had not moved since entering the chamber and in the interim had acquired an entourage of unshielded Riders.

Pollen fell on them as much as it did on everyone else in the room—barring the two envoys, of course, who, each in his own way, was proving immune. But despite this, Leafbright and the contingent of players around her were all at full health.

She's healing them, I thought, watching the constant pulses of soothing energy expanding outward from the druid.

I turned back to Tyelin. *"Will you be able to defeat Malikor on your own?"*

"No," he stated bluntly. *"But I will be able to keep him occupied long enough for you to deal with Leafbright—if you hurry."*

I nodded. *"Then, I better get to it."* Directing my attention inward, I addressed Ghost, *"Time for you to join the fight. Take out the druid's guards. I'll handle the elite myself."*

✳   ✳   ✳

Bern has died.

Void armor charge remaining: 80%. Void thief triggered.

Void negate activated! You are now immune to <u>nature unchained</u>. Stolen spell, <u>slime tentacles</u>, lost.

Void siphon failed to activate. You cannot siphon mana from yourself.

Your familiar has cast explosive manifest. She has 50% mana remaining.

Ghost emerged in the center of the tightly packed ranks of Riders, flinging some aloft, injuring others, but killing none. The pyre wolf was just getting started, though.

Bounding off the body of a downed fighter, she snapped the neck of a nearby lancer, gouged the chest of another, then plowed into a mage.

Her sudden appearance sent many of the Riders scattering, consequentially putting them temporarily out of range of Leafbright's aura. Focusing on the largest such group, I released my next spell.

You have cast slaysight.
You have paralyzed 8 of 10 targets for 60 seconds.

My gaze darted to Leafbright. The elite had not stopped channeling her healing spell. Nonetheless, she was watching my familiar with hawklike intensity.

"*Ghost?*" I prompted.

"*I got this,*" she replied.

I didn't ask if she was sure. There were no sureties in this fight, and I'd done what I could to assist her with the druid's escorts. Now it was time for me to focus on my own objective: Leafbright.

Gathering psi, I shadow blinked.

✳　✳　✳

You have teleported into Leafbright's shadow.

I emerged from the aether behind the elf, with both my blades raised and poised to strike. Amazingly, no magic bubble encased Leafbright. She'd left herself unshielded. I did not for a second believe that meant the druid was unprotected, though.

Ebonheart flew down.

But before the black sword could make contact, a whipcord thin growth shot out from the ground and wrapped tightly around its bladed end.

Leafbright has trigger-cast earthen defenses.
Your attack has been blocked.

In the midst of my attacking maneuver, I started in surprise.

The living rope looked for all the world like one of the vines I'd subverted—a thin, shriveled version, granted, but a vine, nonetheless—and I wondered just how in hells Leafbright had regained control of it. Then, too, there was the question of how the vine had *seen* ebonheart. The black blade was as invisible as the rest of me.

I wasn't about to let the mysteries halt my assault, though, and I brought faithful sweeping down from the left.

But I had scarce set the sword in motion before a second 'vine' shot out from the ground and wrapped around the blade, stopping the blow in the same manner the first had.

Your attack has been blocked.

Damnation, I cursed. Straining my arms, I attempted to force either of my blows to completion. To no avail. The vines gripped my blades too firmly. But they were not vines, I realized a heartbeat later. They were roots. Dark, brown roots that looked entirely too alive and aware.

The roots yanked.

My eyes widened in grim understanding.

Tightening my grip on the hilts of my blades, I resisted their pull. But the roots were stronger, and a moment later, both my swords were unceremoniously wrenched out of my hands.

You have lost faithful. <u>Recall</u> disabled.
You have lost ebonheart. Note: the hostile spell targeting you has temporarily overcome the soulbound properties of this blade. Ebonheart will return to your possession once the spell has dissipated.

I stared down at my empty palms, momentarily dumbstruck. I'd been disarmed, in a manner most unexpected. *What am I—*
"*Prime, watch out!*"

My head whipped up to see the bright shining length of a longsword whistling down. Throwing myself to the left, I rolled out of the way.

You have evaded Leafbright's attack.
A hostile entity has failed to detect you. You remain hidden.

I bounced back to my feet less than five yards away, berating myself for my stupidity. If not for Ghost's warning, I'd be dead. *No more distractions*, I told myself grimly.

Refocusing on Leafbright, I saw the druid had not stopped chanting. That did not prevent her from repeatedly sweeping her blade in glittering arcs over the spot I'd just occupied, though.

She still can't see me. My gaze flickered downward to my two swords, held fast against the ground by the wiry roots wound around them. *I'm not getting them back until I kill her.*

But I didn't need my blades to do that. I had other options—the most obvious one being my psi weapons. Gathering my will, I prepared my next spell.

You have cast astral shurikens.

The luminous psi creations formed in my hand, each a miniature three-pointed star. A deep shade of translucent violet, they throbbed as if eager to be used. Flicking my wrists, I sent them on their way.

Roots shot out to intercept them.

Your astral shuriken has injured 3 ironwood roots.
Your astral shuriken has injured 3 ironwood roots.

My eyes narrowed to slits. *Four* roots had emerged—the first pair to intercept the shurikens, and the second two to absorb the bounce damage. It implied an intelligence on the root's part—an awareness that could analyze incoming attacks and respond appropriately.

As the shurikens faded from existence, their spelled-energy spent, the roots retracted back into the ground. Leafbright was also looking over in my direction, but the druid's attention concerned me less than what I did next.

The roots appeared capable of blocking all incoming attacks. It didn't matter if the weapons were real or formed from psi, the roots would stop them all the same.

I could, of course, try wearing down the roots with my shurikens—the astral weapons had damaged the damnable things, after all—but I had no idea how many roots there were, and doing so would take precious time I didn't have. There was also shatter. But it, too, didn't lend itself to a quick resolution.

That left me with only one option.

Opening my backpack, I extracted my stygian blades. Sheathing them, I reached in again and removed ten stoppered bottles. This was no time to be conservative. I had to end things with Leafbright—and fast.

Glancing around me, I verified that the immediate vicinity was free of threat. The nearby Riders were either focused on Ghost or searching fruitlessly for me.

Right, let's be about it.

Winding back my arms, I flung free the bombs—all ten at once.

Predictably, the roots sprung up to intercept the projectiles. Ten roots for ten bombs. They failed to wrap themselves around the bombs though. Instead, the fragile bottles shattered on contact, just as they were meant to.

You have ignited 10 ice bombs, creating a freezing cloud.
10 ironwood roots have been <u>frozen</u> (duration: 3 seconds).
Leafbright has passed a magical resistance check! You have failed to freeze Leafbright.

The elven druid stopped chanting, her eyes narrowing in anger—or was that concern? Lowering her sword to point in my direction, she sent spell energy racing down its length. Clearly, I'd just been designated a bigger threat than the pollen.

I didn't stop what I was doing, though. I already had another double handful of bombs ready, and without delay, I flung them the way of the first.

Heart in mouth, I watched them go.

The bombs I'd just thrown were the last of my supply of ice bombs. If they didn't work...

More roots shot up.

I counted rapidly. *Eight,* I exulted. *There's only eight!*

A bar of liquid green hit me mid-center. Leafbright's spell.

A blight ray has hit you!
You have ignited 10 ice bombs, creating a freezing cloud.
8 ironwood roots have been <u>frozen</u> (duration: 3 seconds).

The corrosive bar driving into my chest didn't let up, piling on more and more magic damage. I paid it no heed. Gritting my teeth, I spun psi and stepped into the aether.

You have teleported into Leafbright's shadow.

I reappeared behind the elite. Bereft of a target, the blight ray petered out. With a puzzled look on her face, the druid lowered her sword.

"It's because I'm behind you," I whispered into her ear just before I slit her throat.

You have killed Leafbright with a fatal blow.
You and Ghost have reached level 226!
You have slain a Sworn servant of Mammon!

*   *   *

Haiken has died.

Letting the elf's corpse fall lifelessly to the ground, I retrieved faithful and ebonheart, then surveyed the battlefield.

Ghost had matters well in hand with her own foes, and at the north and east doorways, the fighting was waning as both sides' losses from the pollen steadily mounted.

The center of the storeroom was conspicuously empty, Tyelin and Malikor its only occupants. Bern and Haiken were both dead, having fallen at some point during my battles with Zultan and Leafbright. And now, even Tyelin looked in trouble.

Every so often, the Blade envoy's footing slipped as he dodged and weaved around the paladin. The errors were slight, barely perceptible, but they were present, nonetheless.

Malikor, on the other hand, looked none the worse. Frowning, I reached out and analyzed both envoys.

Malikor is at full health, his stamina is at 80%, and his mana is at 50%. Tyelin's health is at 40%, his psi is at 30%, and his stamina is at 15%.

My frown deepened. *"Tyelin, what in—"* I began stridently, then stopped myself.

Taking a deep breath, I began again. *"Tyelin, why is Malikor barely scratched?"* I asked diplomatically instead of what I really wanted to ask, which was: "What the hell have you and your people been doing all along?"

The envoy laughed hollowly. *"Why? It's because the bastard's Class is designed to soak up damage. His armor makes him nearly impervious, and what damage we have managed to inflict, his auras replenish."*

I pursed my lips. *"What was the plan to kill him?"* The envoy had to have had one.

"The plan *was to wear him down,"* Tyelin replied bitingly. *"The plan did not anticipate the early arrival of the others. The plan required Lune."*

The Blade stumbled again, and this time, the misstep nearly proved fatal as Malikor's broadsword came hurtling down. Somehow, though, Tyelin managed to twist out of the way in time.

Drawing psi, I renewed my buffs. *"Is that you?"* I asked as I strode closer. I still wasn't sure how I was going to intervene in the fight, but it was clear Tyelin wasn't going to be able to kill Malikor on his own.

"What?" Tyelin envoy, sounding perplexed by the question.

"Is that really you fighting Malikor and not one of your copies?" I clarified. *"You're not hiding in the shadows somewhere, are you?"*

The Blade Sworn chuckled even as he executed another acrobatic dodge. *"I wish,"* he said wearily. *"But I couldn't withdraw even if I wanted to. Keeping his foes chained in combat is another of Malikor's little specialties. Once you engage him, you, too, will be unable to withdraw."* His lips twisted wryly. *"Unless, of course, you're able to resist a tier six taunt-variant."*

"That's just great," I muttered, my mouth twisting sourly.

The flat of Malikor's blade struck Tyelin a glancing blow and sent the smaller player tumbling across the storeroom.

Watching the display impassively, I drew to a stop a healthy distance away. *"Then I guess you better tell me everything you know of Malikor's abilities while you still can."*

Picking himself up before the paladin could reach him, Tyelin reset his stance. *"Before I die you mean?"*

"Yes," I replied forthrightly.

"You won't intervene earlier?"

I folded my arms across my chest. *"No."*

Across the distance, I saw a smile steal onto the envoy's face. *"Still trying to hide yourself, Jasiah?"*

I shrugged. *"Something like that."* Which was true—as far as it went. No few of my abilities had been at play during the battle, but Tyelin had not seen enough to guess the entirety of what I was, and I wanted to keep it that way.

There was more to my reasoning than that, though.

Mostly, I didn't want to commit myself to a fight from which there could be no retreat, and after seeing how poorly Tyelin and his elites had fared against Malikor, I was beginning to doubt I would do any better.

If I couldn't see a way to kill Malikor, I would not engage. As simple as that.

This was not my fight, after all. And I was fairly confident I'd done enough to ensure the Riders lost control of the sector—in the short term, anyway. Given how many of the faction's players were dead or dying, it seemed almost a certainty that Malikor would not be able to reinforce the sector defenses before the one-hour deadline.

When I didn't add anything further, Tyelin sighed. *"Very well, you win. I'll tell you what I know."* He ducked beneath a whistling blow. *"To begin with, Malikor is not a damage dealer..."*

✱　✱　✱

You and Ghost have killed 1,271 hostile players.
You and Ghost have reached level 232!
Tyelin has died.

The Blade envoy managed to escape death for a full two minutes. He spent the entire time talking non-stop, providing me with what sounded like an exhaustive list of Malikor's capabilities. At the same time, my nature unchained spell whittled down the rest of the Blade and Rider forces to nearly nothing.

"It's done," Ghost said.

For a moment, I thought the pyre wolf meant Tyelin, but then I realized she was speaking of her own task: mopping up the survivors of the pollen— Riders *and* Blades. Tearing my gaze from the tall paladin who was prodding Tyelin's corpse with an armored boot, I studied my familiar.

Ghost's health is at 17%.

The pyre wolf's draining bite had been more successful than I expected, and as a result, her health was not as low as I feared. *"How are you?"*

"Good enough to keep fighting," she assured me.

I wasn't so sure about that, but instead of contesting the point, I threw her a health potion. *"Drink that."*

Catching the stone vial in her jaws, she bit down, sending the life-invigorating liquid coursing down her throat.

Ghost has restored herself to full health.

"Ah, better," she murmured, absently sidestepping a floating pollen.

"That reminds me." Closing my eyes, I momentarily turned my attention inward.

You have deactivated nature unchained. Mana remaining: 9%.

Malikor looked up as the vines shrank back to their original size. I couldn't see his expression—his visor was down—but I couldn't imagine it was anything pleasant.

A second later, the envoy swiveled around, searching the room with his gaze. "That your pet, Jasiah?" he sneered, his eyes coming to rest on the chamber's only other visible occupant—Ghost. "Go on, send it to fight me. It won't last any longer than the Blades, I promise."

Ignoring the Sworn, I retreated toward the north entrance where the pyre wolf waited. *"What's going on in the rest of the fort?"* I asked her.

"There are a few score Riders in the floors above," Ghost answered, *"but either they're not brave enough to enter the basement or they've been ordered not to. They've sealed the doors leading down and have set a guard on it."*

"Come on, Jasiah. Show yourself!" Malikor taunted. "Or are you too scared?"

"Are they enough to be a threat?" I asked.

"No," Ghost replied dismissively.

Resting his bloodied sword on his shoulder, Malikor began to stalk around the room. "The others may believe you a Power, but I know better. You're just a player pretending to be one."

Ghost's gaze slid beyond me to the Rider Sworn. *"Are you going to respond to him?*

I smiled. *"No. Let him stew a bit. It can't hurt."*

"Why are you still here?" the paladin demanded, his gaze flicking back to Ghost. "You must know by now that whatever ploy you and Blythe concocted has failed. Mammon will be here soon. You'd be wise to flee."

"He's lying," Ghost scoffed.

I nodded. *"I think so, too. Wherever Mammon is, he isn't coming to Malikor's rescue. He'd have been here before this otherwise."*

"Do we fight him?" Ghost asked, voicing the question on both our minds.

Lowering my head, I pondered the question. Killing Malikor would be neither quick nor easy.

The red-lacquered armor the paladin wore was a legendary set. It was highly resistant to piercing and would supposedly turn away even empowered backstabs. Worse yet, the set's helm granted Malikor mental immunity—rendering my psi abilities useless.

Then, too, there were the paladin's auras.

There was a whole host of them, from ones that repressed a foe's buffs to others that made Malikor resistant to hostile magics, from ones that slowly burned his enemies to others that healed him. In fact, almost everything about the paladin was designed to increase his survivability while simultaneously reducing that of his foes. In short, Malikor was a player who specialized in defense.

And therein lay the silver lining.

The Sworn was not similarly equipped when it came to offense. Other than the paladin's broadsword, taunts, and limited ability set, I had little to fear from him.

Of course, all of this was secondhand information derived from Tyelin.

But the Blade envoy had no reason to lie when it came to Malikor—and every reason to want me to succeed—and I'd seen for myself the impunity with which Mammon's Sworn strode the battlefield. Nothing had unduly troubled him, not nature unchained, not Haiken's daggers, and not even Tyelin's blades. There was no doubt in my mind: Malikor was one tough bastard.

Difficult to kill. But not impossible.

The most obvious way to defeat the paladin was to open the trapdoor and let in Tyelin's reserves. But such a fight—one against many—was exactly the kind of fight a player like Malikor would excel at.

Even with an army arrayed against him, Malikor would not fall easily, and with his foes packed tightly around him, the paladin's broadsword would not miss—could not miss.

There would be losses. *Significant* losses.

That, in turn, would hurt the Blades' chances of reclaiming the sector, and that was something I wanted to avoid. It made more sense for me to tackle Malikor on my own.

"We do," I said, answering Ghost at last. *"Not immediately, though."*

Tilting her head to the side, Ghost waited curiously for me to go on.

"We slay the remaining Riders in the fort, every last one of them and their hellbats," I explained grimly. *"Malikor is not going anywhere, nor is he likely to be reinforced from outside the sector, and the smug bastard is too arrogant to flee."* I nodded slowly, my strategy solidifying in my mind. *Yes,* I thought, *it'll work.*

"FIGHT ME, JASIAH!" Malikor roared suddenly.

"Why?" I asked mildly, using ventro to disguise my location.

Malikor turned to face the east doorway—the direction from which my voice had emerged. "Why?" he repeated. "Because you'll not claim this sector otherwise."

I laughed lightly. "What makes you think I want this sector?"

My response seemed to give the paladin pause, and while he pondered the question, I ushered Ghost out. *"Let's go."*

Turning tail, the pyre wolf slipped silently into the north corridor. The motion, unfortunately, still drew Malikor's attention, and he spun around. "Fleeing already, craven?" he jeered.

"Oh, never fear," I retorted, hanging back. "I'm still here."

"Where is your pet going?" he demanded.

"To slay the rest of your minions," I answered truthfully, curious to see how Malikor would respond.

The paladin did not budge, which did not surprise me at all.

"By the time I'm done here," I continued, "not a single Rider will remain standing."

"You will have to kill me for that," he declared, readying his sword as he turned about to face the east doorway again.

"I intend to."

"Cheap words," he sneered. "You can't kill me. I'm the—"

"'Devil Himself?'" I mocked.

"Yes!" he hissed, with no trace of embarrassment at the pretentious title.

"We'll see," I murmured. Drawing psi, I flung a casting at his mind.

You have cast slaysight.

You have failed to shatter your target's mental defenses. Malikor's mind is protected by the Helm of Asmod, rendering him immune to all mental manipulations of tier 6 and below.

My spell's failure was not unexpected. Casting it had still been necessary, both to test the truth of Tyelin's words and as a decoy.

"Ha!" Malikor crowed. "Your mind tricks won't—"

Leaving the paladin to spout nonsense at the uncaring room, I raced up the north corridor after Ghost.

I didn't expect my ploy to fool Malikor for long, but it didn't have to, and even a few seconds would've helped.

In the end, it was a full five minutes before the paladin bothered to leave the storeroom. Ghost and I spent that time killing the Riders guarding the entrance to the basement level.

Slaying them was almost laughably easy. Disorganized and leaderless, they put up only token resistance, and by the time Malikor arrived, we'd already moved onto the fort's upper floors.

We stayed one step ahead of the paladin the entire time, and twenty minutes later, when we were finally done, he was still raging about on the floor below.

You and Ghost have reached level 233!
Your shortswords has reached rank 21.
Ghost's magma maw has reached rank 8, her stygian claws and ash armor rank 9, and her death magic rank 5.

"Now what?" Ghost asked, interrupting my perusal of the recent Game messages.

"I restore my spent reserves while you keep watch," I replied. I would need to be at full strength if my plan against the Sworn was going to work. *"Malikor will be here soon."*

"You want to fight him here?" she asked. We were in the hellbat's feeding chamber, having just killed the last of the returned patrols' mounts.

I shrugged. *"This is as good a place as any."* I glanced around. The bodies of those Ghost and I had killed earlier still littered the chamber, but then again, it was less than two hours since I'd entered the fort—a fact I still found hard to believe. A lot had happened since.

I shook my head, dismissing my musings. I didn't have much time before Malikor appeared. Turning about, I headed for the closest stable. *"Let's hide in the pens until we're ready."*

✳ ✳ ✳

"Prime," Ghost said, nudging me with her nose. *"He's here."*
I opened my eyes, but not before checking the latest Game alerts.

You have replenished 72% of your mana.

"Where is he?" I rasped.
"Making his way up the stairs," Ghost replied.
"Damn," I muttered softly. There was no time to channel further. My existing reserves would have to do. Still, there was one other thing I could do to compensate for the lack.

Turning my attention inward, I used all nineteen of my new attribute points to increase the size of my mana pool.

Your Magic has increased to rank 65. Other modifiers: +20 from items.

It had been about time to increase my Magic anyway. Using nature unchained had drained my mana significantly—and consequently, my void armor, too. Nor was it the first time a stolen spell had done so.

In future, I could expect to steal many other such spells, and conceivably, some that were even more powerful. If I was going to employ them effectively, and without compromising my void armor, there was no two ways about it: I needed more mana. Then, too, the additional Magic would benefit Ghost.

Rising to my feet, I made for the door, renewing my buffs as I went.

"You remember the plan?" I murmured.

"Yes, Prime."

"Good. Then it's about time we finish this."

✳ ✳ ✳

Slipping into the feeding chamber, I waited in the exact center of the room. It did not take Malikor long to appear. Standing in the entrance to the stairwell, the paladin craned his neck from left to right.

Probably wondering in which stable I'm hiding.

"I'm here," I said quietly.

Malikor's helmed head swiveled in my direction, tracking my voice.

A hostile entity has failed to detect you!

"That right?" he sneered. "Or are these more of your games?"

"No games," I replied evenly. "I did what I said. You're the last living Rider in the fort."

Unsheathing his broadsword, the paladin strode boldly into the room. "Where's your pet?"

"Behind me," I said, as right on cue Ghost stalked in. Staying near to the door, she sat on her haunches, a silent if intimidating observer.

Malikor stomped closer. I didn't move.

"Are you going to show yourself?" he demanded.

"Why should I?" I shot back. "Can't you reveal me?"

The paladin didn't reply, but listening closely, I heard him mutter under his breath. Smiling, I waited.

Malikor has cast chained-to-combat.
You have passed a magical resistance check!
Malikor has failed to <u>reveal</u> you or afflict you with the debuff <u>no-retreat</u>!

I laughed loudly—and obnoxiously to be sure. "Why, look at that. You've failed."

Malikor didn't say anything, but I could feel the fury washing off him. Drawing to a halt, he started another chant.

Again, I did nothing, simply waited.

Malikor has cast chained-to-combat.
You have failed a magical resistance check!
Malikor has <u>revealed</u> you. You have been afflicted by the debuff <u>no-retreat</u> (cannot hide nor retreat further than 100 yards from the caster).

In one breath, the shadows and my cloak of invisibility were stripped away. I was unfazed though. This, too, was part of the plan.

"Got you!" Malikor snarled.

Saying nothing, I studied him from across the room.

Malikor didn't resume his advance, either my silence or nonchalance giving him pause. A second later, I felt a telltale tingle ripple across me.

You have passed a mental resistance check! An analyze attempt by a hostile entity has failed.

I chuckled. "*Another* failure, Malikor? Tsk. Tsk."

"Who are you?" the paladin all but growled. "Not a Blade, obviously—you let them die. And not anyone named Jasiah, definitely."

"Someone you should never have underestimated."

"What do you want here?" he asked, ignoring my response.

"What does any Power want?" I asked rhetorically. "Power."

"Trite nonsense." Shaking his head, he began crossing the room again. "You're no Power. If you were, I'd be dead by now."

I couldn't argue with that. Staying unmoving, I observed his approach. When he closed the distance to four yards, Malikor slammed his fists together.

Knowing what was coming, I waited.

Malikor has activated the auras: <u>hell's helping hand</u>, <u>doomshield</u>, <u>fiend's taunt</u>, <u>demonic subjugation</u>, and <u>devil's breath</u>.

Malikor is <u>hell-healed</u> and will regenerate 1% of his lost health per second.
Malikor is <u>doom-guarded</u> and has gained 90% resistance to all damage types.

You have failed a physical resistance check!
You have failed a magical resistance check!
You are <u>taunted</u> and cannot retreat further than 4 yards or attack anyone other than the caster.
You are <u>demon-touched</u>, suppressing the benefits of your buffs and auras by 80%.
You are <u>scalded</u> and will sustain 1% fire damage per second.

The triple auras hit me with palpable force, and for a moment, I struggled not to stagger or otherwise react. Still, something in my expression must have given me away.

"Felt that, did you?" Malikor asked so smugly I could almost see beneath his helm to the wide grin splitting his face.

I sighed. Tyelin had not lied. The paladin's buffs were as powerful as he'd described, and already, I could feel my skin itching as if suffering under the effects of a hot wind.

Still, I had a plan.

"*Now*, we fight," Malikor pronounced, raising his sword into guard position.

"Now, we fight," I agreed, drawing my blades.

✳   ✳   ✳

The paladin went on the offensive immediately, and almost before my swords were in hand, he attacked, bringing his weapon crashing down.

I sidestepped the blow easily, shielding my face as the heavy broadsword slammed into the floor beside me and sent chips of stone and sparks flying.

You are scalded. 0.45% health lost (fire damage taken reduced by 55% due to void armor).

Undeterred, Malikor heaved his broadsword around in a sweeping attack that left him wide open. I ducked beneath the blow ignoring the opportunity his exposed back presented, all but certain that my blades would fail to penetrate his armor. For now, my only objective was weathering the storm.

Completing his revolution, Malikor jabbed at me.

I hopped back and out of the way.

You are scalded. 0.45% health lost.

Pursuing me, the paladin executed a triple combo, slashing left, then right, before finally bringing his blade down in another chop from up high.

I bobbed, ducked, and weaved, evading all three successive blows.

You are scalded. 0.45% health lost.

Malikor raised his right leg. Knowing what that boded, I drew psi in readiness.

A split second later, the paladin's armored foot crashed back down with a resounding thud.

Malikor has cast demon stomp.

The floor heaved, sending tremors racing outward like ripples in a still pond. But before the first could touch me, I stepped through the aether.

You have teleported into Malikor's shadow.
You are scalded. 0.45% health lost.

The paladin whirled around, his broadsword leading the way. I bent backward until the back of my head touched the floor and watched the deadly blade pass overhead.

You have evaded a cleaving blow.
You are scalded. 0.45% health lost.

Stepping forward, the Sworn brought his sword back around, attempting to bash my nearly-prone form with its pommel. Letting my already taxed knees collapse beneath me, I fell flat and rolled out of the way.

Malikor turned, tracking me with his eyes as I leaped back to my feet, and for a drawn-out moment, we faced off on one another from four yards apart.

You are scalded. 0.45% health lost.

"You're as slippery as an eel," he said. "But as easily squashed."

I chuckled. "And you lumber about like an ox."

The Sworn fell silent, his thoughts opaque to me courtesy of his helm, but I imagined he was ruminating over my words—or trying to divine my strategy. "You cannot win," he said eventually.

"I beg to differ," I replied airily.

"Why has your pet not joined in?" he asked, his voice a mix of curiosity and suspicion.

"Now where would the fun be in that?"

"You think to use it to ambush me?" he asked, ignoring my quip. "Is that your plan? Well, it won't work."

I opened my mouth, a retort ready on my tongue, but before I could get it out, Game messages unfurled in my mind.

Void thief triggered.

You have acquired the channeled spell <u>devil's breath (stolen)</u> and will retain memory of it for the next 16 hours.

Devil's breath (stolen) is a tier 6 spell that summons the sweltering winds of the hellish planes to the caster's aid, encasing him in a heat haze 5 yards in radius. When hostiles enter the field of effect, they will be <u>scalded</u>. Devil's breath will remain manifested for as long as the caster channels the spell.

Void siphon activated!

A conduit has been forged between you and Malikor, allowing you to steal mana from your foe whenever he casts a spell at you.

Void negate activated!

Your void armor has learned to completely resist the effects of Devil's breath, granting you effective immunity against the spell for the next 16 hours. Note that your void armor must be operational in order for negate to function.

You are no longer <u>scalded</u>.

Void armor charge remaining: 52%. Health remaining: 81%.

I smiled beatifically.

The sweltering heat had vanished as if it had never been. It was still present all around me, but it no longer had the power to touch me.

Seeing my look, Malikor must have mistaken it for mockery because the next instant, he resumed his offensive. Playing my part, I ducked beneath his first slashing blow, sidestepped the next, and swayed out of the way of the third.

You have failed a magical resistance check! Demon-touched reinforced.

You have siphoned a portion of Malikor's mana. Void armor charges remaining: 53%.

This time around, I did better to control my expression, and my face betrayed no trace of my delight at the Game message.

The paladin ground to a stop. "How did you do that?"

I'd done nothing, of course.

It was my void armor, working to siphon my foe's mana. I'd been pretty sure Malikor's devil's breath aura wouldn't trigger siphon—it being negated—but I'd been less sure about how my void armor would react to the Sworn's *other* auras. It seemed I'd gauged correctly, though.

Siphon *did* work against channeling spells.

My strategy, of course, was no different from the Blades. Like them, I intended to wear Malikor down.

Only I could do it faster than they ever could.

Demon-touched reinforced. Mana siphoned.

"Tell me!" Malikor demanded, waving his sword threateningly.

"Tell you what?" I asked innocently.

Even better, it seemed that the Adjudicator had not seen fit to spell things out for Malikor. I'd suspected that might be the case. After all, none of my previous foes had ever caught onto the fact that I'd stolen their castings before, and Malikor, too, appeared none the wiser that his devil's breath wasn't working.

"How did you *siphon* my mana?" he asked, almost spitting out the words.

Staying silent, I watched Malikor carefully. Would he realize there was a link between his auras and what I was doing?

I hope not. Because if he does, this is going to take a whole lot longer than I planned for.

Demon-touched reinforced. Mana siphoned.

"STOP IT!" Malikor roared.

"No," I replied succinctly.

It was the last straw. Throwing caution to the wind, the paladin charged. I was ready for him though and dodged out of the way.

Spinning on his heel, Malikor attacked again. Once more, I evaded him, a crooked grin working its way onto my face.

That only seemed to enrage Malikor further. Stepping up the tempo to a blistering pace, he came at me with everything he had.

It left no more time for further thought. Only move and counter-move.

Our exchanges were nerve-wrenching, but not beyond my ability to navigate, and for every blow the paladin threw, I found a way to avoid being hit. Time was on my side, and for now, I need not do more than dodge.

Sooner or later, Malikor would run out of mana.

And then it would be my turn to pounce.

* * *

Malikor has 21% mana remaining.

While the big paladin was clueless about how I was siphoning his mana, he was not so shortsighted as to not realize he couldn't let that happen.

This was why, when his mana hit twenty percent, Malikor abruptly broke off from his relentless onslaught and backed away. Reaching into the belt at his hip, he withdrew something.

A stone vial.

I recognized it immediately for what it was. A mana potion. *"Now, Ghost!"* I yelled, dashing forward.

I took one step in the real, another in the aether, then I was back out again.

You have teleported 2 yards.

Distracted both by the vial in his hand and by my abrupt change in position, Malikor was unable to stop me from striking my first blow of the battle.

It was not the paladin I aimed for, though, but the vial in his hand.

You have destroyed a full mana potion.

"You misbegotten worm!" Malikor yelled, lashing out wildly with his broadsword in response. "I swear I'll—"

Ghost has knocked down Malikor.

The paladin didn't get to finish uttering whatever threat he had in mind as the big pyre wolf—more than a match for the Sworn in size—bowled into him from behind. She backed away immediately. As did I. Neither of us was so foolish as to try following up on her attack.

Ghost has entered the field of effect of <u>fiend's taunt</u>, <u>demonic subjugation</u>, and <u>devil's breath</u>. She is taunted, demon-touched, and scalded.

I ignored the Game message as I watched Malikor climb back up. I'd expected it. Ghost was now as chained to combat as I was, but that was not an issue—one way or the other, the fight would end soon. Nor was devil's breath a problem either. As high as the pyre wolf's fire resistance was, she'd suffer only minimal damage from being scalded.

"What did that help?" the paladin growled as he finally regained his feet. "You still can't hurt me, and I have many more potions."

"Which we'll stop you from drinking," I replied evenly. "Every time."

Having no answer, the Sworn charged, and our battle resumed.

✳ ✳ ✳

For the next minute, we fought in near silence, with only our grunts of exertion and the clash of steel against stone to mar the peace. Malikor tried drinking a potion five more times, and just like I promised, we stopped him every time.

Malikor has 15% mana remaining.

Frustrated, the Sworn tried turning his ire on Ghost, but with me running interference, the pyre wolf was able to dodge his attacks as successfully as I had.
Then, Malikor changed tactics.

Malikor has deactivated the auras: <u>hell's helping hand</u>, <u>fiend's taunt</u>, and <u>devil's breath</u>.

"Press him," I growled. *"He's going to try and escape."* That could be the only reason the paladin had let his taunt lapse, and indeed, Malikor was already backing away, the words of another spell spewing from his lips.
Ghost and I were not about to let him finish, though.
Stepping through the aether, I re-emerged on the paladin's shoulders and promptly wrapped my arms around his visored face, blinding him.
Malikor stilled, but he didn't stop chanting. Then, he began to bring his broadsword up, no doubt intending to cut me to ribbons.
That's when Ghost hit from the flank.

Your familiar has knocked down Malikor.
Ghost has interrupted her target. Malikor's town portal spell has been disrupted!

I somersaulted off the paladin as he went airborne to land lightly on my feet a few feet away. "A portal spell, Malikor? Really? I'm surprised you have it in you."
The downed Sworn's faceless visor turned in my direction. "You'll pay for this, you worm!" he hissed. "Mammon will see to it."
I shrugged. "Perhaps. Or perhaps not. But no one is saving you today."

Malikor has 5% mana remaining.

Lumbering back to his feet, Malikor glared at me. I said nothing, waiting. Finally, the paladin did the only thing he could: he stopped spell-channeling entirely.

Malikor has deactivated the auras: <u>doomshield</u> and <u>demonic subjugation</u>.

"About time," I murmured.
"You still can't hurt me," Malikor sneered. "Even without my magic, those puny blades of yours are no match for my armor."
"That may be so," I agreed. "But my stygian friend will fare better, I dare say. And then there is always this." On the tail end of my words, I released the casting I'd been holding ready.

You have activated the aura: <u>devil's breath</u> (stolen).
Malikor has failed a magical resistance check!
Malikor is <u>scalded</u> and will sustain 1% fire damage per second.

The Sworn froze. "Th-that's... that's my spell!" he whispered. "You... stole it?" Realization washed over him. "You must've. Just like you did Leafbright's. You *are* a thief!"

I smiled. "I am indeed." Hefting my blades, I advanced on Malikor. "Now, let's finish this."

Things did not end there, of course.

The paladin kept fighting, sparingly using his remaining mana to activate hell's helping hand to heal himself, but the battle's outcome was a foregone conclusion.

And we both knew it.

So, it was no surprise, when a few minutes later, the big Sworn sagged lifelessly to the floor.

Malikor has died.
You have slain an envoy of Mammon.
Congratulations, Michael! You have successfully avoided Mammon's attention despite killing one of his Sworn servants.

You have fulfilled all your Pact obligations to the envoy, Tyelin. The Power Blythe is now Game-bound to provide your persona, Jasiah, with a 200,000 gold promissory note within 24 hours.

You and Ghost have reached level 235!
Your telekinesis has reached rank 19, your channeling rank 21, and your deception rank 23.

"That was easier than I expected," Ghost said, coming up beside me to study the corpse at my feet.

I nodded. Remarkably neither of us had suffered so much as a single blow. *"It's only because we chose the right strategy."* I paused, then conceded reluctantly, *"And for that we have Tyelin to thank. If not for the information he provided, things may have turned out differently."*

Ghost wrinkled her nose. *"I still don't trust him."*

I smiled. *"Me either."*

Crouching on my haunches, I studied the dead envoy. Malikor had been right about one thing. Even without his auras, my blades hadn't been able to penetrate his plate armor. *It's a pity it's heavy armor,* I thought.

"Don't forget the color," Ghost added. *"That red is horrible."*

"There's that, too," I said, chuckling. *"Still, I'm sure we can find a use for it."* Setting my hand to the paladin's helm, I tugged it free.

I had a lot to loot, and the sooner I got started, the better.

✳　✳　✳

It did not take me long to strip the envoy of his armor, and when I was done, I had all five component pieces safely packed away in my bag of holding.

You have acquired the legendary set, <u>Asmod's Suit</u>. Like all legendary items, this set is indestructible and is said to have been the favored battle dress of the renowned hellish commander Asmod. The armor is famed not only for its distinctive blood-red coloring but for the relentlessness of those wearing it.

Asmod's Suit increases your Constitution by +50, your Strength by +50, and your Dexterity by +50 when all pieces are equipped. Additionally, the set grants you the trait: <u>unstoppable</u>, which grants the user immunity to all forms of stuns, paralysis, and entanglement abilities.

I pursed my lips as I considered the armor. The set's bonus trait and attributes alone made it worthy of its legendary title, and that was not even accounting for the benefits provided by each individual piece.

"Malikor is going to miss it," Ghost said.

I laughed. "Oh, he definitely is," I said, considering the fallen envoy's corpse again. Now that I'd removed Malikor's armor, the rich assortment of gear he'd worn beneath was also plain to see. "I suspect, though, it's not the only thing he is going to miss."

Reaching down, I removed a pair of silk-soft gloves from the corpse's cold hands.

You have acquired the rank 6 item: <u>healer's friend</u>. This pair of gloves doubles the effectiveness of any touch-based healing spells you cast. It requires a minimum Magic or Faith of 24 to use.

"Hmm," I mused. The gloves, while interesting, were of no immediate use to me. Stowing them away, I tugged free a gem-encrusted ring.

You have acquired the rank 7 artifact: the <u>Devil's Signet</u>. This ring may only be worn by a Sworn of Mammon. You are unable to discern its other properties. They have been shielded from inspection.

I frowned.

"What's wrong?" Ghost asked, noticing my expression.

"This ring... it's rank *seven*. That's better than any piece of gear I'm wearing." Excluding my own legendary items, of course.

"So, what's the problem?"

"Most of the ring's properties are shielded," I replied. "The only thing I can discern is that it's meant for Mammon's Sworn." I rolled the signet around in my hand. "I've never run across such an item before..." I paused, realizing the denial was false even as it passed my lips. "Actually, I have. Your spirit vessel is similarly shielded."

"The Cloak of the Reach, you mean?"

I nodded. "I will have to remember to ask Adriel about how she managed that." And if the same effect could be applied to the rest of my gear. Thinking about it further, I realized it made sense to obscure an artifact's properties. It added an extra layer of protection to looted items, hiding as it did their true worth.

Reaching out, I yanked off another of Malikor's rings.

You have acquired the rank 7 item: a <u>Brimstone</u>. This ring may only be worn by a Sworn of Mammon. You are unable to discern its other properties. They have been shielded from inspection.

"Huh."

"What?"

"This ring's properties are also hidden."

Ghost's daze drifted back to the corpse. *"Do you think the rest of his gear is like that?"*

I sighed, suspecting that that might be the case. "Only one way to find out."

Bending down, I got to work.

✳   ✳   ✳

You have acquired a cache of 21 miscellaneous items reserved for use by Mammon's Sworn.

You have acquired the champion's belt, +10 Strength.

In the end, my fears proved well-founded.

Barring one other piece, the rest of Malikor's items were unusable by any but Mammon's Sworn. Nevertheless, I still looted them. I also failed to find the envoy's broadsword amongst his remains. Which could mean only one thing: it was soulbound.

My work done, I rose to my feet. From one perspective, the loot was... disappointing. I couldn't use much of Malikor's gear, but I could still sell it.

Unfortunately, the list of potential buyers was vanishingly small. *It'll be a tricky sale,* I thought, a smile stealing onto my face at the prospect.

I turned to Ghost. "Let's go—"

A Game message flashed for attention.

Turning my attention inward, I perused its contents.

You have completed the task: <u>The Tenets of Wolf</u>! You have responded to the Blades' treachery, not with unbridled fury, nor with a forgiving heart, but instead, you have exacted a price for their betrayal.

Those Blades you did not kill outright, you let die. Yet, you still aided the faction to achieve their aims in the sector by forming a Pact with their envoy and slaying their foes as ruthlessly as you did them.

Well done, scion. You have tempered your desire for vengeance but, at the same time, still answered the slight to Wolf. In the process, you have established <u>Just Retribution</u> as a core tenet of your new House. Staying true to this principle in future will see your Wolf Mark deepen.

Straying from it will see your Mark weaken.

Just retribution. I smiled. *I like that.*

Surveying the room, I considered the other corpses in the feeding chamber. I doubted most of them had Sworn-locked items and looting them would likely yield many usable—if lower-valued—items.

"Do we search the others, too?" Ghost asked, guessing my thoughts.

I shook my head. "Maybe later. For now, we have to find Jone. It's past time we finished matters in this sector."

✴ ✴ ✴

Jone was no longer in the kitchen, but as deserted as the fort now was, Ghost and I had no trouble locating him.

"Wait here," I said to Ghost as we drew to a stop outside the closed doors of his quarters. *"Let's not scare him just yet."*

The pyre wolf's ears pricked up. *"Just yet?"*

One corner of my lips twitched upward. *"That's right, just yet. If he proves... uncooperative, doing so may become necessary."*

The pyre wolf sat down on her haunches. *"I'll keep watch."*

Nodding in agreement, I shoved open the door and stepped into the small room beyond. Jone was at the far end, a knife clutched in a white-knuckled grip. The Blade's spy was a man past his prime, with a balding head and a face lined by many years spent outdoors.

He certainly looks like the fisherman Tyelin claims him to be, I thought.

"Who-o are y-you?" Jone stuttered.

"A friend," I replied in a soothing tone as I advanced farther into the room.

Jone shrank back.

Drawing to a stop before the frightened man, I held out Tyelin's package. "I'm here to deliver this."

Consternation flickered across his face. "Wh-what's that?" he asked, his panic easing in the face of my non-threatening posture.

"Cynacilin," I replied.

The fisherman's confusion did not lessen. "What's cynacilin?"

I frowned. "Poison."

Jone's eyes widened as his fear returned. "Y-you're here to k-kill m-me?"

I rolled my eyes. "No. The poison is not meant for you," I said, enunciating each word slowly. "This is a delivery only." It was becoming evident that whatever else Jone was, he was no more than a patsy in Tyelin's scheme. The man didn't even know what I was talking about!

I shoved the white packet closer to him. "Take it."

Once again, Jone made no move to comply.

"Go on, take it. It's safe," I urged. "Tyelin sent me."

Something besides fear grew in the fisherman's eyes. "You're not a Rider?"

I shook my head.

"And you know what I am?"

"Tyelin's spy. Yes."

Jone's gaze flickered back to the packet in my hands. "What am I supposed to do with it?"

I shrugged. "I have no idea, but the Blade envoy wants you to have it."

The repeated invoking of Tyelin's name seemed to do the trick, and this time around, Jone did not refuse as I placed the cynacilin in his hands.

You have lost a packet of <u>unrefined cynacilin powder</u>.

You have fulfilled all your Pact obligations to the envoy, Tyelin. The Power Blythe is now Game-bound to grant your persona, Jasiah, a single favor at a time and place of your choosing. The favor will be equivalent to the worth of sector 75,172.

I exhaled in relief. I'd done it, I had finally completed Tyelin's bogus Pact, and now his Power would be forced to honor the deal we'd struck.

Poor Tyelin. Blythe is not going to be happy with him.

Ghost snorted, eavesdropping on my thoughts. *"It's no more than he deserves."*

Before I could respond, Jone spoke. "Do I open it?"

Glancing at the fisherman, I saw he was staring hard at the innocuous parcel he held.

"Better not," I murmured, then smoothly swiped the packet from his hands.

You have acquired a packet of <u>unrefined cynacilin powder</u>.

"Why did you—" the startled fisherman began.

But I was already halfway out of the room. "Don't worry about it," I called as I closed the door behind me. "It's better you don't know."

CHAPTER 478: TO THE VICTOR GOES THE SPOILS

My next stop after Jone was the storeroom, and I wasted no time hurrying in its direction. I was not on the clock per se, but there were too many unknowns in the current situation for me to be comfortable with taking matters slowly.

With my luck, Mammon might finally decide to turn up. Or Riders from another sector. Or Blythe. Or even those Reapers Tyelin had mentioned.

I shook my head, imagining the possibilities. I wanted no more surprises. And that meant doing things in a strict order of priority so I could leave on a moment's notice if it became necessary.

Reaching the storeroom, I headed straight for Tyelin's corpse, half-expecting to find it missing.

But no, the Blade envoy's remains were still present—and exactly how Malikor had left it. Bending over the corpse, I studied his gear.

... This shirt may only be worn by a Sworn of Blythe. You are unable to discern its other properties.

... This ring may only be worn by a Sworn of Blythe. You are unable to discern its other properties.

... This blade may only be wielded by a Sworn of Blythe. You are unable to discern its other properties.

I groaned unhappily. First, Malikor. Now, Tyelin.

"Damnable Sworn-locked items," I grumbled. Still, there was nothing I could do to alter the situation. Curbing my disappointment, I focused on the equipment that *wasn't* Sworn-locked.

There were five such items.

Four of which were legendary pieces.

That implied something, but I dismissed the thought for later consideration, too fascinated by the pieces themselves. One item in particular held my attention, and I knew immediately it was the one I would take.

Unfastening the piece, I tugged it free from the corpse.

You have acquired a <u>Tiamaten Scalemail Vest</u>. This item is indestructible and is part of the legendary light armor set: <u>Tiamat's Shadow.</u>

Tiamat was one of the last black dragons. Though slain many eons ago, he is still unforgotten. The slayers of the great dragon harvested every last ingredient from his corpse, fashioning items from them that to this day remain unbroken.

This vest has been crafted from black dragonscale hide, making it both lightweight and indestructible while at the same time affording its user protection that is nearly on par with a heavy armor suit. It reduces the physical damage you sustain by 32%, increases your Constitution by +4

ranks, and grants you the <u>slip-through-shadows</u> trait, which increases your chance of evading area-of-effect damage by +20%.

Find the other 4 pieces in the set to increase the benefits received.

"Well, well," I murmured, hefting the vest in my hand. It was barely as heavy as ebonheart, yet provided nearly the same damage reduction as *all* five pieces of the ranger's kit I currently wore.

I definitely need to acquire the full set.

My gaze flickered back to Tyelin's body. The Blade envoy hadn't been wearing the full Tiamaten set, but he *did* have its arm and leg pieces, too, and for a moment—just a moment—I was tempted to strip them off the corpse as well.

No can do.

A promise was a promise. Turning away regretfully, I went looking for the other elites' corpses.

✳   ✳   ✳

You have unequipped a ranger's kit vest, losing 16% physical damage reduction and the set bonus lost: 4 ranks of stealth.

You have equipped a <u>tiamaten scalemail vest</u>, gaining +32% physical damage reduction, +4 Constitution, and the slip-through-shadows trait.

As was the case with the envoys, the gear of Haiken, Bern, Lune, Auris, Leafbright, and Zultan was also mostly Sworn-locked.

"Bloody hell," I cursed, no longer able to ignore the disturbing pattern revealed.

It seemed the Game's elite had ways of protecting their equipment. They couldn't stop others from looting their gear, but they *could* definitely stop unfriendly players from using them.

Sitting down cross-legged, I studied the two piles before me. The first, consisting of four items, were the pieces I'd selected from the Blade elites, and the second, much larger pile, was the Rider elites' possessions.

I picked up the first item, the one I'd looted from Haiken.

You have acquired the rank 5 item: the <u>scoundrel's wristband</u>. This item can be used to configure traps of master tier and below. Additionally, it grants you +5 ranks in thieving.

Each trap can consist of a maximum of 5 components, using any combination of triggers, elements, guides, and keys. Keys can be used to set a trap as dormant. Dormant traps are harder to detect and will not trigger under any circumstances.

Currently stored trap-making crystals: 0 / 300.

Available <u>triggers</u>: pressure plates (for use on floors), sound glasses (omnidirectional), tripwires (between two points), motion pins (cone), remote control (manual trigger), spell detectors (omnidirectional), and psi detectors (omnidirectional).

Available <u>elements</u>: lightning, poison clouds, fire, spring-coiled daggers, bear-trap clamps, small explosives, blots of darkness, ice, spiked pits, and hallucinogenic mists.

Available <u>guides</u>: reflect (redirects an element in the desired direction), split (divide and reflect an element), and funnel (concentrates and directs an element in the desired direction). Note: guides only stay materialized for 5 seconds.

Available <u>keys</u>: remote keys (manual activation) and timed keys (delay-based activation).

As expected, the rank five scoundrel's wristband was an upgrade over my own tier four item. It stored more components and provided greater options when it came to triggers, elements, and the overall trap configurations.

The biggest difference, though, was the addition of the trap keys whose use I'd observed earlier. They, more than anything else, would increase the versatility of my traps. However, since the wristband was currently empty of trap crystals, equipping it would have to wait for later.

Stowing away the item, I picked up the piece I'd looted from Bern. He'd actually had a better wristband than the one I'd taken from Haiken. However, something else on the rogue's corpse had piqued my interest far more.

Picking up the item in question, I inspected it anew.

You have acquired the <u>Seeking Eye of Sylvana</u>. This item is indestructible and is part of the <u>Sylvanain Hunter Seeker</u> legendary device set.

There was no more formidable hunter in the annals of history than Sylvana. She is said to have killed thousands of players and elite monsters during her lifetime. Yet it is not for the quantity of her kills that the huntress is famous but for her success rate. No prey ever escaped once Sylvana was on its trail. The huntress herself attributed much of her success to the hunter-seekers she forged with her own hands.

This item is a tracking and scouting device designed to find and follow a subject by a variety of means, including scent, sight, sound, spirit signature, or mental imprint. The Eye itself is invisible and has no signature or imprint of its own, making it virtually undetectable.

And while the device can communicate and travel an unlimited distance from its owner—within the same sector—its internal store of mana is fixed. After 4 hours of continuous use, the Eye will automatically deactivate, revealing itself.

Available <u>modes of operation</u>: tracking mode (where the Eye automatically searches for the target spirit signature or mental imprint) and scout mode (in which the Eye is manually piloted). Note: the device is more vulnerable to detection in scout mode.

Find the other piece in the set to increase the benefits received.

I rolled the small orb around in the palm of my hand. The artifact was small enough to fit, but in no other way did it resemble an actual eye. Currently inert—and very much visible—the orb was dull gray and inscribed with tiny runes. Rubbing my chin, I considered the small object more carefully.

In many ways, the Seeking Eye was identical to the hunter eyes the mantises in Nexus had used—or rather, the mantises' devices were replicas of it.

Attempted replicas.

There was no doubt the artifact I held in my hand was the superior product. Its invisibility alone assured that. Then there was the Eye's other half, the piece needed to complete the legendary set. I could only imagine how powerful the device would become thereafter.

Let's see it in action, I thought, unable to rein in my anticipation. Reaching out to the orb with my mind, I willed it to life.

You have failed to activate a Seeking Eye.

Before the Eye can be used it must be attuned to its new owner. Equip the item to begin the process. Expected duration: 8 hours.

"Ah damn," I muttered. Testing my new toy would have to wait for later, and I slipped it into one of my pockets.

You have equipped a Seeking Eye. Attunement commenced.

Ignoring the Adjudicator's message, I picked up the next item: Lune's artifact.

Only for it to fall out of my hand.

Huh? I thought, staring in surprise at the item on the floor. It was not clumsiness that had caused me to drop it.

What's going on now?

A Game alert was flashing for attention, and hoping for enlightenment, I focused on it.

Warning: You cannot equip this item at this time. Doing so will exceed the maximum number of 30 wearable Game items.

Note: consumables do not count toward this limit.

Urgh.

I'd known about the thirty-item limit, of course. Ceruvax and Adriel had mentioned it during their lectures on the Game, but I had thought nothing of it at the time, thinking myself nowhere close to reaching it. But examining the Game gear I had equipped—non-player items didn't count—I saw that I was indeed on the limit and sighed again.

"Something the matter, Prime?" Ghost asked from where she sat resting near the north entrance.

I waved aside her concern. *"Nothing important. I just have to unequip some things,"* I grumbled.

Inspecting my gear, I quickly identified a few older pieces that could be removed from active use.

You have unequipped the <u>gift of the unbound</u>, losing immunity to tier 2 entanglement spells, the <u>band of stillness</u>, losing immunity to tier 2 mind spells, and a <u>pioneer's compass</u>.

Equipped items: 27 / 30.

Three free item slots were not enough for comfort, but for now, they would have to do. When time permitted, I would review my loadout in more detail. Storing the unequipped items in my backpack, I picked up the dropped item again.

This time, the Game did not protest.

You have acquired the rank 6 item: <u>icefang</u>. This item increases your water resistance by +20% and grants you the ability: <u>icy steel</u>. Icy steel is an activated ability that allows you to summon a +6 magical weapon of your choice into being. The weapon will be formed wholly from ice and will deal water damage.

Lune's item—cold to the touch and resembling an actual fang—was straightforward enough. It allowed me to summon a magical blade that would inflict more damage than either faithful or ebonheart. It was less for this that I had chosen it, though, and more for the fact that it gave me another attacking option. The additional water resistance was nice, too.

Slipping the fang into another pocket, I inspected Auris' item next. It was a wallet-like object made of leather and about the size of a large book.

You have acquired an <u>elite poisoning kit</u>. This is a rank 6 item capable of storing, manufacturing, and applying tier 6 poisons as well as the alchemical ingredients employed in their creation. Additionally, the kit grants you +6 ranks in poisoning.
Stored poisons: 23 / 100. Stored ingredients: 301 / 500.

The kit was of little use to me, of course, but it would serve Nyra well, if not today, then someday in the future, and I stored it in my bag of holding.

Right, that takes care of the Blades' loot. Turning fractionally, I faced the remaining pile. *Now for the Riders'.*

You have acquired a cache of 3 legendary items and 50 miscellaneous items reserved for use by Mammon's Sworn.

Unsurprisingly, Leafbright and Zultan's gear was less suited to me. That applied to most of their non-Sworn gear, too. Still, there were two items that I found noteworthy.

You have acquired a <u>bishop's ring</u>, +12 Faith.
You have acquired the rank 7 item: <u>Jeweled Pet</u>. This ring strengthens the bond between a player and his pet, be they a companion, familiar, or tamed creature. While wearing the ring, your primary pet gains the trait: <u>mirrored jewelry.</u>
Mirrored jewelry shares with your pet many of the benefits you derive from rank 7 and below jeweled items—rings, bracelets, necklaces, and such. Note: not all benefits are transferable.
This item requires a minimum Magic or Faith of 50 to use.

The bishop's ring was nice, and before realizing how close I was to the item limit, I would've equipped it without a second's thought. If nothing else, the ring would have increased the size of my mana pool. Now, though, I simply stored it in my backpack.

The Jeweled Pet ring, which I'd taken from Leafbright, was more intriguing. For starters, it was the only usable rank seven artifact I'd come across—*ever*. For another, its minimum requirements had more than doubled from that of a rank six item. Beyond that, the ring offered some interesting possibilities for Ghost—assuming it worked the way I imagined it would.

Only one way to find out.

"Ghost," I murmured, holding the ring in the palm of my hand, *"you're ready for this?"*

The pyre wolf yawned, revealing glistening magma teeth. "Yes, Prime," she replied, sounding more disinterested than I thought she had any right to be. We'd discussed the ring earlier, but the possibilities it offered didn't seem to intrigue Ghost as much as it did me.

Shaking my head at her indifference—how could the ring's potential not excite her?—I put it on.

You have equipped the <u>Jeweled Pet</u> ring, granting your familiar the mirrored jewelry trait.

Ghost has gained +8 Strength, +4 Perception, +8 Constitution, +4 Mind, +10 Magic, +6% physical damage reduction, and the ability: spellhold. Note: the benefits from your psi bracelet, farspeaker bracelet, simple potion bracelet, and aetherstone bracelet are not transferable.

"Ah," I exclaimed, rocking back. Ghost had learned spellhold, just as I'd hoped. In of itself, spellhold was of limited use to the pyre wolf—she only had one spell to store—but it was the fact that she'd gained the ability in the first place that interested me.

It meant I could expand Ghost's repertoire of spells using items *I* wore. That was not all, though.

There was something else to consider. A unique possibility that only spellhold offered. *Might offer,* I amended. Much depended on how the ability was being shared between us.

"Ghost, how do you feel?"

"Stronger. Faster. Tougher," she replied. *"You were right, Prime. The differences are appreciable."*

I nodded. *"What about spellhold? Do you understand the spell?"*

"I do."

"Use it," I instructed.

Her ears pricked up in confusion. *"Use it? Why?"*

"You'll see in a moment." I hope.

"But I only have one spell," she protested, *"and it's not even something—"*

"I know. But humor me, please. Go ahead and store draining bite."

"Alright," she replied, sounding dubious.

Stopping myself from fiddling, I waited for the expectant Game message. It was not long in coming.

Spellhold enchantment activated.

Ghost has successfully stored the <u>draining bite</u> spell in the ring, mage's surprise. This spell may now be trigger-cast when required.

"Done," Ghost pronounced.

I nodded excitedly. *"It worked!"*

Ghost scratched the back of one ear with a hindleg. *"I don't understand the reason for all the fuss, Prime,"* she confessed. *"I can activate draining bite through that ring of yours instead of directly. So what? How does that help me?"*

"It doesn't," I breathed. *"But, in this instance, it may help me."* Exhaling in anticipation, I reached into the ring on my right hand and released the spell stored within.

You have trigger-cast draining bite.
You can now leech a portion of your foes' life with each bite.

I laughed aloud at the Adjudicator's response.

Draining bite was less than useful to me, but that might not always be the case. Once we upgraded the ability sufficiently, it might turn into something I could use—*without* needing to bite my foes.

And that was only the beginning of the possibilities spellhold offered. Ghost, though, was still looking perplexed. Taking pity on her, I explained, *"Mage's surprise—the ring whose benefits you are now receiving—has only one storage slot. I didn't expect your new trait to change that, and it didn't."*

I paused for breath. *"What that means is that we're sharing the slot. And that, in turn, has led to some unintended consequences. Beyond me using your spells, I can now use spellhold to transfer my stolen spells to you."*

It took Ghost a moment to process all that. *"So... I could cast something like nature unchained?"*

"If it were stored in the ring, then yes."

"Oh." She lowered her head onto her paws. *"I get it now."*

Grinning, I rose to my feet. *"We'll speak more on the matter later. But, for now, let's see to those mercenaries."*

Chapter 479: Mercenaries

I was halfway to the trapdoor when a Game message interrupted me.

Sector 75,172 has reverted to neutral territory!
The Devil Riders have failed to reinforce the safe zone defenses in the stipulated time and, consequently, have lost control of the sector. All previously applied restrictions have been removed. Anyone may now trade in the safe zone, and you may teleport into and out of it at will.

"About damned time," I said, chuckling.

"We're free to leave?" Ghost asked.

"We are," I confirmed as I drew to a stop before the trapdoor. Tyelin had assured me the traps around it were deactivated, and I saw no reason to disbelieve him. *"Time for you to unmanifest,"* I added, glancing over my shoulder at the pyre wolf. The Blades had already seen her, of course, but that was no excuse to give them time to study her at leisure.

Sighing, Ghost did as I asked. *"Don't delay too long, Prime. I miss the Pack."*

I nodded solemnly. Ghost had been patient—more than patient—while I went about my business in the sector, but I knew she yearned to be reunited with the rest of the dire wolves, and the fact that she'd mentioned it now was testament to how much they weighed on her mind. *"We'll be gone before the day's out,"* I promised.

Not saying anything else, Ghost let her form unravel, but I could tell my response eased her mind.

Ghost has unmanifested.

Alone once more, I kneeled to inspect the trapdoor.

Tyelin had confirmed what I'd suspected all along. The trapdoor and the secret tunnel beyond had been built by the Blades when they'd owned the fort. The passage ran deep beneath the earth and crossed the river to the adjacent sector.

The tunnel was not as large as I'd assumed, though. Only wide enough for two people to walk abreast, its primary purpose was to serve as an escape route.

Which was why the trapdoor could only be opened from the *inside.*

Using the key I'd taken from Auris, I set it into the complicated mechanism that served as the trapdoor's lock. The trapdoor was more than a physical assembly. It had been fashioned from spells of psi and mana as well to prevent unauthorized use.

Here goes, I thought, turning the key.

You have unlocked a hidden door.

✳ ✳ ✳

As soon as I cracked open the hatch, my mindsight was set alight by a long string of mindglows, one that stretched all the way to the river and beyond. It was the minds of the mercenaries in the secret tunnel, hidden up until this point by whatever wards protected the fort and the trapdoor.

Drawing the hatch all the way back, I peered into the deep shaft beneath. A face stared back up at me.

"What took you so long?" Banyen demanded, his face twisted into a scowl.

The Blade's greeting gave me pause as did the mercenary beside him. The mercenary was not a player as I'd half-expected, nor was he one of the more commonly found races in the Game. He had gills and scales, blue iridescent scales that rippled under the light of the glowing bubble of water sloshing above his left shoulder.

He looks just like Devlin, I thought. But the Albion Bank manager was a long way away, and I was surprised to see another of his kind here. Reaching out with my will, I analyzed the mercenary.

The target is Haskell, a level 128 lake warden and tratin.

Tratins are an aquatic species that prefer living underwater, either in the Kingdom's deep oceans or its giant lakes. However, this does not mean they are not as capable on land, and many a land-born foe has found himself undone by a tratin and their inborn water magics.

Ruminating over the Adjudicator's words, I let my attention wander beyond the pair waiting impatiently at the foot of the shaft to those behind. *All* the mercenaries were tratins, not just the one standing beside Banyen. They were also all non-players.

Huh. Fancy that.

"Well?" Banyen demanded, drawing my attention again. "Are you going to just stay there gaping at us or are you going to let down the ladder?"

"You know who I am?" I asked, making no move to release the rope ladder curled up and fastened at the top of the shaft. I didn't know Banyen, and he didn't know me, and at the very least, I'd been expecting to be met with suspicion, not... impatience.

"Yes, yes," Banyen replied testily. "Of course, I do." Before I could ask how, he went on, "Tyelin was in constant communication with the scouts he had posted above ground. The moment it became clear what direction the battle was taking, they crossed the river and reported in." He pinned me with a glare. "So, I know all about you, Jasiah. I know you let our people die. And I know you cut a deal with Tyelin."

"You should be a bit more respectful," an unseen voice called from farther down the tunnel. "Or have you forgotten he is a Power, too?"

Banyen stiffened. "Stay out of this, old man."

"That you, Nicola?" I shouted, already knowing that it was.

"It is," the under-dweller replied. "Is it true you single-handedly killed all the Riders?"

"Not *all* of them," I replied modestly, continuing the shouted conversation much to Banyen's displeasure. "Only most."

"It's safe to come up then?" Nicola asked.

"It is. Malikor is dead. As are his—"

"So, what are you waiting for?" Banyen demanded, interjecting himself in the conversation again. "Let us up!"

Breaking off, I stared at the Blade. His face was an angry shade of red, but that concerned me less than did his smooth, unlined cheeks and low level—he was only rank thirteen. Banyen was young, both physically and in Game terms. What had Tyelin been thinking leaving him in charge?

Probably, that he wouldn't *end up in charge,* I thought morosely.

Still, it looked like I was going to be stuck dealing with Banyen—but hopefully not for long. There was Nicola to consider as well. I liked the underworld merchant, and his presence with the mercenaries set me at ease, no matter that I had no idea what he was doing with them.

"I will," I replied to the impatient Banyen, "on one condition."

He blinked. "Condition. What condition?"

"On condition no one touches any of my loot," I said mildly.

Banyen's eyes narrowed to slits. "*Your* loot? The Blades possessions are not for the likes of you—"

"They are," I said, cutting him off. "Your envoy has already agreed to me taking one item from each of your comrades, and I will abide by my word." I paused for effect. "But the Riders are a different story. Their gear is mine—every last piece."

Banyen's expression darkened. "Those Riders' deaths were bought with Blade blood! I'll be damned if—"

Haskell, the thus far silent mercenary commander, placed a restraining hand on the player, and for a wonder, he fell quiet—but only for a moment. Shooing away Haskell, Banyen continued in a slightly calmer tone. "And if I refuse your demands?"

I smiled toothily. "I'll put someone else in charge."

Banyen's mouth worked soundlessly. But it was rage, not fear, that left him speechless.

I sighed. It didn't look like the young Blade was going to be reasonable. *Perhaps I should've chosen a different tack.* Been more diplomatic. But I was done pandering to the players in this sector. *If he wants a fight, he's going to get it.*

Suddenly, Nicola shoved his way into view. Placing himself squarely in front of Banyen, he forced Haskell back. "Are you really going to risk the sector for the sake of some loot?" he hissed. Clearly, the merchant and everyone else in earshot had been listening intently. "*And* disobey your envoy in the process?"

Banyen swallowed. For all that Nicola was a civilian, he still cut an imposing figure. "Very well," the Blade said, not meeting my gaze. "I accept your conditions."

"Excellent." Letting down the ladder, I backed away. "Then come on up, and we can talk some more."

✳　✳　✳

Banyen was the first one up, followed closely by Nicola. Ignoring the young Blade, I shook the under-dweller's hand. "What are you doing here?" I asked curiously. "A battle is the last place I would've expected to find a merchant."

He grunted. "You'd be wrong about that. My kind flocks to these things all the time." His eyes glittered as he surveyed the corpse-strewn storeroom. "You'll be surprised to hear how many players find the sudden urge to stock up after a close brush with death." His gaze darted back to me, studying my blood-spattered apparel. "Or perhaps not. You seem in your element."

I smiled wolfishly. "Is that an insult or a compliment?"

He shrugged. "Take it as you want."

I laughed, finding his forthrightness refreshing. "You still haven't answered my question, though," I pointed out. "Why are *you* here? Did you just *happen* to be in the neighborhood again?"

"Not quite," he admitted. "This mission was the real reason I was in the Blades' sector in the first place. It's why I was on hand when Tyelin needed someone to meet you at the river. And it's why I had to hurry away when our business was concluded."

I scratched my chin thoughtfully. "So, what are you saying... that you're a Blade?"

He snorted. "Hardly. I'm here on commission." He jerked his thumb over his shoulder. "As are they."

I looked past Nicola to the long line of men and women streaming out of the trapdoor. A colorful, if disparate group, had separated from the mercenaries and were gathering nearby. None of them were tratins, and nearly everything about them was strikingly unique. In one respect, though, they were all similar. Each and every one of them was unarmed.

Civilians.

I turned back to Nicola. "You're heading to the safe zone," I guessed.

He nodded. "That's right. Tyelin has commissioned us to set up shop there."

It made sense. The campaign to claim the sector was far from over. The Blades might have won the first battle, but more were sure to follow once the dead players revived—all of whom would need to be outfitted before they left the safe zone.

"I see," I said, rubbing my chin again. Nicola's words had given me an idea. "When do you have to be in the safe zone?" It would be at least six hours before the first Blade was reborn.

"Not immediately," Nicola replied. "Although getting there sooner would be advantageous." He smiled wryly. "I really don't fancy dallying here and being killed by a stray Rider."

"There are none such," I said, only a little grimly.

The merchant threw me a guarded look but forbore comment. "What makes you ask, anyway? Did you have something in mind?"

Not answering immediately, I surveyed the storeroom again. Banyen had not hung around. Both he and Haskell had left with a long line of mercenaries trailing after them. In all likelihood, they were on their way to secure the safe zone.

The civilians were still huddled together on one side of the room, but I didn't miss the calculating looks they shot in the direction of the chamber's dead.

"Actually, I do," I replied eventually. "How do you feel about taking on a second commission?"

"I'll not say no to more business," Nicola said with a smile, then added more cautiously, "as long as whatever you have in mind doesn't clash with my existing commitments, of course."

"It won't," I promised. "How much time do you have?"

"Before I have to report to the safe zone?"

I nodded.

Nicola thought for a moment. "Five hours, maybe?"

"I can work with that."

"What do you need then?"

"Manpower," I stated bluntly. "Willing and able hands to loot the dead."

Nicola stared at me. "You want me to loot your kills? All—what is it?—one thousand players? There's no way I can manage that in five hours!"

"It's more like two thousand," I murmured. "And don't forget the hellbats and demon aspects. Any gear they're wearing should be collected as well. Not to mention whatever reagents you can extract from the corpses themselves."

Nicola's look only grew more incredulous.

"I don't expect you to do it alone." I pointed at the other merchants. "Use them. The ones you deem trustworthy, anyway."

Nicola's eyes narrowed as his gaze flitted between the merchants and me. "Does that mean you trust me? To loot your kills and keep that bunch in line?"

I smiled. "Who was it that said that an under-dweller would sooner suffer final death than break his word?"

Nicola scowled. "And what is it that you expect us to do with all this loot we're to gather?"

"Sell it," I replied promptly.

"What, all of it?" he asked, looking startled.

"Yes," I said, ignoring the temptation to peruse the stuff first. I would miss out on some interesting items by not doing so, but it didn't always pay to be thorough. There were times when speed counted for more, and this was one of those times. Besides, cold hard cash was always versatile. "Sell all of it," I confirmed, "and as fast as you can."

"What's in it for me?"

"Five percent of what you sell."

His eyes narrowed. "Twenty."

I snorted. "Not on your life," I said, throwing his own words from not so long ago back at him.

"Fifteen," he said. "The others will demand a cut, too."

"Ten," I countered.

Nicola opened his mouth, no doubt with a counter-offer ready.

"There must be more than a few legendary pieces waiting in all that," I said quickly, spreading my arms to encompass the storeroom. "It would be a shame to lose out on them."

Nicola's mouth closed with a snap. "I can sell them?"

"Yes," I replied in a clipped tone. It pained me to lose potentially useful legendary items without even seeing them, but I considered the chances of finding such minuscule, and the 'loss'—if there were any in the first place—would be offset by the extra money earned.

"Fine," Nicola replied, equally curt. "Ten percent. But I get to set the prices, and *I* do all the selling."

I shrugged. "I don't care what prices you demand as long as you sell everything." I paused, thinking of something else. "You will have to wait before putting the Rider gear up for sale, though."

"For how long?"

"A day at least."

"That's ridiculous," he scoffed. "Now is when we would get the best prices. Now, while the Riders are still desperate enough to pay anything to regain their gear and reclaim the sector."

I grimaced. "That's exactly why you will wait. I will not rearm the enemy before the Blades claim the sector."

Nicola looked at me in surprise. "You've allied with the Blades? Listening to young Banyen's complaints, I got a rather different impression."

"We're not allies," I replied. "*But* our interests are aligned as far as this sector is concerned. I will not see it fall to the Riders again."

Nicola sighed. "You're not making it easy, you know?"

I smiled. "Think of whatever you earn through this commission as a bonus. That should make it easier to accept."

The merchant threw me a filthy look, but he refrained from further argument. "Very well, I agree to your terms."

I held up my hand. "One last thing. The Sworn-locked items... are those usual around here?"

"If you're asking if it's normal practice for high-tiered civilian-crafted gear to be enchanted such that only a single player or a single group of players can use them, then yes."

I grimaced. "Is there any way to remove the restriction?"

Nicola frowned. "Not without spending nearly the same amount it cost to create the item in the first place. Why do you ask?"

"Idle curiosity, that's all," I said, sticking out my arm. "We have a deal?"

He clasped my hand. "We do."

Chapter 480: Dire Threats

Nicola and the ten merchants he'd selected got to work immediately. Moving from corpse to corpse in the storeroom, they stripped them with practiced ease.

They've done this before, I thought.

For a moment, I was tempted to stay and watch, but I forced myself out of the room. I'd assigned the task to Nicola, and now that I had, I had to let him get on with it.

"Delegation," I muttered sourly. If I was going to lead House Wolf, it was something I was going to have to do time and again. Better I made my peace with the idea now.

"Are we leaving?" Ghost asked excitedly as I left the basement level.

She meant the fort, I knew. *"Just a few more hours, I promise."*

"Oh! That soon." A pause. *"What about the reward you're expecting from the envoy?"*

"You mean the promissory note?"

"Yes, that."

"We might still have to wait for Tyelin to resurrect before we leave," I admitted, *"but I'm hoping that won't be necessary."*

"Oh." Another pause. *"So, if we're not waiting for the envoy, and if we're not looting the Riders and Blades... what are we doing for the next few hours?"*

"Sleeping," I replied so promptly it surprised her. *"It's been a long night,"* I added ruefully. Which was an understatement. I wasn't swaying on my feet just yet, but I also couldn't remember the last time I'd slept, and that was never a good thing.

"Is it safe to sleep in the fort?" she asked cautiously.

"Ordinarily, it wouldn't be. But this one has a safe zone—an unowned safe zone. We'll be safe there."

✳ ✳ ✳

The safe zone was in the exact center of the fort, and curiously enough, it occupied only the ground floor. As I made my way to it, I wondered why this was the case.

Was it merely a peculiarity of this sector? Or would the same thing happen to other safe zones if entire buildings were constructed around them? But before my thoughts had a chance to venture too far down this path of idle speculation, a message from the Adjudicator flashed for attention.

A faction has staked a claim to sector 75,172!
The Silent Blades have established a cordon of more than 1,000 soldiers around the sector's safe zone. If the cordon remains unbroken for a full 24 hours, ownership of sector 75,172 will transfer to the Silent Blades.

My lips turned up in grudging respect. Hotheaded though he might be, Banyen had moved quickly to complete his objective. "Well done," I congratulated as I drew to stop in front of him and the ten score mercenaries standing guard before the reinforced doors leading to the safe zone's entrance.

The Blade scowled despite my civil words and tone. "What are you doing here?"

I raised one eyebrow. "I'm here to visit the safe zone, of course."

"Safe zone is closed," he said brusquely.

"No, it's not," I replied pleasantly.

"Yes, it is damn well—" The words died on Banyen's lips as he caught the cold look in my eyes.

I smiled. *Wise of him to refrain.* "Let me through," I requested—quite politely, I thought.

"No one is being allowed in," Banyen said stiffly.

"Why?"

"What?"

"Why is no one being allowed in?" I asked reasonably.

"Because they might aid the Riders!"

My brows rose higher. "What about the merchants?"

"They're under commission," Banyen replied, "and Pact-bound not to serve any Riders."

"Interesting," I murmured, even though his statement didn't quite track with Nicola's willingness—eagerness even—to sell to the Riders, but that was not a topic I wanted to pursue now. "But I don't mean the civilians you brought with you. I'm talking about the merchants already inside—the ones contracted by the Riders."

"What? What do you—?" Breaking off, Banyen spun around to see if the doors had somehow magically opened while we'd been speaking. But, of course, they were still closed. "How do you know about them?" he demanded.

I tapped the side of my head solemnly. "You can't hide anything from me, Banyen. I know all your secrets."

The Blade stared at me suspiciously, suspecting he was being made fun of but uncertain.

"Now, tell me your plan for dealing with them," I said, managing to keep a straight face.

Banyen's brows furrowed. "They're civilians. Why would I need to deal with them, much less require a plan for it?"

Bowing my head, I pinched the bridge of my nose. "Tell me, Banyen, which group of players do you think is going to resurrect first?"

"Er... I don't see how—"

"Let me help you," I said, interrupting him. "Thinking back, it started with that group of eight—no, it was the six first, then the eight. After that it was Titus' group—and there were more than a few dozen in that one." I held the Blade's gaze. "What do you think will happen when all those players— every one a Rider, mind you—resurrects and rearms themselves?"

Glaring at me hotly, Banyen said nothing.

My gaze shifted to the mercenary commander beside him. "What about you, Haskell? Do you have an opinion?"

"We die," he said laconically.

"That's right," I said, my gaze returning to the Blade. "You die. *And* you lose the sector. So, tell me, Banyen, how do we stop that from happening?"

He licked his lips. "We get rid of the merchants," he said tightly.

I smiled. "Exactly."

"But I already tried that," he burst out. "The stubborn bastards won't listen. They refuse to leave!"

My smile broadened. "Leave it to me. I'm sure I can convince them."

✳　✳　✳

You have entered a safe zone. Mimic spell not dispelled.

I passed through the doors as I was—in my guise as Jasiah.

I had toyed—briefly—with the idea of impersonating Malikor, but in the end, I decided that was not necessary. 'Jasiah' had garnered enough infamy in the sector to suitably impress the merchants, and with him, there was less risk of being caught out in a lie.

The safe zone itself was nothing more than a large chamber. An ornate, bejeweled chair sat at the far end, and just in case anyone was confused as to the chair's purpose, a lush red carpet led directly to it from the entrance.

"You see that, Ghost?" I asked in amusement. *"It's styled like a throne room."*

There was no immediate response from Ghost, and after a second, I realized none would be forthcoming. The pyre wolf was asleep—in fact, she had been *forcibly* put to sleep.

My amusement faded. It seemed that even when it came to unmanifested familiars, the Game would enforce its injunction against non-players in the safe zone. The bond between me and my familiar had been... not severed but tied down rather.

"Why have you stopped?" Banyen hissed.

I glanced at the young Blade by my side. He'd insisted on accompanying me, and unwisely, I'd acceded to his wishes.

Banyen was not looking at me. Instead, his gaze roved over the two dozen or so men and women lining the throne room's left and right walls. I'd spotted the merchants myself but had pointedly decided to ignore them. It was a tactic I hoped would increase their uncertainty and leave them guessing as to my intent.

Alas, it was also a tactic that had been spoiled by Banyen.

In the place of doubt, I saw fury and anger in the watching faces as their gazes fixed on the Blades by my side. I sighed. *Serves me right for bringing Banyen.*

"Stay here," I ordered, making no attempt to lower my voice.

Banyen's gaze darted to me. "But—"

"No buts. Do as you're told."

The young Blade turned an unfortunate shade of red, but he complied with my wishes nevertheless and stayed unmoving as I strode farther into the room.

Out of the corner of my eyes, I spotted narrowing eyes and tentative smiles. *Good*, I thought, keeping my own expression studiedly neutral. *That should have undone some of the damage.*

Reaching the exact center of the chamber, I turned around in a slow circle. "You all know who I am."

Saying nothing, the Rider merchants stared at me intently.

"I am Jasiah, the one who slew Malikor. I'm also the one responsible for killing every Rider in this fort."

A thickset trader named Alick snorted disdainfully. "A dead man is what you are."

I shifted to face him. "Really? What makes you say that?"

"Mammon is coming," he retorted, "that's what."

I smiled. "Are you sure about that?"

He stuck out his jaw. "Yeah. I am."

My smile broadened. "Excellent. I do hate sitting around doing nothing. How soon can I expect him?"

Consternation flickered across Alick's face, but he didn't back down. "You should run. Because when Mammon gets here, he'll gut you like a pig!"

"I don't fear Mammon," I said mildly. Drawing stamina, I reconfigured my face—and my Marks. "Why should I?"

You have cast mimic, transforming your visage into that of Alick, a human trader.

You have unconcealed your Powerful Initiate Mark.

"Look! His face, it's changed!"

"Forget his face, check his Marks!"

"The rumors were right. He *is* a Power."

Ignoring the whispered comments, I folded my arms and stared down the trader, waiting for his answer.

Alick, however, was still belligerent. "So, you're an Initiate Power, so what? You're still no match for Mammon!"

"An Initiate Power?" I repeated. "Oh, but I'm not that." I gestured to my face. "This is just another façade."

The trader's eyes narrowed. "Show your true face then. Show us who you really are."

I shook my head sorrowfully. "I can't do that, Alick. That'll give the Game away. But never fear, Mammon will know my true name before he dies."

A mix of emotions played across the trader's face, but before he could retort, another merchant spoke up. "Is that why you're here? To kill Mammon?"

"Yes," I replied succinctly.

"Then why bother coming here and telling us any of that?" someone else asked.

"Because," I said, waving in the direction of the almost-forgotten Banyen, "I promised the Blades this sector, and by staying here and rearming the reviving Riders, you lot are only going to delay the fulfillment of that promise." My expression hardening, I swept my gaze across them. "Make no mistake, the Riders are finished. Mammon is finished. Staying here will alter none of that. Only the price *you* pay will change."

"What price is that?" the merchant asked worriedly.

"Final death," I said coldly. "You have my *word* on it. I will hunt you down, no matter how long it takes and no matter where you hide. I will seek you out and see you dead."

On the tail end of my words, a Game alert popped into the minds of the merchants. A similar one appeared in mine.

You, in the persona of Alick, have proposed a Pact with 25 players, pledging to inflict final death upon them unless they immediately leave the safe zone of sector 75,172.

"You wouldn't!"

"How dare you!"

"We're civilians!"

"I would. I do dare. And civilian or not, if you aid my foes, you are my enemy." I paused. "I have no mercy to spare for my enemies. Now leave, before I seal the Pact. This is your only warning."

✳ ✳ ✳

It didn't take the merchants long to make up their minds.

In the face of my dire threats, none of them, not even Alick, were willing to stay, and a minute later, the throne room was emptied out.

"Were you bluffing?" Banyen asked, the only one still in the room beside me.

I shrugged. "Maybe. Then again, maybe not." Not waiting for his response, I made for one of the curtained-off sections behind the throne.

"Where are you going?" Banyen yelled after me.

"To sleep," I called back. Midway to my destination, I paused and turned back. "And, Banyen?"

"Yes?"

"Getting rid of the merchants was a good first step, but on its own, it won't be enough to deal with the initial wave of Riders. I suggest you call back home and beg for some reinforcements." Assuming there was any to be had, of course.

"Won't you help?"

"No," I said tiredly. Turning back around, I resumed walking. "I've already done all that I'm willing to do. The fate of this sector is now in your hands. Good luck."

Chapter 481: Smuggling Ways

You have transformed your visage into that of Jasiah.
You have slept for 5 hours.
Hellfire dome expired.

I awoke hours later, feeling far from refreshed. Nonetheless, I forced myself into motion, knowing I couldn't afford to oversleep. *First things first,* I thought blearily and checked the status of my buffs.

Mimic active. Remaining duration: 5 hours.

Satisfied that my Jasiah-face was still in place, I glanced at the curtains enclosing the partitioned-off space. They were still drawn, and the thin thread I'd hung across them remained undisturbed.

Good, no one's come in.

Drawing open the curtains, I strode out into the chamber beyond. The throne room was occupied again, not only by the merchants Banyen had brought along but also by a handful of players who were clearly *not* civilians.

My eyes narrowing, I studied the heavily armored figures. *Blades. They're Blades.*

It seemed Banyen had taken my advice and called for reinforcements. The Blades had likely teleported in now that the hellfire dome—the ward the Riders had erected around the fort to stop just that from happening—had expired.

Of Banyen himself, there was no sign. Ignoring the inquisitive looks of the Blades and merchants, I made my way to Nicola.

The under-dweller was standing next to the throne, his eyes vacant. *Probably communicating with the Game.* Drawing to a stop before him, I waited patiently.

A minute passed. Then another.

I shifted—less patiently.

Another minute went by.

Realizing that Nicola was not about to reconnect with reality anytime soon, I reached out and shook him. "Nicola? You there?"

"Hngh... wha—?" The merchant's eyes cleared. "Oh, it's you."

"Sorry to pull you out from..." I paused, realizing I didn't know where he'd been. "Where exactly is it that you were?"

"Communing with the auction," Nicola replied, his eyelids fluttering as he split his focus between here and 'there.' "Putting *your* items up for sale."

"On the global auction?"

"No. There are other markets," he replied vaguely. "Ones more... suited to the items we're selling."

I frowned, parsing his words. "You mean like a thieves' market?"

Nicola's rapid blinking stopped as he focused fully on the 'real.' "Lower your voice," he cautioned, his eyes darting left and right to see if anyone was in earshot, "and be careful of what you say."

I looked at him questioningly.

"Yes, I'm putting everything up for sale on the thieves' market. And yes, that is its actual name. The market is an open secret amongst those in the know, but it never pays to talk about it. That can attract the wrong sort of attention or worse, get you booted out."

"Huh-uh," I said, not understanding the reason for his concern. We were literally surrounded by thieves, after all! "How did the looting go?" I asked, changing the topic.

"Satisfactorily. *Very* satisfactorily," he pronounced.

"You didn't run into any problems?"

He shook his head. "No, the Blades' mercenaries didn't bother us, and no Riders arrived to contest the fort. Things went off without a hitch."

"That's good." I paused. "How much do you think we'll net?"

Nicola smiled but didn't answer me.

"Two hundred thousand?" I ventured.

The under-dweller's smile grew broader. "More. Much more."

"Five hundred thousand?" I asked, lowering my voice until it was barely louder than a whisper.

Nicola shook his head. "More still."

My eyes widened. *"One million?"*

He nodded minutely. "Your cut should amount to that much at least. It appears you caught the Riders napping, and some of them were carrying items they shouldn't have"—he grinned—"items they would've done better to leave in a bank."

I whistled softly, marveling at my sudden riches. What was I going to do with so much money? And just as importantly, where was I going to store it? After what Nicola had told me earlier about the banks, dumping everything in the Albion Bank didn't seem all that wise anymore.

Something else occurred to me, too. "Out of curiosity... how much do you think a sector like this is worth?"

Nicola's eyes narrowed. "A sector? I couldn't say, but... more than a million definitely—even for a poor one like this."

"Oh," I said, deflating as I realized how much I'd undersold myself to Tyelin. "Why so much?"

Nicola shrugged. "There are too many factions and not enough sectors. Even a barren region such as this can be turned into a secure base. Not just for the owning faction but for the Powers who run them, too. Where do you think the Powers store their valuables? In a bank run by another Power?" He snorted. "Of course not. They keep it in their own vaults, usually deep inside territories they own."

"I see," I said, nodding thoughtfully. Nicola's perspective ran counter to Adriel's—and Farren and Ceruvax's, for that matter. But then again, the trio still saw the world through the lens of House scions.

The Kingdom had changed much since their day.

Too many factions, Nicola had said. That could be the crux of it. The Houses would have been finite, their numbers restricted by the Primes. There would've been no need for them to claim a barren sector such as this one.

But the factions... There was no natural limit to their numbers. And every faction would want its own base. And from that perspective, the sector's value made sense.

Setting aside further consideration of the matter, I refocused on the conversation with Nicola. "That brings us back to the matter of payment."

He raised his hands, palms up. "I don't have the money yet, and I won't for a few days."

"I know," I said, waving aside his concern. "I wasn't expecting you to pay me now. But that said, I mean to leave immediately, and I don't expect to return anytime soon."

Nicola rubbed his chin. "I see. That could be a problem."

Nodding, I waited patiently to see if he was able to come up with a better solution than I had.

"I can't give you a promissory note," he said. "I don't know the exact amount yet. And besides, the sum is too large."

I chewed the inside of my lip. "Then, assuming we don't use a bank, how do we do this?"

"A bank is a bad idea," he agreed. "What about a third party? Someone like Den Chief Dinara?"

I shook my head. "I prefer not to involve anyone else." The more people we brought in, the greater the chance of betrayal.

Nicola exhaled. "Then, there are two other options. One: we set up a meet for a few days hence."

"Chancy," I noted. "I can't say for certain if I would be able to make the meet."

Nicola nodded. "Me neither. That brings us to option two: set up a drop point."

My brows lifted. "Go on."

"There's not much to it. We choose a sector and a place within it that we're both familiar with—somewhere no one else would think to look. I stash your money there, and you pick it up when you can."

My brows rose higher. "Where are you going to find a place to stash one million gold coins?" That volume of money would require a wagon to haul and transport.

He shook his head. "For a transaction such as this, I won't use gold."

I frowned. "You won't?"

Nicola closed his eyes, and when he opened them a moment later, he was holding a small pouch cupped in his hands. "Have a look."

Leaning forward, I peeked inside the open bag. It was filled to the brim with a fine powder of texture and color I knew all too well.

"Do you know what this is?" Nicola asked.

"Stygian powder," I said, my face carefully scrubbed of animation. "Stygian powder made from stygian seeds or from the residue of dead stygians."

The under-dweller smiled, blissfully unaware of my sudden tension. "That's exactly right. The powder is one of the most valuable substances in the Game. Just a single gram sells for a hundred gold."

"I see. But I'm still not sure what you're driving at."

Pressing his hands together, Nicola caused the pouch to return to whatever aether store he'd summoned it from. "I'm proposing I pay you in stygian powder, of course."

It was exactly what I feared.

Seeing my lack of enthusiasm for the idea, the merchant expounded further. "Look, as expensive as stygian powder is, it's also not as rare as some of the more exotic ingredients in the Game. This means I can acquire the quantity I need to pay you, and just as importantly, you can easily sell it when you need to. Secondly, as widely used as the powder is, its price is stable: one hundred gold for one gram. No need to quibble with any merchants on the price."

Saying nothing, I thought through the matter for a moment.

I couldn't deny that what Nicola said made sense. At the rate he quoted, a million in gold was equivalent to ten kilograms of stygian powder—an easy enough quantity to transport or hide.

And while my own recent experiences had left me leery of anything to do with stygian seeds, I was certain the black powder he'd shown me was inert. Whatever mind the seeds had housed had been destroyed when they'd been crushed to form the powder.

"Alright," I said eventually, "we'll do it that way."

"Excellent," Nicola grinned. "Now to the matter of the drop point. It'll be best to use a Kingdom sector, and we should have more than a few in common. Tell me, which ones are you most familiar with?"

"Err..."

The list of Kingdom sectors I'd been to were vanishingly small. Excluding the two here in the Eastern Marches, I'd visited only three other above-ground sectors: Nexus, the wolves' valley, and the nether-infested sector. And somehow, I didn't think Nicola was going to be familiar with the last two.

"Well?" Nicola prompted. "I know you've been to Nexus. Where else?"

"It'll have to be Nexus," I said, avoiding the question.

"Nexus?" His brows furrowed. "Not a good idea. We should—"

"We can use the plague quarter," I said, interrupting him. "Isn't the den master there as well?"

"He is, but—"

"Good. Then in one visit, I can tick off two things on my list: visiting the thieves guild and collecting my share."

The under-dweller studied me searchingly, no doubt trying to puzzle out the reason for my insistence to use Nexus. "Alright," he conceded at last. "We'll do it your way. Nexus is far from ideal, but I can make it work."

I clapped my hands together. "Right, let's iron out the details then..."

✳ ✳ ✳

Your trap crystals have been fully replenished.
You have acquired 15x rank 4 nether protection crystals.

You have unequipped a veteran's trapper's wristband and equipped a scoundrel's wristband.

You have acquired 51 bombs, 20 miscellaneous skillbooks, and 20 ability tomes.

Ten minutes later, we were done, concluding on not just the location of our drop point but also the arrangement necessary for Nicola to act as my agent and collect the promissory note from Tyelin. As a welcome bonus, Nicola restocked my consumables and supplied the other odds and ends I requested at no cost.

I was trusting the under-dweller with a lot, but trust like delegation was something I was going to have to do more of in the coming days. I was wary of becoming over-reliant on Pacts, knowing myself how well their wording could be manipulated. And, funnily enough, trusting Nicola did not trouble me as much as I expected.

Perhaps that was because the money in question—all one million two hundred thousand of it—was not money I had held in my own hands to begin with. Losing it would hurt, certainly, but not as much as something I already considered mine.

"You will need this to open the drop box," Nicola said, holding out a slim rectangular object. Stretching out my hand, I took the item in question.

You have acquired an unmarked chest key card. It has been enchanted to signal the bearer when they are within 10 yards of the paired chest. This item cannot be stolen, traded, or lost, even upon death.

I threw Nicola a meaningful look. "You've done this before."

He smiled. "I have. Believe it or not, more than a few of my customers have trust issues."

I laughed. "Well, it's always a pleasure dealing with someone who knows what they're doing."

Nicola's smile broadened. "Likewise."

Glancing around the room, I saw that most of the other merchants had drifted to the northeast corner of the room—the one containing the rebirth well.

"What's with the skillbooks, ability tomes, and nether crystals?" Nicola asked suddenly.

I turned back to him. "Hmm?"

"I know I agreed to restock your consumables, no questions asked, but..." He shook his head. "All those books, on top of the ones you already bought before, they can't be for you, can they? And fifteen nether crystals? That's not a quantity you see most players carrying around. You're planning on hunting in the nether and making your own stygian powder or what?"

I smiled. "Maybe." Then before he could pursue the matter further, I jerked my chin in the direction of the congregating merchants. "Expecting company?"

Nicola looked where I pointed. "Yeah. According to the timetable Banyen provided, it won't be long before the first player revives."

"Speaking of Banyen... he mentioned something about there being a Pact not to sell to the Riders?"

Nicola nodded. "Tyelin *did* bind some of the others with a Pact. But in my case, it wasn't necessary." He looked down his nose at me. "As you should know already, I only deal with thieves."

I scratched my head. "Really? I know you said that before, but if that's the case, how were you planning on selling the Riders' stuff?"

The under-dweller waved aside my question. "That's different."

"Different how?" I persisted.

He sighed. "If you must know, I planned on selling the gear back to the original owners. My strictures don't apply when it comes to a player's own equipment. I make an exception in this case, as does every merchant I know. Your Kesh does, too. It's a sort of golden rule. Merchants nearly always give the original owner the right of first purchase." He paused. "Cuts down on the number of revenge killings."

I blinked. "What?"

"Combat players murder civilians, you know. Sometimes because of nothing more than greed, but often it's a case of misplaced blame." He threw me a pointed look. "Threats are common, too. That's right. I heard all about your ultimatum."

"Just a bit of play-acting," I murmured.

He snorted but didn't pursue the matter further.

I stuck out my hand, thinking it was time I left. "Well, I guess this is goodbye."

Nicola looked from my outstretched hand to the merchants gathered near the rebirth well. "You're not sticking around to watch the show? There will be lots of cursing and threats, I assure you."

I smiled. "As fun as that sounds, no. There are places I must be, and I don't want to outstay my welcome." Even though my actions may have directly benefited the Blades, I was certain that many of them would be as upset with me as Banyen was.

Taking my hand, Nicola shook it. "One last thing... if you ever need to get in touch with me, speak to Dinara. He will find a way to pass along the message."

I nodded. "I'll do that."

Pivoting on my heel, I headed back to the curtained-off area, and there, hidden from view, I attended to my final preparations.

Aetherstone bracelet activated. Connection to the ley line network formed. Selected exit: nether portal 1 of sector 75,172.

I was on my way, not to the nether-infested sector, but to rejoin the companions I'd left behind in this sector.

It was past time I checked on them.

Transfer commencing...

...

...

Passage completed!

CHAPTER 482: NO CERTAINTIES

Aetherstone bracelet deactivated. Remaining stored locations: 1. Charged and unetched gems: 3. Uncharged gems: 1.

I stepped out from the selfsame portal I had a few days ago, only this time my passage was a shorter one.

My entry back into the real was not as uneventful, though.

You have entered a tier 6 concealment field.
You have triggered the ward: fly-trap.

Strands of silk that felt as strong as bands of steel wrapped around my torso. Yanking me off my feet, they flung me against the adjacent wall and held me pinned.

You are <u>stuck</u> (duration: 30 seconds).

Yikes. I'd walked right into that one. I was unconcerned, though. Having already spied the two cloaked forms stretched out flat in the far corner of the room, I realized whose trap I'd fallen prey to.

"Uhm, Adriel? Want to let me down?"

The lich sat up, rubbing the sleep from her eyes. "Michael?"

"Yeah, it's me," I said, letting the spell wrapped around my face dissipate. In the next instant, the silk strands trapping me fell away, and I dropped lightly to the ground. "What was all that about?" I asked, rubbing my wrists.

"Precautions," she said with a smile.

"I see," I said, shaking my head. "And you call *me* paranoid."

Adriel laughed. "Well, it seemed only appropriate after—"

She broke off as the figure next to her stirred.

"Who... w-what," Nyra began sleepily then caught sight of me. "Michael! You're back!"

I smiled. "I am. And you've grown in the interim I see." I raised one eyebrow. "Level fifty-three already?"

"Adriel's a slave driver," she said, but there was a smile to her words and no coldness in the look she threw the lich. *Good, they've been getting along.*

"Prime?" Ghost greeted, also stirring. *"Where are we?"*

"We're out of the safe zone and back in the portal tower," I replied. *"You better manifest. I'm sure Adriel and Nyra are anxious to greet you as well."*

The pyre wolf did not respond, but the contentment filling our bond was answer enough.

Chuckling, I strode toward the remains of the campfire someone—Nyra most likely—had started in the center of the room. "Can we get this going again? I'm starving."

Adriel threw me an amused look. "Of course. We have much to discuss."

I nodded. "We do. But first, food."

✳   ✳   ✳

A Seeking Eye has been attuned. You can now activate this item when necessary.

A few hours later, my hunger assuaged, and my throat dry from talking, I finally finished my retelling of the events of the past three days.

"That's quite the tale," Adriel murmured when I was done.

Nyra nodded, looking fascinated.

"So much has changed," Adriel said, her gaze far away. "It's almost a different world…"

"Not everything has changed," I added sympathetically, not missing the strained note in her voice. The Kingdom the lich had come back to was not the same one she'd left centuries ago, and that fact was finally hitting home.

"Enough has though, that you cannot rely entirely on my advice," the lich continued more firmly.

I nodded, having come to the same conclusion myself.

"What I don't understand," Nyra said, "is why those Powers you mentioned—this Blythe and Mammon—didn't appear. Surely, if control of the sector was as important as your merchant friend Nicola made out, they would have wanted to take a direct hand in matters?"

"That one I can answer," Adriel said, speaking before I could. "Even in my day, the Powers were loath to interfere in player conflicts. For one, the Adjudicator's injunction against attacking players would keep them on the back foot. They would *only* be able to react. Then, too, there is the not-so-small matter of being ambushed. If one of the Powers appeared, I can assure you the second would have as well, but it is usually the one fighting the longest that loses."

She glanced at me. "Lastly, there is Michael. To them, he was a wild card. If this were uncontested territory, deep in the heart of a single Power's demesne, I have no doubt that he or she would've turned up and hunted Michael down. But as things stood, both Mammon and Blythe had to be wondering if Michael was an agent of the other, a ploy to weaken them before the true conflict."

I nodded. Adriel's analysis was consistent with my own, but there was one other point to add. "There was also little reason for either Power to risk themselves. For Mammon, the loss of this sector was not particularly significant. His faction owns others in the region, and, as a recent acquisition, sector 75,172 was likely the least of them. Blythe *also* didn't need to turn up since her people were winning."

"I understand what you're both saying, but"—Nyra waved her hands in frustration—"it all sounds so thin. What if Blythe or Mammon were having an off day? Or if anger overcame them? Then…"

"The outcome could have been very different," Adriel finished for her.

"Yes, exactly," Nyra said.

Adriel smiled. "Welcome to the Game. Going forward, the only thing you can be certain of is that there will be *no* certainties." She laughed. "It's nice to see that this much about the Game hasn't changed, at least."

Nyra's lips turned down, not as enamored of the notion as Adriel was, but then again, she, like me, was still a relative newcomer to the Game.

I changed the topic. "I meant to ask, have you ever heard of something like a thieves' guild?"

Adriel shook her head slowly. "There were certainly guilds aplenty during my time. Usually, scions from different Houses gathered under their roof—those who shared similar goals. Of course, House allegiance always superseded guild loyalty. But, as to a thieves' guild, I never heard of one." She bit her lip. "Nor do I know what an 'Under-dweller' could be."

I sighed in disappointment. I'd been hoping Adriel could solve that little mystery.

"A thieves' guild doesn't sound all that interesting," Nyra added. "Now, an assassin's guild...." Her eyes glinted. "*That* I would join in a heartbeat."

I snorted. "Don't be so sure. Remind me to tell you about the Mantises one day. You won't be so enthused by the idea then." Ignoring her curious look, I turned back to the lich. "Now, enough about my adventures. Tell me: how did your own three days go?"

Adriel shrugged. "There's not much to tell. We spent nearly the entirety of the time in the foothills and only got back last night—and that was mostly to check if you'd returned. To be honest, I didn't expect you for a few more days at least." She smiled. "You've been surprisingly punctual."

"A happy accident I assure you," I said with a rueful grin. "How did things go in the foothills?"

Adriel glanced at Nyra, fielding the question to her.

"It went well," the young woman answered, with a sidelong glance at the lich. "Better than I expected, really. Killing the rock trolls was a lot easier than the wisp lords."

"I bet. What skills did you manage to train?"

"All three of my base Class skills: longbows, sneaking, and focus," Nyra replied with obvious satisfaction. "They're all at tier two now."

"Really?" I murmured. "Then these might help," I said, placing a heavy bag in front of her.

"What are they?" Nyra asked, opening it and peering inside.

"Books," I said, pleased that I had remembered to purchase them. "Skillbooks and ability tomes. I wasn't sure which particular skills or abilities would interest you, so there is a wide selection in there: everything from light armor to heavy, from daggers to axes, and from backstab to charge." I paused. "No magic or psi, though. Those are better left to your second and third Classes."

"A wise decision," Adriel said softly. "Keeping each individual Class specialized will improve the chances of a good meld."

It turned out Classes nearly always melded.

Up until the point that Ceruvax and Adriel had set me straight on the matter, I'd been laboring under the impression that they didn't always. What was crucial, though, was the manner in which Classes melded. Bad melds were not unheard of and could be disastrous for a player's existing traits and skills.

Thankfully, my own Classes had synergized well.

I had also kept my Classes specialized—although it had been more an instinctive ploy on my part rather than a defined strategy—and it had led to them blending well together.

It was possible, too, that Nyra's first Class would evolve after she completed its configuration—like mine had—although that was less likely. It remained a possibility, though, which is why I didn't want to distract her with the idea of magic and psi just yet.

Unaware of the thoughts running in my head—and in Adriel's, too, I suspected—Nyra did not look up from her fascinated study of the bag's contents.

Noticing the young woman's distraction, Adriel turned back to me, a wry look on her face. "Which reminds me. While we're on the topic of skills... death magic for Ghost?" She glanced at the pyre wolf resting at her feet. "Not that the choice doesn't please me, but why?"

"*You explain it, Ghost,*" I murmured, and a second later, she began to do so, enthusiastically laying out her reasoning for Adriel.

Leaving the pair to it, I refocused on Nyra. "What about your poisoning?"

Tearing her gaze away from the bag, she looked at me. "What?"

"How is training your poisoning skill going?" I clarified.

Nyra's lips turned down. "My progress there has stalled."

"Well, then, maybe this will help," I said, sliding the poisoning kit across to her.

Her eyes widened. "Is that for...?"

"It is. It's yours now," I confirmed. After a moment's thought, I added a few more trinkets. "As are these."

You have lost 20 x bombs, 3 x full healing potions, a bishop's ring, an elite poisoning kit, the band of stillness, the gift of the unbound, and an enchanted leather armor set.

Nyra blinked, staring down at the sudden wealth of items.

"Use them or don't as you please." I gestured to the bag of books. "Nor is there any reason to rush your choices. Take your time and be certain of the skills you want, because once you make up your mind, there is no going back."

"I will," she said softly. "Thank you, Michael."

I inclined my head in acknowledgment, and when I looked back up, it was to find all three of my companions staring at me expectantly. "Morning is almost upon us, so there is no point going back to sleep," Adriel said, glancing out the window at the lightening sky. "Which begs the question... what next?"

"We leave," I said firmly.

The lich's brows rose in surprise even as Ghost's ears perked up excitedly.

"What, immediately?" Nyra asked. She gestured to the corner where she and Ghost had so recently buried the Blood Talisman. "You aren't going to use that blood-thing first?"

"I can't use the Talisman," I said reluctantly. "Not yet. Worst case, absorbing a new blood memory is going to take three days, and I can't afford to be knocked out that long. By then, the battle for the sector will probably be over, and whoever has won is going to be scouring the area for the upstart Power who upset the status quo. Yes, the odds of them finding us here are low, but low is not non-existent."

Adriel nodded slowly—in agreement, I thought. "And I imagine neither envoy is going to be best pleased with you when they resurrect in a few more hours."

I grimaced. "That, too, is unfortunately true." Why Malikor would be angry was easy enough to understand. I'd stolen the sector from him *and* all his legendary gear. Tyelin's own feelings in the matter were harder to predict, but I didn't see him being happy about the fact that I'd so twisted his own schemes that they came back to bite him.

"So, what are we waiting for?" Nyra asked, sweeping her new possessions into her bag of holding.

"A good question," I said, a smile on my face as I rose to my feet. "There's no point in delaying further. Let's go to the tundra."

We couldn't head directly to the tundra, of course.

With the sector being in a dungeon, we had to use the nether-infested sector as a stepping stone. A few minor preparations were necessary, but completing them took only a matter of moments.

Ghost has unmanifested.
You have acquired a Blood Talisman and a small bag of hiding containing 100 possessed finger bones.
You have unequipped Tyelin's farspeaker.
You have lost 2 x rank 4 nether protection crystals.
You have concealed your Powerful Initiate Mark.

Despite removing the Blades' farspeaker bracelet, I did not replace it with Safyre's, finding myself strangely reluctant to have our first words spoken from afar. It would be better, I decided, if our reacquaintance occurred face to face.

For much the same reason, I hid my Power Mark. Until I got a chance to explain my new status, I didn't want any of my former companions to see it.

"Break your crystals," I ordered Nyra and Adriel.

Ghost, much to her dismay, would be making the trip to the tundra sheltered in her Cloak. She'd fought me on the issue, but it made no sense to needlessly expose her to the nether, and I had brooked no arguments on the matter.

"Do you remember what to do?" I asked, fixing Nyra with a stern look.

She nodded. "Step out of one portal and directly into the other."

"Don't delay for anything," I cautioned her again, "no matter how many stygian creatures are nearby."

"Got it," she replied.

Thankfully, as a New Havener, Nyra was familiar enough with the nether that I didn't need to further impress on her what the dangers were.

I glanced at Adriel. I was less concerned about the lich, she being more able to take care of herself. Besides which, the danger to Adriel was much less. While both Nyra and I risked final death—there being no safe zone in the nether-infested sector for us to resurrect in—the lich still had her phylactery.

"She'll be fine," Adriel assured me.

Nodding mutely, I withdrew a portal scroll. "Then, here goes." Cracking the seal binding the scroll, I drew on my magic.

Unlike the previous time I'd tried using it, no Game message interrupted me, and my mana flowed smoothly into the spelled parchment. It took longer than I expected, but eventually, the scroll was replete and refused further magic.

"It's ready," I murmured to the others, not looking up. Releasing the enchantment in the scroll, I directed its spell weaves to the nether-infested sector—and specifically the location of the Guardian Tower's portal.

Item consumed.

You have opened a greater portal to sector 18,240. This portal is large enough for 4 entities to pass through and will remain open for a maximum of 30 seconds.

The scroll vanished from my hands, and a moment later, a shimmering curtain materialized before me.

"Nice work," Adriel said approvingly. "If I didn't know better, I'd almost believe you a mage."

"Only almost?" I quipped as I advanced on the portal. All my buffs—minus vanish—had been cast, and I was ready as could be.

As the one best equipped to face the nether, it was up to me to draw off the stygians while my companions escaped to the Guardian Tower. To that end, we planned on stretching out the interval between our respective passages through the portal as much as possible. They would delay their entries even as I rushed mine.

Hands on the hilts of my stygian blades, I dashed into the portal. "See you on the other side," I called as the shimmering curtain of white swallowed me.

Transfer commencing...

...

...

Passage completed!

Leaving sector 12,560. Entering sector 18,240 of the Forever Kingdom.

✳ ✳ ✳

You have entered sector 18,240 of the Forever Kingdom.

Warning: this region is under assault by the nether and is in impending danger of being pulled into the Nethersphere!

A young void tree has taken root in the sector, establishing a permanent ley line to the Nethersphere. Until the void tree is destroyed, the safe zone will not form, and the nether toxicity in the sector will continue to rise.

I rolled out of the portal, barely paying the Game message any heed. The nether was a known danger. Less known were the stygian creatures in the area.

Bouncing back to my feet, I pivoted on the heel of my foot and scanned the surroundings with both my mindsight and physical senses.

And found nothing.

I frowned. There was not a single stygian in view.

It was not that they were shielding their minds or hiding. I had nethersight now and could see through the cloying yellowish mists as easily as I could in the dark. And what my eyes were seeing confirmed what mindsight was reporting.

There were no stygians around.

Where are they? I wondered. I'd been expecting the Guardian Tower's portal to be besieged just like it had been on the two prior occasions I'd come this way. That it wasn't...

I shook my head, not knowing what to make of the fact.

The curtain of white behind me parted, and a shape emerged—Adriel. Her hands brimmed with power, but no shield bubble surrounded her. We'd agreed it was best for her and Nyra to be as inconspicuous as possible.

The lich's eyes passed unseeing over me before jerking back, and I knew that even though only a few yards separated us, she was having trouble seeing through the thick mists.

"It's safe," I pronounced.

"Safe?" she echoed disbelievingly.

Nyra staggered through the curtain. Before she could wander astray, Adriel's hand flashed out and latched onto the younger woman's arm.

"Safe," I repeated for Nyra's benefit. "There are no stygians for miles."

My words failed to comfort either woman.

"How can that be?" Adriel murmured.

I shrugged. "I don't know." Lifting the bare stygian blade in my hand—I must've unconsciously drawn it at some point—I gestured to a bright glow only a few yards. "But there's the entrance to the Guardian Tower. Open and unprotected."

"So why aren't we going through?" Nyra asked, her tension unmistakable. "I don't like the touch of this mist. It looks even worse than the nether clouds near New Haven."

Adriel ran her free hand lazily through the air. "The nether here does feel more concentrated than most of the mist in Draven's Reach," she agreed. "What did you say the nether toxicity was?"

"I didn't. But it should be tier two," I said, quoting from memory before double-checking with the Adjudicator.

The nether toxicity at your current location is at tier 4. Your health, psi, stamina, and mana are degenerating at a rate of 0% per minute (damage reduced by 100% due to void armor).

My frown deepened. "It *was* tier two—on my previous visit," I corrected. "Now, it's at tier four."

"That's not good," Adriel observed.

I nodded. The free-floating nether in the area had increased, which could mean the sector was closer to falling to the void. *But how close?* I wondered. And if the nether had tightened its grip on the region, where were the stygians? Calling up the initial Game message, I scrutinized it more closely.

It didn't take long to spot another discrepancy.

"...Is in impending danger of being pulled into the Nethersphere," I repeated aloud.

"'*Impending* danger?'" Adriel asked sharply. "That's the exact phrase the Adjudicator used?"

"Unfortunately, yes." The Game's warning message about the sector had changed since my first visit. While the variation in wording was slight—only the word 'impending' had been added—the implications were potentially catastrophic. "How much time do you think we have?" I asked quietly.

"Months at best," she said definitively. "Weeks at worst."

I swallowed. "That little?"

Adriel nodded. "It could be worse, though. The level of corruption in the sector hasn't reached the final stages yet. If it had, the Adjudicator would've described the danger as 'imminent.'"

"Well, that's something at least," I muttered. Still, there could be no doubt that things in sector 18,240 were worsening and at a faster rate than I'd hoped.

Another complication I don't need.

"What happens when the corruption is complete?" Nyra asked, studying the surrounding nether in horrified fascination.

"The young void tree reaches maturity, and the void rift sustaining it becomes redundant," Adriel replied. "A mature void tree is capable of not only producing enough nether to sustain itself but also of polluting the surrounding aether. Once that happens, the sector will be lost to the nether." She sighed. "And no one, not even the Primes, have ever managed to claw back a sector from the void."

"So, there *is* a rift?" I asked. I hadn't been sure there would be one. "There wasn't any in Draven's Reach."

"That's because Draven's Reach was a dungeon sector—and *already* in the nether. A rift was not required there; free-floating nether could simply seep in," Adriel explained. "This is a Kingdom sector, though. The rift is necessary to bring nether in."

"If we close the rift, we save the sector?" Nyra asked.

Adriel nodded. "Essentially. But it's the tree that anchors the rift. So, to close the rift, the tree must first be destroyed."

I sighed. Adriel's explanation made for a grim picture. But as much as the state of the sector worried me, now was not the time to address it.

I turned to face the Game portal waiting nearby. "Let's move on. Once we've rejoined the others on the tundra, we can decide what to do about this sector." *Hopefully, we'll find them still there. And safe.*

Adriel gestured me forward. "Go on, then. We'll follow on your heels."

I shook my head. "You know I have to enter last." Partly, this was to act as a rear guard, but mostly, it was because of the Guardian Tower's player limit. Only six players could be in the dungeon at any one time. Adriel would have no issues passing through, but Nyra and I might. And while I didn't foresee any problems, there was no point in taking chances.

If anyone was going to end up being stranded in the nether-infested sector, it was going to be me.

Adriel threw me a stern look. She knew my reasoning—we'd gone back and forth on the matter more than once—but she didn't agree with my decision. In her view, I was the least expendable. Still, she didn't argue.

Pulling Nyra along, Adriel entered the shimmering curtain—

—and passed through without hindrance.

I exhaled in relief as the pair vanished. Clearly, the possibility of something going wrong troubled me more than I'd been willing to admit—even to myself.

Now, it was my turn. Striding forward, I faced the portal. What were the chances that there were more players in the dungeon than I expected?

"*None*," Ghost said firmly.

"*Let's hope so*," I murmured and stepped forward. Because if I was wrong, things were about to become inordinately more complicated.

Transfer through portal commencing...

...

...

Chapter 484: Welcome Home

Passage completed!
You have entered sector 107 of the Endless Dungeon. This sector is level 3 of 5 of the Guardian Tower, which consists of 5 unclaimable sectors and 6 one-way portals.
A maximum of 6 players may be in the Guardian Tower at any one time. The dungeon is repopulated daily.
Current number of players in the dungeon: 6 (including you).
Sector bosses remaining: 5 of 5.

I stepped out into a world of white.

The tundra was everything I remembered. Harsh, sterile, and bitingly cold. But I didn't care.

Coming back to the tundra felt like returning home. It wasn't the place—my memories of it were bittersweet at best—no, it was knowledge of those who awaited me.

The Packs, dire and arctic wolves both.

Cara—Safyre now, I supposed.

The twins, Teresa and Terence.

And perhaps even Anriq—hopefully, he'd managed the journey from Nexus safely.

All of them were mine to protect and shelter. All of them were House Wolf. *Family.*

I glanced to my left where a shivering Nyra and Adriel were hastily donning the winter gear I'd warned them to have ready. They, too, were of House Wolf, no matter that Adriel hailed from Death.

It had taken me many long weeks to get here, but I was here finally. "Home," I breathed.

"*Home,*" Ghost echoed.

I smiled. "*Go on, manifest. I know you want to.*"

"*Thank you, Prime,*" the pyre wolf said excitedly.

A moment later, a resounding boom—audible even over the howling winds—rocked the icy plains. Both Adriel and Nyra froze, eyes tracking the sudden shower of snow ten yards ahead of us.

I laughed. "Don't worry, that's just Ghost. She's too impatient to manifest normally."

Both women managed indulgent smiles—only partly marred by their half-frozen faces. It *was* cold, perhaps deadly so. Still, I found the wind's touch... refreshing.

"*Wolves!*" Ghost yipped excitedly. "*I can smell wolves! And hear them, too!*"

Tears swelled in my eyes even as my grin widened. There were no wolves in sight, of course. Even my mindsight was empty, but Ghost's reach had always exceeded mine, and her words were all the confirmation I needed.

The dire wolf Pack was here.

And safe.

Exhaling a tremulous breath, I lowered the mental shields woven tightly around my mind.

A familiar voice whispered through. *"Michael?"*

"Yes, Aira. It's me," I replied, tears streaming heedlessly down my face.

A welter of emotions passed through the link, emotions she made no attempt to hide. *"We thought— I feared—"*

"I know," I replied. *"I wasn't certain we would make it back either."*

"We?" Aira asked, momentarily confused.

Off to the side, I felt Ghost dance fretfully, impatient to join the conversation. Widening the mental link, I let her in. *"Yes, we. I've brought our intrepid adventurer back."*

"IT'S ME, AIRA!" Ghost shouted joyously.

"Welcome back, little one," Aira said warmly, and before Ghost or I could respond, I felt the mental link on the elder's side expand as she let in others of the Pack.

"Pup?" an acerbic voice demanded. *"Is that you?"*

"YES, SULAN. IT'S ME, GHOST! I'M BACK!"

"Stop shouting," Sulan snapped. But despite her attempt to sound stern, there was no hiding the unrelieved joy in her voice.

"Sorry, Sulan," Ghost replied contritely, only hearing the ire in the white wolf elder's tone.

Sulan's regard turned to me. *"You did well, scion. Thank you for returning our lost spirit. The Pack is in your debt."*

"No, it's not," I replied firmly. *"Seeing Ghost safe was my responsibility, too."*

"And I'm not a pup anymore," the pyre wolf chipped in. *"Nor a spirit. I have a body now!"*

"You do?" Sulan asked, taken aback. She was not the only one. Aira, and the other elders listening in, appeared just as startled.

"I do! Adriel made me one. I'm a stygian pyre wolf now!"

Surprise transformed into alarm.

"Is that true, Michael?" Duggar asked, pushing himself to the fore of their mental collective and taking charge of the conversation.

"Hail, Alpha," I greeted solemnly. *"And yes, it's true, but it is not what you fear. Much has happened."* I paused. *"It's better if Ghost and I share the rest of our tale in person."*

"I agree," Duggar said. *"Snow is already on his way to guide you back to the den."*

I squeezed my eyes shut at the mention of Snow. *"Then the arctic wolf pack has survived?"*

"More than survived," Aira interjected. *"They're thriving."*

"You did well by them," Duggar agreed. *"You are at the portal?"*

"I am," I replied faintly, still overcome by relief and joy. I'd done everything I could for the arctic wolves before abandoning them on the tundra—even going so far as to build them a den of ice and bone—yet I had still abandoned them... and I'd been uncertain what state the pack would be in on my return.

"It shouldn't take Snow long to reach you then," Duggar added. *"He'll be there any minute now."*

Lost in my musings, I almost missed the import of the alpha's words. The arctic wolves' den was not all that close to the hidden portal, and I expected it would be a few days hence before we reached the two packs. *"You're not at the den?"*

"We are," Sulan answered. *"Safyre and the others helped us move it closer to the portal. We are not far."*

The last of my tension dissipated. *"Safyre and the twins are safe?"*

"They are," Duggar assured me. *"As is Anriq."*

"Thank the ancients," I murmured. That was the last of my allies accounted for. Only Saya's fate was yet to be determined, but I would have to journey to the wolves' valley before I could assure myself about her wellbeing. *Which I will do as soon as—*

I broke off, as something Sulan had said niggled at me. *"You moved the den? Why?"* And why move it closer to the portal?

Momentary silence.

"That, too, is a tale best relayed in person," Duggar said finally. *"Much has happened while you've been away."*

I frowned, more than a little perturbed by the alpha's response but still willing to wait to hear him out. *"Then we best save further talk until we reach the den."*

Closing the mental link, I opened my eyes and found Adriel and Nyra staring at me expectantly. The pair were kitted out in many more layers than could be comfortable—and yet were still shivering.

"The others are safe and on the way to fetch us," I reported.

"F-fetchh us w-where?" Nyra asked through chattering teeth.

"Somewhere warmer," I added sympathetically. Motion in the far distance caught my eye. "In fact," I said, turning to face the approaching shape, "that must be them."

✳ ✳ ✳

Adriel has cast death's sheltering hand.

Between one second and the next, the wind's howling ceased, strangled to silence by the black dome hovering over us, and the temperature rose appreciably.

I threw the lich a questioning look over my shoulder.

She shrugged. "It's cold. And why wait in discomfort?" she asked rhetorically.

"Thank you," Nyra said fervently, her hunched-over posture straightening.

"Don't thank me yet," Adriel murmured. "I can only hold the spell while we remain stationary. Once we get moving, the cold will return."

The qualification did not appear to perturb Nyra, though, and she closed her eyes, savoring the warmth, temporary though it might be. Facing forward again, I turned my attention to the approaching shapes.

Snow was not alone.

Accompanying him were four smaller wolves. Ice-white like Snow himself, they nipped at each other and yapped excitedly as they followed the alpha's lead.

Snow's offspring.

I smiled. All four had survived. A feat in of itself on the harsh tundra, and while they were not quite full-grown yet, the four were no longer vulnerable pups unable to defend themselves. Now, they were, more rightly, young wolves.

Stepping forward, I went down on one knee to greet the five.

Snow drew to a dignified stop a few yards away, his wary gaze on Ghost. The pups, though, paid the pyre wolf no heed. Surging past their sire, they flung themselves at me. Laughing, I fell back, overcome by licks and wet noses.

"Are those... wolves?" Nyra asked.

"Yes, girl," Adriel murmured.

"What are they doing to him?" she whispered in an aside to the lich. "And why are they so small?"

I chuckled. The young New Havener had never seen real wolves before, and, of course, compared to Ghost, every other wolf would look small. "These are pups," I said, shooing away the four as I rose to my feet. "And they're only a few months old, which accounts for their size." I gestured to Snow. "But they won't grow much larger than him."

"Is that their sire?" Adriel asked quietly.

I nodded as I strode forward to greet Snow. "Yes, he is the alpha of the arctic wolf pack."

Snow watched me approach, his countenance unchanging but his mind replete with images. One after the other, images flickered through my mind, pictures of full-grown wolves, many of whom I'd never seen before. Of those that I recognized, Snow portrayed most as vacant-eyed or with wounds too gruesome to survive. Next came a long string of pup images, some no more than a few days old.

He is reporting, I thought. *Showing me the new recruits, the dead, and the newborn.*

Going down on one knee, I rested a light hand on the alpha. "You did well, Snow," I said gravely. "The Pack has grown strong under your leadership."

The white wolf raised his snout proudly, sensing the intent behind my words if not the entirety of their meaning.

"And how is Star?" I asked.

Another series of images followed, showing Snow's mate snug in one of the igloos. "Leaving you to do all the work, is she?"

Laughing agreement.

Smiling, I rose to my feet and glanced at Ghost. Understanding wolfkin etiquette better than I did, the pyre wolf had deliberately hung back.

"Come meet him," I said.

Ghost slipped forward, her padded feet leaving glistening puddles in the snow. Through our bond, I sensed her anxiety, her earlier joy fleeing in the wake of darker emotions.

Would the Packs accept her? Or would they consider her too strange to be considered a wolf? These and other worries ran rampant in her mind.

"You can trust Snow," I reassured her. Burying her fears, the pyre wolf stepped up to my side, looming over the arctic wolf.

Immediately, four small shapes pounced.

The first launched himself at Ghost's tail. The second scrambled onto her back. The third latched on the underside of Ghost's belly and hung there, trying to bite through her coat. And the fourth went for the jugular.

The sight of the four pups trying to wrestle Ghost into submission made for an amusing picture, and I would have laughed if not for Snow's sudden spike of fear. Hackles raised and teeth barred, the alpha stepped forward, ready to defend his offspring.

"Easy, brother. She will not hurt them," I assured him.

Fighting his own instincts, Snow held himself still. It could not have been easy trusting my judgment over his own, but the alpha did—a fact I found humbling.

"Thank you," I said solemnly. Turning back to Ghost, I watched as she slowly lowered herself onto her belly. Keeping her mouth closed, she gently but firmly nudged the growling pups away.

They threw themselves at the pyre wolf again, of course, making a game of it, only for Ghost to push them away again.

The tension drained out of Snow. He saw what I did. Ghost was indulging the pups, the way any adult in the Pack would. He turned his serious blue eyes on me, a question in his mind.

"This is Ghost," I said, introducing her. "She is my..." I paused, searching for the right word. How could I define my relationship with the pyre wolf in a way the wolves would understand? "My pack sister," I finished. "Consider her a member of the Pack the same as you would me."

Acknowledging my words, he strode forward. The pyre wolf saw him coming and the pups, too. Sensing their sire's mood, they backed away while Ghost dropped her head submissively. It did not matter that she could tear open the alpha's throat with a single bite. This was about more than strength. This was about Pack Law.

Lowering his snout, Snow touched his nose to Ghost's.

I sighed in relief. The alpha had accepted the pyre wolf into the arctic wolf pack.

Ghost was no longer a lone wolf, lost and astray.

She was Pack once more, and knowing how important that was to her, the pure joy streaming through our bond did not surprise me.

"Welcome home, Ghost," I murmured. *"Welcome home."*

Chapter 485: The Wise Old Elders

As we drew closer to the new den—much expanded from the original two dozen igloos I'd constructed—we found a welcome party waiting.

Duggar. Aira. Leta. Sulan.

The dire wolf elders.

But of the rest of the pack, there was no sign. Nor for that matter was there any sign of the arctic wolves or my former human companions. I could sense their minds in the igloos beyond but that they were not present told me all I needed to know.

This was to be a private meeting.

Drawing to a halt, I studied the elders in the distance.

"What's wrong?" Nyra asked. "Why have we stopped?"

"The Pack elders have come out to meet us," I replied softly. She couldn't see the wolves through the howling wind and whipping snow, but I could. They sat waiting, implacable as stone despite the storm raging about the den.

"Aira?" I asked, projecting the question to her.

It was not Aira who answered though, but Leta. *"Bring the lost pup forward,"* she instructed, her mindvoice cold and dispassionate.

Aira must have sensed my unease because a moment later, she added, *"We must be certain what she is before the Pack can meet her."*

The words of the two elders did not reassure me, and I felt Ghost press up against my side, similarly disturbed. Running my hand through her coat, I felt a cold nose push into my other hand.

Looking down, I saw Snow staring up at me. *"Dire wolf business,"* he seemed to say.

I nodded. "Go. Take Nyra and Adriel with you. We'll talk again soon." I glanced over my shoulder at the rest of my companions, but no words were necessary. Anticipating my request, the pair were already striding after Snow.

"No," Sulan interjected. *"Bring the girl."*

I hesitated. *Girl?*

"This matter concerns Wolf," Duggar added. *"She should be present."*

They meant my apprentice then. "Nyra, hold up," I said.

Stopping, the young woman looked at me in surprise.

"They want to see you as well," I told her. I threw Adriel an apologetic glance. "Just her."

The lich, though, was not offended. "House matters, I understand," she said with a shrug. "Good luck." Stepping past, she trailed after the arctic wolves.

"Thank you," I murmured, watching Snow lead Adriel and the pups into a large oblong structure. Unlike the other igloos in the den, it hadn't been constructed as a singular dome. Instead, it looked like it had been internally partitioned into multiple rooms.

"*Come,*" Duggar ordered when the six disappeared from view. Turning around, the elders strode into a smaller igloo set off on the side.

"*Prime?*" Ghost enquired worriedly at the same time as Nyra asked, "What's this about?"

I sighed. "I don't know," I said, speaking aloud for both their benefit, "but everything will be fine." It had to be. Tugging the pair along, I followed in the elders' wake.

And to whatever judgment awaited.

✳   ✳   ✳

It was noticeably warmer in the igloo, but Nyra's sigh of contentment went unremarked by the elders.

They had eyes only for Ghost.

My gaze flickered between the four. The elders were arrayed in a half-circle on the far side of the igloo, leaving me and my two companions to face them across the empty middle. Duggar's face was impassive. Aira appeared intrigued. Leta was actually snarling. And Sulan... Sulan looked forlorn.

"Ghost is not a stygian," I said without preamble, wanting to head off the fears I saw writ large in the elders' faces.

"*She looks like one,*" Leta growled.

"But she isn't," I said, continuing to speak aloud for Nyra's benefit.

"*How can you say that?*" the elder demanded. "*She practically reeks of the nether!*"

I opened my mouth to object, but Sulan spoke first. "*Leta is right. I can smell the taint on her. The void has claimed her. She is one of them now.*"

"I'm not!" Ghost cried, but Sulan looked away, paying her protest no mind.

"*Do you deny she is of the nether?*" Leta demanded.

I ran my hand through my hair. "No, but—"

"*You see!*" Leta snarled. "*He admits it. We should—*"

"*Enough!*" Duggar barked. "*Give the scion a chance to explain. He has earned the right to that much.*" Tilting his head to the side, he studied me quizzically. "*Besides, he is no longer ours to question.*"

Leta stiffened. "*What does that mean?*"

Duggar glanced at his fellow elders, all three of whose gazes were still locked on Ghost. "*Do you not see it?*" he asked, his mouth opening in what looked suspiciously like a laugh. "*Are you three so consumed with our lost pup that you've failed to give our scion more than a cursory glance?*"

That earned him a trio of sharp looks.

"*Elders should be more observant,*" Duggar continued sagely. "*Look at him. Look at the scion.*" At the alpha's command, the gazes of the other three elders drifted my way.

Sulan was the first to see it. Aira followed suit quickly after, and even Leta was not so oblivious as to fail to notice the changes in my Mark.

So that's what a gaping wolf looks like, I thought wryly.

Duggar went down on his belly. *"Hail, Protector, and welcome to the Pack. Know that we stand ready to serve."*

The other three quickly followed suit. *"Hail, Protector,"* they echoed.

"Stop that," I snapped, gesturing impatiently at them.

"Nothing has changed between us," I added as the four elders rose back to their haunches. "I'm still the same Michael I always was. You will treat me no differently."

"As you wish, Protector," Aira murmured, an indecipherable undercurrent in her tone. Was that amusement?

"It's Michael," I said, stressing the point.

Aira inclined her head. *"Of course, Protector Michael."*

I rolled my eyes. No doubt about it—she *was* definitely laughing at me. But I was not offended. In fact, I was relieved. Being made fun of I could handle; bowing and scraping... not so much. I had had enough of deference from the New Haveners, and I didn't want the Pack to start treating me the same way.

More relaxed than I had been to this point, I sat down and indicated Nyra and Ghost to do likewise. The byplay with Aira had served to lighten the atmosphere in the room somewhat.

Ghost, though, was still tense.

"Alright, Aira, you've had your fun," I said, resting my hand reassuringly on the pyre wolf. "Now, can we get back to the matter at hand?"

"Tell us about your Protector Mark," Sulan demanded, her preoccupation with Ghost temporarily forgotten. *"How did you get it?"*

I waved aside her question. "We'll get to that. But first, let's talk about Ghost." I exhaled. "Ghost is... Ghost is no longer a dire wolf. What she is, is a stygian pyre wolf. Her spirit was rehomed in a physical shell created from a mix of organic matter, including the remains of a phoenix and, yes, the nether as well—which is the reason for the taint you smell on her. The void does not impinge on her mind, though. She is still the same Ghost you knew." I paused. "Well, perhaps a bit more grown up."

Not unexpectedly, my explanation unleashed a flurry of questions.

"Rehomed? What you say is impossible."

"A phoenix? Where did you find such a creature?"

"How was this done? And by whom?"

"Why use the nether? Why not give her a dire wolf body?"

I opened my mouth to reply, answers at the ready, but before I could respond, Ghost took it upon herself to do so. *"Time was short,"* she said, raising her snout defiantly. *"Adriel—the one who fashioned my new body—had no choice but to use the material she had to hand."*

Momentary silence.

"Adriel... she is the other human who accompanies you?" Aira asked.

Sulan sniffed. *"She is no human. She stinks of death."*

Ignoring Sulan's interjection, I nodded mutely, choosing not to delve into the details of exactly who and what Adriel was. There would be time enough for that later.

"But why use nether?" Sulan demanded again. *"Why not wait until—"*

"I told you, there was no time," Ghost interjected angrily. *"If Adriel waited, I would be dead."* She glared at the white wolf. *"Or would you have preferred that?"*

Sulan shrank back from the raw hurt in Ghost's words. "No," she whispered, hanging her head. *"Not that. Never that."*

"Then why...?" Ghost asked, her own voice just as small. *"Why shut me out? Why not let me in?"* She was referring to Sulan's mind. Like the other elders, Sulan held hers firmly shuttered.

Sulan took a tentative step forward. *"I'm sorry, pup. The fault is not yours but mine. Just an old wolf being foolish."* She touched her nose to Ghost's while simultaneously baring her mind. *"Will you forgive me?"*

Ghost rubbed her chin against the older wolf's. *"Of course, Sulan."*

"Tell us about the phoenix," Duggar said, deliberately drawing away my attention—and that of the other elders—in a bid to give Sulan and Ghost a semblance of privacy.

I shook my head. "We'll get to Sunfury in due time. My tale is a long one, and it's best if I relate it to everyone at once."

The alpha inclined his head in acceptance. *"What can you tell us of this one then?"* he asked, his gaze shifting to Nyra.

"Nyra is my apprentice," I replied.

Hearing her name, the sniper straightened. Despite me speaking aloud, she was understandably having difficulty following the conversation. Unlike me, Nyra lacked the beast tongue trait. Her Wolf Mark notwithstanding, she would require a skill like telepathy to communicate with the dire wolves.

In fact, I suspected that in the times of the ancients, telepathy had been the primary means by which most scions communicated with their Houses' beastkin. Only a few Houses—such as Death—would've had no beastly counterparts. This, in turn, led me to wonder if the prevalence of telepathy amongst the ancients also explained its relative absence in the modern era.

Do the new Powers and their players—whether knowingly or not—shun the psi disciplines because of its tainted association with the Primes of old?

It was an interesting question but one meant for later pondering. Refocusing on the here and now, I saw Duggar rise to his feet.

Padding forward, the alpha walked a slow circle around a nervous Nyra. *"She is young,"* he noted.

"But still bears the Mark," Leta added in a more subdued tone than she'd used thus far. Of all the elders, she seemed the most affected by my new status as a Pack Protector.

"And yet she cannot communicate with us," Aira observed.

I nodded. "All those things are true, but Nyra is still new to the Game. She will learn, both to speak to the Pack and to understand the ways of Wolf."

"Then it is not to enter the Trials that you've brought her here?" Aira asked.

I shook my head. "No. Nyra is not ready for the Trials. But one day, she will be."

"Soon, hopefully," Nyra added unexpectedly. "Michael is teaching me. I have given him my allegiance and will follow wherever he leads. But I hope to be a friend of the Pack in my own right someday."

"She speaks truly," Leta noted.

"Her thoughts are free of deceit," Duggar agreed. He glanced at me. *"Please welcome her in the name of the Pack and tell her that we, too, look forward to that day."*

"The alpha has extended his welcome," I told Nyra with a smile. "You are free to come and go amongst the Pack as you wish, and unless you prove otherwise, you will be treated as a trusted pack member."

Nyra did not miss the warning implicit in my words. "Thank you," she said, bowing in the direction of the elders. "I will not betray your trust."

I rose to my feet. "Now that that is all out of the way, will you see to Nyra's introduction to the rest of the Pack?" I asked, directing the question to Aira specifically.

"Of course, Michael," she replied warmly. *"Oursk and the others are most impatient to meet her."* She paused. *"And you, too."*

I nodded. "As I am them." I glanced in the direction of the structure Snow had taken Adriel. "But there are a few others that I must greet first."

Aira laughed. *"Go. I know you are anxious to be reacquainted with your human friends and... perhaps one in particular?"*

Ignoring her teasing note, I ducked out of the igloo, safe in the knowledge that Ghost and Nyra were in good hands.

CHAPTER 486: REUNITED

On closer inspection, it was obvious why the oblong building differed from the rest of the structures in the den. It had been constructed for human habitation and, no doubt, had been internally subdivided as well.

There was even a chimney, I noted as I drew closer, watching the cheerful plumes of smoke puffing out the thick steel pipe poking out the top of the structure. The building itself was mostly constructed from hard-packed blocks of snow. But bone and animal fat had also been used to increase the structure's overall sturdiness and density.

A proper ice bunker, I thought, drawing to a stop in front of the door. And it was a *real* door—made from animal skins, sinew, and reinforced with bone—no less.

I raised my hand to knock, then stopped. *Much better to surprise them,* I decided.

Pushing open the door, I advanced into the room.

The chamber beyond was small, cozy, and crowded. Fur rugs lined the floors and curving walls, magelights hung near the roof, lighting the windowless room, and a fire blazed in the central stonepit, its fumes funneled away by the steel pipe I'd spotted from outside.

Five figures were locked motionless around the fire. Four were gathered on the right side while the fifth stood alone on the left. I sighed. The tension in the room was palpable, and it was not hard to guess what was going on.

"Took you long enough," Adriel said, not looking over her shoulder as she spoke. "I was beginning to think I might have to kill someone."

While the words were clearly spoken in jest—to my ears, anyway—none of the four facing her took it that way.

Anriq's hands curled into fists while Teresa and Terence tightened their grips on their swords. Only Cara—Safyre—reacted with any semblance of calm and stopped short of raising her wand. It was Safyre, too, who Adriel watched most closely, I noted. Which was not unexpected, given that she was the only other elite in the room.

What *was* surprising was how little attention my entry had drawn. Only Anriq had bothered to glance my way, and that was simply to nod in acknowledgment before he returned to watching Adriel.

Clearly, my former companions deemed the lich too much of a threat.

Sighing again, I shut the door and strode deeper into the room. Of Snow and his pups there was no sign. The arctic wolf alpha was a wily one, though, and no doubt he'd sensed the simmering tension. For his pups' sake, he must have vacated the area.

"Hello, everyone," I said brightly. "I'm back." Which fact was glaringly obvious already, but I was hoping it would cut through some of the tension.

Sadly, it did not.

Safyre's brown eyes slid in my direction as she looked me over. My heart thudded loudly. The aetherist was exactly as I remembered her.

Her hair—meticulously pinned and with no strand out of place—shone blue-black under the harsh glare of the magelights, while her sliver-white garb was as spotless as the last time I'd seen her, every piece of gear glittering with magic. Safyre was clearly flourishing despite the hardship of life on the tundra.

"Who is this?" she asked dispassionately, waving one negligent hand in Adriel's direction.

Uh-oh.

No 'hello.' No 'how are you?' Not even a demand of where I'd been. It did not bode well.

My trepidation increasing, I took a second longer look at Safyre's face. Despite her smooth, unruffled expression, her cheeks were flushed and her eyes fierce.

Right. She's angry.

"Adriel is with me," I said. "She's a friend."

"She's a lich," Safyre said in the same monotone voice.

"A fact of which I'm well aware," I said, the grin slipping off my face. "Nevertheless, Adriel is a *trusted* companion."

Once again, there was no give in Safyre's expression. My gaze flickered to the others. There was no change in their stances either. All four of my former companions remained tense and alert.

What's gotten into them?

"What about the stygian traveling with you?" Safyre asked. "Is it a trusted companion, too?"

I blinked. "*She.* Not it. And how do you know about Ghost?"

It was Safyre's turn to blink. "Ghost? The lost spirit wolf?"

"Not any longer, obviously," Adriel murmured.

Ignoring her interjection, I kept my gaze fixed on Safyre, who it seemed was the four's nominated spokeswoman. "Well?"

"I scryed your approach from afar," she replied stiffly.

I nodded. That explained some of their apprehension, but not all of it. "Ghost is no nether creature. She is a stygian pyre wolf." I paused. "And my familiar."

However, instead of allaying Safyre's fears, my words appeared to have the opposite effect. "The Michael I knew was no mage," she said, her fingers tightening around the end of her wand.

"The Michael you knew?" I repeated, my brows furrowing. "Wait, wait! Don't tell me you think I'm an imposter?"

"Aren't you?" she challenged. "You're traveling with an undead—a lich no less—an unknown player, and a stygian." She paused. "Pardon, a stygian pyre wolf."

"As if that makes it any better," Teresa muttered under her breath.

"Nyra—the unknown player—is my apprentice," I said simply.

"Your apprentice," Safyre repeated, disbelief writ clearly in her tone. "So why take her to the pack elders?"

"You saw that, too? *They* don't think I'm an imposter—and they're telepaths! Don't you think the elders would know if I wasn't who I said I was?" I demanded.

Safyre nodded. "That the dire wolves have accepted your identity is the only reason you're still alive." Before I could think up a response to that, she went on, "I'll ask again: why did you take your apprentice to the elders?"

"Because she bears a Wolf Mark," I said flatly.

Safyre's gaze sharpened. "Anriq, go check."

Obediently, the werewolf swung toward the door.

"Stop," I growled.

Anriq froze.

Safyre glanced at him. "Anriq?"

The werewolf's eyelids fluttered. "I c–can't, Safyre," he whispered. "Not if he forbids it."

Safyre's gaze slid from Anriq to me.

"Tell her why, Anriq," I replied, just as softly.

He gulped audibly. "He's a Pack Protector. Even Duggar and Snow will have to obey his commands now."

Safyre's eyes grew cold. "That explains the Pack's acceptance then."

I threw up my hands in exasperation. "This has gone on long enough, Cara!" I snapped, deliberately using the name I'd bestowed on her when we'd first met. Rounding on Anriq before she could respond, I ordered, "Tell her how many player alphas you've met."

"Two," he whispered. "You and Dathe."

"And how many Pack Protectors?" I demanded.

"One. You."

"Do you believe I am who I say, Anriq?"

He licked his lips. "Yes."

I swung back to Safyre, a challenge in my gaze. "You see. The odds that I'm *not* Michael are vanishingly small." Now was definitely not the time to bring up the mimic spell and its ability to alter my spirit signatures.

Some of the frost in Safyre's gaze thawed, but she still looked far from convinced. She shrugged. "You could be under a compulsion."

"A compulsion?" I asked, nonplussed.

"Like the one Loken's envoy used on Oursk," Terence added helpfully.

Elbowing him in the ribs, Teresa nudged him into silence. "Let Saf handle this," she whispered to him.

"But Loken's envoy is not here," I pointed out—very reasonably, I thought.

Safyre's gaze slid back to Adriel. "But a lich is."

Adriel laughed abruptly. "She's not wrong, you know. Lichs have always had quite the reputation. Compelling a player is well within their—our— means."

I glared at her. While the lich's face gave nothing away, her eyes were swimming with laughter. *She's enjoying this,* I thought morosely. "That's not helpful, Adriel," I ground out.

She smiled. "I haven't told them anything they don't already suspect, albeit incorrectly."

Ignoring the byplay, Safyre addressed me again. "Tell us where you've come from."

Sighing, I turned back to her. "From Sector 18,240—which you know already."

"Is that right?" Teresa interjected, ignoring her own prior admonishment of Terence for the selfsame offense. "Do you seriously expect us to believe that the three tagging along with you were living there? In a sector overrun by the nether?"

I stared at the young woman. "Still, brash as ever, Teresa," I murmured.

She glowered at me. "Answer the question!"

"I wasn't in sector 18,240 the entire time," I said evenly.

"Then where were you?" Safyre asked, taking charge of the interrogation—because that was what it felt like—again.

"Trapped in a dungeon," I said curtly.

Her eyes narrowed. "What dungeon?"

"Draven's Reach," I replied, not expecting the name to mean anything to her.

"How did you get there?"

I hesitated, not wanting to reveal the existence of a second dungeon portal in sector 18,240. Equally, though, I didn't want to lie to the four. Being caught out would make it that much harder to allay their suspicions, and besides, these four were amongst those I trusted most in the Game. They were... pack. If I couldn't trust them, who could I trust?

"Through a portal in the nether-infested sector," I said at last.

Safyre's reaction was not what I expected. Instead of expressing surprise, she exchanged a knowing glance with Anriq. I frowned. *Now what is that all about?*

"Describe the portal's location," Safyre instructed.

I shook my head. "I can't do that. It's not my secret to—"

She cut me off. "It's on the eastern bank of the river, isn't it?"

My eyes narrowed. How could she know what?

Safyre's lips twitched upward. "Don't bother answering. I can see that I'm right. Why did you—"

Adriel stepped forward. "Not that I don't find all this entertaining, but this has gone on long enough."

Safyre spun to face her. "Don't interfere, lich," she warned.

Adriel threw her an amused look. "You don't want to fight me, child."

Safyre raised her wand, and the twins went as far as to draw their weapons. But if anything, their actions only seemed to amuse Adriel more. Reaching into her cloak, she pulled out a slim object and held it before Safyre. "Do you know what this is?"

Recognizing it for what it was, I started. "No, Adriel!"

Shooting me a quelling look, the lich turned back to Safyre. "Well?"

"I don't see what that has—" the aetherist began.

"Analyze it," Adriel commanded.

Safyre's lips thinned at the lich's peremptory tone, but she did as ordered, and a moment later, her eyes widened as the Adjudicator identified the object as Adriel's phylactery.

Adriel held out her arm. "Take it."

Safyre did not move.

"Go on," Adriel said, smiling at the naked shock on the other woman's face. "Take it."

Safyre studied the lich searchingly, trying to divine her intentions. "Why?"

Adriel shrugged. "Isn't it obvious? You believe us a threat—you believe *me* a threat." She shook the phylactery. "If you know enough of lichs to know what I'm capable of, then you also know that my phylactery holds the power of real death over me." She swept the four with an imperious gaze. "I haven't compelled the Wolf scion as you fear. If handing over my phylactery is what it takes to prove that, if it's what it takes to prove my good intentions, so be it."

Safyre still didn't move.

"It's him, child," Adriel added more gently. "Michael. He really has returned. This is no trick."

Ignoring Adriel's outstretched hand once more, Safyre turned around to face me. More than one emotion raced across her face—doubt, consternation, fear, anger, and finally, hope. Her eyes locked on mine, she advanced until she was within arm's reach. "Truly?" she whispered. "It's you?"

I nodded, my throat too tight to speak.

Taking one final step, Safyre closed the distance and wrapped me in a hug. Throwing Adriel a grateful look over her shoulder, I hugged her back.

"Welcome home, Michael," Safyre whispered in my ear. "I missed you."

Safyre's acceptance broke the impasse, and the next few minutes passed in a blur of handshakes, hugs, and backslaps—all of which Adriel was conspicuously excluded from. Despite my companions' joy at my return, the lich was still an outsider to them.

Eventually, though, reality intruded, and the questions began.

"What took you so long?"

"Why didn't you return sooner?"

"How could you just abandon us?"

"You didn't think to send back word? Really? The entire time—"

"Woah, woah," I said, holding up my hands. "I'll answer all your questions, I promise. Just give me a chance."

The four exchanged glances, then seeming to come to some sort of accord, they reseated themselves around the fire. Beckoning Adriel to join me, I did so, too.

Waiting on me, no one broke the silence.

Not letting the opportunity go begging, I scrutinized the four carefully. Anriq, Terence, and Teresa were dressed in the same equipment I'd gifted them what felt like a lifetime ago.

Terence's plate armor sat easily on him, and the broadsword at his hip bore the telltale signs of heavy use. Despite this, his gear looked well cared for.

Teresa's chainmail fitted her like a second skin, and the crossed longswords sheathed across her back appeared as much part of her now as her armor did. Her eyes, too, told a story, filled with the lazy confidence of a master swordswoman.

Outwardly, Anriq looked no different from the last time I'd seen him. He wore the same shapeshifter armor I'd given him and still carried the big two-handed axe which I'd encouraged him to learn how to use. And from the many chips, dents, and scratches along the weapon's length, he'd taken my advice to heart.

The axe had seen hard use. *As has Anriq,* I thought.

Yet, it had appeared to have done him some good. The haunted, lost look of the werewolf I'd found in the swamp was gone. In its place was a confident, contented, and dangerous player.

"You all look well," I said at last. "Life on the tundra appears to suit you."

Terence snorted. "I wouldn't go *that* far."

"It's too damn cold," Teresa complained.

"The cold's nothing," Anriq said with a grin. "Wait until you're forced to live in a swamp."

Teresa shuddered. "No thank you."

I smiled, gladdened to see how well they were all getting along.

"We wouldn't be doing nearly so well if not for the packs," Safyre murmured. "They've kept us... sane."

The three younger players nodded emphatically.

"Oh, yes," Teresa said in heartfelt agreement. "Snuggling close with the wolves is way better for staying warm"—she threw Terence a sideways glance—"than using this oaf."

"Hey!" he protested. "That was uncalled for!"

I chuckled. "I've slept with the pack myself a time... or three." My amusement faded. "I guess everyone has questions."

The fours' expressions grew serious. "We do," Safyre said softly.

"Lots of them," Teresa interjected.

"So, where to begin?" I wondered aloud.

"You can start with where you've been all this time," Terence suggested.

"And how you acquired a Protector Mark," Anriq added.

I glanced at the werewolf. "That tale will have to wait for later. It's a long one and better told once everyone has gathered to hear it." I sighed. "As for where I've been... I'm sorry. I know I've been gone longer than any of you expected. Hells, longer than *I* expected, but—"

"Thirty-nine days," Teresa said.

My brows rose. "What?"

"Thirty-nine days. That's how long you've been missing," she replied.

It had felt much longer. *Only thirty-nine days?* I wondered. It didn't seem all that long. "In any case, I was not missing. I was stuck in the dungeon."

Safyre shook her head. "From our perspective, you *were* missing, Michael."

I inclined my head, acknowledging the point.

Teresa leaned forward. "But why did you enter Draven's Reach instead of coming here?"

I sighed. "Did Safyre tell everyone about the stygian overlord? The one I told her about over the farspeaker bracelet?"

Anriq, Terence, and Teresa nodded.

"It was the overlord that drove me to the other dungeon," I explained. "I barely escaped the creature's clutches, and I only managed that much by diving into a river. At that point, there was no turning back. I was too far away from the Guardian Tower's portal to reach it." I shrugged. "It was either enter Draven's Reach or perish."

"So, you knew of the portal's existence beforehand?" Safyre asked. "It wasn't happenstance that you found it?"

I winced, realizing what she was driving at. "I did," I said quietly.

Her lips thinned. "Why didn't you think to tell me about it? You could have with the farspeaker bracelet, you know."

"I know," I said, not denying the fact. "But by the time I realized I had to make for Draven's Reach instead of the Guardian Tower, it was too late."

"What did you do then?" she asked, not berating me further.

"I had to find a way out of the dungeon"—my gaze flickered to the lich—"which is how I met Adriel. She is as much my ally as any of you are."

Teresa harrumphed. "So, you leave her in the dark as much as you do us?"

I chose to ignore Teresa's aside this time, as did Safyre. "But why didn't you leave the dungeon by the same portal through which you entered?" she asked.

"The portal was one way," I said simply.

Anriq's face creased. "You were stuck in Draven's Reach all this time?"

"By and large, yes," I replied.

His frown deepened. "When did you get out?"

"Three days ago."

Safyre inhaled sharply. "Why didn't you return here sooner?"

"I couldn't," I answered forthrightly. "The sector I arrived in was under the control of a hostile faction. Teleporting out from the safe zone was not an option. It took me nearly three days to find a merchant, buy a scroll, and deal with the other complications I ran across." I met Safyre's gaze. "I came as soon as I could."

She sighed. "We feared you were dead."

I bowed my head, realizing that from their perspective that was the most logical conclusion. I hadn't told anyone about Draven's Reach, nor had I given them any reason to believe escape was possible from the nether-infested sector.

"Despite this," Safyre continued, "we launched daily forays into the nether sector."

Startled, I jerked my head back up. "Daily?"

Safyre nodded soberly. "Yes, daily. That's why we moved the camp. Day in, day out, we ventured through the gate, each time killing the stygians guarding the area. Eventually, they gave up and retreated." She paused. "But *we* didn't. Even though most of us believed you dead by then, no one even suggested giving up. We entered the sector time and again." Safyre fell silent for a moment, and when she resumed, there was a distinct tone of hurt—or was it anger?—in her voice. "But we didn't know where to search."

She met my eyes, and unable to hold her gaze, I looked away.

"You hadn't told me where you were going or even thought to mention the dungeon's existence when you had the chance, after all."

I winced. This time there was no mistaking the accusation in Safyre's voice. Worse yet, it was justified. I *had* been too secretive. Truly, she and the others had every right to be angry.

I'd uprooted them from their homes and their quiet—if imperfect—lives, promising them something better, only to promptly vanish and leave them facing the possibility of spending a... well, a very long time in the inhospitable tundra.

In their place, I would've been furious.

"Even the dire wolves had trouble tracking you," Safyre went on remorselessly. "The nether's stink confused their sense of smell. And besides, we were limited by how far we could venture from the portal. I could only shield them for so long. Nevertheless, we tracked you to the river, but there we lost your trail." Another pause. "We almost gave up that time."

Safyre exhaled heavily, under the grip of strong emotions. "Then, three weeks ago, Anriq arrived, giving us new hope. He entered the nether-infested sector, and on his own, he searched the river shores."

I glanced at Anriq. "How?"

The werewolf didn't need me to elaborate further. "My regeneration skill kept me alive," he replied.

The werewolves famed regeneration again. The skill was powerful enough to keep Anriq alive despite the nether's corrupting touch. Still, it would not have done anything to stave off the mist's energy drain.

While the werewolf's health might have stayed intact, his stores of stamina, mana, and psi would have plummeted, leaving him all but defenseless against any stygians he encountered.

I shook my head, awestruck by the risk Anriq had taken—that they had *all* taken. And for what?

To find me.

I licked suddenly dry lips. "I'm guessing from what Safyre said earlier that you found the portal to Draven's Reach?"

Anriq nodded. "I did. Only five short days ago. But I couldn't enter."

I tilted my head to the side. "Why?"

"The gate to Draven's Reach is besieged," Safyre answered in his stead. "It seems that the overlord chose to remain there after your escape. Not only that, a small army of stygians have joined it. There will be no using the portal until they've been cleared out."

"Damn," I said softly. Closing my eyes, I worked through the implications. *What does it mean for my plans for Draven's Reach? How am I going to get everyone into the dungeon now? But, more importantly, what am I—*

"Is that all you're going to say?" Teresa demanded suddenly.

I opened my eyes to find the four of them staring at me expectantly.

"I'm sorry," I said solemnly. "Truly, I am. I should've been less... secretive. In my defense, my secrets were as much to protect you as they were for anything else. Knowing what I am, knowing about the wolves, my bloodline, the nether sector, all of it, would only have endangered you." I inhaled deeply. "But I realize that in trying to protect you, I only left you less equipped to deal with the situation." I held each of their gazes unflinchingly in turn. "No more secrets. I promise."

"Not good enough," Safyre said bluntly.

I looked at her in surprise.

"For better or worse, we've thrown in our lot with you, Michael, and our lives are as much at risk as yours. At the very least, that entitles us to some say in all our futures."

She was right, of course. None of the four were my followers, and I couldn't unthinkingly assume that they wanted what I did. "I agree," I said quietly. "What are you suggesting?"

"You take us into your confidence, and more importantly, you let us *help*," she said. "You may be the best equipped to tackle some of the things we face, but that's no reason to go at it alone. We should work together from now on."

"I cannot agree to that," I said flatly. "Not always."

Safyre closed her eyes. "Then are you ready for the alternative?"

"What alternative?"

She opened her eyes. "We part ways."

I stared at her in shock. Was she being serious? *Or is she bluffing?* But there was no give in Safyre's gaze, only steely determination. *She'll do it.*

"I plan on heading to Nexus next," I said tightly. "You cannot accompany me there."

Safyre arched one eyebrow. "Why not?"

"You know why," I growled. "You're forsworn."

"I am," she agreed. "But that only means I *shouldn't* enter the safe zone, or any of the districts under the direct control of the factions. But there is no reason for me to do that, is there? With the Guardian Tower, we have a means of entering and exiting Nexus via the plague quarter. The Triumvirate will be none the wiser."

"No," I refuted, jutting out my jaw stubbornly.

Safyre, though, remained adamant. "What do you plan on doing in Nexus?"

"Things," I said evasively.

She smiled, looking truly amused for the first time. "Come, Michael, did you not just promise: no more secrets?"

My mouth turned down sourly, but I didn't refuse to answer. She had a point—*damn her!* "I plan on finding the swamp dungeon. There's also an inn I must visit. And there are werewolves to attend to as well," I replied, laying out only the bare facts. The details would come later.

Anriq stirred. "Then you will need my help, too."

"Definitely not," I snapped.

"You will not find the swamp dungeon without me." He held out a key. "And you will need this if you intend on dealing with Dathe."

Lowering my head, I rubbed at my temples. *Hells, if allies aren't more trouble than they're worth.* Still, even if I wanted to, I couldn't take Anriq and Safyre to Nexus.

The pair would be killed on sight. And there were other things I intended on doing in the city. My plans for them were still nebulous, though, which was the only reason I hadn't mentioned them yet. And I couldn't attend to any of those things if I was dragging Safyre and Anriq along behind me.

I opened my mouth, intent on saying just that when the twins spoke up. "We want to come, too," they sang in unison.

I groaned. "God damnit, no!"

"Your companions have a point," Adriel said unexpectedly.

My head whipped in her direction. "*Now*, you decide to join the conversation?"

She shrugged, unfazed by my anger. "You will need someone to back you up in Nexus." Her eyes turned sad. "And as much as I'd like that to be me, you know why that cannot be."

My mouth worked soundlessly. Adriel's fate was something else I needed to address, but now was most certainly not the time to open that can of worms.

"We'll discuss the matter later," I said to the others, bending a little, "*after* I've spelled out—in detail—what you'll be getting into, and *after* I've laid out all my plans for the future of House Wolf. Then each of you can decide if you still wish to accompany me to Nexus. I wager you won't, though. Does that sound fair?"

Safyre smiled. "It does."

"Good. Then, now that we've got all that out of the way, can we set aside further serious discussion for later and enjoy a quiet meal together, please? There'll be time aplenty to discuss the future once we rejoin the elders."

Safyre's smile broadened. "Of course, Michael," she murmured. "Whatever you say."

Tyelin has delivered a promissory note for 200,000 gold to your representative, Nicola, thereby fulfilling his Power's Pact obligations. Your Pact with Blythe is closed!

My reunion with the rest of the wolves was as emotionally charged as the one with my human companions—if for different reasons—and the day flew by as Ghost and I reacquainted ourselves with both Packs.

Nyra's introduction to the others was another occasion for tension, but the New Havener handled matters well enough on her own, and no intervention was required on my part. Still, it was close to midnight before all the reunions were completed, and I decided to postpone the recounting of my adventures until the next day.

"Are we all here?" Safyre asked when everyone had gathered in the large central igloo the next morning.

Sitting down cross-legged atop a thick stack of furs, I glanced at those on either side of me. Wolves and humans both, we sat in a large circle.

Ghost, the dire wolf elders, and Snow lounged on my left, while Adriel, Nyra, Anriq, Teresa, and Terence were on my right. "I think so," I said to Safyre, who'd sat directly opposite me.

"Then go ahead, Michael," she replied. "Whenever you're ready."

Nodding, I gathered my thoughts.

It was Safyre who I had asked to set up the promised 'serious discussion.' She had not demurred, for which I was glad. Safyre was already familiar with everyone invited—except for Adriel and Nyra, of course. Tellingly, she had spent more time with any of them than I had, and it was clear to me that the twins, and even Anriq, trusted her.

But then so, too, did I.

We hadn't had as much time to speak last night as I'd hoped. Still, we had managed to smooth over some of the biggest misunderstandings between us. The air hadn't been cleared entirely, though, and much had been left unsaid.

Chief in my mind was Safyre's threat.

It had not been an idle one, I knew. She would leave if she felt I was holding out—and that was something I definitely did not want. *So, let's not mess this up.*

Exhaling, I began. "All of you are aware that I plan on reviving House Wolf. Until yesterday, I thought I knew what that meant. A bit of delegation here and there, trusting everyone to do their part, appointing a custodian, arranging a successor, and so on. But at the end of the day, I would still be the one holding all the cards. The only one to grasp the whole picture."

I sighed. "Today, I've come to the realization that I cannot rule alone, that House Wolf cannot be steered correctly if I am the only one who understands what needs to be done. I have decided that House Wolf needs a council." I scanned their faces. "And that you are it."

Silence.

"*Us?*" Terence finally blurted. "You want us on House Wolf's council?"

"While some of you might not have been my first choice," I said, with a pointed look at Terence that set the others chuckling, "fortune did bring us together." My face grew solemn. "But on a more serious note, each of you has my trust. And make no mistake, what I'll be trusting you with is the future of the House no less."

The laughter died down.

"There are still a few faces missing," I continued, thinking of Ceruvax, Algar, Regus, and Farren, "but otherwise, yes, you are it: the inner council of House Wolf."

"Really?" Adriel murmured. "You'd be so bold as to allow a lich on your council?"

I smiled at her. "But you're not just any lich, are you?"

She shook her head. "Michael, I'm no Wolf, you know that. If Ceruvax was here... well, I'm sure you can imagine what he'd say. Death should not sit on Wolf's council."

No one contested Adriel's words, and if anything, I sensed the others agreed with her. Despite my assurances yesterday, an undercurrent of tension remained between the lich and the rest of my companions.

I was not about to let it sway me, though. "If you haven't already noticed, there is a dearth of Wolf candidates right now," I said wryly. "And besides, you've more than earned your right on this council. But if it makes you feel any better, we can designate you a visiting dignitary."

Adriel laughed. "Whatever you wish, Michael. I will serve your House while I can, but you know I will not be around for much longer."

I nodded, not missing the pointed nature of her last remark. It was not, however, a subject I wanted to address just yet.

"But what *is* a House?" Teresa interjected.

I turned her way, glad for the distraction. "I'm not sure what you're asking," I admitted. "What is House Wolf? It is whatever we say it is."

Adriel shook her head. "Not quite."

I glanced at her curiously.

"Houses are—or were, rather—like special factions. They were more than just that, though. To be of House Wolf was synonymous with having *awakened* Wolf blood. Every House member would have already gone through an awakening and subsumed his other bloodlines."

Terence frowned. "Then neither Teresa nor I could ever be true Wolves?" The pair already knew they had no Wolf blood.

"Not by the old definition, no." Adriel shot me a glance. "In fact, the only one here qualified to be a member of House Wolf is Michael himself."

"What about a player's Marks?" Safyre asked, looking intrigued.

"What about them?" Adriel asked rhetorically. "Marks don't factor at all when it comes to House membership. They provide an indication of a player's relationship with a particular bloodline, Power, or Force, and they influence how a player may evolve, but they *don't* automatically confer House membership."

"Interesting," Safyre murmured, sitting back.

"Don't get me wrong," Adriel added after a moment. "Marks *are* important. They can, if sufficiently deepened, suppress other Marks and awaken—or suppress—bloodlines."

Anriq sat up. "What does that mean for me?"

"Under the rules of the old Primes, you, too, would not have qualified for House membership," Adriel told him bluntly. "Your bloodlines—all of them—have been suppressed by your Force Marks and can never be awoken."

"But the old Primes are no more," I said flatly.

Adriel inclined her head, acknowledging the point. "And there are no higher-ranked Wolves around to gainsay you. So, it's as you say, Michael: House Wolf is whatever you say it is."

My lips tightened fractionally. I would not have put it so baldly, but she had the right of it. Not wanting to dwell further on the topic, though, I glanced at Safyre and signaled for her to proceed.

Taking my meaning, she moved things along. "Alright. As Michael has said, we are now, each of us, part of House Wolf's inner council. It will therefore fall on us to decide the House's future." She paused. "But before we get to that, there is another matter we must attend to first." She smiled, somewhat bitingly I thought. "As most of you are no doubt aware, our dear scion is all too fond of his secrets."

That spurred another round of chuckles.

"The secrets end today," Safyre continued. "As a member of the inner council, you will be privy to *all* the House's secrets." Her face grew more serious. "There is a 'but' however. A big one. Notwithstanding my previous remarks, there are consequences to being one of those in the know. You are all already aware of some of them. You will be branded a criminal and hunted—relentlessly—across the breadth of the Kingdom for the information you hold."

Safyre fell silent again, weighing up each person before continuing. "But those are only the external consequences. There are internal ones, too. Restrictions we must place on ourselves to safeguard against betrayal."

Teresa shifted restlessly. "Betrayal? How can you even suggest that? No one here would betray Michael!"

Safyre waved aside her protest. "You're missing the point, Tes. It's not just Michael who would be betrayed but *all* House Wolf. Each of us has already been tainted by Michael's heresy." She held up her hand, stilling Teresa' burgeoning objections. "Oh, I know no one here considers it that, but the new Powers do—and they will spare no effort to wipe out anything that smacks of the ancients. No one will escape their wrath. Not you. Not the dire wolves. Not the arctic wolves. Not even their pups. Everyone will be put to the sword. *That* is what betrayal will cost us. Do you understand what I mean?"

Teresa gulped. "I do."

"There is something else to consider," Adriel interjected softly, drawing all eyes to her. "Betrayal need not be willingly performed. Everyone, even Michael, can be made to betray our cause. There are players in the Game who can extract your deepest, darkest secrets—without consent." She gestured to the pyre wolf. "Ghost, here, can do that to an extent. But there are also others who can do it more fully and more brutally."

"The lich is right," Safyre said. "And don't forget the Powers themselves. What they can do does not even bear mentioning."

Anriq lifted his chin. "So, what are you driving at?"

Safyre looked at him. "Just this: there is a price to being a member of this council. A price to knowing all the House's plans." She swept the room with her gaze. "If you choose to remain, you must also accede to your movements being controlled."

Anriq snorted. "My movements are already curtailed. I'm a criminal, remember?"

"And I am a forsworn," she said. "But the restrictions I speak of will be more onerous."

"More?" Terence asked disbelievingly.

"More," Safyre confirmed. "If you decide to stay in the council, you will swear a Pact with the House's leader, giving him the right to decide where you go and when."

"That would be Michael, presumably?" Nyra asked softly.

Safyre nodded.

"But... but... if we do that, he'll just force us to stay here," Terence protested. "Safe and out of the way, just like he wants!"

"It has to be this way," I said, speaking up at last.

What Safyre had proposed came as no shock to me, of course. We'd discussed the matter yesterday, and if I was being honest, it was more my proposal than hers. Yet she had agreed to its necessity. "Not just for my sake but that of everyone," I added.

Teresa stared at Safyre, looking betrayed. "You made him promise last night not to leave us behind. Now you're giving him the means to do just that!"

"That's not what this is about, Teresa," I said gently. "I will keep my word. You *are* being given a choice, but like Safyre said, there can be consequences—ugly consequences—to being captured by our enemies." I sighed. "If you wish to accompany me to Nexus, it's better to step outside now and not know everything." I held her gaze. "You can't betray what you don't know."

The young fighter looked away.

"The same applies to all of you," I said, addressing the others. "I will tell you everything, but only if you're willing to pay the price for holding such secrets."

In the renewed silence that reigned, I studied the rest of my companions, measuring their reactions.

Terence looked troubled, Anriq not so much—he met my gaze unflinchingly—Safyre appeared resigned, and Nyra was simply bored— none of this was new to her. The twins, then, were the biggest holdout. But despite their reservations, neither so much as glanced at the door.

"I guess that settles that then," I murmured, when after the drawn-out moment no one moved. "I will be honored to hold your Pacts."

"How?" Anriq asked abruptly.

I glanced up at the werewolf. "How?"

But it was not to me he directed the question but Safyre. "How is Michael going to form a Pact with us? I thought only Powers could do that?"

Safyre threw me an opaque look. "That is the same thing I asked him yesterday, but he refused to divulge any details, promising to do so today." She gestured to me with a gloved hand. "Michael?"

All eyes turned my way.

Ignoring their stares, I took my time gathering my thoughts. I'd not discussed what I had become with any of my tundra allies—not even with Safyre or the dire wolves—and with my Power Mark hidden, none of them had had cause to suspect the truth.

Now, though, the time had come to reveal myself. But for some reason, I still found myself hesitating.

"Trust them," Ghost said suddenly. *"They will not look at you any differently after this."*

I glanced at her. *"How can you be so sure?"*

"I'm a mind reader, remember?" Her eyes twinkled. *"And yesterday, just about everyone wanted to touch me."*

I snorted, caught between scolding and thanking her, and while I couldn't tell whether Ghost was being serious or not, her words still reassured me. *She's right. There is nothing to fear.* Inhaling deeply, I turned my attention inward.

You have unconcealed your Powerful Initiate Mark.

"Inspect my spirit signatures," I said quietly.

For a drawn-out second, no one said anything.

Then the twins gasped, Anriq's eyes grew wide, and Safyre, who I looked to most keenly, paled. "You're a Power?" she mumbled.

"Technically, I'm not one yet," I replied. "But I'm on the path to ascension."

"Semantics," she muttered, color returning to her cheeks.

Her initial shock had passed, I thought. *What will follow in its wake?*

"When?" she demanded.

I shrugged. "I don't know. I could become a Power a week from now, a month, a year. It all depends on—"

Safyre slashed her hand downward. "No. I mean, when did you become a Powerful Initiate? Since before we spoke at the wolves' valley?"

My eyes widened. "Of course not! I would not have kept something like that a secret for so long."

The suspicious glint in her eye did not dim.

"It happened while he was in Draven's Reach," Adriel said, jumping in.

Safyre's stare swapped to the lich.

"Michael told me you were an elite," Adriel went on, "and that you're someone who was once sworn to one of the new Powers. Is that true?"

Safyre nodded curtly.

"Then, I take it you know how one earns the Power Mark?"

Again, Safyre merely nodded.

"Well, *we* don't," Teresa interjected loudly. "Care to enlighten us, lich?"

"Why not," Adriel murmured. "It has always been an ambition of mine to educate unruly children."

Teresa reddened at the rebuke but didn't back down from Adriel's challenging stare.

The lich chuckled. "That one is going to be trouble," she said in an aside to me.

Teresa's flush deepened, but I steadfastly didn't react. While I appreciated Adriel coming to my rescue, I wasn't about to redirect Teresa's ire my way. *I have enough people angry at me as it is.*

"There are two ways one may step onto the path of Power, young lady," Adriel began, and to her credit, her tone was only slightly condescending. "The first, and perhaps easier, is to reach level two hundred and fifty."

Terence's gaze whipped in my direction. "You're a tier six player?" he asked in an awed tone.

I shook my head. I could well understand Terence's amazement. When we'd parted ways, I had only been rank fifteen. To gain another ten ranks on top of that—in what amounted to little more than a month—was a nearly impossible feat, even for me.

I'd come close, though.

"Not yet. I'm rank twenty-three at the moment," I said, knowing that none of them would be able to overcome my deception skill and successfully analyze me.

Terence's face grew puzzled. "Then, how—"

"The second method of becoming a Power," Adriel said, speaking over him, "is to kill a Power."

This time around, Terence, Anriq, and Teresa were too stunned to voice further questions.

"There was a Power in Draven's Reach?" Safyre asked quietly.

"Not a new Power like you're thinking," I answered, "but a stygian one."

Her brows creased. "There are stygians in the dungeon?"

"There *were* stygians in the dungeon," I corrected. "Including a harbinger and a void sapling."

Safyre's face went blank. "You killed a harbinger?"

"I did," I replied, "but not without assistance. Adriel helped. As did... a few others."

Safyre pursed her lips at my evasive response, but all she said was, "I see we're going to have to wait for the full tale to hear all the details. But for now, I've heard enough." She scanned the faces of the other players in the room. "What about everyone else? Has your curiosity been satisfied, and can we proceed with the Pacts?"

Anriq and Terence nodded, but Teresa was not done yet. "What about the packs? Michael may be able to bind us to obedience through a Pact, but what about the dire and arctic wolves?"

"Like I said yesterday, no wolf will dare disobey Michael," Anriq replied before I could.

Teresa rounded on him. "You didn't explain why, though."

"As a Pack Protector, Michael's Wolf Mark is stronger than even an alpha's," he said softly. "Pack hierarchy demands they acknowledge his dominance."

"Really?" Teresa asked.

Duggar rose to his feet, as did Snow. All the pack elders had been following the conversation closely, but inhibited by the players' inability to speak mind to mind, they'd been relegated to the position of silent observers.

Yet, they could still communicate without words—which was what Duggar and Snow were choosing to do now. Going down on their bellies, both alphas submitted to me.

I inclined my head, acknowledging the gesture.

"That clear enough for you?" Anriq asked, smirking at Teresa.

She glared at him. "It is," she said in a clipped tone.

"Good," Safyre said. "Then there is no point in delaying further. Let's proceed with the Pacts."

There was no point in attempting to craft a Pact that stopped the others from betraying me or the House, so I didn't try.

Any Pact could be broken, after all.

Safyre was living proof of that. And while the consequences for breaking a Pact were dire—which, again, Safyre could attest to—if a player was sufficiently motivated or tortured, they *would* break their Pacts.

So, instead, I tried for a softer approach and bound the others in a manner that *should* prevent them from ever falling into a situation where they were forced into betraying their convictions.

You have sealed a Pact with Anriq, Teresa, Terence, and Safyre. In exchange for a place on the inner council of your House and being privy to its secrets, the four have agreed to let you direct their movements from here on, limiting the sectors they may visit. This Pact may be terminated at any time but only at your discretion.

You have 5 / 20 active Pacts.

It took only a few minutes to complete the agreements between the others and me. The moment I was done, though, Teresa picked up on an anomaly.

"What about her?" she demanded.

Looking where she pointed, I saw that Teresa was gesturing at Nyra. Finding herself the subject of the other young woman's ire, Nyra scowled. "What about me?"

"Why aren't *you* being bound by a Pact?" Teresa retorted.

I sighed. It was just like Teresa to notice something like this. Knowing I had to intervene before things could escalate, I said, "Nyra's my follower. There is no need to bind her further."

Teresa's mouth opened in an 'O' of surprise. It did not stop her from probing further, however. "Why does *she* get to be your follower and we don't?"

"There are reasons. *Valid* reasons."

Teresa squinted at me suspiciously. "I thought you said no more secrets?"

I pinched the bridge of my nose, striving for patience.

"Perhaps if we gave Michael a chance to explain?" Safyre suggested.

Inclining my head in thanks to her, I turned back to Teresa. "What do you see when you study Nyra's spirit signature?"

"Hmm, just a Shadow Mark."

"She has a Wolf Mark, too," Anriq added, sounding both envious and curious at the fact.

"That's right," I said. "She has both those Marks. But what none of you see is her *third* Mark: the Mark of Michael."

Terence laughed. "Mark of Michael? Good one." Spotting my unsmiling face a moment later, his humor faded. "It's not a joke?"

I shook my head. "No. It's not. When you give your allegiance to a Power, you become Marked for all the Game to see. Which is why I did not suggest follower Pacts for you and Teresa."

"Why don't we see your Mark on her then?" Anriq asked.

"Because I have a secret blood trait that conceals my followers' allegiance—but only if they themselves are of Wolf."

He sat up straighter. "Then there is no reason for *me* not to become your follower."

I glanced at Adriel. "Would I be able to pass on the secret blood trait to him?"

She shook her head adamantly. "You won't. Like I said earlier, his Marks have suppressed his bloodlines. For all intents and purposes, the werewolf is not a Wolf." Her lips turned down. "A strange contradiction, I know."

Anriq's shoulders sagged, but he made no further complaint.

I nodded, in light of everything I'd learned about the ancients, I was not at all surprised by Adriel's response. I knew Anriq was disappointed, and despite what Adriel had said, I considered him a Wolf. Still, the werewolf could not become my follower, not until such time as the need for secrecy had passed.

I turned back to Safyre. "I think we can continue."

She nodded. "The first order of business is for Michael and"—her gaze slid in the lich's direction—"Adriel to relate their stories." She turned to me. "If you will begin, Michael?"

I marshaled my thoughts. "This is going to be a long tale, so brace yourself," I warned.

"It began with the stygian overlord and the river..."

✻   ✻   ✻

It took Adriel and me the better part of the day to lay out the events of the last month and a half.

My promise to the others had not been an idle one, and I didn't hold out, not even about New Haven. My companions already knew about the portal to Draven Reach, so there was little point in concealing the city's existence. I left out nothing else either, not of what I'd done nor my plans and aspirations for the future. If I fell, they would be the ones to take up the mantle of the ancients.

And I was not about to let them do so unprepared.

Unsurprisingly, my tale evoked strong emotions and reactions from my companions on more than one occasion.

...

"A Wolf envoy?" Anriq exclaimed. "What's he like?"

...

"How old did you say you are again?" Teresa asked, looking aghast at Adriel.

...

"So many dungeons lost to the nether..." Safyre rued. "What have the new Powers done?"

...

"Wolfmen, that's more than passing strange," Terence mused. "What do you think the chances are of creating, uhm... cat-men?"

...

"A phoenix!" Teresa exclaimed, her eyes shining. "I want to meet one!"

...

"Possessed..." Terence muttered, throwing Adriel a sidelong glance. "They sound like abominations."

...

"An entire city," Safyre marveled. "Exiled and living in a dungeon. How is that possible?"

...

Snow listened intently to everything I said, but I knew much of my tale was beyond his understanding. Still, he grasped the gist, and more importantly, he understood what it meant for the arctic wolves.

"*War. Coming,*" he said.

"*War is coming,*" I agreed.

"*We. Ready. Support. Protector.*"

"*Thank you, Snow,*" I murmured.

The dire wolves, of course, understood everything, yet they had held themselves steadfastly silent during my tale, and it was only as I ran down, that they stirred.

"*Ah, Michael,*" Aira said. "*I fear for the Pack. Trouble lies ahead for us.*"

"*Not just for the Pack,*" Sulan muttered. "*For all wolfkind.*" She shook her head. "*Guardians. Lost Primes. Stygian Powers. There is little that I fear in this world, scion. But your tale scares me, I admit.*"

"*This is not a task the Pack is equipped to face,*" Leta added worriedly. "*Protecting Wolf's line is one thing, but this... this is beyond us.*"

"*Perhaps, it is,*" Duggar said. "*But it is not a task we will shy from. We have a debt to repay. We will follow the commands of the Primes.*" His gaze met mine. "*Both the old and the new.*"

"*Whatever it takes,*" Sulan said in agreement.

I ducked my head. "*I thank you for the support, Duggar. But this is not your fight. I will not put the Pack in harm's way and will do my best to shield you.*"

"*Which is why, despite everything, we will follow you,*" Leta growled.

I looked at the elder in surprise. She was the last one I'd expected to voice any kind of support for me.

Leta snorted. "*Oh, wipe that foolish expression off your face, or I will begin to believe Sulan right and you are a pup.*" She shook her head. "*How can humans be so ignorant?*"

Duggar chuckled. "*What Leta is trying to say, Protector, is that we will fight for you and on your behalf.*" His mindvoice grew serious. "*And yes, we will die for you, too. But wolves are no strangers to death. For the Pack to survive, some must die. That is the way.*"

"*That has always been the way,*" Sulan pronounced.

"*But,*" I protested, "*it is not necessary for—*"

"No buts," Aira interjected gently. *"The others are right. We know you will not spend our lives foolishly. Which is why we will follow you."*

Duggar rose to his feet, as did Snow—almost as if the other alpha's motion was a cue he'd been waiting for.

"The Primes of old gave their lives for us," Duggar said as he and Snow padded to a stop before me. *"We will do no less for you."* The pair lowered their heads.

"This is really not—" I began.

"Shh," Leta commanded, *"the Pack has decided."*

Images flashed through my mind as Duggar and Snow conveyed their intent—the dire wolf alpha communicating through pictures and not words for Snow's sake—and a Game alert unfurled.

Duggar and Snow have offered you their allegiance. Do you wish to accept their oaths on behalf of the Forerunners faction?

I sighed, realizing the futility of trying to dissuade the pair. Nevertheless, I gave it one more shot. *"Are you sure about this?"*

"We are," Duggar replied, speaking for both of them. Closing my eyes, I laid my hand on each wolf in turn.

You have accepted the arctic wolf and dire wolf Packs into the Forerunners faction. As non-players, the wolves are free to break their pledges at any time and without consequences. As are you. However, until such time as the Forerunners disavow the Packs—or vice versa—they will be considered the faction's sworn soldiers, and their actions will reflect on it.

I opened my eyes to find my human companions staring at me.

"What was all that about?" Safyre asked.

Sadly, none of my companions could communicate directly with the wolves, lacking both telepathy and beast tongue. *Another thing we will have to find a solution for going forward, I suppose.*

"The wolves have just joined the Forerunners," I murmured. The two packs had grown in my absence, the arctic wolves substantially so. Being dungeon creatures, the Adjudicator himself saw to it that their numbers were replenished by bringing in new wolves from outside.

The net effect of this was that the arctic wolves now numbered two hundred, overtaking the dire wolves whose numbers had remained stable at one hundred and thirty.

Another three hundred and thirty recruits for the faction. Not bad.

"Then we should join as well," Teresa said, stepping forward.

I eyed the four. There was no reason for them not to join the faction. It would not alter their spirit signatures in any way, and I saw no other reason to object. "Alright, let's get it done."

✳   ✳   ✳

You have accepted the players, Safyre, Terence, Anriq, and Teresa into the Forerunners faction.

A few minutes later, we were done, and everyone had reseated themselves. Unsurprisingly, Adriel had not seen a need to join the faction, expecting as she did for her time on the council to be short.

"So, now that that is all out of the way, what's next?" Terence asked.

I held up my hand. "Before we move on, there is something else to discuss." When I'd related my story, there was one topic I'd not broached. Now the time had come to do so.

"I said no secrets, and I meant that." Withdrawing a slim object from my bag of holding, I held it up. "It's time to discuss House Death."

Adriel stilled. "What do you mean, 'discuss House Death?'"

Not answering her directly, I placed the sealed envelope in her hands. "From Farren," I said without further explanation.

There was no mistaking Adriel's consternation as she took the envelope from my hands, nor her trepidation when she saw the numbers— coordinates to House Death's home sector—stenciled on the front. Breaking open the seal, the lich withdrew the letter inside and began to read.

I could see the questioning looks in the others' eyes, but I ignored them, my gaze fixed on Adriel as she grew steadily paler. "No," she breathed, "No, no, NO."

Unbidden, Ghost rose to her feet and lay her head in the lich's lap. Adriel buried her hands into the pyre wolf's coat, clinging to her as if to a lifeline. Her gaze rose to mine. "Did you know... about this?"

"I haven't read the letter." I exhaled heavily. "But Farren told me the gist before we left Draven's Reach. He made me promise not to give it to you until..." I broke off, searching for the right way to put it.

"Until too late?" she asked in a voice stripped of emotion.

I nodded wordlessly. That was not exactly what I'd promised, and technically, I was not breaking my word to the archlich, but I'd kept this secret too long already, and it was time to speak openly.

"I'll kill him for this," Adriel said tonelessly.

She was joking, of course. At least, I hoped she was.

"This changes things, you realize," I said, searching for something to say. But only a second later, I wished I could take back the words.

Saying Farren's revelation had changed things was an epic understatement. Of course, it had. Right now, Adriel's world must feel like it was crumbling all around her, and here I was uttering trite nonsense. "Sorry, that was stupid of me," I muttered.

But Adriel didn't appear to hear.

She stared unseeing past me, her eyes cold and her back unbending, and for a moment, I thought she would deny the undeniable, but duty still held her. Duty to a dead House.

"It does change things," she agreed, shoulders sagging. "It changes everything. Damn him."

My gaze flickered across the room. All the others had turned away—even the ever-inquisitive Teresa. Knowing something was wrong, but not understanding the cause, they were doing what they could to give Adriel and me some semblance of privacy.

Which they would not have to do if you picked a more appropriate time to raise this.

I lowered my gaze. "I'm sorry, Adriel. I should have waited before bringing this up."

"No," she said sharply. "Delaying bad news never helps." She paused. "What you should have done was tell me sooner."

I hung my head further. She was right.

Adriel sighed. "But this is not your fault, and it's wrong to blame you." She held out her hand, offering me the letter.

I glanced from the parchment to her face. "Are you sure...? There's nothing, uhm, personal in it?"

Something akin to a wry smile touched her lips. "In a letter from Farren? Definitely not."

Taking her at her word, I flipped open the letter and began to read.

Dear Adriel,

What I have to say is going to be hard, and something I'm sure you don't want to hear, but for the sake of Death, hear me out. There is no easy way to say this, so I'll say it plain.

You need not remain a lich.

There, I said it. And no, dear sister, I do not joke. I've preserved your body using a spell—you know the one—that will let it outlast even the guardians. Until you get to it, your body will remain untouched and unageing.

I've hidden it away, too, of course, somewhere no one would ever find. And if you think but for a moment, I'm sure you will realize where that is.

'Why me?' I can hear you asking. 'Why did he choose me?'

But you know the answer to that, too, don't you? You were always the best of us—in every sense. With you at the helm, Death can only grow stronger. However, I am not blind to your own desires in this matter, nor do I dismiss them. I understand, I truly do.

Which is why I've an alternative to suggest. Remember Stayne? The ascendant dead the scion informed us about?

He may be a viable candidate for the House if you believe yourself... unfit. You're not, trust me, but I will leave the decision in your capable hands.

Death must rise again. Whether by your hand or another's, it must. Our House's ancient debts demand nothing less. I know I need not speak to you of duty. Yours has always been stronger than mine.

And as much as I hate doing this to you, I will rest easier knowing Death's fate is yours to decide. Do what you think is right, as I know you always will.

Your brother in death and life,
Farren

I perused the letter, then turned it over, but it was blank on the other side. "He is a bit scant on the details, isn't he?"

Adriel laughed, sounding a bit more like her old self. "That's Farren. He always did enjoy making people read between the lines."

An answering smile flickered on my face, but only for a moment. I didn't want to be the bearer of more bad news, but nor did I want Adriel to give false hope. "I would not advise leaving Death's fate to Stayne. I can't claim to have known him well, but I believe him to be wholly Erebus' creature."

Adriel sighed. "I believe you. But I don't think Farren meant me to take his suggestion seriously. He mentioned Stayne as a reminder only."

I raised an eyebrow. "Oh?"

"Where there is one Death scion," she said softly, "there may be more."

I ruminated over that for a second. *More Death scions? Alive—sort of, anyway—and working for Erebus?*

If that were true, it would explain a few things. Things like the Awakened Dead's sudden rise in the Game, which Loken had attributed to the dungeon they'd discovered.

But what if it was not just the dungeon that accounted for the Awakened Dead's success? What if Erebus *did* have more scions in his pocket?

Loken had to suspect the truth. He was too canny not to. And it would be just like the trickster to mislead me about the source of his interest in the Awakened Dead. Was the Death scion—or scions—the real reason 'Hamish' had been spying on Erebus?

Huh. Interesting.

Answers would have to wait, though. "I see," I murmured, dismissing my musings.

Turning back to the letter, I began to read it again but stopped before the end as something else caught my eye. "What does Farren mean by 'ancient debts?' It seems an odd turn of phrase."

"It was a House motto of sorts, one shared by many Houses," Adriel replied, her emotions under tight rein again. Nothing disrupted the lich's equilibrium for long. She glanced at me. "Including House Wolf's actually."

My brows rose higher. "Care to explain?"

"I will." She scanned the room and noticed the others' turned-away faces. "But I think you should reconvene the meeting first. This is something everyone should hear."

"Now that everyone is caught up," I said, after I'd explained the contents of the letter and its implication, "Adriel has something that she wants to share."

I turned to the lich. Her eyes were closed and her face smooth. If I didn't know better, I would've said she was sleeping.

"The Primes broke the world," she said without preamble.

I stiffened, shocked by the stark statement.

"What do you mean by that?" Safyre asked slowly.

Adriel opened her eyes. "Just that. The aether, the nether, the sectors—islands floating in a void—they're all the Primes' doing. The ancients fractured the world in a titanic war long before I was even born."

"How do you break a world?" Teresa demanded.

Adriel chuckled. "A good question. Sadly, though, it's one to which no one living knows the answer."

Pressing my palms tightly together, I rocked back and forth, one thought running through my mind: Loken had been telling the truth—at least, in part.

When we'd last met, he'd told me the Primes were the ones who'd shattered the Kingdom. That that was why he and the other new Powers had rebelled.

"If the Primes did that, why are we trying to bring them back?" a confused Terence asked.

"Another good question," Adriel murmured, but it was not to Terence but me that she looked, almost as if she could tell what I was thinking.

"Why didn't you tell me about this earlier?" I asked softly, not oblivious to the irony in me asking her that.

Adriel's lips quirked. She, too, recognized the reversal in our roles. "At first, I didn't know you well enough. Then, I feared it might affect your determination to set things right." Her amusement faded. "But no excuses. I should have shared this tale with you when you told me about Loken's version." She stared at me steadily. "But the trickster did not tell you everything. There is more to the story."

"Go on," I said, willing to hear her out.

Adriel turned back to Terence. "Like I said, the world's breaking occurred a long time ago. Before the Houses became a thing, actually. It happened when the Primes roamed the world, sometimes alone, sometimes in packs, seeking out and destroying their rivals, whether of their own bloodline or not. It was an evil era by all accounts." She sighed. "And ever since, the Houses have been trying to make restitution."

"Restitution?" Anriq asked.

Adriel nodded. "*Forget not the breaking. Forget not the dead. Forget not our ancient debts,*" she quoted. "That was House Death's motto. Most Houses had something similar. It served as an unsubtle reminder of the breaking and our duty to fix it."

"Fix it?" Safyre asked, a trace of disbelief in her voice. "How can you fix the aether? The nether? How can you fix a world split apart?"

"With the Game," Adriel replied succinctly.

My eyes widened. "What?"

"The Game, the guardians, the Adjudicator, they were all created with one purpose in mind," Adriel said, "and that purpose was—*is*—restoring the world."

"How?" I demanded. "How can the Game do that?"

Adriel laughed ruefully. "I don't know. I'm not even sure most of the Primes knew. But there *is* purpose behind the Game. There is purpose behind the Adjudicator. The Game was not created on a whim."

"What about the stygians?" Nyra asked, breaking out of her shell to join the conversation. "How do they fit into all this?"

Adriel's lips turned down. "That, too, is something I don't have the answer to. But by every documented account I've read, the stygians did not exist before the breaking. Whatever happened when the Kingdom was shattered brought them here, and ever since, they've been trying to make the world theirs."

"And the new Powers?" I asked, intrigued despite myself.

"While the Game began with the noblest of intentions, it did not stay that way. Over time, it became corrupted. The new Powers are the ultimate manifestation of that corruption. Power for the sake of Power."

Teresa scowled. "What are you saying, then? That we"—she spread her arms to encompass the players in the room—"that all of us were brought to the Kingdom to fix the Primes' problems?"

Adriel shrugged. "Maybe. Like I said already, I don't know how the Game is supposed to mend things."

"Where does that leave us?" Safyre asked quietly, looking at me.

"The same place we started," I replied just as softly. "Except, with a different perspective, maybe."

✱　✱　✱

We took a short break thereafter.

After Adriel's revelations, everyone felt the need to clear their heads, myself included. Standing alone in the snowstorm—it didn't bother me like it did the others—I stared out onto the tundra.

Thus far, I'd been operating on the assumption that the Primes were good and the new Powers evil—a naïve world view admittedly, but not one I had questioned too closely. Now, though, I was forced to face the question head-on...

If Adriel was to be believed—and I didn't doubt her—Wolf and his kin had committed deeds as black, if not blacker, than Loken and his fellows. In fact, nearly everything about our present circumstances could be traced back to them and the decisions they had made.

The Game. The world's breaking. The stygians.

It was all the Prime's doing. Of course, I didn't doubt the new Powers were any better. But Adriel's story *had* called into question my commitment to restore the Houses—just as she feared it would.

I sighed. *Why is nothing simple?*

A soft chuckle sounded in my mind. *"Perhaps because nothing is ever black and white."*

Glancing to my left, I saw Duggar approaching.

"Deep thoughts?" he asked as he drew to a stop next to me.

"Maybe. I've just realized the task I set myself is not as simple as I anticipated." I laughed. *"On second thought, it was never simple to begin with."* I rubbed my chin. *"Only now..."*

"You're wondering if it's the right choice?" Duggar suggested.

I nodded. *"I am Wolf. I am certain of that as I am of little else in this world. He sings within me."*

"He does," Duggar agreed.

"But about the Houses..." I laughed sharply. *"I'm less certain about them. After Adriel's revelation, I find myself wondering if I should bring back the Houses, or if it would not be better for the Kingdom if they stayed dead."* I glanced at Duggar expectantly, waiting to hear what he had to say.

But the big dire wolf said nothing. Standing companionably next to me, he stared off into the tundra.

"What?" I prompted. *"You're not going to convince me otherwise?"*

He snorted. *"I'm not Sulan. I respect Wolf, but I don't revere the ancients the way she does."*

"I see," I murmured, staring out contemplatively over the horizon. *"You know,"* I said after a moment, *"I thought by raising House Wolf, I was being true to the Primes, doing what they wanted."*

"And you probably were," Duggar agreed. *"House Wolf was the old Wolf's dream."* He turned his great head my way. *"But you forgot one thing."*

"Oh?" I asked, meeting his gaze.

"Wolf always follows his own path." His piece seemingly said, the alpha turned tail and headed back to the den. *"It's too cold out here,"* he growled.

I smiled. *"It's refreshing."*

Snorting disdainfully, Duggar didn't bother to reply.

"You know you haven't made my decision any easier?" I called after him.

The alpha chuckled. *"Who told you it was going to be easy?"*

Before I could think of an apt rejoinder, Nyra stuck her head out of the central igloo. "Michael?" she yelled. "You coming? Everyone is already gathered. We're just waiting on you."

Swiveling about, I followed after Duggar. It was time for some decisions. Difficult though they might be.

✱ ✱ ✱

"So, what's next?" Terence asked the moment I seated myself.

"We decide our next move," Safyre replied.

"Which is no easy task," Teresa said heavily. She gestured at me. "Considering how many open tasks you have."

I nodded. "That is true enough."

"Then, let's start by defining our priorities," Safyre said. "What are they?"

"Cleansing sector 18,240 of the nether," Teresa declared immediately. "If the sector falls to the void, we lose access to Draven's Reach."

"Reclaiming sector 12,560," Terence added. "Erebus' dungeon is too important a resource to ignore." He gave me a lopsided smile. "And I miss Saya."

"Gaining more blood memories," Anriq volunteered. "Without Michael getting stronger, we'll be hard put to hold any sector."

"We also have to secure the Guardian Tower and restore the Nexus guardian," Adriel put in. "Even if I am not the one to take Kolath's place, someone has to."

"Why bother with the tower at all?" Safyre asked curiously.

"Nexus is the heart of the Game and the key to everything, and what the Guardian Tower has to offer in this respect cannot be ignored: a means to enter and leave Nexus without alerting the Triumvirate," Adriel replied. "With a guardian in place who's friendly to our cause, we secure the Tower the same way Draven does the Reach."

Safyre nodded thoughtfully. "Good point." She scanned the room. "What else?"

"Returning to Draven's Reach," Nyra said softly, "and convincing New Haven to join our cause."

"*Awakening Draven's brethren,*" Duggar said in my mind, and acting as his voice, I repeated his words aloud for the benefit of the others.

"Reclaiming the Wolf Torc from Dathe," Anriq said.

"Getting Michael's money!" Terence added with a laugh.

"Don't forget about the lost Prime," Safyre said. "We have to find her."

"There is also House Death to consider," Adriel said. "We must raise it—and the other Houses, too, if we can manage it."

Safyre nodded. "By my count, all that makes ten." She made a face. "We're not short on priorities, at least."

Laughter rippled across the room. "Does anyone have anything else to add?" Safyre asked when it subsided.

No one replied.

Safyre looked at me. "Michael, you've been quiet." She smiled. "But I've never known you to be without an opinion. You must have some thoughts as to our next move?"

"Just working through some stuff," I replied. Duggar's words were still ringing in my head, and the more I considered them, the more they resonated with me.

"Care to share?" Safyre asked pointedly when I didn't go on.

I held up my hands, palms up. "Sorry, you're right. I should share. Keeping my own counsel has become... habit, I suppose."

"We know," she said solemnly. "But tell us, please."

"Alright." I exhaled. "I agree with everything everyone has said. Those are all priorities. But there are even more things we can throw on the list."

Raising my right hand, I began ticking off points on my fingers. "Things like acquiring allies—be they the bounty hunters, the Blades, the under-dwellers, or even the brotherhood. And learning everything we can of the stygians. Or finding out what is so important about the artifact Loken wants, or going one step further and figuring out what game he is playing. Then there is exploring Erebus' dungeon and making contact with those already resisting the new Powers—I even have an inkling where to start with that one."

I threw up my hands as I ran out of fingers. "Let's not forget leveling up and skill training. I can go on, but sixteen different priorities are already too many."

Safyre tilted her head to the side. "So, what are you saying?"

"I'm saying..." I began, then stopped.

"I'm saying," I said more slowly as my thoughts crystalized, "that it's premature to focus on our next step just yet. We can't do that. Not until we agree on what we're trying to achieve."

"I thought we already knew what that was," Anriq said, looking confused. "We're trying to restore House Wolf." When no one said anything, he looked around. "Aren't we?"

"That's part of it," Teresa agreed, "but we're not all Wolves." She jerked her chin in Adriel's direction. "Nor can we ever be—as the lich pointed out earlier. Our goal should be broader. What we should attempt to do is resurrect *all* the Houses."

"Including whichever Cat one we spring from," Terence put in.

"But reviving the Houses is not all that we're about, is it?" Nyra asked. "We also want to defeat the stygians."

"And vanquish the new Powers," Safyre asserted, "freeing ordinary people and creatures from their stifling rule."

"All of those things are just a means to an end, though," Adriel said softly, her eyes on me. "Ultimately, we want to settle the ancients' debts, don't we?"

I met her gaze. "Why?"

Her brows drew down. "What do you mean why?"

"Why do we want to do that?" I asked.

"To fix what's broken, of course," Teresa said, almost scornfully.

I turned to her. "And what good will that do?"

"Well, for starters, the world will be whole again!" she snapped.

"How is that good?"

She glared at me. "It'll get rid of the stygians for one."

"We don't know that," I pointed out. "Even if we can fix what's broken, it doesn't mean things will go back to the way they were before the breaking."

"What are you getting at, Michael?" Safyre asked.

"That it has been eons since the world shattered," I said, spreading my arms wide. "People have adapted. The *land* has adapted. Tribes and nations that were split apart have evolved and developed separate identities. Sectors have been resettled. Those who preferred isolation fled to the deepest darkest corners of the world." I brought my hands together. "Now imagine, if we forced all those disparate peoples, places, and cultures together again. What do you think will happen?"

"Chaos, mayhem, war," Anriq replied.

I nodded. "Exactly." I turned back to Adriel who was watching me intently. "It's too late to fix the Kingdom. Trying to right that ancient wrong will only inflict a greater wrong on the world."

She stared at me unblinkingly. "What do you suggest then? Leaving things as they are?"

"No," I said firmly. "The new Powers are tyrants, I agree with you on that much." I paused. "But the Primes were no angels either. They and the Houses are largely why we are where we are today."

Teresa, Anriq, and even Terence opened their mouths in protest, but Safyre raised her hand, silencing them. "Where does that leave us, Michael?"

I exhaled sharply. "With no choice but to start something new."

Silence.

"Something new?" Nyra asked tentatively.

"Yes, new," I repeated. "Why should we follow the same tired old patterns? Why should we try resurrecting something that we know does not work? Why should our goals be the same as those of Primes long dead?"

"Because the bloodlines give us power," Adriel rasped. "The power to change things."

I waved aside her words. "I'm not suggesting we abandon the bloodlines. On the contrary, we have to do everything we can to gather strength, and that means reviving the bloodlines. What we don't need are the Houses."

"Which means what?" Adriel asked with growing impatience.

I leaned forward. "Don't you see? With all this talk of Houses and bloodlines and already our goals have started diverging. The twins want to raise their House. You need to raise Death. *I* want to revive Wolf. How much longer before we part ways entirely? And how much longer after that do you think it'll be before we start warring against each other?"

I sat back. "For better or worse, the Houses are gone, long dead, and that leaves us with a unique opportunity. Why recreate separate Houses for Wolf, Death, and so on? Why divide non-players from players and Forcesworn from scions? Why not bring everyone under one roof?" I blew out a slow breath. "No artificial separation. No unequal rights. No special privileges."

"Keep the bloods, do away with the Houses, is that what you're suggesting?" Adriel asked, not sounding convinced.

"Something like that." I opened my arms wide. "We've already started down this road by appointing all of you—non-Wolves—to the inner council of House Wolf, but I realize now that that doesn't go nearly far enough. We should assume a common identity, one that does not favor any bloodline."

Adriel shook her head. "You're ignoring the reason the Houses were formed in the first place. It's true the ancients' system was not perfect, but there can be no question that the Houses *worked,* that they stopped the endless cycle of wars that was so prevalent before them. Without the Houses, the world would have suffered a second breaking, I am sure of it."

I smiled. "You've just proved my point."

Her brows furrowed.

"What did the Houses bring?" I asked rhetorically. "Unity and structure, that's what. Both of which reduced the conflicts that flared up, and when they did, they provided a mechanism for regulating them." I stared hard at the lich, willing her to understand. "What I'm suggesting is the same, only I propose taking it a few steps further."

"One House in the place of many?" Safyre murmured.

I nodded, not looking away from Adriel. The naked skepticism had disappeared from her gaze, and I could only hope she was actually thinking through my words.

"You think it will make a difference?" Adriel asked eventually. "You think it will stop the infighting and power grabs?"

"Maybe, maybe not. But if we don't try..." I shrugged.

Adriel sighed. "I'm too old for this," she muttered.

I straightened, sensing capitulation in her words. "Then you agree?"

"I won't go *that* far," she said dryly. "But I'll allow that your idea has potential." She paused. "You do realize you're going to have a hell of a time convincing Ceruvax, though? That old wolf is unbending."

My smile broadened. "Leave Ceruvax to me."

CHAPTER 491: ONE HOUSE

On the heels of Adriel's agreement, a surprising Game message unfurled in my mind.

The Adjudicator has allocated you a new task: <u>Found a new House</u>! Your determination to bind disparate players, Powers, and bloodlines into a single united whole has not gone unnoticed. While it is a worthy ambition, it's also one fraught with risk. Beware Wolf, that it does not bring about your downfall.

Objective 1: Convince 2 Powers not of Wolf blood to join your House. Note: completion of this task may have unpredictable consequences.

"Ah," I exhaled.

"What is it?" Safyre asked, seeing my focus turn inward. "Did the Adjudicator object to your plan?"

"Not exactly," I murmured and read the Game message aloud for everyone's benefit.

Adriel's eyes narrowed. "Cryptic," she muttered. "And somewhat ominous."

I agreed wholeheartedly with the sentiment and waited to see if she had anything else to add. But despite her pronouncement, Adriel did not reverse her previous decision as I half-feared she would.

I turned to the others. "What about everyone else? Do you agree with my proposal?"

Nods followed all around—which was not surprising.

Lacking the lich's own storied history, the others had no great attachment to the Houses to begin with. The wolves did not object either, and I got the sense that Duggar had spoken harshly with his fellow elders to bring them in line. The alpha's support did not surprise me. It was his own words, after all, that had given me the idea. His and Adriel's.

"What should we call ourselves?" Terence asked.

"The Forerunners," I said, seeing no reason for a separate name. "Unless anyone disagrees?"

No one did.

"Good," I pronounced. "As for our motto. *One house, one people.* That has a nice ring to it, don't you think?"

"Sounds great," Teresa muttered. "But what does it mean—practically speaking?"

"It implies we're not a loose collection of separate groups but a single united people." I smiled. "But practically speaking? Practically speaking, it means our new House already has three potential Powers within its ranks."

Terence's eyes widened. "Three?"

I nodded. "Me." I glanced to my left. "Adriel." I faced forward again. "Safyre."

She gasped, looking more shocked than I'd ever seen her. "You can't be serious? But my blood can't be awoken! I'm sworn to the Light!"

"You cannot be a Prime," I agreed. "But you *can* become a Power." I chuckled. "I wasn't just spouting rhetoric earlier, you know. I meant every word. We will be a House for everyone—new Powers included."

I heard Adriel's sharp intake of breath but didn't turn her way.

"You will invite the likes of Loken and Tartar to join our cause?" the lich asked.

"No," I said, somewhat exasperated, "but Forcesworn like Safyre"—my gaze drifted left—"and Anriq should not be left out in the cold. That their path differs from ours is no reason to abandon them or limit their growth. Assuming they have the potential to do so, both *should* become Powers. It will only strengthen us."

For a drawn-out moment, Adriel didn't say anything.

"You're a damn revolutionary, that's what," she muttered at last.

I grinned. "Perhaps."

"But I'm forsworn," Safyre protested, drawing my attention again.

"True," I conceded. "But that is irrelevant. What matters is that you're *unsworn*."

"How does that—" she began.

"He's right," Adriel cut in. "Since you're not pledged to any Power, you can gain the Powerful Initiate Mark." She glanced at me. "What level did you say she was again?"

"Level two hundred and ten," I replied. Everyone I'd left behind in the tundra had progressed—largely, I knew, from the campaign they'd waged against the stygians. Some, though, had advanced more than others. Calling up the analyze data of my fellow players, I reviewed it once more.

The target is Teresa, a level 85 human blade devotee. She bears a Mark of Minor Light.

The target is Terence, a level 84 human swordsman. He bears a Mark of Minor Light.

The target is Nyra, a level 53 human sniper. She bears a Mark of Lesser Shadow, a Mark of Michael (hidden), and a Mark of Wolf-friend (hidden).

The target is Anriq, a level 125 were-rampager. He bears a Mark of Greater Dark, a Mark of Lesser Shadow, and a Mark of Wolf pack-brother. Anriq is Darksworn. Note: as a Forcesworn, Anriq's blood has been indelibly suppressed and cannot be awakened.

The target is Safyre, a level 210 human aetherist. She bears a Mark of Supreme Light. Safyre is Lightsworn and forsworn. Note: the forsworn are offered no protection by the Game. Powers are not constrained from acting against them. They may not carry soulbound items, and while they may visit a safe zone, the forsworn are unprotected from harm within one.

Like Adriel had said, and the Game had just confirmed, Safyre and Anriq could not awaken their dormant bloodlines, but that did not mean they could not follow the ascendancy path of the Forcesworn.

The options when it came to Nyra and the twins were more interesting, but all three were yet young in Game terms, and they had a long way to go before ascendancy became a possibility.

"Huh, rank twenty-one already," Adriel remarked, drawing me out of musings. "She doesn't have far to go before she gains the Power Mark by default then. She should be able to hit rank twenty-five within the year."

"She may not even have to wait that long," I murmured.

The lich glanced at me sharply. I suspected she knew what I was thinking, but she didn't voice any objections—not aloud, anyway.

My comment went unnoticed by Safyre, though. Still reeling at the idea of becoming a Power, she was staring down at her hands in shock. "I never imagined that..." She looked up at me. "Do you really think I have it in me to become a Power?"

I nodded solemnly, then turned to face the group at large. "Helping Safyre and Adriel ascend should also factor high on our list of priorities."

"So, we're back to priorities again," Teresa remarked, arching one eyebrow.

"Seems so," I murmured.

"Well, it's all well and good that we're one House, faction, or whatever else you want to call it, but what is our goal?" she demanded. "What do we want to achieve? You raised the question earlier but didn't supply an answer."

I inclined my head. "You're right, I didn't. And for what it's worth, I think our goal should simply be to take care of our own."

She blinked. "That's it?"

I laughed. "Sorry. It's not earth-shattering, I know. But it's the heart of what I've been doing since I've entered the Game—protecting myself and those I consider mine."

"Safeguarding your pack, you mean," Anriq supplied.

I nodded. "Exactly. We are all one pack now, and I mean the entire forerunner faction when I say that. Our objective should be to see ourselves and every like-minded soul—be they a player, scion, Power, Prime, or non-player—protected."

"And once we achieve that?" Terence challenged.

"Achieve it?" I asked in a bemused tone. "Oh, I don't think we'll ever *achieve* it. Protecting a pack is the work of a lifetime. Never-ending."

Teresa rolled her eyes. "Alright, so what's the first step then?"

I threw her a lopsided grin. "Now look who wants to talk priorities again." Before she could do more than scowl, I added, "If you ask me, our first priority is carving out a home for our new faction. There are three options for that."

"The wolves' valley," Terence volunteered.

"The nether-infested sector, of course," Teresa added.

"And Draven's Reach," Nyra finished.

I smiled. "Correct. Of the three, Draven's Reach is the most secure, the wolves' valley is the most palatable, and the nether one has the best potential."

"It is also the gateway to both the Reach and Nexus," Adriel said.

"And the sector under the gravest risk," Safyre put in softly.

I nodded. "Which is why I believe that our first step must be investigating how deeply entrenched the stygians are in sector 18,240. If we can force them out, we must."

"And if we can't?" Nyra asked, a strange note in her voice.

Glancing at her, I could tell from her face that she already knew the answer to the question. "If we can't," I said for the benefit of the others, "then we'll have no choice but to abandon Draven's Reach and sector 18,240." *And evacuate everyone we can from the dungeon.*

"In which case, we fall back to the wolves' valley," Safyre said.

Before I could answer, Anriq spoke up. "What about the Blades' sector?"

I hesitated. "It's an option," I allowed. "Although it's one that comes with many complications, which is why I didn't suggest it to begin with."

He nodded, not contesting the point.

"Are there any more questions or objections?" I asked, scanning the faces around me.

No one said anything.

"Let's get down to the planning then. By my reckoning, it's going to take us at least a week to survey the stygians. However, given the nether mist, not everyone is going to be an effective scout, so here is what I think we should do..."

✳　✳　✳

Finalizing our plans took a few hours. Although most of that time was not spent considering how to scout the nether sector but what everyone else should be doing in the meantime.

There was no use in anyone standing idle, after all.

By the time we were done, it was close to nightfall, and no one objected when Safyre proposed beginning our campaign tomorrow.

That night, everyone—including a large contingent of wolves—gathered in the largest igloo. It made for a tight fit, but we managed. The evening passed in a relaxed manner as we shared food and tales, whether of recent days or days long past.

Ghost proved to be a firm favorite with the packs' pups, and under the watchful eye of Aira and Star, she let them stalk her around the den. Adriel, too, fit in better than I expected and passed the time regaling the pack elders with tales of the ancients from her day and before. Much of the tension between her and the others had dissipated.

Most surprising of all—or perhaps not considering their relative ages—was the friendship that began to develop between Nyra, Anriq, Teresa, and Terence, and I scarce spotted a moment when the four were not together. What they had to talk about, I don't know, but every time I drew close, they clamped down.

I spent the greater part of the night moving from group to group, reacquainting myself with everyone and making sure all my companions were getting along. We were a disparate House, and one that would only get more so once we expanded the Forerunners' ranks.

One House. One people.

The concept had sounded great when I'd come up with it, and it still did. Yet, I couldn't help but wonder if I was doing the right thing. How would the Adjudicator react to me abandoning House Wolf? The confounding new task seemed to imply there would be *some* impact, but how significant that would be, I couldn't tell. Would it affect my ascendancy path? And how would I stop the new House from fracturing from internal strife?

Was Adriel right? I wondered. *Am I trying to do too much? Change too much?*

"There you are," a voice said from behind.

Smiling, I turned around to face Safyre. She, like me, had spent most of the night crisscrossing the room. I'd not missed the affection the wolves showed her and she them. It only reinforced my own opinion of her. She would make for a strong leader if the need arose.

"Why are you hiding here, alone and in the dark?" she asked.

I opened my mouth to protest, then noticed that I *had* gravitated to the darkest and most isolated spot in the room—something hard to do in a chamber as crowded as this one was right now. I grinned. "Habit, I suppose."

Safyre shook her head. "Mind if I join you?"

Moving over, I made space for her atop the large pile of furs I'd climbed onto. "Not at all."

"We haven't had a chance to talk," she said, sitting beside me. "Not really."

I nodded. "I know what you mean." Our conversations since my return had, of necessity, been focused on the wider group, the doings of the pack, the logistics of surviving on the tundra, and catching up on recent events. We hadn't just... talked.

"I'm sorry I abandoned you here," I said, staring out at the wolves below. "Matters spun out of control."

"They always seem to with you," she said with a laugh. "But don't be sorry. I've enjoyed my time in the tundra."

I turned to face her. "Really? That I don't believe."

She laughed again. "You forget what my life was like before this. Standing around all day, hidden behind that awful hood and selling wares to low-level players was..." She shuddered. "If not exactly horrible, close enough. It was good—*is* good—to do something for a change, to be part of something again." She paused. "And it doesn't hurt that our cause is one I believe in."

I searched her eyes. "You do? Truly?"

"I do," she said, not shying away from my gaze. "The players and Powers have run amok in the Kingdom for too long. No one opposes them or curbs their excesses."

"The world needs balance," I agreed.

"That's exactly it." Facing forward, she stared out into the room. "But not everything about life on the tundra was great," she said, returning to her previous comment.

"Oh?"

"Well, I certainly didn't find worrying about you entertaining."

I glanced at her sideways. "You were worried about me? There was no need really. I was—"

"Oh, shush, Michael."

I blinked. "What?"

"If we're going to be friends"—she threw me a sharp glance as she said that—"you're going to have to stop pretending you're above everyone's concern. Above *my* concern."

"I don't do that," I protested. "Do I?"

"You're... aloof, Michael. Don't get me wrong, I get it. As a leader, as Wolf, you have to be that way sometimes, but not always." She held my gaze, her own serious. "And not with me."

I swallowed. "Right."

Safyre gestured outward at the room. "You can be their protector all you want. But you don't have to be mine." A smile touched her lips. "Let me worry about you if I want. Deal?"

I returned her smile. "Deal."

She placed her hand on mine. "Good, then tell me more about this New Haven. It sounds like an intriguing city."

I laughed. "What do you want to know?"

"Well, for starters..."

Chapter 492: Memories

You have lost 10 x rank 4 nether protection crystals, the seeking eye of Sylvana, the spectacles of ward seeing, a mirror shield, Asmod's Suit, a champion's belt, icefang, and healer's friend.

Anriq set off for the nether-infested sector early the next morning, alone and with little more than some enchanted crystals for protection. I'd loaned him the seeking eye, too, and had tasked him with mapping out the sector's terrain and discovering the location of every stygian nest.

It was a dangerous mission, but it was one which Anriq assured me that after his many days in the selfsame sector, he was well-equipped to take on. It went against my nature to send others into danger in my stead, but I sent him anyway, however reluctantly.

Delegate, I reminded myself. *Must delegate.*

The twins set off at nearly the same time with Adriel and a small group of wolves for company. Terence wore Malikor's armor—those pieces he could—making him an unmissable red target on the snow-white tundra.

On hearing of Malikor's prowess, the young swordsman had been more than a little besotted, and I wouldn't be surprised if he pursued a paladin Class himself. With Asmod's armor, the mirror shield, and the champion's belt, he was well-equipped to do so, anyway.

Teresa was still dead set on becoming a druid, and after giving the matter careful thought, I realized icefang would suit her better than me. The twins' mission was a simple one: gaining their bloodline Marks. Adriel had more than a few ideas about how they could go about that. In the lich's day, acquiring your Marks was something of a ritual, and according to her, it was all about finding the right situation...

Nyra also left the den. She took with her two sleds, each pulled by a different team of arctic wolves. Her task was at one time simple and complex: leveling up, gathering supplies, and generally aiding the Pack in whatever way she could. Both she and I were hoping this would deepen her Wolf Mark.

Lastly, there was Ghost. Not about to be left out, she too set out to train her skills. That in itself would not have concerned me. Her choice of targets, though, did. The pyre wolf was intent on hunting down the tundra's yetis. And while her nature and her flame attacks made her admirably suited to such a task, it also left her vulnerable to the yetis' own attacks. Which is why I'd made sure Sulan, Oursk, and Aira accompanied her.

That left Safyre and me as the only players remaining behind to guard the den—not something that was strictly necessary. *And besides*, I thought grumpily as I sank down cross-legged on the bed of furs I'd prepared, *soon I am going to be in no condition to guard anything.* Which was why Safyre had insisted on staying behind in the first place.

To guard me.

"You're sure you don't want to venture out with the others?" I asked her for the tenth time.

She shook her head firmly. "No. Someone has to make sure you're alright."

"Duggar and the rest of the dire wolves can do that well enough," I pointed out.

Lifting her right arm, she pulled back her sleeve to display the farspeaker bracelet she wore. "Someone also has to be on standby in case any of the others get into trouble."

I nodded, conceding the point.

Every group that had set out had a player wearing a matching farspeaker bracelet—only Ghost's group didn't, of course, but the dire wolves had their own means of communicating. Safyre's set consisted of four bracelets—I'd returned mine to her—and now Anriq, Nyra, and Teresa each wore one.

"And besides," the aetherist went on, "I'm curious."

I raised one eyebrow. "Curious?"

"To see how all this works," she said, gesturing to the Blood Talisman in my lap. "This is my first chance to witness your blood magic at play."

"It's not blood magic," I muttered, but I knew she was only teasing.

She smiled. "It might as well be, given everything Adriel says it can do."

"True," I admitted, taking up the talisman in my left hand. I glanced up at Safyre. "Remember I might be out for as long as three days, so don't start worrying before then."

"Nice to know I have your permission to do that this time around," she said with a straight face.

I grimaced. "You know what I mean."

She laughed softly. "I do." Reaching out, she squeezed my hand. "Good luck."

"Thanks," I murmured. Closing my eyes, I willed my intent to the Adjudicator.

It was finally time to get my next blood memory.

✸　✸　✸

Contact established between Blood Talisman and the anointed Wolf scion, Michael. Reading the candidate's blood signature...

My breathing still and controlled, I waited patiently. Above me, I sensed Safyre hovering. And she was most definitely worrying already. I chuckled. "You couldn't even—"

I broke off as another message unfurled in my mind.

Scion, your blood is ready for its second awakening.

Remember, the blood of an ancient is a fearsome thing. Memories of traits, skills, and abilities lie long dormant within them. When sufficiently awoken, your blood can be made to 'remember' its ancient lineage and perform feats you had not thought possible before. Do not forget that blood memories are powered by your blood itself and consume neither psi, mana, nor stamina.

It is up to you to determine which of your blood memories to awaken. At this time, you may recall either 3 lesser blood memories or 1 greater blood memory.

Lesser memory: <u>Ancestral Knowledge</u>. Your blood recalls ancient knowledge. This blood memory grants you a once-off boost of +5 ranks in any skill of your choice. Note: attribute thresholds still apply. This is a generic blood memory.

Lesser memory: <u>Blood Pet</u>. Your blood can infuse your pet. This blood memory will grant you the ability: duplicate. It can be used once per day to grant your familiar all your own skills, abilities, and traits for one hour. This is a generic blood memory.

Lesser memory: <u>Rabid Blood</u>. Your blood can infect the minds of your foes. This blood memory turns you into a carrier of a mind-affecting disease that is highly contagious. Henceforth, direct contact with your blood will cause your foes to become deranged and confused. This blood memory is unique to Wolf.

Greater memory: <u>Blood Harvest</u>. Your blood can reap your foes. This blood memory will grant you the ability: level drain. It can be used once per day to leech 1% of an enemy player's levels. Leeched levels are permanently transferred to you. Note: this ability only works against players slain by yourself. This is a generic blood memory.

Greater memory: <u>Blood Puppet</u>. Your blood can enslave your foes. This blood memory grants you the ability: enslave. It can be used to permanently dominate a foe whose level is equal to or lower than your own. Note: you may only have one enslaved subject at any one time. This is a generic blood memory.

Greater memory: <u>Alpha's Command</u>. Your blood reinvigorates your allies. This blood memory grants you command of the power word, rally, which consists of two stages: clarity and invigorate. Clarity dispels all negative effects of every ally in a 100-yard radius, while invigorate imbues them with a buff that fully replenishes their health and energy pools over 60 seconds. The power word can only be used once per day and is unique to Wolf.

Choose which memory you wish to recall for your second awakening.

"Ah," I exhaled, my eyes still closed.

"What is it?" Safyre demanded, her voice strained.

"Nothing bad," I assured her. My lips twisted. "Just an excess of choices." Ignoring the insistent throbbing of the Talisman in my left hand, I recited aloud the descriptions of the blood memories on offer.

Safyre whistled softly. "That *is* a dilemma. Those lesser memories sound nearly as tempting as the greater ones. And you said you can pick three of them?"

"Yes, but the memories the Game will offer when I consult the Blood Talisman again might be entirely different."

"I see," Safyre muttered. "That makes things trickier, I suppose." She paused. "Which way are you leaning?"

"I'm not sure," I admitted. "The lesser memories are tempting, especially considering that I can have three of them *and* their effects will be doubled by my champion trait. There is also my commander trait to consider. With it, I can grant my Wolf followers a lesser variant of the blood memory."

"But?" Safyre prompted, seeming to sense there was one.

"But the greater memories' effects will also be doubled and shared, and according to Adriel, it's the better option."

A drawn-out moment of silence, then, "I would heed the lich's advice if I were you."

My eyes almost snapped open in surprise, but I caught myself in time. Both Ceruvax and Adriel had warned me not to disrupt my connection with the Talisman once I started my blood awakening. The consequences, they'd informed me, could be disastrous.

"Really?" I asked aloud. I wouldn't say that Safyre didn't like Adriel, but there was definite friction between the pair.

"Really," Safyre replied dryly. "Adriel and I might not see eye to eye on everything, but I don't pretend to have her level of expertise when it comes to this"—she laughed wickedly—"blood magic stuff." Her tone grew more serious. "Besides, if blood memories scale in the same manner as abilities do, the high-tiered options are invariably better."

"That makes sense," I allowed. "Then, too, greater blood memories are only the second tier." There were three more beyond them—godlike, ancient, and ultimate.

Safyre repressed a shiver. "Yes, and I can only imagine how powerful *they* are."

I chuckled. "So, that narrows my options down to three."

"Two," she countered. "Blood harvest sounds nice, but its use is strictly limited. Once you hit level three hundred and can no longer attack players, you're going to struggle to find anyone to employ it against."

She was right. I wasn't all that far away from level three hundred, and while I had no doubt the blood memory would speed up my progress to that milestone, once I became a Power in truth, the only viable targets for blood harvest were other Powers—and they were not the sort of foes I expected to be battling on a daily basis.

"The other options are both nice," she continued, "but of the two, I'd say blood puppet is the better."

My brows rose. Again, she'd surprised me. On first glance, blood puppet sounded... evil.

And it was. Or rather, it could be.

If the spell was misused, I had little doubt it could inflict great harm. But then again, that was true of many things in the Game. Yet no weapon was evil in and of itself. It was always the wielder that made it so.

"Why do you say that?" I asked.

"Well, from the Game's description, it doesn't sound like the buffs from the alpha's command will apply to you." She laughed ruefully. "And it's you that we're talking about here. How often do you think you're going to go into battle surrounded by an army of allies?"

"A valid point," I murmured. "Then, too, my champion trait will probably synergize better with blood puppet than it will with alpha's command."

"Exactly."

At a guess, my champion trait would increase the power of alpha's command by doubling the reach of the spell or halving the time it took to reinvigorate my allies. It could also increase the spell's stages, but I had no idea what the additional stages might do.

Whereas when it came to blood puppet, I foresaw only two ways the spell could be made more powerful: either by changing the level limit applied to the spell's victims or by doubling the number of subjects I could enslave. Both changes would be immediately useful.

I inhaled. "That decides that then. Blood puppet it is." Reaching out to the Adjudicator, I made my choice.

Blood awakening initiated. Activating fallen scion essences...

...

...

The energy I'd siphoned from the fallen scions in the Ritual Combat Circle—lying dormant in me all this time—abruptly burst free of their confines and seeped into my blood.

Setting it afire.

"It's begun," I gasped as my limbs began to contort, and my muscles started to lock up. Falling over, I curled into a ball. "R-re...mmember.... wha-at... I... said. T-thr-ree...," I began, mangling the words as I forced them out through a suddenly uncooperative jaw.

"Three days, I remember." Safyre placed a soothing hand on my forehand. "Don't worry, I have everything well on hand here, Michael. See you on the other side."

I tried to nod or otherwise acknowledge her, but the fire raging in me reached a crescendo, and I knew no more.

Blood awakening completed.

Congratulations, Michael! You have awakened the greater memory: <u>blood puppet</u> and have gained the ability: <u>enslave</u>.

Enslave (champion variant) is a touch-based ability that allows you to permanently dominate 2 subjects whose levels are equal to or lower than your own. In the event that either subject is a player, the effect will last until the player's death. When the player revives, they will have no memory of their time as a blood puppet.

Note, this spell will only remain active while you and the dominated subject remain in the same sector. The spell may be canceled at will.

This ability's activation time is very slow. It consumes neither mana, stamina, nor psi and cannot be upgraded.

Congratulations, Michael! You have awakened your first greater memory, advancing your bloodline trait from anointed scion to <u>House Elite</u>. This trait not only furthers your binding to Wolf, but it also improves your ability to sniff out a subject's blood. When reading another player's signature, you can now sense if they possess any Wolf blood.

Lifting my head, I opened my eyes.

My thoughts were clear and my eyes sharp. My second blood awakening felt nothing like the first. I'd come out of that one barely able to walk. This time around, I felt... alive and energized. Clearly, the fugue that had been raging in me had long since passed.

"Michael!"

My eyes jerked to the left, recognizing Safyre's voice. Then I frowned. She was not alone; Adriel was with her. "What's wrong?" I asked, knowing something had to be if the lich was here.

"You've been out for five days," Adriel replied bluntly.

Five days? Querying the Game, I saw that was indeed so. My frown deepened.

Safyre slipped closer. "Are you alright?"

I nodded slowly. "I feel perfectly fine. But"—I turned to Adriel—"why was I out for so long?"

She shrugged. "I'm not sure. It might be because of some peculiarity associated with the blood memory you chose." She glanced at the other woman. "Safyre told me your choice... blood puppet?"

I nodded.

"An interesting memory," Adriel murmured. Then shaking her head in dismissal of her musings, she resumed her interrupted explanation, "Or it could be a result of your champion's trait."

"I see." That meant I would have to plan for future blood awakenings taking as long, if not longer. *Not good,* I thought, sitting up. *Not good at all.*

"Tell us about the blood memory," Safyre asked with undisguised interest. "Is it everything you hoped for?"

"In some ways it is," I replied, "but in other ways, it's more limiting." Recalling the Game's description, I relayed it verbatim to the two women.

Safyre pursed her lips. "Hmm. That it's touch-based does render it less useful," she mused. "And the slow casting time doesn't help either."

My lips turned down. "It doesn't," I agreed.

"Nevertheless, it's a powerful ability," Adriel noted, "especially given how your champion trait has modified it."

"That it will scale with my level doesn't hurt either." I paused. "Nor does the fact that it will work on players. That's going to allow for some interesting possibilities."

Safyre's eyes twinkled. "Already planning further mayhem?"

I smiled. "Perhaps." I turned to Adriel. "You didn't tell me my anointed scion trait would change," I said, almost reproachfully.

The lich blinked. "Oh. I forgot about that. It was a fairly trivial upgrade in my day. Although, I suppose," she allowed, "that in these times, it will come in more handy."

"Oh definitely," I said. As a recruiting tool, if nothing else, it would be invaluable. It would also help when it came to selecting candidates for were's bite. I paused, struck by an altogether startling thought. Was Safyre such a candidate?

Giving in to the sudden urge to find out, I reached out with my will and analyzed her.

The target is Safyre, a level 210 human aetherist. She bears a Mark of Supreme Light and is both Lightsworn and forsworn. Safyre carries a minor wolf bloodline strain that has been permanently suppressed.

Needless to say, the Game's response was disappointing. Deflating, I said nothing of my impromptu inspection and studied the two women anew. "Tell me what has happened while I was away."

"No disasters have befallen, if that's what you're worried about," Safyre assured me immediately.

"That's something," I said lightly. "Where are the twins?"

"Still out on the tundra trying to acquire their Marks," Adriel replied. "Don't worry, they're not alone. Duggar has taken over my role as chaperon."

"That's good." I turned to Safyre. "And the others?"

"Nyra is progressing well," she reported. "Her Wolf Mark hasn't deepened yet, but her skills and level are advancing nicely. She asked to stay out a few days longer, and I didn't object." She looked at me questioningly.

"Good decision. The additional training can't hurt," I replied. "What about—"

"Prime? What's happening?"

Breaking off, I held up my hand. "One second, that's Ghost," I told the two women. *"My awakening ran late it seems,"* I said, replying to the pyre wolf across our familiar bond.

"Oh. Are you alright?"

"Perfectly fine," I assured her. *"Adriel is here now. How are things progressing on your end?"*

"Great!" she said brightly. *"I've earned us a level!"*

"You have?" I asked, a little startled.

"Yes," she said excitedly. *"Sulan, Aira, and Oursk have been a great help. We've been killing yetis almost non-stop for five days. Did you know..."*

With a half-smile on my face, I let Ghost ramble on while I checked on my older Game messages, and sure enough, they confirmed what the pyre wolf was saying.

You and Ghost have reached level 236!

Ghost's magma maw and telepathy have reached rank 9, her stygian claws and ash armor rank 10, and her death magic rank 7.

"Well done, Ghost," I murmured as she ran down. The pyre wolf's training was progressing better than expected, but I could already tell her skills were beginning to plateau—as mine had during my own time hunting on the tundra.

"Thank you, Prime." A pause. *"Should we return to the den?"*

"No, keep at it until all your skills hit rank ten," I told her. *"I haven't determined what my own plans will be yet. Once I do, I'll let you know."* Refocusing on my surroundings, I passed on the pyre wolf's report to Adriel and Safyre.

"Ghost is doing well," Adriel remarked.

I nodded. "She is, and she's happy, too. But I suspect that's less to do with her skill advancements than the fact that she's able to hunt with the pack at long last." I met Adriel's gaze. "You gave her that."

She waved aside my words. "What's the point of being a master of death if you can't use your powers for good?"

Chuckling, I turned to Safyre. "What about Anriq? Has he checked in?"

"He has," she replied. "Three days ago. Right on schedule. I have his report on the overlord and the nether creatures surrounding the Reach gate." She hesitated.

"And?" I prompted, sensing the news wasn't good.

"It's bad," she admitted. "The stygians have reinforced their forces again. There are now a little over a thousand of them guarding the gate."

I sucked in a breath. That was a lot of stygians, but it was a far from unassailable force. What concerned me, though, was how long it would take to clear the creatures out—and what the stygians would do after that. If the void had seen fit to reinforce the gate once, there was no reason why they wouldn't do so again.

"What about the void tree?" I asked. "Has he found it yet?"

Safyre shook her head. "No, but I told Anriq you were still under, and he returned to the nether sector to resume scouting. I expect his next report in two days."

Nodding absently, I rose to my feet and began pacing the small room. If the void tree had allocated a thousand stygians to guard the Reach's gate, how many had it kept to protect itself?

Surely more. Lots more.

The two women exchanged glances before Safyre asked the question on both their minds. "What are you thinking?"

I turned to face her. "That I should go to Anriq," I admitted.

Safyre opened her mouth, then closed it before very obviously restraining herself from questioning me further.

"Why?" Adriel asked after a pause.

"Because we're running out of time."

"You, yourself, set the timetable," Adriel pointed out. "One week you said."

"And it has been five days already." I resumed pacing. "I expected us to have located the main stygian nest by now."

"But you ordered Anriq not to rush things," Safyre said.

"I did," I agreed.

And there had been good reason for the order. The void tree would undoubtedly be surrounded by a swarm of stygian spores, just like the one in Draven Reach's had been. The spores had truesight, which would negate both my own invisibility and that of the Sylvanain eye Anriq was using. And while the legendary artifact was indestructible, it was not immune to capture.

"I'm not blaming Anriq," I continued, "but like it or not, scouting the nether is a task he is less suited to than me."

Neither woman disputed my claim.

I inhaled. "Which is why I think I should replace him."

Safyre sighed. "We agree."

I blinked. "You do?" I knew neither of them wanted me venturing into the nether alone. "Wait. You said *we*. When did you two reach this decision?"

Adriel laughed. "While you were sleeping, wolfling."

My gaze flickered between the two. Safyre was smiling knowingly. It seemed the pair had anticipated my intentions.

Looks like you're not as unpredictable as you fancied yourself, Michael.

"What else?" I asked.

Safyre looked at me innocently. "What else?"

I rolled my eyes. "I know you two will not want to just let me go traipsing into the nether sector without laying down some extra conditions. What are they?"

"No conditions," Safyre replied easily. "Just this." She extended her arm.

Glancing at what rested in her open palm, I saw that it was a farspeaker bracelet, and if I was not mistaken, it was the very same one I'd been wearing all along. I frowned. "How is that—"

"We've enchanted it," Adriel said. "While you're wearing it, we'll be able to track your exact location."

"And at the same time, you'll be able to use it to stay in communication with Anriq who'll be stationed at the Guardian gate," Safyre added.

"Safyre and I will be waiting on the tundra side of the same gate," Adriel went on. "If you run into any trouble, we'll cross over and open a portal to you."

"And if for some reason the bracelet doesn't work, Anriq will also track you with the Sylvanain eye," Safyre said. "That way we can be doubly sure of your location."

I nodded slowly. "It's a good plan," I admitted.

"Did you expect any less?" Adriel asked sardonically.

I shook my head ruefully. "No. No, I did not."

CHAPTER 494: HIDDEN IN THE MIST

We set out for the nether portal less than an hour later, Adriel and Safyre having already seen to the necessary arrangements. Our party was larger than I expected and included Adriel, Safyre, myself, and a team of arctic wolves.

I eyed the sled piled high with supplies sitting next to the lounging wolves. "What's all that for?"

"Emergencies," Adriel replied laconically.

Clearly, she and Safyre were determined to be prepared for every eventuality—an attitude I could not fault. Not bothering to question the lich further, I swung around to face Snow and Star. They and the rest of the arctic wolf pack had come to see us off.

"I'll be back soon," I said, kneeling before the alpha and his mate.

Snow sent back a questioning image.

"No, I won't be gone as long as last time," I replied. I gestured to Safyre and Adriel. "They'll make sure of that."

Seemingly reassured by my answer, the alpha turned about and led the wolves back into the den, sending me a last flurry of images in farewell.

I watched them go for a moment. Saying goodbye was unfortunately something I found myself doing frequently. Since entering the Game, I'd rarely found the opportunity to stop moving. But someday—soon, hopefully—I hoped circumstances would allow me to make a real home.

Wherever that might be.

Sighing, I made a silent promise to Snow to keep my word to him this time around.

"Michael?" Safyre called.

Glancing over my shoulder, I spotted the two women sitting in the sled and ready to go.

"Coming," I replied. Trudging through the snow, I took my place at the front of the party and led the way to the portal.

* * *

Adriel has cast death's sheltering hand.

A little later, we reached our destination, and while Adriel saw to setting up our 'camp'—which task primarily consisted of configuring her wards—Safyre and I approached the portal.

"You're sure about this?" Safyre asked as we stopped in front of the shimmering curtain.

"It has to be done." My lips quirked up. "And as many precautions as you and Adriel have taken, I won't be in any danger."

Safyre nodded, though she looked far from convinced.

"I'll be fine," I assured her.

"Don't underestimate the nether," she warned. "If there is one thing I've learned through my own rift dives, it is that the void is never predictable." She bit her lip. "And after what you told me about the void fathers, I worry that the stygians will be ready for you."

I threw her a puzzled look. "Oh?"

She met my gaze. "You said the void sapling from Draven's Reach escaped. Assuming the void fathers can put two and two together, they should realize that the player who fled this sector and the one who defeated them in the dungeon are one and the same." She shrugged. "If I was a void father, sector 18,240 is where I would expect you to show up again."

I grimaced. "That makes a horrible sort of sense."

"It could also explain why the nether toxicity in the sector has increased so much since your last visit," Adriel said, coming up from behind.

I glanced at her. "Because the stygians have ramped up their efforts to claim the sector?" I hazarded.

She nodded. "Exactly."

"Well, that's just great," I muttered. It meant that we might have even less time to reclaim the sector than I'd anticipated.

"There's one more thing," Safyre said.

I looked at her sideways. "Somehow, I don't think I want to hear whatever you've to say next," I murmured.

A smile flickered across her face in brief acknowledgment of my quip before she turned serious again. "After hearing Anriq's report on the Reach gate and the sheer numbers they've dedicated to blockading it... I wonder if we beat them back too easily from the Guardian one."

My brows drew down. "You fear a trap?"

"I do," she said simply.

I rubbed my chin. "That would make sense," I allowed. "It would be awfully hard to spring an ambush at the portal itself. Retreating to safety is too easy. But if the stygians managed to draw their quarry farther in..."

"Then they just might catch him," Adriel finished for me.

I sighed. "Right, you two have certainly given me food for thought." I pressed my palms together. "And as much as I appreciated all that, please don't tell me you have anything more to add."

Adriel laughed. "We don't. Besides, given all our preparations, you should be fine."

"Just be careful," Safyre warned.

"I will," I said solemnly. Removing my Cloak of the Reach, I handed it to Adriel who took it mutely.

Ghost would not be accompanying me on this trip. Her nether resistance was not up to the task of a prolonged excursion in the nether. Given that, it made sense to allow her to continue her training in my absence.

Fortunately, the nature of our spirit binding allowed us to be separated. It was only Ghost and her spirit vessel that had to remain in the same sector, not me and her. And while no one else could use the Cloak in my absence, that did not preclude someone like Adriel from keeping it on her person—with my permission, of course.

Unequipping a few other crucial items—the Blood Talisman amongst them—I handed them over to Adriel and Safyre for safekeeping. It was too dangerous to take them with me into the nether.

Then, bidding one last farewell to the pair, I turned back to the shimmering curtain of white and stepped through.

Transfer through portal commencing...
...

...
Passage completed!
Leaving sector 107. Entering the Forever Kingdom.

✻   ✻   ✻

You have entered sector 18,240 of the Forever Kingdom.
The nether toxicity at your current location is at tier 4.

I stepped out of the portal into a familiar world of smog and immediately spotted Anriq. The werewolf was sitting cross-legged within touching distance of the portal. His eyes were closed, and I suspected he was communing with the seeker.

He looks ready to flee at a moment's notice.

On my arrival, he opened his eyes. "Michael," he greeted, a weary smile touching his lips.

"How are you?" I asked. "You look spent."

His smile widened a fraction. "Not quite," he murmured. "I've managed to keep my stamina from touching zero." He shook his head minutely. "But it only works if I don't move much."

"Wow," I said, impressed. "You shouldn't speak then, not unless it becomes strictly necessary. And when you need to, rather use the farspeaker bracelet. Did Safyre share the plan with you?"

He nodded.

"Did she also share her and Adriel's concerns about the mists?"

He nodded again.

"Alright, good. What about the seeker? Have you recalled it?"

Another nod.

"Perfect. When it gets here, return to the tundra. Safyre and Adriel are just on the other side of the portal. They'll restore your spent reserves and recharge the seeker. I won't wander far until you're back." I paused. "Any ideas about where I should look?"

"*Follow. River. North,*" he whispered.

"That's good advice," I replied. The portal to Draven's Reach was south of our present location, and to get to it, I had followed the river downstream. It would not be a bad idea to check what lay in the other direction.

Squeezing Anriq's shoulder in passing, I walked farther into the mists. "I'm going to scout the surroundings. Don't worry if you lose sight of me. I'll be close."

"*Tracks. Heading. River.*"

"Got it," I called as I vanished from sight.

✳   ✳   ✳

You have cast enhanced reflexes, load controller, vanish, and trigger-cast quick mend.

I found the tracks Anriq had mentioned easily enough. No effort had been made to conceal them, and without the mists to obscure my sight, they were glaringly obvious.

Looking up, I studied the sky and spotted the sun hanging low in the east. It was not that I could not see the mist anymore—I could. Only now, it was mostly transparent, nothing but a gentle haze across my vision.

Which was why I could just as easily see the distant river and the rolling hills on the far shore. But of the stygians, there was no sign.

Crouching over the tracks, I studied them for a moment. I was no tracker, but at a guess, I'd say they had been made by a pack of stygian hydras. Their heavy feet had left deep impressions in the soil. It was clear, too, that the creatures were making their way westward, toward the river.

Alert and with my mindsight extended, I trailed after.

✳   ✳   ✳

"Michael, I'm back, and the seeker is in place."

Anriq's communication came just as I reached the river. Glancing up, I searched the sky but failed to spot the tiny orb with either my physical sight or mindsight. *Huh, fancy that. Just as advertised.*

"Where is it?"

"Above your right shoulder."

I grunted but didn't bother looking again. *"Do you see me?"*

"I do."

"Good. I'm going to follow the tracks you mentioned. Looks like they were made by a pack of hydras. They've turned right at the river and appear to be following the river north. I'll contact you when I have something else to report."

"Got it," he replied.

Falling silent, I refocused on my surroundings. It was time to find out just what we were up against.

CHAPTER 495: TROUBLE COMES IN FOURS

Your nether absorption has increased to level 203.

Six hours later, I was still following the river. The hydras had not deviated course even once, which I took to be an encouraging sign. They were obviously heading *somewhere*, and it was a good bet that that somewhere was a nest.

Every three hours or so, I halted as Anriq recalled the seeker, skipped over into the tundra, and had Safyre or Adriel recharge it—and him. It made my task more tedious, but only slightly, and I was not about to complain given the risks associated with exploring the nether-infested sector.

The enforced rest stops were also an ideal opportunity to restore my mana reserves. While my void armor saw to it that I was protected from the surrounding mists, there was an associated cost. Every bit of damage my void armor repelled drained my mana a little. Thankfully, though, the rate at which I could regain my spent magic through channeling was significantly higher, so much so that whenever Anriq returned from the tundra both my void armor and mana were at full capacity.

Around the seven-hour mark, sometime after my second stop, I drew to a sudden halt.

In front of me, the hydra tracks continued their unrelenting march north. To my right, the ground rose sharply, creating a narrow and heavily shadowed corridor that was about two hundred yards long. A cliff wall bordered it on one side, open water on the other.

Something is off.

Frowning, I tried to figure out what. It was not the corridor itself that disturbed me. Yes, it made for an ideal ambush spot, but it was definitely empty. As was the water to my left and the clifftops to my right. Both my mindsight and senses attested to this fact, and unless the stygians had found some new way to hide themselves, I was certain the corridor was safe.

So, why am I hesitating?

Ordinarily, I wouldn't have. I would have dismissed the niggling worry and continued on, confident I could handle whatever came at me. But I had taken Safyre's warnings to heart, and a new wariness infected me.

Nothing *seemed* off, but *something* definitely was. Remaining stock still, I scanned the area once more.

And came up empty again.

Nothing was nearby, I was sure of it. Although, I supposed it was always possible that a group of stygian spores lurked in the corridor. The things were nearly impossible to detect. When I'd run across them in Draven's Reach, it was only thanks to the Adjudicator's warning messages that I had managed to find them.

But the spores were harmless on their own. Yes, their truesight would reveal me, but unless there were other stygians nearby to take advantage of that fact, the spores were no threat.

Still, I did not set foot in the corridor.

Maybe the ground's trapped? Maybe the shadows are hiding—

I broke off.

The shadows.

That was what was off. It was just past noon, which meant the corridor should have been brightly lit, not occluded in shadows.

A cold chill ran up my shoulder as realization set in.

The threat was above—from something hanging in the sky. Craning my head back slowly, I peered up.

And spotted an overlord.

I'd not seen one properly before. *And if not for my nethersight, I wouldn't have spotted this one either,* I realized. Nor the trap it had set.

The mammoth stygian creature was exactly as Ghost had described it all those many days ago. It was a round ball, with hundreds of gray tentacles extending from its bottom half—all presently motionless. It hung high above, perhaps at an altitude of three or four hundred yards. Still, I managed to perceive a few more details.

Thick reddish hide. Crate-like pockmarks. No eyes. No limbs—unless you counted the tentacles. And no obvious explanation for how something that large was hanging motionless in the sky. *Has to be magic.*

The most startling thing about the overlord, though, was its size. It was larger than Sunfury. Larger than the harbinger. Hells, it was larger than ten harbingers all rolled together.

How do I even kill something like that? For sure, my blades—tiny by comparison—were going to be next to useless. Reaching out with my will, I inspected the stygian.

The target is a level 308 stygian overlord.

I exhaled a troubled breath. The Adjudicator's response contained a distinct lack of information, and other than for the stygian Power's level, I had little else to go on. Yet, given that the overlord hung motionless, I could only assume it was not aware of my presence. *I bet that'll change if I enter the corridor, though.*

"*Are you seeing this, Anriq?*" I asked, reaching out to him through the farspeaker bracelet.

A pause. "*Seeing what?*"

I sighed. His words confirmed my suspicion. Despite its otherwise superior abilities, the Sylvanain seeker obviously couldn't see through the nether like I could. "*Never mind. When last did you check on the overlord at the Reach gate?*"

A longer pause. "*This morning.*"

Well, damn. Based on my own experience and what Safyre had told me, I knew the overlords moved slowly—which made it unlikely that this was the same creature Anriq had observed earlier in the day. "*I guess that means there are two of them.*"

"Two?"

"There's a stygian overlord almost on top of me. Mark the location and send the coordinates to the others."

Alarm shot through the link. *"Don't engage it!"*

I chuckled. *"That's the furthest thing from my mind right now,"* I assured him. I thought for a moment. *"I'm going to circle around."*

"You should head back," he protested.

"I will soon," I promised. *"But wherever those hydras' trail ends, it isn't here. I have to find the nest."*

"Be safe," he said, sounding resigned.

"Always," I replied and cut the link.

✳   ✳   ✳

Just to be safe, I backtracked a few hundred yards before I cut a wide arc around the corridor.

The entire time, I kept one eye skyward. Now that I knew it was there, the overlord's presence was impossible to ignore. The thing did not so much as twitch. It was unnatural, but then again, that could also be said about every other stygian.

An hour later, with the overlord behind me, I rejoined the river, where, to my delight, I found the hydras' footprints once more.

"I'm back on the trail," I murmured for Anriq's benefit.

"Alright." He paused. *"What's the nether toxicity like? Has it increased again?"*

Before answering, I turned my attention inward and queried the Adjudicator.

The nether toxicity at your current location is at tier 5.

"Not since the last time," I replied. About thirty minutes ago, the concentration of the surrounding mists had increased—which I took as a good sign. From my previous encounters with the void sapling, I knew the nether was always stronger in the vicinity of the void's 'chosen.'

Something lay ahead, and if I was lucky, it would be the void tree itself.

✳   ✳   ✳

The nether toxicity at your current location is at tier 7.

Five hours later, I was still heading north, following the hydra's tracks. About an hour ago, the stygians' and river's paths had deviated, with the first continuing north, while the second turned west.

Of necessity, my rest stops had become more frequent as my mana drained faster. Full night had fallen, too, but despite both these things, I had no intention of turning back.

The nether toxicity had increased twice over, and I was sure the void tree couldn't be far off. The only thing that led me to doubt this was the case was the absence of stygians. Except for the lone overlord, I had yet to encounter another nether creature.

That changed, though, as I crested an incline peppered with dead trees. Spread out before me was a shallow valley.

And it was teeming with stygians.

"Wow," I exclaimed involuntarily.

"What is it?" Anriq asked tersely.

"A stygian nest." But I had discovered more than that. *"I've also found the void tree."* I paused. *"And two more overlords."*

"Two more?" Anriq asked in a strangled voice.

"Yes," I replied. *"That makes four."* Four stygian Powers—well, five if you counted the void tree itself, all in the same sector.

Damn.

The two overlords hovered mere yards above the valley floor, which is why I had not seen them from afar. The thick mass of tentacles on their underside was buried deep into the ground, either anchoring the two in place or doing something more nefarious. What's more, the pair were belching a near continuous stream of nether, saturating the entire valley in thick, yellow smog-like plumes.

Bracketed between the two stygian Powers, was problem number two: the young void tree.

In many ways, the tree was the same as the sapling I'd encountered in Draven's Reach. Only this one was larger. Much larger.

The tree was ash-white and tall enough that its uppermost branches overtopped the adjacent overlords. And just like sapling, its rail-thin branches were covered in ebon-black thorns.

"Get out of there!" Anriq urged.

"In a minute," I replied absently, scanning the valley. It was not just the stygian Powers that was cause for concern. The ordinary nether creatures were just as troubling. Or rather their numbers were.

There were at least ten thousand stygians in the valley.

And here you were thinking of reclaiming the sector. No way was that going to be possible. Not against a force of the size of the one below. Not yet.

And certainly not with that, I thought, my eyes drifting to the fourth point of concern in the valley.

The rift hanging behind the tree.

Its inky blackness framed the tree's ash-white limbs perfectly. The rift was active too, and a near continuous stream of stygians drifted both in and out from... elsewhere. Tearing my eyes away from the void of nothingness, I took in the rest of the valley.

The river that had turned west earlier had returned to form a horse-shoe-shaped valley in which the stygians nested. It made the nest unassailable from the north, west, and south. The valley itself was huge, too, with the nest's closest corner some four hundred yards northwest of me.

"Michael, it's too dangerous," Anriq tried again. *"You should retreat."*

Sighing, I conceded he had a point. I had already seen everything I needed to, and going in for a closer look was not going to add anything substantial. Still, there was one more thing I had to do.

Reaching out with my will, I inspected the three nether Powers.

The target is a level 325 stygian overlord.
The target is a level 321 stygian overlord.
The target is a level 340 young void tree.

I sighed again. The harder I looked, the grimmer the picture grew. *"Alright, I've seen enough. I'm on my way back."*

The next day, everyone gathered in the den again. It was time for some hard decisions.

I surveyed the faces around me. On my right were the dire wolf elders and Ghost. Farthest left from me were the twins. Both wore smug looks of satisfaction, and it was no secret why either. The pair had gained their bloodline Marks.

They were Lions.

"Hmpf," Sulan sniffed. *"More like cubs really."*

I had not bothered shielding my surface thoughts from the dire wolves, and some, like the white wolf, felt no shame in eavesdropping.

I smiled at her. *"What do you know of the bloodline?"*

"Lions, urgh," she replied. *"They're brash. Prideful. Lazy."*

I chuckled. *"Well, the last one at least doesn't apply in this case."* For all their faults, the twins worked hard and were diligent about improving their skills.

"But perhaps the first two do?" Aira suggested.

"No comment," I murmured and returned to surveying my companions.

Nyra sat next to the twins. My apprentice had sadly not deepened her Wolf Mark yet, but she'd grown in other ways and, importantly, had completed the configuration of her primary Class. Turning my focus inward, I called up her analyze data.

The target is Nyra, a level 67 human virulent shade. She possesses the skills: longbows, sneaking, focus, poisoning, light armor, and daggers.

Nyra's Class had evolved but in an unexpected direction. Instead of favoring her Wolf heritage, her new Class appeared to be inspired by the synergies between her skills. The Adjudicator had perhaps also taken into account her previous vocation as an assassin. In any case, the Game now labeled her a virulent shade—a Class that specialized in poisoning its victims from either afar or up close.

Seeing my gaze resting on her, the young woman nodded. Inclining my head in acknowledgment, I turned to the werewolf sitting beside her. *He* was perhaps a bit closer than strictly necessary.

Of the four younger players, Anriq had progressed the least, but that was largely because he'd spent nearly all his time in the nether-infested sector, while the seeker scouted the region.

Lastly, there was Safyre and Adriel. My two lieutenants. Both women returned my gaze steadily, their faces grave. Only they knew the question I was about to pose to the group.

I inhaled deeply. "Right, let's begin. I suppose by now, everyone is aware of what we've discovered in sector 18,240?" I waited for their nods before continuing.

Raising my right hand, I ticked off points on my fingers. "Overlords. Tree. Rift. Nest. That's what we have to deal with if we want to reclaim the sector."

"Sounds like a tough set of challenges," Terence said offhandedly.

"But we know you'll find a way around them," Teresa added with a grin. "You always do."

"It's more than tough," I said, not returning their smiles. "They are impossible obstacles to overcome."

"Impossible?" Anriq asked, stirring. "Surely you don't mean that?"

"I do. It is impossible with the forces at our disposal." I paused to let my words sink in. "Which leaves us two choices."

No one said anything, but I could feel their anticipation build. They were waiting for some sort of crazy scheme, I realized. Sadly, I was going to have to disappoint them.

"Our first option is to abandon sector 18,240," I said softly.

"What? Why?" Terence cried.

Nyra straightened. "But what about New Haven?"

"We can't do that," Teresa protested. "We'll lose—"

I held up my hand for silence. "Let me finish. Like I said, option one is that we abandon sector 18,240, ignoring the void tree and the stygians swarming around the rift. Instead, we push through the force besieging the Reach gate. That *we* can do. However, we should expect the trip to be one way. I have no doubt that the void will install an even larger blocking force thereafter, and by the time we muster enough allies to defeat it, the sector will fall to the nether."

"Why would we even want to do that?" a puzzled-looking Anriq asked. "We'll be stranded in the dungeon with no hope of escape."

Nyra shook her head. "We won't be stuck. We'll still be able to leave via the portal exiting onto the Eastern Marches. What we won't be able to do is re-enter Draven's Reach."

"Nyra is correct," I added. "In essence, option one transforms the dungeon into a single-shot resource. After we use it, we can never do so again."

Terence frowned. "But what use is there in us entering Draven's Reach now? Except for Safyre, the rest of us are too low-leveled to run the dungeon successfully."

I turned to him. "You *can* run the dungeon—with help—but admittedly it will be slow going and dangerous to boot. But there are other benefits. The packs can make a permanent home in the dungeon. You, Teresa, and Nyra can safely grow your Marks and even awaken your blood there. And Anriq, Safyre, and I can grind our skills and levels until we're all as close to level three hundred as possible."

"And then what?" Teresa asked. "We leave?"

"Correct," I said. "The New Haveners, if they choose to come with us, will have to abandon their city. The same applies to the wolfmen and the packs. They, too, will have to leave behind whatever home they've made in the Reach. It may take years before we're ready, but eventually, we will rejoin the Game."

"But we could never return," Adriel said softly.

I nodded. "Adriel is right. Once we leave, we won't be able to go back or contact the guardian there again. The Reach will be lost forever."

Everyone fell silent as they digested that.

Option one was a good option, there was no question of that. As a group, we could grow safely while sheltered in the dungeon, and more importantly, we could control the timeline. *We* would decide when to leave. *We* would decide when we were ready. In the Kingdom, there were too many outside forces beyond our control that might push us in directions we didn't want to go.

"You really think entering Draven's Reach is the best option?" Ghost asked quietly.

I glanced at her. *"For us, personally? No. For the Forerunners as a whole... yes."*

The pyre wolf's ears flattened. *"So, why don't you tell them that?"*

I nearly laughed aloud at that. *"Because if I do, they'll resist. Our fellow councilors are strong-willed, and they won't like being pushed."*

"You could always order them," Ghost pointed out. *"Then they would be Pact-bound to obey."*

"I could," I allowed. *"But that would be misusing the Pact I sealed with them. The choice we face today has nothing to do with protecting House secrets and everything to do with the course the Forerunners chart in future."* I paused. *"And like it or not, that is not for me alone to decide."*

Ghost didn't have anything else to add, and I turned my attention outwards again. No one had spoken yet, and folding my arms in my lap, I waited patiently for someone to do so.

Predictably, Teresa was the first to break the silence. "What's behind door number two then?"

I sighed. I had known we'd have to broach the subject of option two eventually, of course, but I'd been hoping to delay speaking of it until after I'd convinced them of the wisdom of retreating into the dungeon.

"Michael?" Teresa prompted when I didn't immediately respond.

"Our second option is to try and close the rift in sector 18,240," I said heavily. "That, though," I added before they could grow excited, "is going to take a great deal of work."

"And the chances of failure are significant," Safyre put in.

"Again correct," I said. "We also stand to lose much more by attempting option two. It won't be just the two sectors at risk but also the lives of everyone in this room."

"How would we go about it, though?" Anriq asked quietly.

"We gather allies," I said simply. "But we'll be limited both by whom we can trust and by time—we can't assume we will have more than a few weeks to assemble the forces necessary to assault the rift."

"We can expect a warning from the Adjudicator when the sector is in imminent danger of falling, though," Adriel added.

I nodded. "That will be our cue, to either launch our assault on the rift—assuming we're ready—or abandon the sector altogether if we're not."

"But who could we turn to for help with something like this?" Terence asked.

"The werewolf pack in Nexus for one," Anriq said, looking at me. "They can't be trusted, but they *can* be coerced with the Wolf Torc."

I nodded in mute agreement.

"There are also the possessed," Adriel said. She raised the pouch in her hand. "This bag contains the spirits of one hundred potential allies. All former scions and all capable fighters in their own right." She glanced at Duggar and the other elders. "I will have to inspect the Rings of Astral Walking to be certain, but there is a chance I can rehome them permanently."

The dire wolves said nothing, but I sensed their grudging assent. The rings were a touchy subject, but we had discussed the matter at length prior to this.

"Then, there are all of you, too," I added. "Adriel needs to regain her own body, and Safyre must gain a Power Mark." I faced Anriq. "You must become an elite." I turned to twins. "You two must strengthen your Marks, and awaken your blood, but even more importantly, you must acquire your secondary and tertiary Classes." I glanced at my apprentice. "The same applies to Nyra."

"And all that will be enough?" Teresa asked skeptically.

I shook my head. "Sadly, no. We will need more allies. Thankfully, we have a few other options: the Bane Wolves, the wolfmen, New Haven, the Blades, the under-dwellers, Kesh, the lost Prime, House Pestilence"—Anriq flinched involuntarily at their mention, something I didn't fail to notice, but now was not the time to question him about them—"the bounty hunters, and the brotherhood." I exhaled heavily. "However, there is a large element of risk associated with all of these options, be it of exposure or failure."

Terence tilted his head to the side. "And we have to get everything done in a month?"

I nodded. "Something like that."

He frowned. "What about Saya?"

"I don't plan on abandoning her," I assured him. "Nor Shael for that matter. Whether we proceed with option one or two, I will reestablish contact with them first."

"Having a tavern nearby would be nice," Safyre remarked, sounding almost wistful at the prospect.

I smiled. "A merchant wouldn't be a bad idea either," I murmured.

Terence's face lit up. "We could get Saya to set up shop in sector 18,240 or even Draven's Reach!"

I held my hand. I hated to quell his enthusiasm, but I knew I must. "We should also prepare for the possibility that Saya may not want to join the Forerunners."

Terence's face fell. "Why wouldn't she?"

I spread my arms. "Look at this place. The tundra is inhospitable. Draven's Reach is not much better, and who knows how long it will be before the nether in sector 18,240 fully dissipates?" I studied his face. "Saya is a civilian, too, remember. Danger and risk are not things she craves. And as yet, she knows no dangerous secrets, nor is she at any great risk where she is. There is no need to uproot her life—especially if it's not something she herself wants."

"If you ask her to come, she will," Terence insisted stoutly.

"I'll give her the choice," I allowed, "but I won't *ask* her nor pressure her in any way. Acceptable?"

Sighing, he nodded.

Teresa squeezed her brother's hand sympathetically, then asked, "What about the wolves' valley? Is relocating to the sector not an option?"

"I considered it—briefly," I replied. "But I no longer believe the sector is a suitable stronghold for the Forerunners. What with the Bane Wolves, the wolfmen, the wolves, and the rest of us all there, our true aims and nature would not stay undiscovered for long."

Teresa cocked her head to the side and, for once, had no disagreement to voice. "Does that mean you're abandoning your tasks in the sector?"

"Definitely not," I said firmly. "The wolves' valley may not be a viable location for a secret base, but that does not mean exerting some measure of control over it won't be beneficial."

Nodding slowly, she fell silent.

"About those allies you spoke of," Anriq said, pulling the conversation back on track, "we can't contact them from here. Someone—you?—will have to leave the tundra."

I shook my head. "Most of the preparations we need to complete cannot be done from here. If we go with option two, nearly all of us will have to leave the tundra at some point."

That got their attention.

"Explain," Teresa said, almost quivering with eagerness.

I waved aside the question. "I will, later—*if* we go with option two. The crucial thing to realize is that if even one of us leaves the tundra for somewhere like Nexus, the risk of exposure increases significantly. It is partly why going down the route of option two is rife with danger. However, the choice is not mine alone to make. It's all of ours." I met the gaze of each of them in turn. "So, what will it be? Option one? Or two?"

"Option two," Teresa called out immediately.

"Are you sure?" I asked. "Because once we—"

"I agree," Terence blurted out.

"Me, too," Anriq added, less enthusiastically but just as firmly.

I closed my eyes. "What about you Nyra?"

She shifted uncomfortably. "I know I chose exile over staying in New Haven, but…"

"Go on," I encouraged.

"But I still consider the city home. I know my fellow citizens. Most will not leave New Haven, even on your say so." She sighed. "I will not see them abandoned and isolated. We have to save sector 18,240 if we can."

"Thank you, Nyra. Adriel?"

The lich took her time answering. "It's been many centuries since the Primes' defeat, and even longer since the stygians began gobbling up sectors, but I get the sense that matters are coming to a head." She shook her head. "I believe the longer we wait, the more difficult our task will become. I vote option two."

I inclined my head in acceptance. "Safyre?"

"You know my feelings on this matter, Michael. Option two is undoubtedly the more dangerous path before us, but if we're to succeed in our objectives, it will be far from the most dangerous thing we do. We should start as we mean to go on. Option two."

I opened my eyes. "Thank you, everyone," I said, not needing to poll the elders. The wolves would follow my lead no matter what.

I scanned the faces of my companions. The conclusion they'd reached did not surprise me. Still, I had mixed feelings about the decision.

On one hand, I didn't want to abandon sector 18,240 either. On the other... I wanted to keep everyone safe. Sadly, both of those things were not mutually achievable. I couldn't help but wonder, though, if my companions had grown too cavalier about what we faced.

But they understood. I had made sure of that. And yet, they had still chosen the more dangerous path.

I will not be able to protect them all. Some will die.

It was their choice to make, though, and they had made it. "Very well," I said, my voice studiedly neutral. "Our goal is set.

"We will close the rift in sector 18,240."

✳ ✳ ✳

THE END.

Here ends Book 7 of the Grand Game.
Michael's adventures will continue in **The Lost Reclaimed**.
Coming 01 February 2025!

I hope you enjoyed the story! If you did, please leave a <u>review</u> and let other readers know what you think.
<u>Click here to leave a review</u>.
Happy reading!
Tom Elliot.

MICHAEL AT THE END OF BOOK 7

Player Profile: Michael
Level: 236. Rank: 23. Species: Human. Lives Remaining: 4.
Ghost's Lives Remaining: 4.
True Marks: Powerful Initiate.
True Marks (hidden): Worthy Adversary, Wolf Protector, Wolf Progenitor.
False Marks (fabricated): Lesser Shadow, Lesser Light, Lesser Dark.
Followers: 2 / 200. Active Pacts: 5 / 20.

Faction Data: Forerunners
Office held: Faction Leader. Sectors claimed: 0 / 2.
Players pledged: Nyra, Ceruvax, Safyre, Terence, Teresa, Anriq.
Non-players pledged: Pack of the Reach (500), Bane Wolves warband (2,000), arctic wolves (200), dire wolves (130).

Active Buffs
denotes boosts affected by items.
Damage reduction (DR) (reduces damage incurred only):
Life: 20%. Death: 25%. Air: 55%. Earth: 55%. Fire: 55%. Water: 55%. Shadow: 40%. Light: 40%. Dark: 40%. Nether: 100%. Physical: 62%*.

Resistances (RES) (negates damage and/or rebuffs spell effects):
Life: 10%. Death: 12.5%. Air: 27.5%. Earth: 27.5%. Fire: 47.5%*. Water: 27.5%. Shadow: 20%. Light: 20%. Dark: 20%. Nether: 70%*. Physical: 0%.

Ghost (DR / RES): Fire: 45% / 72.5%. Nether: 45% / 22.5%. Physical: 51%* / 22.5%.

Other Benefits derived from Items
Damage: +30% damage (ebonheart), +40% damage (faithful).
Abilities: perceive tier 6 spelled wards (sorcerer's coif), move soundlessly (wayfarer's boots), hands immune to hazardous substances (wayfarer's gloves), spellhold: none (mage's surprise), psi-feed (psi bracelet).
Traits: +20% aoe evasion (tiamaten vest).
Skills: +5 ranks in thieving (scoundrel's wristband).

Attributes
Available: 6 points.
Strength: 28 (20)*. Constitution: 36 (24)*. Dexterity: 137 (113)*.
Perception: 94 (90)*. Mind: 135 (123)*. Magic: 86 (65)*. Faith: 0.

Classes
Available (Michael): 0 points.
Available (Ghost): 8 points.

Primary-Secondary-Tertiary tri-blend: voidstalker (fabricated). voidstealer XIII (hidden).
Ascendant Class: wolf lord (rank I, hidden), sire wolf (rank I, hidden).
Familiar: stygian pyre wolf VI (unique, hidden).

Traits

void heritage II (wolf, hidden): +4 Dexterity, +4 Strength, +8 Mind, +8 Perception, +12 Magic.
voidwalker II (wolf, hidden): improved senses in all conditions, nethersight, immunity to blindness.
arctic wolf II (wolf, hidden): +10 Constitution, +4 Mind, +6 Strength.
were's bite II (wolf, hidden): 0 to 30% chance of granting another player the were-trait.
sire's strain (wolf, hidden): boosts your other wolf traits by +1 tier.

house elite (bloodline, hidden): bound to House Wolf, detect dormant wolf bloodline strains.
secret blood (bloodline, hidden): conceals the wolf blood of yourself, your followers, and your familiar.
blood puppet (bloodline, hidden): grants you the enslave ability.

beast tongue: can speak to beastkin.
Marked: can see spirit signatures.
inscrutable mind: +8 Mind.
mental focus IV: increases effectiveness of Mind skills by 40%.
budding explorer: all key points in newly discovered sectors logged.
spell illiterate: cannot cast mana-based spells.
potion resistance II: potency of potions reduced by 2 ranks.
spirit talker: can speak to spirits.
bold blood: +1 attribute per level.
higher evolution: can evolve Class beyond master ranked.
commander: can share bloodline traits or blood memories with your followers.
champion: increases the strength of blood memories.
spirit familiar: can bind a willing spirit as your familiar.
mage-host: +10 Mind, +10 Magic.
slip-through-shadows*: 20% chance to evade AoE damage.

spirit familiar (Ghost): mirrors player attributes and level, and shares ability slots with them.
psionic being (Ghost): retains telepathic skills and abilities from her former incarnation as a dire wolf.
free spirit (Ghost): can roam an unlimited distance from her host, but only within the same sector.
born again II (Ghost): grants your familiar 2 additional lives, will resurrect in spirit vessel.
pyreborn (Ghost): +50% fire magic resistance and +50% fire damage.

mirrored jewelry*: gains benefits of accessories rank 7 and below (rings, bracelets, and necklaces).

<u>Skills</u>

Available skill slots: 0.
light armor (current: 163. Constitution, basic).

dodging (current: 207. Dexterity, basic).
sneaking (current: 226. Dexterity, basic).
shortswords (current: 212. Dexterity, basic).
two weapon fighting (current: 186. Dexterity, advanced).
thieving (current: 150. Dexterity, basic).

chi (current: 185. Mind, advanced).
meditation (current: 214. Mind, basic).
telekinesis (current: 190. Mind, advanced).
telepathy (current: 222. Mind, advanced).

insight (current: 246. Perception, basic).
deception (current: 230. Perception, master).

channeling (current: 216. Magic, basic).
elemental absorption (current: 115. Magic, master).
null force (current: 82. Magic, master).
null life (current: 44. Magic, master).
null death (current: 53. Magic, master).
nether absorption (current: 204. Magic, master).

magma maw (Ghost) (current: 93. Magic, master).
stygian claws (Ghost) (current: 102. Strength, master).
ash armor (Ghost) (current: 103. Constitution, master).
telepathy (Ghost) (current: 94. Mind, advanced).
death magic (Ghost) (current: 76. Magic, advanced).

<u>Abilities</u>

<u>**Constitution ability slots used:**</u> **15 / 24.**
greater load controller (15 Constitution, master, light armor).

<u>**Dexterity ability slots used:**</u> **101 / 113.**
crippling blow (Dexterity, basic, shortswords).
minor piercing strike (5 Dexterity, advanced, shortswords).
deadly backstab (30 Dexterity, elite, sneaking).
improved trap disarm (5 Dexterity, advanced, thieving).
superior lockpicking (5 Dexterity, advanced, thieving).
superior set trap (10 Dexterity, expert, thieving).
superior whirlwind (15 Dexterity, master, two weapon fighting).
vanish (30 Dexterity, elite, sneaking).

<u>Mind ability slots used:</u> **111 / 123.**
mass puppet (15 Mind, master, telepathy).
stunning slap (Mind, basic, chi).
improved windborne (15 Mind, master, telekinesis).
enhanced reflexes (15 Mind, master, chi).
superior astral shurikens (15 Mind, master, telepathy).
extreme shadow blink (15 Mind, master, telekinesis).
improved quick mend (15 Mind, master, chi).
improved fortified mind (15 Mind, master, meditation).
astral bite (Ghost) (5 Mind, advanced, telepathy).

<u>Perception ability slots used:</u> **86 / 90.**
powerful analyze (30 Perception, elite, insight).
greater trap detect (15 Perception, master, thieving).
conceal small weapon (Perception, basic, deception).
mimic (30 Perception, elite, deception).
superior ventro (5 Perception, advanced, deception).
lesser imitate (5 Perception, advanced, deception).

<u>Magic ability slots used:</u> **1 / 65.**
draining bite (Ghost) (Magic, basic, death magic).

<u>Other abilities:</u>
adept slaysight (hidden) (Class, elite, telepathy): paralyze, shatter, sleep, terrify, blind.
greater void thief (hidden) (Class, master, any void skill and telepathy): steal, siphon, negate, redirect on direct-damage, channeled, damage over time, aoe).
manifest (Ghost) (Class, advanced): explosive.
diresight (Ghost) (Class, advanced, telepathy).
direshield (Ghost) (Class, advanced, telepathy).
enslave (hidden) (blood memory, greater).

<u>**Known Key Points**</u>

Kingdom Sector 1 (Nexus) safe zone.
Kingdom Sector 12,560 (wolves' valley) nether portal and safe zone.
Kingdom Sector 18,240 nether portal 1 (guardian tower), and nether portal 2 (Draven's reach).
Kingdom Sector 75,172 nether portal 1 (Draven's Reach) and safe zone.

Dungeon Sector 101 (scorching dunes) exit portal and safe zone.
Dungeon Sectors 102, 103, and 104 (haunted catacombs) exit portals and safe zones.
Dungeon Sector 105, 106, 107, 108, and 109 (guardian tower) exit portals.
Dungeon Sector 14,913 (candidate's dungeon) exit portal and safe zone.
Dungeon Sector 73,102 (Draven's Reach) one-way entrance portal, safe zone, and exit portal.

<u>**Aetherstone Bracelet Stored Points**</u>

sector 24,401 safe zone.

<u>**Equipped**</u> (27 / 30 Game items)
<u>**Weapons**</u> (2 equipped)
ebonheart (+30% damage).
faithful (+40% damage).

<u>**Armor & Clothes**</u> (12 equipped)
tiamaten scalemail vest (+32%, +4 Constitution, slip-through-shadows).
sorcerer's coif (perceive tier 6 wards).
ranger's kit (+24% damage reduction, 4 pieces).
bomber's belt (5 x acid bombs, 5 x smoke bombs, 5 x ice bombs, and 5 x fire bombs).
belt of the chameleon (10 x rank 4 nether protection crystals, 11 x rank 4 disease protection crystals, 7 scent concealment crystals, 5 x mental concealment crystals, 4 x rank 6 disease protection crystals, 2 x rank 5 poison protection crystals, 1 x rank 4 strength enhancement crystals, 0 x rank 4 dexterity enhancement crystals, and 2 x rank 4 magic enhancement crystals).
wayfarer's boots (legendary item, +8 Dexterity, move soundlessly).
wayfarer's gloves (legendary item, +8 Dexterity, hands immune to hazardous substances).
cloak of the Reach (legendary soulbound item, +10 Magic, +20% fire magic resistance, +20% nether magic resistance).
scoundrel's wristband (+5 ranks thieving, 300 / 300 trap-making crystals) (<u>triggers</u>: pressure plates, sound glasses, tripwires, motion pins, remote control, spell detector, psi detector. <u>elements</u>: lightning, poison clouds, fire, spring-coiled daggers, bear-trap clamps, small explosives, blots of darkness, ice, spiked-pit, hallucinogenic mist. <u>guides</u>: reflect, split, and funnel. <u>keys</u>: remote, timed.)

<u>**Rings & Accessories**</u> (12 equipped)
goliath's ring (+8 Strength).
acrobat's ring (+8 Dexterity).
sharpshooter's band (+4 Perception).
hale stone (+8 Constitution).
savant's ring (+4 Mind).
troll's talisman bracelet (+6% damage reduction).
mage's surprise (+10 Magic, spellhold: trigger-cast tier 5 spells).
psi bracelet (legendary item, +8 Mind, psi-feed).
simple potion bracelet (3 / 3 full heal potions).
aetherstone bracelet (1 / 5 stored locations, 3 stone charged).
jeweled pet (grants Ghost: mirrored jewelry trait).
farspeaker bracelet (Safyre set, 1 of 4).

<u>**Other**</u> (1 equipped)
large bag of holding (200 slots).

seeking eye of Sylvana (legendary item, +invisible, 4 hours use, track & scout).

<u>Ghost (1 equipped)</u>
shadow's friend (+4 ranks stealth).

<u>**Backpack Contents (Key Items)**</u>

<u>Money</u>: 1023 golds, 5 silvers, and 3 coppers.
1 x coil of rope.
cat claws.
5 x full healing potions, 2 x rank 4 cure poison, 1 x rank 6 cure disease potions.
simple map of Nexus.
commune rod.
10 x acid bombs, 10 x smoke bombs, 10 x ice bombs, and 10 x fire bombs.
small bag of hiding (tier 6 concealment ward).
stygian shortsword, +3.
stygian shortsword.
netherstone.
underworld promissory note (12,000 gold).
4 x upgrade gems.
piercing strike tier III, IV, & V.
trap disarm tier III.
lockpicking tier III.
ventro tier III & IV.
2 x greater portal scrolls.
packet of unrefined cynacilin powder.
ranger's kit vest (16% damage reduction).
veteran's trapper's wristband.
Blood Talisman.
small bag of hiding containing 100 x possessed finger bones.
farspeaker bracelet (Tyelin set, 1 of 15).

<u>Soulbound Items</u>
Tartan token.
Vivane token.
Kesh Emporium access card.
tavern bill of ownership.
BHG ID (junior member, 1 / 10 active jobs).
phoenix's feather shaft (soulbound, Sunfury's feather).
apprentice rogue's underworld token.
pioneer's compass (soulbound, attuned to safe zone).
unmarked chest key card (from Nicola).

<u>**Miscellaneous Loot**</u>

3 x legendary items.
73 x miscellaneous items reserved for use by Mammon's Sworn.

<u>Alchemy Stone Contents</u>
(14 / 500 ingredients stored).
4 x orbs of petrification, 10 x Shadow ectoplasm.

<u>Bank Contents</u>
Money: 1,655 gold, 0 silvers, and 0 coppers.
2 x full healing potions.
2 x full mana potions.

<u>Tavern Money</u>: 9,850 gold, 0 silvers, and 0 coppers.

<u>Open Tasks</u>
Heist in the Dark (steal chalice from the Power, Paya).
A Perverted Trial (stop the Triumvirate abuse of the Combat Trial).
Brokering Peace (establish peace in sector 12,560 within 4 months).
Brotherhood Obligations (report to the brotherhood after 4 months).
Restore the Nexus Guardian (replace Kolath with Adriel).
Revive the Guardians (awaken Draven's brethren).
Locate the Lost Prime (find the hidden Prime).
Resurrecting Death (make Adriel a scion again).
Seedy Side of Life (become a full member of the thieves guild).
Found a new House (persuade Powers from three different bloodlines to join your House).

<u>Open Pacts</u>
Deliver cynacilin. Status: pact obligations fulfilled. Blythe owes Jasiah a favor equivalent to the worth of sector 75,172.
Inner Council Pacts with Safyre, Anriq, Teresa, and Terence.

Books by Tom Elliot

By Tom Elliot

The Grand Game (series page)
Book 1: The Grand Game: ebook | audiobook
Book 2: Way of the Wolf: ebook | audiobook
Book 3: World Nexus: ebook | audiobook
Book 4: House Wolf: ebook | audiobook
Book 5: Wolf in the Void: ebook | audiobook
Book 6: A Scion's Duty: ebook | audiobook
Book 7: Ancient Debts: ebook | audiobook (coming soon)
Book 8: The Lost Reclaimed: ebook (coming soon)

The Grand Game Box Set (series page)
Book 1-3: Birth of a Player: ebook.
Book 4-6: Rise of the Elite: ebook (releasing 31 December 2024)

The Grand Game, Elana (series page)
Book 1: Empyrean's Rise: ebook
Book 2: Empyrean's Flight: ebook

By Rohan M. Vider

The Dragon Mage Saga (series page)
Book 1: Overworld: ebook | audiobook
Book 2: Dungeons: ebook | audiobook

The Gods' Game (series page)
Crota, the Gods' Game Volume I
The Labyrinth, the Gods' Game Volume II
Sovereign Rising, the Gods' Game Volume III
Sovereign, the Gods' Game, Volume IV
Sovereign's Choice, the Gods' Game Volume V

Tales from the Gods' Game
Dungeon Dive (Tales from the Gods' Game, Book 1)

AFTERWORD

Thank you for reading the Grand Game!

If you enjoyed the book, please consider leaving a review on <u>amazon</u> <u>[click here]</u>. I'm already at work on Michael's next adventure.

If you have any questions, comments, or want to support my writing, please feel free to contact me through my site, <u>TomLitRPG.com</u> or <u>Discord</u>.

Alternatively, if you wish to learn more about the world of the Forever Kingdom, understand the system of the Grand Game better, or are just looking for the latest news on the Grand Game, please visit my site at <u>TomLitRPG.com</u> or signup up here for my: <u>Newsletter</u>.

Regards,
Tom
Support my writing on **PATREON**
<u>Amazon Author page</u> | <u>Goodreads</u> | <u>Facebook</u> | <u>Reddit</u> | <u>Discord</u> |

DEFINITIONS

Accord: old agreement between new Powers ceding control of Nexus to the Triumvirate.

Adjudicator: controller and arbitrator of the Grand Game.

alchemy stone: a device used to store alchemical components.

ancient: old Power.

anointed scion: a scion who has bound himself to a bloodline.

ascendancy: process of being a Power.

ascendant: descriptor often applied to Game aspects involving higher evolution.

ascendant undead: term the Adjudicator used to describe Stayne, meaning unknown.

blended Class: a combined Class.

blood awakening: the process of recalling blood memories.

blood infusion: the absorption of the essences from former scions.

blood memories: gifts from your forebears containing the power of the ancients themselves.

bi-blend: a combination of two melded Classes.

bloodline: reference to the ancient from which the player is a descendant.

breaking: refers to the breaking of the world, the fracturing of the Forever Kingdom into sectors, aether, and nether.

Circle: aka Ritual Combat Circle.

civilian player: a player without a class or combat abilities. Civilians do not have a player level.

class-unique skill: a skill that is unique to a Class and can only be acquired through a Class stone.

closed sector: a landmass that does not physically border another, making the area inaccessible except by portal.

composite spell: a multi-stage spell made up of two or more individual spells.

controlled sector: a sector owned by a faction. Ownership of a sector gives the faction's players increased privileges in the region.

Class: a defined path or vocation that gives a player access to specific skills.

Class evolution: the advancement of a Class, generally to a better-ranked one, due to particular traits, skills, or Marks acquired by the player.

Dark: one of the three Forces.

Darksworn: a player pledged to the Dark who values the self over the collective.

deathwish: An ability that is triggered in the instant between a creature being dealt fatal damage and the spirit fleeing the body.

Elite: a tier five player, i.e. someone above level two hundred.

ebonblade: soulbound weapons found in the Twilight Dungeon.

envoy: a trusted representative of a Power authorized to speak on their behalf.

Endless Dungeon: A section of the Nethersphere where dungeon mechanics are active.

Everborns: term used to describe players.

evolution: the advancement of a player's core characteristics.

familiar bond: a permanent spirit binding between a spellcasting player and a creature, allowing them the transfer of Game-gifted knowledge from host to familiar.

follower: a player who has pledged themself in a binding vow to a Force or Power.

Force: Light, Dark, Shadow. The building blocks of the cosmos and energy in its rawest form.

Forcesworn: Collective term referring to Darksworn, Lightsworn, and Shadowsworn players.

Forever Kingdom: the world of the Nethersphere and Kingdom.

forsworn: a sworn who has betrayed their Power.

Game: refers to the Grand Game.

gatekeepers: holders of ancient lore, guardians of the ancients' trials.

half-form: the in-between state where the player is in a mix of his two forms (man-form and beast-form).

House: House of the Ancient.

House of the Ancient: a grouping of followers pledged to one Prime.

Kingdoms: the collective name given to sectors located in the aether.

lycan: werewolf.

ley line: magic threads connecting nether sectors.

Light: one of the three Forces.

Lightsworn: a player sworn to the Light that champions the cause of the many, even to his own detriment.

marshmen: mysterious dwellers in the saltmarsh district.

meld: the process of combining multiple Classes into one.

mindglow: the visible signature of a mind as seen with mindsight.

neutral sector: a sector unowned and unclaimed by any faction or Force.

Nethersphere: collective name given to the sectors in the nether.

Netherspawn: stygian creatures.

nethersight: ability that allows stygian to see through free-floating nether.

new Power: one of the Powers that usurped the ancients.

oath breaker: one who has broken a Pact.

Pact: a binding enacted between a Power and player, overseen by the Adjudicator.

Power: an evolved player.

power word: a blood memory ability.

Prime: head of ancient bloodline. An ancient.

Prime Conclave: a gathering of Primes referred to by Kolath.

Primehood: the act of becoming a Prime.

rift: unstable portal from the nether. Ley line created by stygian seed.

scav: short for scavenger. A player who loots kills not his own.

scion: one bearing the blood of an ancient.

scion abilities: the abilities Michael had earned during the Wolf trials: astral blade, chi heal, mind shield, shadow blink.

seeking spell: spell that distinguishes friend from foe.

Shadowsworn: a player pledged to Shadow.

stolen spell: a spell acquired from another and cast using their skills and attributes.

soulbound: an item that remains with the player after death.

sworn: as in sworn servant. A sworn is a follower of a Power who has sufficiently deepened their binding Mark to benefit from the binding.

the real: reference to the physical realm.

trap-making crystal: crystal in trapper's wristband. Can be manifested as different trap components.

tratin: underwater sentient species with gills and blue scales.

trials of the ancients: tests created by the Primes for their successors.

tri-blend: a combination of three melded Classes.

trigger-cast: a spell held in readiness and invoked under specific conditions.

unsworn: not a sworn servant, and not bound to a Power.

upgrade gem: a game item used to advance an ability a single tier.

voids: informal term used to reference players who possess a void Class.

void Classes: a rare subset of Classes that specialize in damage reduction.

void's chosen: term by which the stygians address the stygian seeds.

void fathers: void trees.

Watcher: a Game artifact typically used to uncover deception players.

windslide: ramp of air formed by windborne spell.

were-trait: a trait carried by all were-players, fueling their ability to shapeshift.

weres: short for werewolves and other were-players.

wolfmen: hybrid species, non-player werewolves.

wolf trials: ancient trials created by Wolf Prime.

wolfkind: used interchangeably with wolfkin.

KEY CHARACTERS & FACTIONS

Albion Bank: major non-aligned bank in the Forever Kingdom.
Awakened Dead: A Dark faction.
Axis of Evil: An alliance of Dark factions.
blackguards: Policing force in the Dark quarter.
dawn brigade: Policing force in the Light quarter.
Devil Riders: small Dark faction.
Forerunners: Michael's faction.
gray watch: Policing force in the Shadow quarter.
Mantises: A Dark faction of assassins.
Marauders: small Shadow faction.
Reaper Clan: small Dark faction.
Silent Blades: small Dark faction.
Shadow Coalition: A power bloc of Shadow, made up of like-minded Shadow Powers.
Tartan: the faction of Tartar, the god-emperor.
Tartan legion: the military forces of Tartar.
Triumvirate: A unique faction composed of Light, Dark, and Shadow that control Nexus.
Unity Council: the governing body of Light, made up of all Light-affiliated Powers.

Guardians

Draven: centaur construct in Draven's Reach.
Kolath: mysterious construct in the Guardian Tower.

Guilds and Non-Factions

Bane Wolves: mercenary band out of New Haven.
Bounty Hunters Guild (BHG): headquartered in the plague quarter, mercenaries.
Information Brokers: a gnomish organization in the plague quarter.
Pack of the Reach: wolfmen pack.
Kesh Emporium: merchant company owned by Kesh.
Stygian Brotherhood: headquartered in the plague quarter, experts in all-things-nether.

House Wolf

Atiras: Dead Prime Wolf.
Ceruvax: Former envoy of Atiras.

Non-Players

Adriel: lich, Farren's sister.
Arden: Gnome information broker.
Algar: human captain, New Haven.
Avery: New Haven magister.
Castor: Possessed mage.
Cilia: First amongst the dark elves of New Haven.
Cyren: Gnome senior information broker.
Elron: dark elf marshal, New Haven.
Everard: dark elf master archer, bane wolf.
Farren: lich, Adriel's brother, new archlich.
Gamil: New Haven shopkeeper.
Lorn: Orc Chief in New Haven.
Loskin: Archlich.
Megtir: dwarven captain, bane wolf.
Minakawa: dark elf captain, New Haven.
Regus: court's security chief.
Sunfury: A phoenix.
Sienna: Human lord in New Haven.
Stormhammer: Dwarven Thane in New Haven.
Zorgulg: orc captain, bane wolf.

Players

Anriq: werewolf criminal.
Barac: crusader, male centaur.

Beorin: senior BHG member, dwarf.
Bornholm: Michael's companion from Erebus' dungeon, dwarf.
Cara: alias given to Kesh's agent in plague quarter by Michael.
Dathe: unknown werewolf player.
Devlin: Viviane's guard, unknown aquatic species.
Dinara: underworld den chief in Nexus.
Ent: guard outside emporium, armsmaster, giant.
Eyes: The BHG HQ doorkeeper, species unknown.
Jasiah: duelist, human male.
Genmark: ward architect, gnome male.
Gintalush: mantis assassin, insectoid.
Hannah: BHG client liaison officer, human female.
Kartara: huntmistress at Stygian Brotherhood Chapterhouse.
Kesh: master merchant, owner of the emporium, human woman.
Lake: guard outside emporium, berserker, giant.
Malikor: Mammon's envoy.
Michael: protagonist.
Misha: Marauder tracker, aka the Hound.
Moonshadow: aeromancer, male elf.
Morin: Michael's companion from Erebus' dungeon, the painted woman.
Nicola: under-dweller and underworld merchant, civilian.
Nyra: sniper, Michael's apprentice.
Orlon: Triumvirate knight-captain in the plague quarter, human.
Pitor: rank 15 warrior, Kalin sworn, human, Marauder sub-boss.
Richter: constable in Triumvirate citadel, human civilian.
Saya: apprentice alchemist, tavernkeeper in wolves' valley, gnome.
Shael: red minstrel, half-elf.
Simone: sharpshooter, half-elf female.
Stayne: Erebus' henchman.
Stonebeard: Triumvirate captain, dwarf.
Talon: the captain, Tartar's envoy.
Tantor: Michael's companion from Erebus' dungeon, high elf male.
Teg: Michael's escort in citadel, human.
Terence: rank 2 human fighter, swordsman.
Teresa: rank 2 human fighter, blade devotee.
Tevin: Marauder knight.
Toff: player outside haunted catacombs, ogre
Trion: Triumvirate holy knight, Herat sworn, human.
Trexton: herbalist in Triumvirate citadel, Simone's contact, dark elf.
Tyelin: Blythe's envoy.
Wengulax: mantis assassin, blade dancer, human.
Wilsh: Blackguard captain, human.
Yara: Silent Blade, Tyelin's lieutenant, orc.
Yzark: Marauder boss.

POWERS

Arinna: Light Power.
Artem: Shadow Power. Goddess of nature.

Blythe: Dark Power, faction leader of the Silent Blades.
Erebus: Dark Power, leader of the Awakened Dead faction.
Herat: Light Power, member of the Triumvirate.
Ishita: Spider goddess, Dark Power, member of the Awakened Dead.
Loken: Shadow Power.
Kalin: Minor Shadow Power, faction leader of the Marauders.
Mai: Unknown Power and collector of artifacts.
Mammon: Dark Power, faction leader of the Devil Riders.
Menaq: Dark Power, leader of the Mantis faction.
Muriel: Light Power contesting Wolf Valley.
Mydas: Shadow Power, member of the Triumvirate.
Paya: Dark Power, junior member of the Awakened Dead ruling council.
Rampel: Dark Power, member of the Triumvirate.
Tartar: Dark Power, also known as the God-Emperor.
Viviane: Power owning the Albion Bank.

WOLFKIN

Aira: dire wolf dame.
Barak: dire wolf elder.
Cantur: half-mad wolf.
Duggar: dire wolf alpha.
Oursk: dire wolf sire.
Leta: dire wolf elder.
Monac: dire wolf elder and former alpha.
Moonstalker: Oursk's pup.
Shadetooth: Oursk's pup.
Snow: arctic wolf pack alpha.
Star: Snow's mate.
Stormdark: Oursk's pup.
Sulan: dire wolf healer.
Suva: dire wolf elder.

LOCATIONS

bounty hunters guild headquarters: in the plague quarter.
court of the dead: archlich's stronghold. Also court.
Dark quarter: eastern side of Nexus.
Eastern Marches: collection of open sectors Draven's Reach exits onto.
global auction: auction in the safe zone.
guardian tower: public dungeon.
haunted catacombs: public dungeon.
highlands: arid northern grasslands and hills of the Eastern Marches.
information brokers office: in the plague quarter.
Kesh Emporium: merchant house in the safe zone.
Light quarter: western side of Nexus.
lowlands: fertile southern lands of the Eastern Marches.
market square: square housing global auction.
New Haven: city in Draven's Reach.
plague quarter: southern side of Nexus.
saltmarsh district: area in the southeast of plague quarter.
scorching dune: public dungeon.
Shadow Keep: central castle in the Shadow quarter.
Shadow quarter: northern side of Nexus.
Sickening Ooze: dungeon in saltmarsh.
Sleepy Inn: Michael's tavern, aka Wyvern's Roost.
Southern Outpost: tavern in plague quarter.
Wanderer's Delight: hotel in the safe zone.